D0058310

Nanjing Never Cries

Nanjing Never Cries

A Novel

Hong Zheng

The Killian Press

Library of Congress Cataloging-in-Publication Data

Cheng, Hung, 1937– author.
Nanjing never cries : a novel / Hong Zheng.
Cambridge, MA : The Killian Press, 2016.
LCCN 2016016584 | ISBN 9781944347000 (hardcover : alk. paper)
LCSH: Nanking Massacre, Nanjing, Jiangsu Sheng, China,
1937 Fiction. | College teachers China Nanjing (Jiangsu Sheng) Fiction. | College students Massachusetts Cambridge Fiction. | Chinese United States Fiction. | GSAFD: Historical fiction.
LCC PS3603.H4597 N36 2016 | DDC 813/.6--dc23 LC record available at https://lccn.loc.gov/2016016584

10 9 8 7 6 5 4 3 2 1

I dedicate this book to Jill, who has taken very good care of me.

Contents

Book II

Book III

Preface

Many people I know are surprised that an MIT professor who has spent his entire academic life as a theoretical physicist would use ten years of his spare time writing an English novel. He has no qualification to do such a thing.

Getting an English novel published has gotten increasingly difficult, people told me. There has been a sea change in recent years. People rarely read novels these days. Publishers rarely accept first-time authors. A Chinese individual who knew little English at the age of twenty cannot possibly command enough language skills to warrant a chance in this difficult field. Expect rejection after rejection from literary agents, and eventually self-publish. Then the book will be read by few and remembered by no one.

Yet, I had no choice but to plunge into such a foolish endeavor.

The idea started the afternoon of April 13, 1995, when two of my colleagues, Harvey Greenspan and Willem Malkus, walked into my office and said, "Hong, you better go over there. Those historians are distorting history!" They were talking about the one-day symposium being held at MIT in memory of Hiroshima.

I went to room 9-150 and saw four speakers on the podium, three of them Caucasians, one Japanese, no one from China or Southeast Asia.

After hearing them repeating the story of American guilt over dropping the bomb, I raised my hand, stood up, and said, "I would like to ask you distinguished speakers: if a group of bandits broke into your home, raped your wife, killed your children, and were about to slit your throat before being subdued by the police, would the story be police brutality to you?"

After a long awkward silence, one of the Americans on the podium said a few words, then the speakers resumed the discussion of American guilt, completely ignoring my objections.

After the symposium was over, I was walking through the door of the lecture hall when a hand fell on my shoulder. I turned and saw the Japanese speaker who had been on the podium moments earlier. Professor Rinjuro Sodei told me that he agreed with everything I had said. He also asked me to sign a petition urging the Japanese government to apologize for Japan's past war crimes.

I went home and composed a letter to MIT's *Technology Review* describing the holocaust the Japanese had inflicted on the Chinese during the Sino-Japanese War. The magazine edited down my letter before publishing it. Another letter, written by one of the speakers in the symposium, was also published in an earlier issue. Its many pages dwarfed my letter's half page.

Being a physicist, I understand the horror of the atomic bomb, but history should be presented with no ideological tilt. The prejudice I encountered made me realize that English novels about the Sino-Japanese War are needed. The true nature of this war must be brought to a higher level of Western consciousness. At least some such novels must be written by the Chinese, who have the right to tell the world their side of the story. In particular, people in my generation, having lived through the Chinese holocaust, have the responsibility to pass down this lesson of history to the next generation.

I spent several months in Nanjing (also Nanking) during my next sabbatical leave, trying to learn how the Nanjing people lived. My proudest moment came when someone in the street asked me for directions. I had become one of them.

In Nanjing, I had the good fortune of interviewing two of the massacre survivors. These old men could not help crying when they recounted what had happened to their families one day sixty-two years earlier. My wife, who was with me during the interview, cried with them.

I couldn't possibly have completed the project without the help of many special friends and acquaintances. Alexa Fleckenstein sat with me every Tuesday afternoon for almost a year, reading and editing the whole manuscript. Before then, I had no idea how poor my English was, nor how the canons of Western literature differ from their Chinese counterparts.

I was fortunate that this woman with a heart of gold had the patience to teach me everything I know about English fiction writing.

Another friend I have to especially thank is Dr. Ping-Yeh Wang, who read every draft of the story—there have been more than ten of them—giving me his opinions and pointing out errors. Most important, he gave me the unfailing moral support that kept me going in the face of insurmountable odds against my getting the novel published.

Virginia Li and Dennis Porche deserve my heartfelt thanks for their time-consuming efforts reading my manuscript and offering good advice.

I have benefited from talking to Ji-wei Sun and Teh-ying Lee, historians of the Nanjing Massacre. I thank Mr. Lian-Hong Lee, staff member of the Nanjing Massacre Memorial Museum, for introducing me to the massacre survivors. Professor Fan Wang was my gracious host in Nanjing. He and Dr. Xin Zhang took me to several scenic spots described in my novel.

Other friends and acquaintances who read my manuscript and made useful comments were Dave Benney, Jim Carrol, Elizabeth Chadis, Bill Cheng, Rosine Green, Harvey Greenspan, Mei Hu, Bob Laronga, Kelvin Lee, Annabel Liu, Caroline Mei, Russ Phillips, Ron Probstein, Diana Tsomides, CC Wang, Wei-ming Wang, Gunther Winkler, Suh-jen and Winston Yau, Terence and Margaret Yen, and Alison Yung. Their interest is appreciated.

I am thankful that Elizabeth Chadis took my manuscript to the MIT Press. Ellen Faran, then director of the Press, told Elizabeth that the MIT Press does not publish novels, but she would take a look at the first and last chapters and advise me where to send my manuscript. Two months later, she told me that she did not glance at these chapters; instead, she read the prologue word for word and went on to read the rest of the chapters word for word—twice. She suggested that I give my manuscript to the MIT Press, to be published by a new imprint that she tentatively called the Killian Press.

After news of the publication of my novel appeared in the media, thanks to Cynthia Huang, ChiaLi Tang, and Li Zhou, I soon got an offer to publish my Chinese translation of the novel by Yilin Press, which belongs to Phoenix Publishing and Media Group, the largest publishing group in China. I hope that this will mean more than a handful of people will read my novel.

Readers who want to learn more facts about the Nanjing massacre can go to Google, search for John Rabe or John Magee, and proceed from there. The former was the chairman of the Nanjing International Safety Zone, whose diary was discovered by Iris Chang as detailed in her book *The Rape of Nanking*, while the latter was an American Episcopal priest who had taken films and pictures during the Nanjing Massacre. The readers may also find out from Google the facts about the Panay Incident described in my novel, in which an American gunboat was sunk by Japanese bombers near Nanjing four years before Pearl Harbor. They may also be interested to watch a Universal newsreel of this incident taken by American newsmen, which miraculously survived.

There are two excellent books about the Nanjing Massacre: *The Rape of Nanking* by Iris Chang, published by Basic Books, a subsidiary of Perseus Books, L.L.C., 1997; and *The Nanjing Massacre* by Honda Katsuichi, published by M.E. Sharpe, 1999.

Prologue

Nanjing, Capital of the Republic of China, 1937.

The Yangtze River was a dragon curling around its rear, Bell Mountain a tiger guarding its flank.

Nanjing, the city of misty rains! Fish grew in the lakes filled to the brim with warm rain water. Musical sounds floated in the air as drizzle fell on the rice stalks at night. On spring mornings, in cobbled alleys, little girls sold bouquets of dewed apricot blossoms for two coppers each.

During the fourteenth century, the First Ming Emperor Zhu Yuan-Zhang had built China's strongest city wall here. The base of the wall was constructed with granite and rocks, the brickwork a concoction of rice glue and tung oil. The ramparts, twenty miles long and sixty feet above the ground, allowed two horses to gallop side by side.

For almost six centuries, the wall had made the city difficult to sack. Then, in July 1937, the Sino-Japanese War broke out.

On December 9, Japanese tanks arrived at the wall and bombarded the city. Four days later, they crashed through the giant stone gates and rolled into the streets littered with jagged tiles and broken bricks. Fifty thousand Japanese soldiers marched behind the tanks. A commander waved the flag of a startling red sun, and the soldiers raised their rifles and howled, sending the hungry crows fluttering into the sky.

* * *

Nanjing's Jinling Women's College had been a peaceful world of green lawns, red moongates, curved tile roofs, and a lotus pond. It was now a scene of screaming women jostling with one another getting into a refuge sanctioned by foreigners.

Inside a small office in a large hall of a red brick building, John Winthrop was frantically assigning beds to the refugees.

The twenty-seven-year-old brown-haired professor had been a co-leader of a research project carried out at another university. Calvin Ren, the principal investigator of the project, had collapsed in exhaustion and had left the city, as had other project workers. For almost a week, the American had turned his attention to helping refugees settle into the women's college.

In a dark overcoat, a blue necktie showing through the collar, and a large red cross on a piece of white cloth tied to his left arm, John Winthrop presented a sharp contrast to the women waiting anxiously outside the office he shared with Minnie Vautrin, acting president of Jinling Women's College.

The refugee women in the hall wore baggy pants and dark jackets. They carried blue sacks, broken umbrellas, rice, hams, salted vegetables, even cackling chickens, which sent a stale smell across the room. As sounds of distant cannons penetrated the walls, they winced and gathered their little children around them.

Male adults had been turned away. A drooling teenage boy crying "*ah ah ah ah*" refused to let go of a woman's sleeve. The woman, having to choose between possible rape and abandoning her retarded son, kowtowed on the pavement. Miss Vautrin relented and lent them a tent. Mother and son would spend the wintry night on the snowy bank of the lotus pond shivering inside the leaky shelter.

John stepped out of the office and glanced about the hall, hoping to see May Chen, an eighteen-year-old girl who had lived a few blocks away from him.

John had helped May with English, and May had helped John hunt for antiques. They had become friends.

People in May's neighborhood called her *Heimao,* which meant *Black-Hair*. Her *Baba* owned a small convenience store. That shoebox of corrugated metal was also where May's family of eight slept at night.

Six months ago, on a hot and sweaty summer day inside the beehives of antique booths, John suggested that they buy two cups of sour plum juice to quench their thirst. May's eyes lit up like the finest black onyx. But she wanted only one cup to share with him.

"I am not that thirsty," she insisted.

May was shy with men. She did not have a boyfriend. Indeed, John seldom saw her talk to young men of her age. Her father probably would not allow it.

So it surprised him one day when it began to rain, and she grabbed his arm to run for shelter. It was an inadvertent declaration of how she had come to regard him. People in the street stared disapprovingly. No wonder. She was growing into a woman's body, fresh as the apricot blossoms on a spring morning.

* * *

When John came back to the office, Minnie Vautrin, the fifty-one-year-old missionary from Minnesota, was cocking her head to listen to a woman who had just arrived from Changzhou—a city taken by the Japanese a few weeks earlier.

"We lived outside the city wall," said the peasant woman with deep lines on her dark brown face. "One morning my husband wanted to buy some herbs for our daughter, who had a high fever. He was stopped at the city gate. From our window we saw several Japanese soldiers surround him. Before long he was struggling to ward off the soldiers stripping him. Two of them tied him to the rear end of an army truck and drove off, his body bumping up a trail of dust. The soldiers being left behind stomped their feet and pointed at one another, bending to their bellies laughing."

"The Japanese soldiers can do any awful thing for no good reason," commented the American woman.

"How is your husband?" John asked the peasant woman.

"We fished his body out of a river several days later."

* * *

From the lotus pond a series of rapid-fire pops broke out. It sounded like soy beans dancing on a flaming wok in the Red Cross kitchen: *da da da da da . . . da da da da da*.

Women screamed and dropped to the floor, covering their heads. The hall was like water boiling over.

Violent poundings on the moongate. More screams.

A Chinese worker ran into the office, breathless. "Miss Vautrin, Japanese soldiers."

"What do they want?"

"*Hua-gu-niang*, what else?"

"They will get *young girls* over my dead body," the woman missionary seethed.

"Miss Vautrin, Japanese soldiers don't take *no* for an answer," the worker said.

"Let me talk to them, Minnie," John said.

"Thanks, John. I'll handle them myself."

The worker rolled his eyes.

"I'll go with you, Minnie," John Winthrop said.

A mustached Japanese officer wearing a monocle stood outside the front door of the building. He wore a double-breasted, mustard-colored military uniform with red straps on the shoulders, a dagger and a pistol at his waist. Behind him stood ten or twelve Japanese soldiers in sloppy khaki uniforms and tapering wool hats, their bayonets glistening.

"Good afternoon, officer," Minnie said. "What can I do for you?"

"Who are you?" the officer asked in broken English.

"My name is Minnie Vautrin. I am in charge here."

"Chinese soldiers hide in your buildings! We search!"

"We accept only women and children here. No men allowed, let alone soldiers. You've been misinformed, sir."

"The Intelligence of the Great Japanese Imperial Army never makes mistakes."

"I am very sorry, sir. You can't enter this building. The entire campus is in the Nanjing International Safety Zone."

"You lie! Kneel down!"

"How dare you! I certainly will not."

Whack! The Japanese slapped the missionary woman, who staggered back holding her cheek.

"Hey! She is telling the truth." John stepped forward and shielded Minnie with his body. "You don't have the right to search an American property." He showed the officer the American flag planted at the door.

"You have Chinese soldiers! You violate Red Cross rules! Get out of my way!" The Japanese shoved two thick fingers at John's chest.

John had played varsity football in college. He easily brushed the fingers away. His expression changed when he noticed something on the bank of the lotus pond. "What the devil did you people do?" He raised his voice, pointing at the bodies lying near a crumpled makeshift tent.

"We shot Chinamen." The officer glanced blandly at the corpses of a young boy and an older woman partly submerged in the lotus pond, streaks of blood slowly expanding in the water.

"Why?" John demanded.

"The man ran from us."

"He was only a boy, with the mind of an infant," John lamented. "He ran because he was frightened. No civilized man considers it reason enough to kill. What about the woman?"

"She attacked our soldiers."

"With the deadly weapons of her bare fists? You ought to be ashamed of yourself!"

Minnie gasped as the angry Japanese took a swing at John. The American blocked the bulky hand. Furious, the officer drew his dagger and lunged for the young professor. John dodged and knocked the dagger to the ground.

The soldiers behind snapped their rifles—all of them aiming at John's head.

Wheezing loudly, the Japanese officer stared at the indignant American towering over him by half a foot. Then his bulging mustard uniform deflated like a punctured balloon. He raised his right hand, and the soldiers lowered their guns.

The officer stooped to pick up his dagger. "You tell Chinese soldiers surrender. Hear? We will not harm. We give food and shelter."

The officer returned his dagger to the sheath and departed with his men.

* * *

John went to the Red Cross kitchen with Minnie for a quick lunch. On rushing back alone to the reception hall, he noticed a feeble figure leaning against the wall of his office. His first thought was: *Why is this young woman wearing an ugly pink blouse twice her size?* Then he realized she was May, the girl he had been looking for.

May's long hair covered her swollen face, her eyes bloody and almost completely closed. Her arms hung at her sides. Her torn pants revealed her naked thighs. Her lips quivered; her whole body shook. Her eyes darted left and right but did not see him. She jumped when he gently took her hands. When recognition came to her eyes, she tried to raise her arms but slumped to the ground without a sound.

He picked her up and helped her into his office, his heart pounding. "Oh Lord, please tell me you have spared this innocent girl from the shame she considers worse than death!"

His shoe caught the threshold of the office door, and he almost tripped.

"Careful, John!" Miss Vautrin was returning from the kitchen.

"Thanks, Minnie," John looked up and tried to relax his jaw into a smile. "I'm as blind as a bat. Five years of graduate school at MIT did that to me, you know."

Minnie gasped when she saw the badly injured young girl John was carrying. "John, what happened to her?" she asked, helping John lower the girl onto a couch.

"I'm afraid to even think about it."

"There are no doctors to call; most of them have left the city," Minnie said. "We should take her to a hospital"—she poured tea from a thermos bottle and handed it to him—"but let us give her some tea first."

The hot cup burned John's fingers, but he welcomed this diversion from the ache in his chest. "How are you doing, sweetheart?" he asked May, giving her the tea.

No answer.

"Where is your family?"

Still no answer.

"It's all right, love. You are safe now. You're here with me."

The girl shivered.

"You'll be fine, you'll see." He tried to be reassuring, if only to himself. "I am glad you knew you should come here." He studied her face. "Are you in pain?"

She nodded.

"Can you walk?" Minnie asked.

She shook her head.

John felt the ache in his chest again. "I'll go to get a rickshaw."

On his way to the street, John ran into John Rabe, chairman of the Nanjing International Safety Zone Committee. The balding middle-aged man offered him the use of his personal car with Germany's national flags on its windshield.

When John rushed back to fetch May, he was surprised that she was no longer slumping on the couch. Instead, she was limping along the floor outside his office like a wounded animal. She began screaming the moment he appeared, "They *killed* Baba! John, they killed my Baba!"

Heads turned all over the hall.

"Why? When?" He sounded like an idiot, and he knew it.

"I hate them, John," she said. "I hate them with every bone in my body! I will never forget any of their faces."

He saw the fire in her eyes, and it scared him.

He patted her back. "Cry it out, Nanjing girl. Cry out all of the rage in your body. You will feel better."

"I don't cry when I am down, John. No, no, no, no! That's not how it works. *Nanjing doesn't cry!*" She threw away his hand. "I'll hunt down those animals one day! I will choke all the breath out of their bodies with my bare hands! I'll pluck out their hearts, their livers, and their lungs, and eat them whole and raw. Then I'll burn their bodies into ashes and throw them to the pigs. That's what I'll do, John!"

A Chinese worker came running, "Mr. Winthrop, Japanese soldiers are setting up machine guns at our gate."

John spun around and ran to the front door.

Book I

Chapter 1

The Story of Chen May

Chen May, born in 1919, was the first child of a boat couple. Her Baba named her Heimao. As a little girl, she lived in a wooden junk not much more than ten feet long.

Her mother had haunted eyes and high cheekbones, looking like the opium smokers in yellowed photographs displayed in novelty shops. People living on the water gossiped that she must have used the narcotic once shipped to China under the auspices of the British Navy.

In the spring Mama coughed constantly. In the winter she complained of the cold. But Baba made it clear that she must do whatever she could to earn money—even when pregnant. So she went out every morning looking for any odd job.

When Mama looked unhappy, Heimao tried to lie low and avoid her.

One afternoon Mama went to help prepare for a dragon boat race, leaving Heimao in the junk alone. Nanjing was very hot and very humid in the summer, with the dubious distinction of being one of China's four furnaces. The three-year-old girl, sweating rivulets, scooped up water from one side of the boat and sprinkled it on herself. She kept giggling until a large wet spot grew on her pants. Then she was worried: Her mother would be upset with her. So she took her pants off to sun on the deck.

On returning, Mama shrieked at the sight. She meant to run over and give the girl a whack, but the ship wobbled under her feet and she slipped.

"Put your pants on, you damn fool!" Mama yelled from the deck as she crept toward a corner of the boat. "Don't you dare let any man see your bare bottom again!" She lay down and groaned loudly, a dark splotch of blood slowly staining her thin cotton pants.

Heimao was scared. She pulled a blanket over her mother's belly hoping to stop the blood.

Baba was livid when he came home and saw the scene. He ran off and dragged a midwife back to the boat.

Mama screamed all night before giving birth to the first of Heimao's younger brothers.

The midwife told Baba: "You were lucky to find me. Nobody else could have saved your son and your wife too. I need one hundred coppers."

The payment cleaned Baba out.

* * *

Baba named the newborn *Damao*.

Heimao was upset: *Da* meant *big; mao* meant *hair*. So her brother, a good three years younger, was the *Big-Hair* of the family?

"I am the eldest. Why didn't you name me Damao?" she demanded of Baba.

"Because you were born with a head of beautiful *black hair*," Baba said.

Grandaunt Nainai told her, "Don't worry, child, you are almost as important as your brother! On the day you were a month old, your Baba bought dozens of eggs and had them dyed red."

"Why did he do that?"

"Babies die prematurely. You were still alive and kicking a month after birth. That was reason enough for your Baba to celebrate!"

"What did he do with the eggs?"

"He gave them away to everyone he met."

"So wasteful?"

"Well, it was none of my business to tell him that—or how silly a grown man looked holding a baby in his arms all day!"

Heimao understood. Indeed, during last spring's festival, Baba had carried her on his shoulders to see the lantern procession. Excited to be in a crowd, she wrapped her arms around Baba's head and kept calling into his ear: "Hello, Baba! Hello, Baba! Hello, Baba!"

Baba never stopped smiling.

Still, she wished she had been named Damao.

Mama held a grudge against her little daughter. "Bad girl! Because of you, we lost every copper we had saved."

If the little girl was slow bringing Mama the salt she must have, Mama would yell, "Heimao! What hole did you drop dead in?"

A slap would land on the girl's behind.

Many a time Mama argued with a peddler for the amount of oil she had paid a copper for. The fight always ended with Mama hitting her daughter's back. "Watch where you are going, you *dumb egg*!" she shouted and glared back at the peddler.

Out of the blue, Mama would beat Heimao with the bamboo handle of a chicken-feather mop. Such a beating was *very* painful, leaving the girl's body with long, purplish swellings. Heimao never knew what she had done wrong.

Heimao took the punishment without flinching. She never begged for mercy. Finally Mama gave up: there was no satisfaction hitting a rag doll.

* * *

A year later, Mama gave birth to a second son. Baba named him *Ermao*—Second-Hair.

Every night the two little boys wet their slit pants. Baba scolded his wife for the mess around the boat. Mama hung her head. But the woman had worked to her limits and got angry. "Look here, I don't have three heads and six arms. Can I slave day in and day out and make your boat shine like a palace too? Go earn some serious money, you gorilla, and buy yourself a concubine you can bully!"

Once she had gotten started there was no stopping her. She rattled off his other sins, including but not restricted to the sweater he had promised and never bought her. Baba could hardly get in a word.

"Enough!" Baba shouted.

Mama smashed a dish on the floor.

She got a slap on the cheek.

Mama stomped off the boat yelling, "I will never come back to this filthy junk again!"

When Mama snuck back at midnight, Baba acted as if she were a ghost who could not be seen or heard. The next morning Mama wept quietly at the back of the boat.

* * *

They never ate more than twice a day.

To prepare dinner, Mama measured two handfuls of raw grains from a lidded urn and poured them into a pot.

Eyeing the grains suspiciously, she would return some of them to the urn. After adding water and bringing the rice to a boil, she would serve it with a dish of bean paste. Nothing else was on the dining stool. Mama hit Damao's hand when he dipped his chopsticks once too often into the bean paste. "An expensive son!" she declared.

On the days the bean paste ran out, she made do with a bowl of heavily salted water.

Baba liked the way Mama managed. "On a sunny day you prepare for the cloudy days. On a cloudy day you prepare for the sick days."

Heimao figured it a sunny day if Baba came home drenched in sweat. Mama would count out five coppers and go to the market. She brought back a bag of tofu and stir-fried it with the mushrooms she picked from the riverbank. The boys squatted around the dining stool waiting. They stopped beating each other over the head the moment Mama appeared with her wok. She dumped a big spoonful of tofu into Baba's bowl and gave the rest to her sons. Heimao didn't get any.

Baba would move a large portion of his tofu into Heimao's bowl as Mama stared.

The day was definitely cloudy if neither parent found any work. Baba said, "Good luck arrives singly while misfortune doesn't walk alone." Sure enough, the rice urn would run empty on this same day. A man could not lose face. So Mama went out to beg.

Never fully fed, Heimao was thin as a weed.

* * *

At the age of seven, Heimao was told to mind her brothers.

A little boy walked by their boat licking a lollipop, and Heimao's brothers nagged her for one too. She gathered wildflowers and taught them how to suck the nectar out of the stems.

Another day a girl half a head taller than May walked by. With a bob of hair barely covering her earlobes, she looked like a little samurai. "My name is Ren Kemei. I live five blocks from here," she said brightly.

Heimao warmed to her friendliness. She told the girl her name and added: "My father carries bags of rice to the harbor every day. He is very strong! What does your father do?"

"My father is a college teacher," Kemei said. "He is very smart. My brother's even smarter. He studies in America!"

Heimao was incredulous: "How did he get there?"

"He took an exam and won a scholarship!"

"That's crazy! What's his name?"

"Ren Kewen," Kemei said. "He has an English name, but I forget how to say it."

"What does he study in America?"

"Physics."

Heimao had absolutely no idea what that was.

"It's funny," Ren Kemei said and laughed, "but he was a middling student till the eighth grade."

"What happened?" Heimao was all ears.

"One day he went to the city library, picked up a math book for high school students, and found that he could understand most of what it said."

"I would die if I could do something like that!" Heimao sighed.

"Well, he began to read something called calculus. Several months later, his teacher entered him into a citywide math contest. He walked away with the second prize."

Heimao had had only Baba to look up to. Now she must add Kemei to the short list. The girl had an incredible brother!

A few weeks later, Grandaunt Nainai dropped in with a round loaf wrapped in lotus leaves. "*Babaofan* for your thirtieth birthday." She beamed at Baba.

Babaofan was a sweet and sticky cake imbedded with a million kinds of dried fruits and nuts, a dessert delicious beyond belief. Nainai unwrapped the lotus leaves to reveal its multi-colored syrup. Baba sliced it on the dining stool. The little boys hopped. The largest piece was offered to Nainai. Then Baba beckoned the children to come and get their share.

The two boys jostled each other running over. The smaller boy ducked and snatched the biggest piece left on the stool, but Damao grabbed it away holding it above his head. The smaller boy bawled, shaking every eardrum on the boat with his healthy lungs. Baba looked embarrassed but did nothing.

Heimao understood. The eldest son of the family must be given face.

"Ermao can have my piece," Heimao said.

Baba must be given face too.

* * *

Baba worked as a coolie in Xiaguan Harbor. He carried a bamboo pole on his right shoulder with a rattan basket at each end. Walking in quick little steps, he hissed *hee-hoo-hee-hoo-hee-hoo-hee-hoo* all the way to the harbor, passing most of the pedestrians.

One day Baba borrowed money from a loan shark and bought a pushcart. Now he could transport a large load of rice with less effort. Every time he made a delivery to the harbor, he was rewarded with three pounds of rice and a pat on the back.

But he couldn't find enough work to feed five mouths and pay interest on the cart loan too. "My head bloats to twice its size every time the loan shark gives me a tongue lashing!" he would say.

"What a great buy!" Mama hissed.

Mama warned Heimao to watch out: Baba was going to sell her. She would be living with a family of strangers and be married to one of the family's sons when she reached thirteen.

Heimao went to tell Baba she was not going.

Baba's eyes widened and his large body shook. Heimao covered her head, thinking that he was going to strike her. But after a long time had passed and no blows came, she looked up and found Baba crying. A pain stabbed her heart. She wanted very much to wipe away his tears. Unable to reach him on tiptoes, she was readying herself to jump when Baba squatted down and held her waist with both of his hands.

"Heimao, Baba owes a lot of money! I fear all of us will starve to death. You will be spared if you go to another home."

The little girl began to sob.

"Heimao, Baba cannot bear to see you cry. Please don't!" Baba said in a coarse voice.

Heimao immediately dried her eyes with her hands. "I won't, Baba," she said obediently.

"The family I've found for you are not boat people," Baba said. "They live on land! I've made sure that their son has all limbs and round eyes and all."

"Please wait a month, Baba."

"Why?"

"I will show you I can earn a living by myself."

"Child, you don't know what you are saying."

"Give me a chance, Baba," the little girl begged. "I don't want to leave your boat."

Baba wiped his face with his fingers and kept nodding. Heimao was happy. Now she knew that Baba did not really want to sell her.

A boy in the neighborhood often boasted to Heimao that he knew how to make a lot of money. One day the secret came out: Trains dumped furnace dregs, and you could find *er-tan* on the railroad tracks.

"What's that?" Heimao asked.

"Coal chunks only half burned!" the boy whispered. "Really good stuff. You can sell them and get rich!"

After that talk with Baba, Heimao got up early the next morning and went to the railway station, a basket on her arm. The tracks were full of roaming children. After a train had arrived and unloaded the furnace, children swarmed to the black heap left behind. They looked like the gulls near the riverbank, swooping down in droves, pecking at the spoils that had been dumped. She had no chance.

Heimao went home after the afternoon meal had been served.

"I have already eaten," she lied to Mama.

The gnawing in her stomach kept her tossing and turning all night. She got up before daybreak and went to the train station. It was as quiet as a graveyard. She immediately spotted a little pile near the track. Even in the dim morning light she could tell er-tan from the thoroughly burned coal dregs: The former were black while the latter were gray. Her heart pounding, she picked out the good ones and filled half her basket.

By the time the other children drifted in, Heimao had already planted herself at the most strategic spot she could determine. She fought tooth and nail with the boys who tried to shove her away—and bit their hands when they tried to pull her away. She was surprisingly strong and had no fear.

A uniformed man came out of an office and yelled, "Hey, you tough guys, showing off your muscles, eh? If you have any balls, you'll go to Shandong and kick those Japanese assholes out of China, not shame my eyes beating up on a pea pod of a girl, fuck your mother!"

The boys backed away.

Late in the afternoon, Heimao dragged her full basket to the noodle stalls nearby. The owners of these stalls were tough-looking men wearing oily aprons around their fat bellies, black tunics covering only part of their hairy chests.

"Please, sir, could you use some coal?" the girl asked in a small voice, choosing the man with the least hair.

"Go away!" the man bellowed. But his features softened when he saw her face. "A girl, for heaven's sake!" he exclaimed. "OK, OK, don't look at me like that. I'll give you a bowl of sunny-spring noodles."

Such kind of noodles had neither meat nor vegetables to go with it, but before long she began to belch loudly, scraping the bottom of the ceramic bowl.

"Just this once, alright?" the man said, emptying the er-tan into a barrel. "Don't you come back to me no more!"

But as she licked her lips and clucked her tongue, the man swallowed hard and told the little girl she could bring er-tan to him the next day.

That evening she asked Baba, "What did the Japanese assholes do in Shandong, Baba?"

"Watch your mouth, Heimao!"

"But, Baba, that is what the uncle in the train station said. He was hopping mad at the Japanese."

"So am I."

"Why?"

"Those midgets killed tens of thousands of our people in Jinan last year." Jinan was the capital of Shandong Province.

"And our police uncles just let them?"

"Chiang Kai-shek sent a representative named Cai Gongshi to talk to them. The Japanese gouged his eyes out, cut off his ears, nose, tongue, and limbs, and did the same to the people accompanying him."

"Noooo! Did any of those people live?"

"Nah, the Japanese soldiers killed all of them."

"Where were our soldiers?" Heimao cried.

"Chiang Kai-shek moved all of them out of the city."

"Why?"

"He did not want a fight."

"Why?"

"He's afraid of the Japanese!"

"Baba, do the Japanese kill people everywhere they go?"

"You go and ask Nainai."

"How does she know?"

"She used to live in Southern Manchuria. One day the Japanese came and chopped off her husband's head."

"They dared to do that to my granduncle?"

"They killed almost everybody in the seaport where your Nainai used to live."

"Why do the Japanese kill, Baba? Aren't they people like us?"

"They sure don't act like it."

"Why?"

"I don't know."

"Will they come here, Baba?'

"I hope not."

"No worry, Baba. If they do, I will chop off their heads."

"Ha!" Baba gave her shoulder a pat.

Heimao learned to rummage through the dumps for old newspapers and empty bottles. She bound the papers with a string, cleaned the bottles in the river, and sold them for a copper or two. Other times she collected *zai-bian-ze*, tall water-reeds that had withered and fallen into the water. She sunned them dry and hauled them home as cooking fuel for Mama.

One late afternoon on her way home, Heimao ran into Baba, who thrust into her hand a small loaf wrapped in lotus leaves.

"Babaofan!" she cried, knowing that a bite of the rice cake meant as many as eight delicious tastes in her mouth!

"I broke the deal with the family I had talked to," Baba announced. "You are staying with us."

The loaf fell to the ground. Baba picked it up and put it back into her hand. Heimao meant to unwrap the lotus leaves, but this was sort of hard to do when you were looking lovingly at Baba muttering, "Thank you, thank you, thank you."

Chapter 2

The Best Student at MIT

In 1910, John Winthrop was born to a China trade family in Salem, Massachusetts.

He didn't distinguish himself very much during elementary school. The smallest child in his class, he often fell prey to bullies. Motivated by several such incidents in school, he did physical exercises at home to get bigger. But nothing much happened until the summer before his last high school year, when he sprouted three inches. The following fall he tried out for football. He was cut. So he hit the books hard, and, a year later, made valedictorian. He was subsequently admitted to MIT, the best engineering school in America, where he met Calvin Ren, Kemei's brother, a month into his first semester.

MIT students came mostly from New England. Very few of them had lived in other parts of the country, let alone a nation across the Pacific. John was surprised one evening when he saw an Asian student eating silently by himself in the dining hall of the East Campus Dorm. Other students at his table talked with one another—none to him.

Having encountered similar situations in his early school years, John didn't like what he saw. He walked to the chair next to the foreign student and sat down. They introduced each other and shook hands.

"Glad to know you, Calvin," John said. "This is quite a coincidence. My grandfather once served as bishop of the Episcopal church in the very city you came from."

"Is that right?" the Chinese student exclaimed. "How did your grandfather happen to go to Nanjing, may I ask?"

John heard the delight in the heavily accented voice. It must be difficult to come to a foreign country so young and all alone.

"His father used to be a supercargo—a business agent, on an American vessel buying teas and silks from China," John answered. He was about to describe the family house his great grandfather had built, but decided that the Chinese student would have a hard time understanding what Queen Anne style was.

Calvin said he had arrived in Boston that morning. John looked at the small face that had not made the transition from a juvenile to a grown man. He wondered if this boy could handle the rigorous MIT academic program.

"You've missed a month of lectures," John said. "The calculus exam will be held in Building Ten tomorrow, under the Dome at the center of the campus. Since you don't have time to prepare, I would ask to be excused from it."

The following morning John went to the exam and saw hundreds of students already settled in their seats in the large hall. Others were looking for theirs. Calvin sat quietly among them, his round, silver-rimmed glasses blinding when he looked up.

The exam was difficult, and John soon lost himself in it. After twenty minutes, a faint murmur rose in the hall. John looked to the podium and saw Calvin handing in his paper. Several students snickered. The Chinese boy was obviously in over his head.

Students gossiped who was the best among them. By consensus, that person was an epileptic sophomore named Arthur Efron. Walking with a cane and carrying a typewriter for taking notes, Efron was incredibly brilliant. Many students struggled to reach the GPA of 2.0. Efron's was 4.33. He had gotten an A+ for every one of his courses—including English Lit!

"Who can compete with Arthur?" was the saying around the campus.

But soon John heard the rumor that a Chinese freshman might run a close second. This came about after Professor Mathew had been overheard telling a teaching assistant in the undergraduate math office: "He scored a perfect one hundred, while the next highest score in the entire freshman class was seventy-eight!"

* * *

The housemaster of the East Campus dorm called on John. Dennis, Calvin's present roommate, had hidden a twenty-dollar bill inside his chemistry textbook. Today he had found it missing. The angry student stormed into the housemaster's apartment demanding that Calvin be moved to another room. The young assistant professor talked to several students, but none was willing to share space with Calvin. Could John help?

"Gosh!" John said. "I'd better apologize to Calvin for the rudeness of my dorm-mates."

He exchanged beds with Dennis, giving up a river view glistening with the reflection of red maple leaves.

Few knew about the incident. No one talked about it.

John discovered Calvin's uncanny power of thinking. The Chinese student was able to see the answer to a scientific problem without going through all the logical steps. It seemed that he could take a gigantic leap over a scientific hurdle yet manage to land on his feet. The leap was made instinctively, and most of the time he couldn't explain why. More than once John Winthrop and classmates got together to fill in the steps Calvin had not provided. They would find Calvin's solution correct.

John also found it remarkable that Calvin did not regard a rigorous mathematical proof to a scientific problem necessary. To Calvin, only the result counted. Rarely did he bother to justify his procedure. Instead, after making up some special numerical tests, he would consider his result validated if it passed them. Calvin's approach contrasted with the methodology emphasized by almost all MIT professors.

John spent an inordinate amount of time in the MIT engineering library. But Calvin could do his calculations anywhere—even sitting on the toilet bowl.

It was obvious that the Chinese student had a passion for mathematics. On the other hand, he soon fell behind in his Shakespeare reading. Such a student could never reach Efron's rarified level.

Living with Calvin had a few surprises. He insisted that the room must be pitch-dark when he went to sleep. It was not enough just to turn off the lights. All curtains must be drawn. He even sealed the bottom of their door with towels.

"I have sensitive retinas," Calvin explained.

"Calvin, you are difficult!"

Nor did John understand Calvin's eating quirks. While not particular about the kind of foods he consumed, Calvin wanted his broccoli to have wholesome stems and leaves, his pork chop a perfect square.

"The way Confucius liked it," Calvin said.

* * *

John had no interest in girls before his last year in high school. There were simply no common grounds. For example, he liked sports while they didn't. But in the fall term of his senior year, he suddenly became consumed by the sight of their breasts. Being younger than many of the girls in his class, he spent hours working up the courage to ask one of them for a date. His awkward manner didn't help. More often than not, the girl would decline.

His situation in college did not improve much. MIT students liked to say they worked hard and played hard, but the truth was that their social environment was drab. Few female students applied to MIT. With the classrooms filled mostly with males, life was not unlike that of sailors at sea. While pretty women could be found off campus, students from Harvard's business school or law school usually took the first picks.

Billy Silver, John's former high school classmate, attended Caltech—MIT's West Coast equivalent. When Billy came home for the summer after his sophomore year, John showed him around campus. The guided tour ended with a leisurely stroll on Massachusetts Avenue. When they needed to know the time, John went to seek help from a young woman waiting at the bus stop across the street.

That turned out to be a mistake—but John found out too late that she was very pretty. He froze, his words turning into stutters. With his face becoming redder by the second, he feigned a coughing fit and fled.

Billy took this incident as proof that Caltech was superior to MIT.

"*We* are better off than *you* are," he told John gleefully.

Chapter 3

Going to School

On a summer morning in Nanjing, half a globe away from Boston, a merchant had a rice shipment to deliver to the harbor, but could find no one to help except a large coolie.

Baba ran all day. That evening, he came home with a bag of rice weighing as much as five pounds—the most he had ever been paid for a day's work. As he emptied the bag into his urn, a purse fell out. His jaw dropped when he found it filled with silver dollars!

Mama had a rare smile, counting out two coppers, and disappeared into the night. She came back with three eggs. The boys cheered when their mother carried to the dining stool a dish of steamed tofu capped by yellow shreds of fried eggs!

The next morning Baba got up and muttered that he had not slept well. "I must return the money."

"After eating the eggs?" his pregnant wife said. "Please think of the little one in my belly."

"I'm thinking of the three bouncing around us," Baba said. "If I cheat the employer who gave me rice, the thunder god will strike all of them dead!"

The rice merchant had hidden the purse containing the silver in the bag of rice to conceal it from his own wife. But somehow he had forgotten all about it. He couldn't stop talking to other merchants about the good work the honest coolie had done for him. Baba got more work. He cleared his debt with the loan shark in a couple of months. In a few more months he bought another cart and hired a coolie to work for him. Silver dollars rolled in. Baba hid them inside his waist belt. Every night when May heard clinking sounds, she knew it was Baba laying out the coins and counting them.

In Baba's neighborhood there was a small convenience store. One day after work Baba came to take a break under a tree by the store. The store owner came out to offer him a cigarette. They squatted together and smoked without exchanging a word. As Baba finished and was about to get up, the owner held his arm.

"I need money to pay my gambling debts."

"Can we talk inside?" Baba asked.

He came out owning the store.

Baba sold his boat and his carts. During the day he worked as storekeeper. At night he boarded up and turned the place into his family's sleeping quarters. Heimao was his lucky star. After keeping her, his family had become land people.

* * *

Good days flowed by as easily as the water in the Yangtze River. Mama was in labor again.

But it was all thunder and no rain. The labor went on for a full day—but nothing happened. By the evening Mama had groaned herself hoarse. Nainai came over to help. At night Baba took his children next door to stay with Qian Ma, a woman who owned a spare cot on which her teenage daughter had once slept. The young girl had been sold to a wine house two years earlier.

Heimao slept on the cot. In the middle of the night, she was wakened by a rocking hand. In her drowsiness she saw Baba bending over her with a scowl on his face. She quickly got up and dressed. Baba woke up his two sons stretching on the ground and herded everybody back to his house.

Nainai, Qian Ma, and Sun Ma, another neighborhood wife, were whispering in the shadow behind a dim oil lamp. The midwife held a bawling baby. Heimao asked Baba if it was a boy.

"Yeah," Baba replied impatiently before pushing Heimao to a corner of the house. Mama was lying on a mat covered by several layers of blankets. The glow on her face reminded Heimao of a glorious sunset. For the first time Heimao thought Mama beautiful.

Mama cast her glance on the two boys rubbing their eyes. A wan smile appeared on her lips. Then she said in a weak voice, "Heimao, your mother has a bad temper and didn't treat you right. But sometimes she did not feel good herself, you know." Her voice trailed off.

Heimao was stunned. What brought this on? And why was Mama referring to herself in a way she had never done before?

After a moment of silence, Mama turned to Baba and whispered something into his ear. Then she turned back to Heimao. "In another month the clothes will need to be sunned," she said. "There is a fish head in the wok. Eat it tomorrow or it will spoil, which would be a great pity."

"I think that's all," she told Baba. "I am sorry I never took good care of you. After I go, my soul will look after you and your family."

Then her head fell to one side and her eyes closed.

Baba cried out, "*Ahmei! Ahmei!*"

Little Sister was the endearing name Heimao had heard Baba call Mama in their better moments. Not hearing any response, Baba fell on his knees covering his face and howled, "Answer me, all you gods in heaven! I burn incense to honor you every New Year's Day, and I never step on the beetles crawling under my feet. Why do I deserve this?"

Heimao and her brothers also went down on their knees.

Baba angrily pushed away the hands pulling him up. Heimao knelt for so long her knees became numb. Her mind was more so. She wondered how her mother, alive one moment, could be dead the next. When told to stand up, she collapsed.

* * *

The chores of caring for the baby fell on Heimao's thin shoulders. She boiled porridge, but the baby spat it out. She took the soiled clothing to the pebble beach, but the two brothers she brought with her kept running into the water, paying no heed to her frantic shouting.

Neighbor Sun Ma offered to wet-nurse the baby. The heavy-set woman, married to a military officer named Sun Chi, had just given birth to a daughter. She brought her newborn to Baba's house and breastfed the two babies together.

The cries of two infants soon shook the house. No one dared to say that Sun Ma's milk was inadequate. Still, she was humiliated. The chaos affected the store business.

Salvation arrived in the form of a widow with large hands, large feet, and a baby son of her own. Rumor had it that her zodiac, not dysentery, was the true cause for the early death of her late husband. Good families wouldn't let her enter their doors, lest the evil spell she carried with her would ruin their households.

But the woman was robust, so Baba asked a matchmaker to take his proposal to her. The wedding banquet was held in the store. There were two guests: Nainai and the matchmaker. The bride wore a blue tunic, the highlight of her attire being the red silk flower in her hair. Each of Baba's children got a bowl of noodles to eat in a corner. Marrying a widow deserved no hearty celebration, and she got none.

Baba told his children to call her *Ma.*

* * *

Ma knew her place. Although her own baby was already five months old, she called him *Didi*, or younger brother, and Baba's newborn *Gege*, or older brother.

The next day Baba's baby stopped crying. In a few weeks, neighbors marveled at how fat he looked.

In order to prevent the older children from wetting their bedding, Ma got a piss pot and made the rounds several times a night. The two boys were unhappy to be roused from the comfort inside their blankets. Ermao would grab his prick and refuse to pee into the pot. Ma had to do a lot of coaxing to make him cooperate.

No matter how little sleep she got at night, Ma would look perfectly rested in the morning and cheerfully carry out her daily duties.

* * *

Baba's business thrived. Good times came back to the family again! But Heimao never forgot how close she had come to being sold. She was determined to become independent.

An opportunity arrived one summer day. A Caucasian woman came to the store introducing herself as Miss Minnie Vautrin of Jinling Women's College. She told Baba that her college had founded a school for neighborhood children. She would waive tuition for his.

Heimao was overjoyed. But her happiness only lasted until Baba told Ma to make preparations for the *boys* to go to school. The children Baba had in mind did not include his eldest.

"Why do you leave me out, Baba?" Heimao demanded.

"School is not for girls," Baba said. "The boys will *touch* you. Who will marry you after they do such a thing to you?"

"Baba, there were plenty of boys in the train station. All of them stayed away from me. Indeed, none of them dared to look at me in the eyes."

"That's enough! I must make sure your future parents-in-laws will have nothing to complain about you."

"I will never marry," Heimao shouted, "not even to a diligent student."

Before this confrontation, Heimao had not imagined herself capable of hating Baba. Now it became difficult just to sit at the same table with him for dinner.

* * *

Chiang Kai-shek had succeeded in defeating most of the warlords, and China's strongman chose Nanjing as his capital. Automobiles, movie houses, and fashionable shops grew in the city.

Baba's business thrived. Now he could afford to go to the bathhouse to get his feet rubbed. He even bought a wide-band gold ring from Qian Ma's courtesan daughter, who got it as a gift from a client.

For many days people complained that the store was stinking with human waste. Ma found the culprit: Damao, who had not taken a bath for days. After that, Baba took Damao to the bathhouse with him.

Baba gave the children some coppers to spend. Flushed with riches, Ermao was swindled into buying a fake antique coin with his first monthly allowance.

The streets of Nanjing were full of pushcarts selling steaming sweet rice cakes. These peddlers held a device called *bangzi*—bamboo slabs bound together with strings. When the slabs were twisted against one another, they issued a sharp screeching sound that made people wince and cover their ears. As soon as the children heard it, they flew out to surround the cart and took turns to shout at the peddler. Other peddlers carried large bamboo baskets on their heads. They sang out the goods they were selling: buns with sweet bean paste, stinky tofu, or shrimp wontons. The children imitated the songs. Each of them would say, "No, listen, it sounds more like this," and give his own rendition.

Baba's youngest son, Sanmao, heard the peddlers, but he was not allowed to go out—he was too small. Ma asked one of the peddlers to come into the store and sing for him. This turned the little boy into a happy bundle of squeals and energy. Doling out a precious copper to buy a bowl of sweet lotus soup, he would not shake hands with his idol despite Ma's repeated encouragement.

Heimao was the only child who refused the coppers from the hateful Baba. Her silent war with him stretched first to days and then weeks. She wanted to hurt him. But she was hurting herself more.

The evening before the fall semester began, Heimao heard Baba telling Ma in a loud voice to prepare a satchel for *daughter* to carry to school. Although he was looking at Ma while he spoke, Heimao knew he was actually talking to her. She felt a pain. Baba must be hurting inside losing face in front of his family. Then a tide of gratitude swept over her. She ran to him and went down on her knees kowtowing furiously.

* * *

Heimao went to the school's registration office the next morning. Miss Vautrin was sitting behind a desk chatting with a Chinese man in a Zhongshan uniform—gray pants and gray jacket with four pockets. A few children hung around a corner of the office.

The American missionary saw the little girl and seemed delighted.

"I-I would like to register," Heimao stammered, intimidated by the presence of educated adults.

Miss Vautrin asked for her name and age.

"My name is Chen. I'm ten," Heimao replied, then gave Miss Vautrin her date of birth.

"And what did you say your first name was?" Miss Vautrin asked again.

The little girl blushed. "I have none," she said. Heimao was a nickname, not a name that could be used in an official situation.

Everybody laughed, all except Miss Vautrin. Visibly shaken, she stood up and went around the desk to hug the little girl. "You said you were born in the fifth month of the year," she said hoarsely. "Your English name will be May. But I still need a Chinese name for you."

The man in gray uniform muttered "May . . . May," then wrote a Chinese character on a piece of paper. "This word is also pronounced as 'May.' You know what it means?"

Heimao shrank into a small ball.

A tiny girl came over. "Why, it is winter plum, China's national flower!" she exclaimed.

Heimao was jealous that a girl so little could read so well.

The man added the Chinese character "Chen" in front of the character "May" he had written. "Family name before first name," he said. "Your full Chinese name will be Chen May."

Miss Vautrin made May register for the second grade. The girl would have to make up a year's lessons on her own.

* * *

On the first morning of school, May looked for Damao but couldn't find him. When the same thing happened the following morning, May got the message: Damao did not want to be seen with her.

Neither did Damao call her *Jiejie* (elder sister) in front of his schoolmates. He warned her to stay clear of the places in which he spent time and pretended not to see her if they happened upon each other. Laughter would ring out behind her as soon as she walked past him.

But May was happy. She counted every school day a sunny day—unaware of the storm gathering in China's Northeast.

Chapter 4

The Boxer Reparation Foundation

One Saturday evening at the end of his sophomore year, Calvin put on a suit and tie and told his roommate that he would be going out. Upon questioning, he admitted that it was for a party sponsored by the Boston Chinese Student Association.

Told that the party would cost fifty cents, John was surprised. Calvin had rarely taken a nickel out of his pocket to buy coffee. Why was he willing to spend a large sum of money for such an occasion?

After Calvin left, John decided to get dressed and go to a fraternity house mixer to meet girls. At the door of the dorm, he was told that attendance was limited to fraternity brothers.

Next morning in the bathroom, John told Calvin about his wasted evening and asked Calvin about his.

"Oh, so-so." Calvin shrugged.

"Did you meet some nice Chinese girls?" John asked, half in jest.

"Sure, sure. There was one sitting next to me at dinner."

John looked up from the washbowl. "Did you talk to her?"

"Sure, sure. She talked to me, so I talked to her."

"And?" John asked.

"We talked some more in the Public Garden."

John almost dropped his toothbrush on the floor. "You went with her to the park, *alone*?"

"Well, Judy wanted to show me some places she liked."

"Judy? Is she from China?"

"No. She grew up in Boston's Chinatown."

"What does she do?'

"She is a freshman at Boston University."

"Is she pretty?"

"I don't know," Calvin said.

John thought the answer strange. He interpreted it as *yes*.

"Where does she live?"

"I don't know."

"For heaven's sake, Calvin! Why didn't you ask her?"

"John! The ratio of male to female is ten to one in the Boston Chinese community. A Chinese girl here doesn't give out her address—not to someone she meets for the first time. I would have to beg to get Judy's, and even then the chance is slim. I've never begged in my whole life, John, and I'm not about to start now."

John shook his head: A young man without a girlfriend could not afford to worry about losing face!

The next afternoon at the dorm, the front desk called John to come down: A girl was waiting in the lobby.

John's heart leaped: A girl?

In the narrow foyer, he found a skinny Asian young girl with a dimple on her left cheek. She held a thick textbook over her skirt with both hands. The thin brown arms outside her white sleeves looked like two long twigs.

"May I help you, Miss?" John asked, disappointed.

"Is Calvin in?" the girl asked in a small voice. As if explanations had been demanded, she added, "He promised to help me with calculus."

"I'm sorry. He's out," John said, wondering which high school she was from.

"When is he expected, please?" the girl asked in an even smaller voice, her hands twisting on the textbook.

"He didn't say."

The girl was almost reduced to tears.

"Could you come again next Sunday, about the same time?" John said. "I'll make sure that Calvin will be here to help you. What's your name?"

"Judy."

She came back the next week—and continued to do so for many Sundays.

* * *

Early in the next academic year, John was elected vice president of the junior class. Elated by this unexpected honor, he joined the MIT debating club to improve his speaking skills. On the academic front, though, he remained a B student. One day Professor Edwin Dickinson praised his lab reports. Later on, several graduate students talked to him about their experiments. It did not take him long to realize that his mind had a practical bent. Abstract concepts were not his forte. Possessing neither the talent nor the mathematical skills for theoretical work, he should channel his energy into becoming a good experimentalist.

* * *

John didn't think Judy a *looker*. But she became almost beautiful when she talked about Calvin.

One Sunday afternoon Calvin went out to mail a letter, and John was alone with her in the dorm's living room.

"The moment I laid my eyes on him, I knew he was the man for me," Judy said, a glow coming to her cheeks.

"Falling in love at first sight?" John grinned.

"Not that. But Calvin was the first person who saw me as a woman," Judy said.

"What do you mean?"

"I mean . . . no one had paid attention to me. I didn't get to go to the prom." She blushed. "I felt pretty for the first time when I met Calvin at that dinner."

"What happened?"

"He stole a glance at me and looked away. I thought he wasn't pleased with what he saw. But he stole another look at me soon after. It was out of the corner of his eye, but I caught it!" Judy giggled.

"Son of a gun!" John said.

"His face turned as red as the tomato in his salad bowl. I had to do my best to draw him out of his shell." Her eyes shone.

"Did you?"

"No! But he looked so cute in his dark suit!" Judy giggled again. "That's why I decided that I'd marry him." She covered her face with both hands, seemingly shocked by the words coming out of her mouth. Then she gave John a smile so tentative and yet so enticing it sent his heart pumping.

To John, though, Judy's prospect for marriage was distant. Although Calvin seemed interested in her, he was more into his studies. He rarely took the initiative to spend time with her.

* * *

At the beginning of his senior year, John realized with some wonderment that he had grown to six feet tall. He tried out for the school's varsity football team, the MIT Beavers. It took half a semester, but he made cornerback on a team described as having a higher IQ than body weight.

But soon afterward, in a football game between MIT and Babson College, John suffered a shoulder separation, which took a long time to heal. For advice, Judy introduced him to a pretty nurse named Cynthia. John found that Cynthia was also raised in Salem, his hometown, and that the two had some mutual friends. Cynthia lived in an apartment in Back Bay, a couple of miles from MIT, and John often took public transportation to go see her.

One day a research assistant took John and Calvin to Professor King's office. The Nobel Laureate grabbed a piece of chalk trying to solve the problem the graduate student had brought him. Since the undergrads were supposed to be there to gawk at the famous professor, nobody bothered to explain anything to them. When Professor King stopped and rubbed his chin, Calvin stood up and went to the blackboard. "May I try it?" he asked—and proceeded to solve the problem.

John became convinced that Calvin would have a distinguished career in theoretical physics.

John and Calvin applied to MIT graduate schools. After waiting for a few months, John heard the good news: He had been accepted by the aeronautical division of the mechanical engineering department. Hired as a full-time research assistant under Professor Dickinson, he would be earning his living.

A few weeks later, Calvin also heard from the physics department, offering him a part-time teaching assistantship.

John told Calvin that he would talk to Professor Franklin, chairman of physics.

Calvin asked, "What can you tell him?"

"That you are the best student at MIT."

"But, John, that person is Arthur Efron, not me," Calvin cried.

"Sorry, pal, I've changed my mind. I think you are the more original."

When John came back, Calvin asked anxiously, "Did Professor Franklin laugh you out of the office?"

"Well, he said your GPA is not high enough for full financial support."

"He's right!" Calvin said.

"Calvin, that was an excuse. You've got to understand this: You are Chinese."

"I'm a guest in your country. I'm thankful for anything my host gives me. One day China will become strong, and we will have our own MIT."

"I know, I know," John said. "But that will be a long time away. What are you going to do in the meantime?"

"I'll apply to the Boxer Reparation Foundation."

The Boxer Rebellion took place in Northern China at the turn of the century, when angry mobs killed foreigners and burned Christian churches. In its aftermath, the United States extracted from the Chinese government reparations equal to twenty times the American losses as recorded in the US congressional records. Years later, a Chinese diplomat named Liang Cheng succeeded in persuading the Congress to establish an educational foundation in China with the excess money.

One afternoon Calvin returned to his dormitory room holding a letter in his hand. He looked sick.

John looked up from the book he had been reading. "What's wrong, Calvin?"

"I can't bring myself to open this letter," Calvin replied.

John did it for him. "Calvin, the Boxers Reparation Foundation has granted you a stipend!" he said after reading the letter inside.

Calvin leaped into the air. "Thank God! Thank God! Let's go out and celebrate tonight!"

"You mean going to the Old Howard Theatre in Scollay Square?" John said with a wink.

Students often joked about the theater that offered the only striptease in Boston. John had never ventured into its dark arena. When he occasionally walked by the lamppost in front of the theater, heavily made-up women would beckon him, and he would walk away quickly.

That evening, John and Calvin took the subway to downtown and walked several blocks to a Chinese restaurant. John ordered egg drop soup, chicken chow mein, and egg foo young, and shared them with Calvin.

The Chinese student insisted on paying the bill: "It is my invitation."

On the subway ride back to MIT, John said: "I enjoyed the dinner, Calvin. Thank you very much."

Calvin frowned. "But the food is horrible. It's not Chinese!"

* * *

Three months later, both John and Calvin finished their undergraduate studies. After attending the commencement ceremony in June, they had to move out of the East Campus Dorm. John had heard of a vacancy in Cynthia's apartment building in Back Bay, and convinced Calvin to move into it with him.

Chapter 5

The Invasion of Manchuria

Early one September morning, May came out of her front door, as usual, and took a deep breath. The air was so fresh! Most stores on the street were still closed. Several men hurried on the road, their Zhongshan uniforms telling May that they had some official capacity. A crowd practiced tai chi on a small lawn, an old man with three strands of white beard leading the rhythmic motion.

Her classroom was ten minutes away on foot.

The thirty-six desks in the classroom were arranged in six rows. The smallest students took the desks in the front. May, the tallest, was assigned a desk in the back. She was self-conscious about her position. Everyone in school must be gossiping that she was too old for second grade!

May sat down and recited the five letters taught the day before: *f*, *g*, *h*, *i*, *j*. Missionary schools offered English classes early. Baba was proud about that. He told his neighbors, "My daughter's going to make a lot more money than I."

May liked the sounds she was making. She was speaking English! Feeling good, she gradually dozed off. Then her eyes felt warm and bright. It was the sun on her face. It must be late. Why was the classroom empty? She looked out the window and found many of her classmates in the yard talking and gesticulating excitedly.

Kemei, Calvin's sister, walked past the classroom window. The girl loved spicy peanuts and dropped into Baba's store frequently.

"What's going on?" May called out.

"Someone bombed the South Manchuria Railway early this morning!" Kemei shouted to May over the din.

May rubbed her eyes and yawned. "Who?" She didn't get enough sleep the night before, and Manchuria was northeast of Nanjing, like a million miles away!

"Who else? The Japanese!" Kemei hissed.

May walked to the window and put her elbows on the sill. "Why would they do a stupid thing like that?"

"They not only did it. They also blamed it on *us*!" Kemei spat out the last word with vehemence.

"I don't understand." May's mind was still a blank.

"Idiot, don't you know anything? Those Japanese wanted an excuse to attack Shenyang. They created one!" Shenyang was Manchuria's largest city.

It got May's attention. "That's so wicked!" May cried. "I hate cheats. I hope they will be punished."

"Well, those cheats are doing very well, thank you very much," Kemei said. "They took over Shenyang without firing a shot!"

"How could such a thing have happened?"

"Have you heard of a man called Zhang Xue-liang?" Kemei asked.

"Isn't he the 'young marshal' who controls all of our troops in Manchuria?" May asked.

"That's right. The man's a prick! When Japanese troops stormed his city, he was dancing with a movie actress and couldn't be disturbed," Kemei said.

"He ought to be shot!" May exclaimed.

The bell rang, but most students still hung around the schoolyard. Miss Vautrin came out of her office and yelled at them.

May's arithmetic teacher didn't start the session with a rehash of the multiplication table. Instead, he told the students about the forests and the mineral reserves of Manchuria.

A messenger hurried into the classroom. The teacher took a glance at the delivered message and announced, "All of you will wear white dresses and white caps to the auditorium tomorrow. Professor Ren Guo-hua will deliver a speech on Manchuria."

The professor was Kemei's father. He must be a very wise man to teach in a university. May looked forward to learning more about the unfolding events.

The next day May put on the dress she had worn to her mother's funeral. The auditorium was quiet with occasional nervous coughs. One would have been able to hear a pin drop when Kemei's father began to speak.

The professor told the students that China had been among the richest nations in the world. China's gross national product exceeded those of Western Europe, Eastern Europe, and the United States of America—combined.

"Till the nineteenth century," Professor Ren said gravely, "when England brought opium to our shores. England became the greatest drug cartel in human history, and China the sick man of Asia."

May's blood boiled.

The professor went on to recount how other powers had joined the fray against China. He named, in particular, France, the United States, Japan, and Czarist Russia, which had stripped China of vast territories in Siberia. It was like a gang of thugs taking their turns hitting a defenseless man.

"They killed our soldiers, seized our land, burned our palaces, robbed us of our most valuable antiques—and asked *us* to pay *them* reparations," the silver-haired professor said. "Please remove your hats and lower your heads to mourn the state of our nation."

The professor's lips still quivered when he resumed his speech: "Japan is the worst offender among the powers. At the turn of the century, they took Taiwan from us. Yesterday they invaded Shenyang. Tomorrow it will be all of Manchuria."

Minnie Vautrin raised her hand. "Pardon me, Professor Ren. The Japanese government has assured the West of its disinterest in occupying Manchuria. Are they lying?"

"I'm afraid the Japanese government cannot speak for the Japanese military, who take their orders from the Japanese Emperor," Professor Ren replied.

"Assuming that you are right, what do you think Japan will do after occupying Manchuria?" Minnie Vautrin asked.

"Conquer all of China, Madame," Professor Ren replied.

May recoiled in horror. Would the Japanese be coming to Nanjing? Would she still be going to school?

Minnie asked: "What will happen after China?"

"Japan will attack the Philippines, Hong Kong, Dutch East India, British Malaya, Burma, and India, in no particular order."

Minnie was incredulous: "Do you seriously believe Japan will dare invade these Western colonies, challenging the military might of the United States *and* the European Powers?"

"Japan's national goal is to replace the Western Powers as Asia's sole master," Professor Ren answered. "She needs Asia's oil and mineral resources to reach equal status with England and America."

That evening May went home and told Baba that the Japanese would be coming to Nanjing.

Baba said, "We are four hundred and fifty million strong. When our people get together, we can drown those midgets with our spit alone!"

But Nainai said, "Those little demons chop the heads off anyone they come across. I would run away before they can find me."

"Any place we know?" May asked.

"The Min Province!"

She was talking about Minnesota, Miss Vautrin's hometown.

"But there is an ocean separating China and the Min Province," May said. "You can't get there by running."

Nainai panicked.

Chapter 6

The Genie in the Bottle

On this same September day in Cambridge, Massachusetts, Calvin came home and declared that he wanted to transfer to the aeronautics division of the department of mechanical engineering! He asked John to help him fill out the application forms; he couldn't do it himself because he had just injured his hand in a fit of anger. He refused to explain what had upset him.

John thought it foolish. No one should give up the credits of five years of a physics program. Relativity and quantum mechanics had just come into their infancy. Breakthroughs in physics were waiting to happen. A physicist had a chance to leave his mark in history. "You are making a big mistake," he said.

"But I want to do something practical," Calvin said.

John understood this feeling very well. As a child, his favorite toys had been airplanes. And he had chosen aeronautical engineering as his own major. John stopped arguing.

After his transfer had been approved, Calvin lost the financial support granted him by the physics department. In an effort to cut expenses, he started walking to school from home and back.

As his farewell to physics, Calvin wrote a paper on heavy atoms. Professor Tucker, his physics adviser, told him to type up the manuscript and submit it as his thesis for a masters degree.

Since Calvin did not know how to type, Judy volunteered to help. John had been working in the lab at night, so she used the men's living room in the evenings to do the work.

One night during a break, Judy made tea for both of them and talked about her widower father, who owned a small restaurant in Chinatown. "Sally, his mistress, just left him," Judy said, putting lemon in her tea.

"How did your father take it?" Calvin asked.

"He was devastated. But I think it was good riddance!"

"Was Sally not a good fit for your father?"

"She was a slut!" Judy hissed. "But the way my father went after her, they deserved each other. What I hated most is how this sordid affair spoiled the romantic story between my parents."

"What's that?"

"Well, my father met my mother through a family friend, and he proposed to her the next day."

"A man of quick decisions, eh?" Calvin exclaimed.

"Well, he told me that Mother was the girl he had met by a country well one bright spring morning. Not in this present life, mind you, but in his former life—the one before the present one."

"He must have been joking! Things like that just don't happen."

"I didn't believe him either," Judy said. "But after Sally moved in, I left home and never went back."

Calvin asked if she missed her father.

"Honestly? No," Judy said. "I hate the way he speaks to me: Lecture, lecture, lecture, and then repeat, repeat, repeat."

"Judy! You are talking about the man who is putting you through college."

"I have a part scholarship," Judy said, "and I type letters and manuscripts to make my living. I don't depend on him."

"Doesn't he help you at all?"

"He wanted to, but I don't need to hear him telling everybody what an expensive daughter he has." Judy put down her tea cup too quickly, spilling a little.

"Sounds to me he is very frugal," Calvin said.

"You are frugal. He is crazy!" Judy said.

"What's the difference?"

"Well, my father wouldn't throw away anything, so junk piled up to the ceiling. I was living in squalor. One day I decided to clean house. He was furious when he came home and found out. He went to the dump with a wheelbarrow and brought every item back."

"He must've saved up quite a bit of money. What does he want to do with it?"

Judy said that her father had talked about founding a school.

"That's a good idea," Calvin said.

"Talk. That's all he does!"

"He must've taken care of you when you were little."

"If you call that taking care!" Judy exclaimed.

When she was a little girl, Judy said, her father left her in the basement of his restaurant, where she daydreamed or colored with a crayon. In the evening, she fell asleep on a cot until her father closed up shop and carried her home.

"Didn't you attend school?"

"Of course, but school was just as boring. During recess, I watched my schoolmates laugh and flirt, but I was never a part of it. Although I spoke English, they took a look at me and yelled, '*Go back to China*!'"

"I know how that feels," Calvin said in a low voice.

"There I was, born in New York City, raised in Boston, and didn't belong in America," Judy said. "I have no China to go back to! The only Chinese place I came from was my mother's belly. I couldn't have gone back there even if she had been alive!"

Calvin was silent.

"Every afternoon after school, I went to my father's restaurant, cleaned the kitchen, and took care of orders," Judy said. "After dinner I hung around the Boston Public Garden. The park was filled with people, but it might as well have been empty. No one talked to me. I was the genie in *Arabian Nights*, swearing my loyalty to the first person who would un-bottle me."

"For a while I felt the same way," Calvin said with a hoarse voice.

"One day five or six girls came up to me and surrounded me," Judy said. "Two of them stretched my arms out and a third hugged me from behind. I was so grateful I couldn't stop thanking them for taking the trouble to play with me. One of the girls seemed surprised. Then she turned around and ran away. Others followed. A little girl stayed behind and told me they had been there to rob me. I found a nickel and two pennies in my pocket and held them out in my palm. She picked up the silver coin and left."

"Did it get better for you in college?" Calvin asked after pausing for a long time.

"College students are more civil, and I feel like I belong. Still, my best girlfriend is Korean. I feel completely comfortable only with her."

That night, after John had come home, Calvin told John that he had grown accustomed to the sound of the typewriter keys and felt restless when the apartment was completely quiet.

The following Saturday Judy came to work in the afternoon. She packed up to leave before nightfall.

"Why do you want to go so early?" Calvin asked.

"Ask me no questions and you will hear no lies," Judy said.

"I was just curious," Calvin said.

"Well," Judy said, "I'm seeing someone tonight, if you must know."

Calvin's face turned red. "Who, if I may ask?"

"A Harvard law school student."

"I see, I see. All right. Go, go!"

Judy came again the next afternoon but wanted to leave early again. Calvin asked if she was seeing that Harvard guy again.

"Why . . . yes."

"I don't want you to!"

"What?"

"I mean, if you leave now, don't bother to come back!"

"But I'll finish the thesis for you tomorrow."

"Screw the thesis!"

"What's the matter with you, Calvin? You never notice what I wear. You never tell me how I look. The question you ask me is always how much typing I've done that day. Why do you suddenly care about that law student?"

"I don't notice women's dresses. They look the same to me. If you want my opinion about anything, why don't you ask me? Look, I have nothing against your law student. I mean, I don't give a damn about him. Listen, you will not see this fellow again. I forbid it. Never, never, never! You hear me?"

"I hear you, loud and clear." Judy started to cry. "Calvin, that was the nicest thing you've ever said to me!"

Calvin and Judy broke the news of their engagement to John and Cynthia, the nurse John had been seeing. The next morning John took his roommate to shop for a diamond ring.

After asking for prices, Calvin said, "Diamond is not Chinese."

"Which precious stone is Chinese, Calvin?" John asked.

"Tourmaline," Calvin said.

"But, Calvin, tourmaline is not a precious stone."

"Believe it or not, it is among the Chinese Imperial jewelries."

Calvin selected a Maine tourmaline. According to Calvin, its red color was auspicious.

Judy showed her ring to everyone she knew.

Chapter 7

The Boils

Over in Nanjing, news about Manchuria continued to pour into May's school. When a messenger delivered a bulletin to her classroom, the teacher would stop the lecture and read it aloud to the students.

The League of Nations decided against imposing economic sanctions on Japan. No nation wanted to lose trade at a time when the world economy had been affected by the US depression. The *New York Herald Tribune* called the League's decision an unconditional surrender of principle.

The "young marshal" Zhang Xue-liang, unable to match Japan's air power, pulled his troops out of Manchuria.

Hearing this news from his daughter, Baba kicked a chair to the front of his store.

* * *

In January 1932, the League of Nations appointed a special commission to investigate the Manchurian affair. A year later, the committee chairman, Lord Lytton, completed the fact-finding.

Lytton wrote the final report from a hospital bed in Beijing. He had to negotiate every syllable of its wording with the French commissioner, who insisted Japan's position be presented in as favorable a light as possible.

Miss Vautrin read the commission's conclusion in a schoolwide meeting: "Without declaration of war, a large area of what is indisputably Chinese territory has been seized and occupied by Japanese forces and has in consequence of this operation been separated and declared independent of the rest of China."

The League of Nations would declare Japan the aggressor. Japan would have to leave Manchuria! The students cheered.

In March 1933, the League of Nations called a meeting of its member nations to vote on the report. The proceeding would be broadcast from Geneva, Switzerland.

Not having a radio of her own, May went to Miss Vautrin's office. Teachers and students packed the room, breathing nervous white steam into the chilly morning air.

The chief delegate from Japan delivered a powerful speech to refute the report. A number of other chief delegates, including China's, also spoke.

Then the roll call began:

"Argentina."

"Oui."

"Australia."

"Oui."

"Belgium."

"Oui."

One by one the chief delegates to the League of Nations voted affirmatively on Lytton's report.

"Chile."

"Oui."

"China, the disputing party."

"Oui." The firm voice of the chief Chinese delegate resonated in the great hall. The room buzzed, and it took a few seconds before the clerk resumed the calling.

"Colombia."

"Oui."

The roll call continued, and so did the *oui*, until the clerk announced, "Japan, the disputing party."

A pause. Then the voice of the chief Japanese delegate broke the air: "Non!"

The roll call went on. All of the remaining chief delegates voted *oui* with one exception. "Siam has been a friend of Japan for five hundred years," Siam's chief delegate declared. "Siam abstains."

The roll call ended with the clerk shouting: "Yugoslavia."

The response came firmly: "oui."

The broadcaster explained that, by the rules of the League of Nations, votes of the disputing parties and that of abstention would be discarded. Then he announced the final count: forty-two to nothing. The League of Nations had unanimously condemned Japan for her aggression on Manchuria!

May and everybody else in the room leaped to their feet cheering.

In the ruckus, the broadcaster announced that the Japanese delegates were walking out of the meeting.

* * *

When summer came, May realized that her body had shot up by three inches. Her black hair had become longer and thicker, reflecting light like the finest lacquer.

But fine hair also appeared around a sensitive part of her body.

Confucians held chastity as an unmarried woman's highest virtue, the loss of which was considered a fate worse than death. Confucian etiquette dictated that hands should not touch when a man and a woman exchanged an object between them. Although May had had no Confucian schooling, she had heard enough whispers and titters to develop an inhibition over this kind of matter. Once she shrieked hysterically when her eleven-year-old brother Damao ran into a covered corner of the store. The boy had stumbled into his sister while she was changing clothes.

May did not want Baba to find out about her physical development. Now that she was maturing, sometimes she wondered if Mama had been jealous of her. She did not feel comfortable alone with Baba in the house.

Almost as certainly, neither should Damao suspect anything. Being occasionally fed with eggs and even meat these days, the eldest son in the family had become a husky boy. He stopped harassing her after she had grown to tower over him. He beat up boys who shouted unsavory words at her.

Neither would she allow Ma into her confidence. She was not her real mother.

Then May found to her alarm that her nipples had grown, the area around them becoming very painful and very itchy.

Boils!

Their large size, though, worried her. When everybody else was asleep, she got up, tiptoed to the front counter, and stole two medicine pads from a jar. She slipped back under her blankets, peeled off the covers from the pads, and stuck them over her swellings.

But the *boils* continued to grow.

A horrifying bleeding followed. She quietly washed out the stains on her sheets and garments, her heart in her throat, wondering if she was being punished for doing something sinful.

One day Ma came to her. Without asking any questions, she taught May how to take care of herself. May couldn't open her eyes when Ma wrapped her up. She was overcome by Ma's kindness, now thinking the older woman so wise and so deserving of respect.

Although Ma told her that the growth of all parts of her body was normal, May used a long strip of cloth to wrap up her breasts as tightly as she could. She looked down at herself to make sure that she would draw no attention.

Still, aunties in the neighborhood began to describe her as a green bulrush sprouting out of the river. Matchmakers called on Baba to inquire about her availability.

May began to have strange dreams. Incoherent and never making much sense, they were always about being kissed. While unable to make out the face of the person doing it to her, she had the feeling that he was someone familiar. She meant to push his face away, but her arms would not obey her command. As his lips fell on hers, she would close her eyes, a sweetness sweeping over her entire body. Waking up, she was hot, even perspiring.

"I must be a bad girl!" Now she was certain.

She was curious about the identity of the person in her dreams. A young man her age was living a few blocks down the street from her. She always thought of him as 'sort of good looking.' They never talked, but he often followed her home after school, and she could feel his gaze burning her back. She wondered if the person in her dream was this young man.

May decided to seek the counsel of a wiser person. Kemei had graduated from high school and gone on to attend St. John University in Shanghai. When she came home for the summer, May approached her to ask the delicate question.

"Don't worry, May. Even grandmothers have erotic dreams!" Kemei whispered.

Chen May was shocked. "How do you know *that*?"

"I went to the Nanjing City Library and borrowed all the books on such matters," Kemei gave her a wicked smile.

"Good grief! How did you have the nerve to check them out?"

"I kept my straight face on." Kemei laughed. "You should have seen the old-maid librarian when I asked her to stamp the books for me. She went back and forth from my face to those books."

May changed the subject. "How is your brother doing?"

"He will be coming home, after getting his doctoral degree!"

"What school is he attending?"

"MIT!" Kemei said.

"What's that?" May asked.

"It's a famous university, stupid!"

May was wild with anticipation over seeing this legendary young man in person. She had heard of famous people, but they were many years ahead of her and didn't count. Kemei's brother belonged in her generation.

"Will you point him out to me when you get the chance?"

"Better—I will introduce you to him," Kemei promised.

Chapter 8

The British Were No Smugglers

In the spring of 1934, Calvin passed his thesis defense.

John congratulated Calvin. "Now you can relax and buy some groceries. I'm tired of the leftover salads from the seminar room you keep bringing home."

"I can't wait to try the key line pie you talked so much about."

"Key *lime* pie, Calvin."

"OK, OK," Calvin said. "John, Professor Henderson offered to send me to Caltech. He said one must work with the present leader of the field in order to become the future leader of the field. Von Karman is the leader of aeronautics right now."

"I agree," John said. "Calvin, Von Karman was trained as a theoretical physicist. Your background will match his beautifully."

"But I told Professor Henderson I'm going back to China."

"And throw away this opportunity of a lifetime?" John was flabbergasted. "You better have a darn good reason."

"The project I'm going to do can only be carried out in my country."

"Aha, you are dying to go home!" John said.

"I really don't want to leave, John. I'll be losing the opportunity to work with the best engineer produced by MIT in years."

"Whom are you talking about, Calvin?" John asked.

"You, John!"

John felt blood rushing into his head. "Are you pulling my leg, Calvin?"

"Engineering is a practical science," Calvin said. "All the theories I've spun are worth nothing until someone turns them into applications. I always envy your pair of hands, John."

"Stop it, pal!" John stammered. He was blushing like a plain little girl who has just been told she's very pretty.

* * *

Calvin applied to several universities in China. Two months later, he received an answer from Nanjing Central University. Professor Zhu, head of the Department of Mechanical Engineering, offered Calvin an associate professorship. The university would also pay for his traveling expenses. He accepted it without waiting for other offers.

Judy had not planned on leaving America so soon. Having graduated from Boston University two years earlier, she had been working as a lab technician at Massachusetts General Hospital. Did hospitals in China have labs? If not, what could she do in Nanjing?

At noon the next day, munching a sandwich in the MGH cafeteria, she shared her problem with Cynthia.

Cynthia saw a different concern. Judy would be starting a family in a foreign country, living under the same roof with her parents-in-law. That had *trouble* written all over it! Cynthia finally found a silver lining. "Don't worry, Judy. They will be eating out of your hands when you give them grandchildren."

"But I may never have a baby," Judy protested.

Whatever doubts she might have for her future, one thing was certain: Calvin's career was first priority. She would follow him wherever he went. There was no second thought about that.

* * *

Two weeks later, Judy's father sold his restaurant and booked a freighter to Guangzhou, China.

"He has been complaining about chest pains," Judy told Calvin.

They went to South Station to see the old man off. Calvin was shocked to see that the gray hair of his future father-in-law had turned snow white.

"I will board the ship in Philadelphia. It will sail down to Central America, cut across the Panama Canal, and make stops at Hawaii and the Philippines before docking at Guangzhou," the old man said, rubbing his pouch.

"How long will it take you, Mr. Lee?" Calvin asked.

"Three months."

"That's wasting a lot of time," Calvin said. "Why not take a faster ship?"

"Too expensive," the old man said, hawking up a mouthful of phlegm. "I'm no *fangui*."

"My father thinks all *foreign devils* are spoiled rotten," Judy said.

* * *

Two months afterward, Judy and Calvin got married in Cambridge City Hall. Only Professor Henderson, John and Cynthia, Judy's Korean friend Mary, and a few of the couple's American schoolmates attended the ceremony.

That evening, Cynthia served a buffet in her apartment. Professor Henderson brought a bottle of wine. Judy had a glass, got a bit tipsy, and could not stop giggling all evening.

A few days later, the new couple boarded a train for San Francisco, where they would be taking an ocean liner to Shanghai.

John and Cynthia said goodbye to them at Boston's South Station. Cynthia looked at Judy and said, "I know you don't enjoy watching women touch your husband. But I won't be seeing him for a while. May I kiss him just once?"

Calvin laughed nervously when Cynthia gave him a peck on the cheek. Then Cynthia hugged Judy and cried.

Judy patted Cynthia's hand. "We'll meet again, I promise!" Then she kissed John and whispered into his ear, "Visit us in China!"

* * *

A month later, a stocky customs inspector at the Shanghai harbor took his time checking over every one of Calvin's books in his suitcase.

"He will be disappointed," Calvin told his restless bride. "We are bringing no communist materials into China."

Outside, a young woman with a bob of short hair jumped up and down behind the barrier. Calvin ventured, "Kemei?" The sibling he had last seen eight years earlier still looked like the child she had been at ten—only taller.

"That's probably the way you would fix my hair if I let you," Judy whispered to Calvin.

Kemei said a few words in Mandarin to Judy, drew a blank, and switched to English, laughing nervously when her brother corrected her grammar. She got a coolie to carry the luggage. Warned of pickpockets, Calvin held his briefcase close to his chest. On the street, Kemei hailed two rickshaws and squeezed into one with Judy. Calvin got into the other.

In the tight space of the cab, her hair in the wind tickling Kemei's cheek, Judy felt close to Kemei.

The rickshaw turned into a wide avenue bordering a river on one side. Broad stone buildings lined the opposite side, a few of them more than twenty stories high.

"Where are we, Kemei?" Judy asked.

"This is the Huangpu River," Kemei answered. "You are in the Bund, the British settlement."

"You mean this is *not* China?"

"The Manchu government ceded this area to the British in 1842," Kemei said. "See the dark man with a bright red turban standing on that street corner?"

"The Sikh?"

"Yes, people like him are keeping the law here."

"Funny!" Judy exclaimed. "The buildings are Art Deco, Gothic, Renaissance, Romanesque, but not Chinese."

"This is the Shanghai Club, Judy, where the British hold their social gatherings," Kemei said. "Over there is the Nissan."

Their rickshaw turned into a narrow street hugged by shabby stucco buildings. Garments and underwear hung from windows waving like international flags. On the ground, stores displayed strange merchandise: live turtles, dried fish, leaping frogs, cackling chickens. They stretched out into the road, leaving barely enough room for their rickshaw to get through. The puller slowed to a walk, yelling out warnings to the pedestrians.

The scenery reminded Judy of New York's Chinatown, although something was vaguely different. Then it dawned on her: there were no Caucasians in the streets.

"I've never seen more people of my own race in one place," Judy told Kemei.

They boarded a train for Nanjing. Because of the many stops, Kemei said, the trip of two hundred miles would take eight hours.

Kemei whispered to Judy a family secret: "The eldest of our uncles was a well-to-do man, comfortably married to a young wife who bore him two lovely daughters. Then he was introduced to opium. It enhanced his sexual prowess ten times, enabling him to ride a whore shooting like a machine gun for an hour."

Judy felt her cheeks burning.

"He was hooked," Kemei continued. "Running out of money, he borrowed from a loan shark. When the loan was due, he asked for three days of reprieve—then disappeared into an opium den."

"Pitiful!" Judy said.

"On New Year's Eve—when all debts must be settled, the loan shark came to Uncle's home with two thugs," Kemei said. "They caught Uncle in his dining room partaking of the New Year's Feast with his family. Uncle begged for two more days, promising on his ancestors' portrait that he would pay up. The thugs dragged Uncle to the kitchen. One of them spread Uncle's middle finger on the cutting block, and the other took a cleaver and chopped it off. Uncle yelled and fainted."

"No!" Judy cried.

"When Uncle came to," Kemei said, "the loan shark warned him to pay up the next day, or they would be back and cut off another finger.

"My aunt, who had wrestled with the thugs and been thrown to the floor, ran into the kitchen. She handed over her jewelry box and wept: 'Take all of it, and please don't bother us again!'

"On his knees, Uncle vowed that he would stop smoking opium.

"But you know what? Uncle just couldn't quit. He sold his house to pay for his habit. Then he sold his wife and his daughters to a whorehouse. At the end he hanged himself."

"Where are the poor woman and her daughters now?" Judy asked breathlessly.

"Who knows?"

"Where did your uncle get his opium?"

"It was available in the open market during Uncle's time. There were plenty of opium dens on the streets too."

"And the policemen didn't close them down?" Judy cried.

"Grandfather went to the police station and demanded just that. The police chief refused."

"What was wrong with him?" Judy screamed.

"He said that if he had done that, the British merchants wouldn't have liked it. When they complained to the governor, his head would roll on the *noongate*."

"You mean the governor would execute his police chief if the British smugglers so demanded?"

"The British were no smugglers, Judy," Kemei said. "They had the legal right to bring as much opium into China as they pleased."

At the Nanjing train station, two young men in suits and ties grabbed the newlyweds' luggage. Everybody laughed when Calvin hugged his briefcase again. The strangers were Calvin's cousins.

A boxy black sedan took them to a road flanked by lovely stucco houses surrounded by silent, mossy brick walls. Dreading the prospect of meeting Calvin's parents, Judy wished the taxi would keep going. But it stopped at one of those houses.

Judy shuffled to its gate, feeling as if she were going to court to face a judge. She almost stumbled when popping sounds suddenly burst out behind her. Calvin took her arm: "The servants are setting off firecrackers to celebrate your arrival."

Judy turned and saw a leaping snake of firecrackers hanging from a tree, the point of explosion moving rapidly from its head to its tail. Thousands of tiny paper shreds danced in the air. Judy fanned the sulfur smell away from her nose.

"How do I look?" she asked her husband anxiously. "Should I put on more lipstick?"

"No!" Calvin said impatiently. "You are good."

She was led to a large room filled with people. Calvin's father had eight siblings, all brothers; his mother had nine siblings, all sisters. There were at least thirty pairs of eyes trained on Judy's face, the most somber ones belonging to the old man and the old woman in two large, yellowed photographs above a shrine. Judy was told to hold a candle and bow three times to Grandpa and Grandma.

Then she was made to turn around and give three bows to the crowd. Calvin made introductions: "This is third grandaunt, the paternal side; this is seventh aunt, the maternal side; this is the cousin of the husband of second aunt, the maternal side." Judy's head spun. Occasionally Calvin hesitated, and people broke out laughing as Kemei stepped in to help him with the names.

Generally, white hair implied granduncles and grandaunts, gray hair uncles and aunts, and black hair cousins. But there were exceptions. A young woman about Calvin's age was introduced as Calvin's grandniece. Even after a long-winded explanation, Judy was still confused.

Judy was taken to the adjoining study to meet Calvin's parents, who were sitting in black-lacquer armchairs studded with shiny mother-of-pearl decorations. A servant came in with a red-lacquer tray, and Judy offered tea to her parents-in-law with both hands. The elderly couple took a sip of the tea and smiled at each other. Both groped in their robe pockets, each producing a little red envelope for Judy.

The senior Mrs. Ren put on her glasses, grabbed Judy's right wrist, and examined her palm. Pandemonium broke loose as people in the living room rushed to the study to join the palm reading. After a long chatter, all agreed that Judy would have five children—at least two of them sons. Mrs. Ren nodded solemnly and released Judy's hand.

That was when Mr. Ren held court. The professor with silvery hair and gray beard sat in his armchair like an old saint asking questions in Mandarin—the official Chinese spoken language. Calvin translated for Judy. A granduncle joined the questioning but fell asleep by the time Judy's answer was translated back to him. Another granduncle shouted himself hoarse pointing at the bride, but in the commotion no one paid him any attention. Meanwhile, a few women held Judy's hands, caressed her back, and touched her hair, their Nanjing accents adding to Judy's giddiness.

In the noisy banquet, Judy followed Calvin from table to table to toast the guests. She received loud well-wishes and understood none of them. After the second cup of yellow wine, she kept the smile on her face and stopped listening.

Late at night, Judy retired with her husband to their chamber. She dropped on the bright-red embroidered bedspread and immediately fell asleep. Waking up the next morning, the only thing she remembered was the lecture Mr. Ren had given her on how not to forget her Chinese origin. She found two red envelopes in her purse. Inside them were crisp bills equivalent to almost twenty-five dollars!

For a month, her new relatives took turns giving banquets in Judy's honor. Luxuriating in attention for the first time in her life, she felt like a celebrity.

But the daily squats over the smelly toilet hole brought her self-importance down to earth. She had no stomach to look down, and she was surprised that a professor's home had no flush toilets.

"Calvin, can we have an apartment with a flush toilet?" Judy begged.

Her husband promised to apply for a university apartment with modern amenities.

Judy went out looking for a job and hit the wall everywhere. After a few frustrating weeks, she stopped trying.

Calvin's father asked a friend in the Ministry of Education to write Judy a letter of introduction. Judy carried the letter and a fruit basket to visit a Mr. Yang who, luckily, spoke Cantonese. Mr. Yang read the letter and talked to Judy for an hour, during which time she nodded and laughed a lot. The principal gave her a job teaching English in his middle-school.

To Judy's students, *between* was *bechween*, and *name* was *nam*. Judy stayed after school to tutor them.

One day a reporter came to interview Judy. A week later, an article about "the woman who returned home to educate the children of her motherland" appeared in a newspaper. Some people in her school came to ask her about the fabulously rich country where she had been born. Others tried their English on her. She made friends—mostly female teachers wearing no makeup. They came to her house, helped her grade papers, and did a lot of gossiping in between. Judy's Mandarin improved so much she even dreamed in Mandarin.

Friendship was not an unmitigated blessing. Her friends asked about her salary and told her theirs. She was not happy to find that hers was lower than theirs.

The university granted Calvin an apartment with a flush toilet. Judy went around the neighborhood shopping for her new home. A young girl in a convenience store kept asking Judy about her professorial husband. Calvin was with her the next time Judy went to the store. She introduced the girl to Calvin.

The girl hung on every one of Calvin's words. "Professor Ren, could you lend me a book on calculus?"

"Which grade are you in, May?"

"Seventh."

Calvin said calculus was for older students.

The girl blushed. "I just wanted to follow your example the best I can."

"You are too young for calculus now—perhaps in five or six years." Calvin said. He added that a student at her stage only needed to learn the fundamentals well and enjoy what she was doing. "Don't spoil your appetite for learning."

"Don't I need to work hard?"

"The hardest you can, but that's for later. Conserve your energy now and pour it out after you find your calling."

"When will that be?"

"That may come as late as after college."

"Professor Ren, do you think I am good enough for all that?"

"Absolutely. You are already curious about calculus. You will do fine."

Afterward, Calvin often dropped off books at the store for the girl to read.

Judy told Calvin that he was acting like a father to May.

Chapter 9

Qianlong, Mark and Period

In the spring of 1935, John Winthrop finished graduate school. It had taken him five years to get his doctoral degree—one more than Calvin.

Professor Dickinson, his faculty adviser, offered him an instructorship at fifteen hundred dollars per year.

"You have a PhD, and your salary is lower than mine?" Cynthia, now his fiancée, said. "How much would an aircraft company pay you?"

"Probably twice as much," John said, avoiding Cynthia's eyes.

"Why don't you go for the better pay?" Cynthia asked.

"Calvin once said: 'A spring worm doesn't die until it has spun all its silk.' I want to publish as many papers as I can before I go to pasture."

"What for?"

"Being fortunate enough to have an education, I've derived the intellectual's curse: I feel guilty if I fritter away my time," John said.

Professor Dickinson asked John to come to his office. After learning what John had in mind for his career, Dickinson said, "You've already spent ten years at MIT, much too long to be in one place. American universities discourage inbreeding.

They prefer faculties with broad experiences. I suggest you spread your wings and apply for an assistant professorship elsewhere."

Over dinner that evening, John told Cynthia about the conversation. His fiancée pushed the salad bowl toward him. "Why not a professorship at MIT?"

"Professor Dickinson thinks I'll have a better chance to get tenure at another university," John answered.

"What's tenure?" Cynthia asked.

"It's the privilege to hold a teaching position permanently."

Cynthia agreed that tenure would be nice. John's father, a former partner at a small bank, remained unemployed after his bank had gone under after the Great Crash of 1929.

"How much does a tenured professor make?" she asked.

"Probably twice what I'm making," John said.

"How long will it take you to become one?" Cynthia passed John the plate of meatloaf.

"Seven years—if I'm lucky," John said.

"You mean, we can't get married before then?" Cynthia put her fork down.

"Sure we can. It won't be lavish living, but we'll get by."

"But, John, *getting by* for seven years, I don't think it will work. I would like to own a house in a few years!"

Cynthia enjoyed looking at houses. The one that had caught her eye was a little red brick at Chestnut Street near the hospital. It had three bedrooms, two baths, and a small lawn in the back. Perfect! The asking price was nineteen thousand dollars, thirty-eight hundred dollars for the down payment. She would love to quit her job and raise a family in such a house.

From the kitchen where she was doing the dishes, Cynthia called over her shoulder: "So, Dickinson thinks you have no chance for tenure at MIT?"

Although his feelings were hurt, John knew Cynthia spoke the truth.

John received a letter from Calvin, who invited him to spend some time at Nanjing's National Central University.

John liked the challenge of bringing a backward department to the forefront. Moreover, he had always wanted to see the Orient, which had been a subject of conversation during family reunions.

John prepared a simple dinner for Cynthia to come home to from a nursing class. Over soup and a sandwich, he showed his tired fiancée Calvin's letter.

"What? You want to work in a foreign country?" Cynthia's spoon stopped before her mouth.

"I don't." John found himself on the defensive. "I mean, I didn't. Calvin's idea."

"And what am I supposed to do while you go sightseeing in China?"

John replied that they could get married and sightsee together.

"John, you know I can't leave!" Cynthia exclaimed. "I'm making money so that we'll have a yard for our children to play in. Why don't you look for a job right here in Boston?"

John saw the dilemma.

An official letter from China arrived. Signed by Professor Zhu, head of the Mechanical Engineering Department at the National Central University, it read: "We are happy to offer you an appointment as a visiting associate professor, teaching a course on thermodynamics and organizing our laboratories."

The professorship was one rank above what he was seeking!

"The term for the appointment is three years. The salary is twenty-five hundred US dollars for the first year, with annual increases of five percent in each succeeding year."

This handsome salary came as a surprise!

Professor Zhu concluded, almost as an afterthought: "You will be expected to work with Professor Ren on a research project, sharing the responsibility of supervising a team of engineers."

"Oh no! Not three years!" Cynthia cried when John showed her the letter. "I can take one year of separation, but that's all. You're not going to accept the offer, are you?"

John wrote Professor Zhu and explained he couldn't work in China for so long.

John applied to several local universities: Harvard, Northeastern, and Boston University. Just in case, he threw in a number of colleges out of state.

For months he received no responses. As days went by, he dreaded more and more Cynthia's inquiries about them.

The world of antique Chinese porcelain provided him an escape.

John's interest in it had begun at home in Salem, Massachusetts. As a child, he loved the blue-and-white Chinese porcelain sleeping peacefully in the family cupboard. The mountains, trees, and bridges painted on the porcelains reminded him of the sapphire on his mother's ring finger. Little John Winthrop could not imagine a home without old blue-and-white porcelain in its curio cabinet.

"The Nanjing mayor gave this set to your grandpa when he retired and headed home," his father had told him.

But by the time John entered graduate school, his father had declared bankruptcy, and the antique porcelains had gone, along with their Queen Anne house.

One day, months after the foreclosure, John walked by a small, crammed antique shop on Charles Street not far from Cynthia's hospital. He saw a blue-and-white soup bowl displayed in its window.

John's heart leaped. It had been one of his family's heirlooms!

But during the Great Depression that had followed the Crash, few people would buy non-essentials. John walked on.

Several days later, he took the subway to Charles Street and asked the store owner questions about the bowl: Do you think it was produced in Jingdezhen, capital of Chinese porcelain? Are there any imperfections on this bowl? How do you rate the quality and rarity of the decoration? How about the glaze and the paste?

The antique dealer was as patient as a saint. Still, John couldn't make up his mind. He went back a third time and learned that the bowl had been made in the eighteenth century.

The store owner showed him another blue-and-white bowl for comparison. "Both are exports, but the one in my hand was produced a century after the one in yours. China got into hard times and the quality of her porcelains declined."

John saw the difference and finally decided to ask for the price of the older one.

"Five dollars."

"Would you take four?" John asked.

"It cost me more than that. Tell you what. I'll take four-fifty. You know that's a good deal!"

The owner wrapped the bowl up with layers of newspaper and gave John's back a pat. "Congratulations! You've got good taste."

John went home happy for a whole week.

He searched other antique shops, but couldn't find another of his forgone heirlooms.

But to ease the anxiety about his job prospects, John visited more antique stores in Boston and New York City, where he occasionally went to give seminars. He loved the porcelains displayed in Yamanaka and C. T. Loo, both exclusive galleries. All of the items sold by these dealers were superior to his bowl, many of them costing more than his monthly salary.

Cynthia showed little interest. "If you would at least look at furniture," she said. "Antiques are like jewelry. They are for the wealthy. The dealers make money on you when you buy and when you sell. You lose twenty, thirty percent each way."

During one of the visits to Yamanaka's Boston store, John couldn't take his eyes off the display in a lit glass case. The multicolored Chinese porcelain vase had four medallions of floral sprays painted on a blue sgraffito scroll ground.

"Jim, how much is it?" he asked the salesman with whom he was on a first-name basis.

"Two thousand dollars. Shall we wrap it up?" The salesman gave John a wink.

John whistled. "That's more than half the down payment I need for Cynthia's dream house."

"Well, there is a Qianlong mark at the bottom of the vase with provenance to boot." Qianlong was an eighteenth-century Chinese emperor. "This vase is mark and period."

"Sure," John said. "I'll go to the race track at Suffolk Downs tomorrow and get you the money."

Jim laughed. "If I were you, I'd go to China. You can probably buy a vase like this for an apple and an egg. You can trade it for your mansion upon your return."

Most universities turned John down. The only favorable response came from Texas: a two-year instructorship at sixteen hundred dollars per year. John wondered what Dickenson had written in his letter of recommendation.

Cynthia took John to visit her childhood friend Emma Simon. Emma's dentist husband gave them a tour of their apartment on Beacon Hill. Cynthia sang praises about the high ceilings, the elaborate moldings, and the spectacular view of the Boston Public Garden. She was quiet on the way home. John understood. Engineers were no princes on white horses. Young women had good laughs over how MIT students went to mixers with slide rules hanging on their belts and danced like robots. John counted himself lucky. Judy must have put in some good words for him.

Cynthia's expectations were reasonable. He felt inadequate being unable to meet them.

* * *

Another letter from Professor Zhu in Nanjing arrived. "If the problem is the length of the appointment, we can make it one year. You will be welcome to stay for longer if you change your mind at any time."

John could read between the lines how badly they wanted him. It did wonders for his self-esteem, which had been beaten down by repeated rejections.

"No matter which choice I make, we will be separated for a year," he told Cynthia during dinner. "Nanjing pays better, and living expenses in China are lower. I will be able to bring two thousand dollars home!"

Cynthia stormed out of the room.

But John had made up his mind. He went to see his parents and shared his decision. His father was thrilled. His mother cried when she hugged him goodbye. On the train back to Boston, John worried about his mother sitting in that small living room. She belonged in the Queen Anne house built by a China trade merchant, not a dingy apartment on a back street in downtown Salem!

Suddenly he sat up, the voice of salesman Jim ringing in his head. He had figured out a way to buy back the family house for his mother!

Chapter 10

An American in Nanjing

The longest trip John had ever taken was from Boston to Manhattan. It was five hours by train.

Going to China was in a different league. It took three days on land to cross to the West Coast, three weeks on water to reach Shanghai, and eight hours by train to get to Nanjing.

When John was near his final destination, he suddenly had an anxiety attack. *What am I doing here?*

A little girl kept chewing a dry squid, spreading a strong aroma. A woman nursed a baby with her blouse wide open, her breasts very full. A whiff of sulfur hung in the compartment, probably having seeped into the car when the train passed through a tunnel. The occasional chatter among his fellow passengers was not understandable.

Everything around him was strange and foreign.

The train made a long hoot. White steam passed John's window. People inside the train began talking. The buzz heightened as the train slowed down. John felt sick to his stomach.

It would be just like Calvin to forget my time of arrival. Where am I going to spend the night if he doesn't show up?

* * *

When John stepped down from the train, a Chinese couple waved at him from a distance.

Calvin was no longer the scrawny graduate student with short cropped hair. His face had grown fuller but paler. Wearing a long gray Chinese robe, long hair separated in the middle, he looked the part of a Chinese professor.

Judy Lee now wore a blue *qipao* and a pair of gold-rimmed glasses. Her brown arms had become more round.

"It's so good to see you," John said, putting down his luggage, and hugging Judy and then Calvin.

"You look exhausted," Judy observed.

"You both look great," John lied.

Walking out of the train station together, they were immediately surrounded by shouting rickshaw pullers. John watched with admiration how deftly Judy haggled with them.

"The apartment Professor Zhu provided for you is only a few blocks from ours," Calvin said as he steered John toward one of the three rickshaws Judy had chosen. "It has a flush toilet."

It was a fine evening to sit in an open vehicle. A nice breeze tousled John's hair. The only discomfort he felt came from being pulled by a skinny man probably weighing less than a hundred pounds.

The rickshaw turned into a spacious avenue lined with two-story houses behind walls of roses. With hardly any automobiles on the streets, the only sounds John heard came from crickets, frogs, and the coolie's bare feet slapping the pavement.

When the rickshaw turned a corner, John suddenly found himself in a world of loud noises and bright lights—a Times Square filled with sallow faces and boisterous restaurants. His eyes were drawn to the steaming buns stacked up over a large boiling wok. For a moment he thought they were young women's soft breasts.

Darkness engulfed him again when his rickshaw entered a dark area of low-lying houses, whose windows showed not electric lights but flickering candle flames. The idea that there might be no electricity depressed him.

The rickshaws stopped at a two-story building. Everyone alighted. Calvin paid the coolies. John carried his luggage and followed his friends up the grim concrete staircase. Calvin unlocked a squeaky door and flicked a switch. Warm light flooded the foyer. John's spirit lifted.

Entering the foyer, he smelled ammonia. Poking his head into the adjoining bathroom, he saw a concrete floor stained with water marks. The moldy wall was completely bare and didn't even have a nail to hang a towel. A solitary dripping resounded from the bottom of the yellowed porcelain tub.

"Where's the living room?" he asked as soon as he entered the bedroom.

"Those are two sofa chairs in this room in case you want to entertain your guests," Calvin said.

The small bedroom also had a desk, two wooden chairs, and a narrow bed, all filthy.

"I guess the desk will double up as my dining table?" John said.

"You bet." Calvin laughed.

Calvin answered a knock at the door. He returned with a limping middle-aged man in dirty overalls, a long chain of keys dangling on his belt.

"This is Old Yen, your custodian." Calvin introduced the man in Mandarin. The short, stocky man said a few words to John in a high-pitched voice. John had taken Mandarin lessons before coming, but the custodian's accent was heavy.

Calvin stepped in. "He asks you not to use the bathroom faucet. The sink is clogged. He'll get it fixed next week." He lowered his voice. "Not sure you can trust him. He just started working for us a few weeks ago."

* * *

Fifteen minutes later, John walked out of the building with his friends. They went to a noodle shop a few doors down the street. John ordered a large plate of steaming buns.

After the buns had disappeared from sight, Judy asked, "Are you sure you don't want anything else?"

John could only shake his head, his mouth stuffed with food.

After paying, they visited the convenience store several blocks away.

"Buy yourself plenty of tissue paper," Calvin said. "Carry some with you at all times." He explained that it was not available in public toilets.

"You should also get at least two thermos bottles," Judy added.

"What for?" John asked.

"One for tea and one for the hot water you will need to wash your face."

Calvin introduced John to the store owner. The man almost as tall as John put his left fist into his right palm and bowed his head, the gold ring on his finger glistening.

Calvin pointed to the young girl reading behind the lamp. "Chen May. She is the eldest daughter of the store owner."

The girl stood up and bowed. John was fascinated by the way her black hair played with the light of the oil lamp. She wore a pair of black trousers and a white, long-sleeved tunic, a line of pretty black buttons coming down from her right armpit.

Calvin told May: "Professor Winthrop was my roommate at MIT."

May's vivid black eyes shone. "Hello, Professor Winthrop."

"How is school, May?" Calvin asked.

"Oh, I must thank you, Professor Ren. Mr. Zhao praised the solutions I handed in last week. He said they were most clever. All the girls were jealous until I told them I got the hints from you."

"You did most of the work yourself, May," Calvin said to her happy smile.

Judy introduced a large woman on a stool. A baby girl, her cheeks reminding John of the apples in New England, sat on the woman's lap. The woman gave John a bashful nod.

The baby wanted to touch John's hand. Her mother held her back, telling her not to bother the professor. The baby struggled till her face wrinkled. John went over and patted her hands. She grabbed his fingers, her eyes like two pools of crystal water. John asked to hold her, planting a kiss on her cheek.

Judy took the baby from John. "All of us fight to hug her, spoiling her terribly."

"What's her name?" John asked in awkward Chinese.

"*Wumao*," Judy said, adding that *Fifth-Hair* was ten months old.

John walked around the store and picked up various items. The store owner didn't charge "Professor Ren's friend" for the toilet paper.

"Heimao, wrap them up for the American *lao-shih*." The American teacher.

"Ai, Baba," the young girl answered obediently, putting her book down.

* * *

John woke up at three the next morning. In his grogginess, he almost bumped into a wall on his way to the bathroom.

After peeing, he turned on the faucet. The water did not go down. John recalled what Old Yen had said. He went to the kitchen and opened the rusty tap over the cement sink. The spout spat furious yellow foam before the water cleared. He scooped up some and splashed it over his face.

He swept the floor, dusted the furniture, and proceeded to fix the bathroom sink. Then he climbed back into his bed for another bit of shut-eye.

"Do all Nanjing girls have hair as black and shiny as those?" he wondered before losing consciousness.

* * *

On his second evening in Nanjing, John Winthrop wrote his fiancée a letter:

October 12, 1936

My dearest Cynthia,

I arrived in Nanjing last night, my love! Calvin took me to our department this morning, and Professor Zhu told me there are more than one hundred students registered for my course.

I asked if classes in China were usually this large.

"Not for upper-class courses," Professor Zhu said. "Some students are curious about 'the American professor.' Those will drop out soon. Others don't know much English and will not understand enough to keep up. They will disappear too. Please don't be discouraged when the attendance dwindles. Most definitely, don't blame yourself."

Professor Zhu took me to Dean Zhang's office.

The dean was ebullient. "Professor Winthrop, thank you, thank you, thank you for coming to Nanjing to help us!" He grabbed my hand with both of his. "Our nation needs aeronautical engineering—even Generalissimo Chiang Kai-shek said that!"

He took Professor Zhu and me to a restaurant for lunch. Hostesses in qipao greeted us at the door. One of them led our party to a private room with a large round dining table. Several senior faculty members were already there waiting. Soon dishes arrived one after the other. They were removed only half finished. I have never eaten many of the dishes! I definitely had too many cups of white wine. You should have heard all the toasts with clinking glasses!

Dean Zhang told me that Mr. Lu, President of the National Central University, would like to see me in the privacy of his house. That surprised me. Karl Compton, our counterpart at MIT, would never do that for a visiting junior faculty member.

Then Dean Zhang surprised me more by saying that the First Lady, Madame Chiang Kai-shek, will receive me next week. Madame Chiang Kai-shek! Does Chinese hospitality know no bounds?

Professor Zhu told Calvin and me to come to his house that night for dinner.

When we arrived, the expression on the face of the woman opening the door told me that the invitation had been impromptu. Mrs. Zhu quickly went out and came back with a live chicken.

Now, I am exhausted and must go to bed.

Miss you terribly.

Love,

John

* * *

The next evening John called on President Lu, an elderly man with streaks of silver in his hair. The presidential residence was an old wooden house inside the campus. The living room was surrounded by walls of books encased in little blue boxes. Sitting in his rattan chair, President Lu talked about his recent trip to Beijing.

"The Japanese government has forced us to demilitarize Northern China," the Confucian scholar said. "Their strategy is to devour China in the manner a silkworm consumes a mulberry leaf, bit by bit and not giving pause. If you ask me, the war between China and Japan is unavoidable. But, as our 'young marshal' found out in Manchuria, you can't fight a modern war without a good air force. If we lose, China will become another Japanese colony—a second Korea."

President Lu alluded to Madame Chiang Kai-shek's tea invitation. John asked, "Do you know her well?"

"You may say I know the Generalissimo better," President Lu replied. He explained that twice a year he reported to the national leader on the progress of the university and ended up discussing Confucianism. "He may be more interested in the latter," President Lu said with an amused smile.

"You mean the Generalissimo is a Confucian scholar?" John was astonished.

"I wouldn't go that far," the president replied. "As a young man, he did study Wang Yang-ming, a philosopher in the Ming dynasty, and derived a healthy respect for all things Confucian."

"I heard new thinkers in China reject the Chinese culture. They want to tear down the temple of Confucianism and replace it with everything Western."

"Ironic, isn't it, the Generalissimo calling himself leader of the Chinese revolution?" President Lu said. "Not many people realize how genuinely he embraces traditional Chinese values."

John asked President Lu how he had befriended the Generalissimo. President Lu explained that he had been the dean of the School of Humanities and Sciences in Beijing University. One day he went to Nanjing to attend an Academia Sinica meeting. As he stepped off the train with his aide, men in blue uniforms came up to him. They politely ushered him into a huge Cadillac, explaining that the Generalissimo wanted to meet him. Mr. Lu's aide recognized that the car was the only bullet-proof limousine in China—a gift sent to the Generalissimo by President Franklin D. Roosevelt.

Mr. Lu was taken to the presidential suite at the Jinling Hotel. As his aide arranged his glasses, papers, and brushes on the desk for him to do his work, a few light knocks came from the door. The aide answered it and was shocked to see a smiling Generalissimo in a formal Chinese long robe standing outside! A group of aides lined up behind him.

After tea had been served and some pleasantries exchanged, the Generalissimo came straight to the point: "Mr. Lu, I came to ask you to take over the presidency of the National Central University."

"Thank you very much for this great honor, Generalissimo," Mr. Lu replied. "But I have given my word to President Cao to serve as his dean for five years. I still have two years to go."

"Mr. Lu!" the Generalissimo said. "The National Central University is the major university of the capital. I would like to see it grow into the major university of the nation under your leadership."

Mr. Lu said he had no desire for any more administrative duties. He was planning to return to studying and teaching after fulfilling his deanship.

"In this pivotal time when the survival of our nation is at stake," the Generalissimo said, his voice growing solemn, "a scholar must carry a load that is as heavy as the journey is torturous. I promise you all the funding you will need."

Mr. Lu remained silent.

"I have another reason for my request," the Generalissimo added, his voice turning softer. "It's a personal one. I admire your treatises on the thoughts of Wang Yang-ming. If you come to Nanjing, I will have a chance to learn from you and become a better person." The Generalissimo added that he had already called President Cao and had obtained his consent to relieve Mr. Lu of his obligation.

Mr. Lu said he needed time to think it over. China's strongman did not press the issue further. On parting, he invited Mr. Lu to have dinner with him and his wife that evening.

The meal consisted of a fish, a little meat, some rice, and lots of vegetables. Madame Chiang Kai-shek sent a servant to the kitchen for a bottle of *maotai*. She told Mr. Lu that the Generalissimo did not consume alcohol, but tonight was a special occasion: he was meeting the scholar he had revered for a long time. The First Couple of China toasted Mr. Lu and drank to his health.

Two weeks later, Mr. Lu accepted the offer.

* * *

John's toilet overflowed in two days. He borrowed some tools from Old Yen and got it fixed. But the problem happened again the next day.

The short and stocky man growled in his high-pitched voice, "Flush toilets are fickle. You must not throw junk into the bowl."

John protested that he hadn't.

But soon John realized he had been guilty as charged. He should have put the soiled toilet paper in a wastebasket and thrown it out with the other garbage.

* * *

John bought a bicycle. Now he could navigate Nanjing's broad streets by himself.

His classroom was packed. There were not enough chairs for all the students. Some of them were standing; others sat on the floor. When he tried his Chinese on them, he was greeted with laughter.

His first job in the lab was to construct a wind tunnel. He worked in the basement of an old building. There was a locked door with a rusty chain. No one could tell him what was behind that door.

At MIT, his project would have been routine. Many of the parts he needed would be ordered from outside. Here he had to drill and saw all of them himself.

* * *

One day he went to the neighborhood convenience store to do some shopping. May greeted him with a sunny smile. "Baba told me not to charge you for paper," she said in English. "You are a *lao-shi.*"

John liked the way she said *teacher*, a calling that was much revered in China.

He felt a tiny warm hand touching his knee. He looked down and saw a little baby on the floor, her eyes shining. "When she grows up, she's going to be as pretty as her sister," he thought.

Seeing that the baby girl had no toy to play with, John decided to get her one.

* * *

October 15, 1936

My dearest Cynthia,

For the last two days I have been trying to locate the church where my grandfather once worked, but the descriptions my father gave me have not been much help. Calvin promised to ask his father to look into city files.

I found a church to go to worship. It is inside a school campus not far from where I live. Sunday services are practically the same as those back home, but I feel strange being the only "big nose" sitting in the midst of the attendees.

The school of some three hundred kids is run by Minnie Vautrin of Jinling Women's College. Seeing how hard this woman works at two jobs, I begin to appreciate Grandfather's sacrifices serving Our Lord in Nanjing.

Here is a kiss for you. How are you, my sweetheart?

Love,

John

* * *

The following day Calvin went to Beijing on business. In the evening, Judy came to John's apartment carrying a pot of soup. John invited her to sit on one of the sofa chairs in his bedroom.

"Your apartment needs some decoration," Judy looked around and frowned. "Live a little, John!"

"You're right, Judy, thanks," John said. "Say, how has China treated you?"

"Gosh, people here are warm. I like my friends in school, but sometimes I feel the need to have some space."

"Are you managing all right financially?"

"Salaries in China are low, but professors are among the best paid government employees. We don't spend much money, and Calvin's twenty dollars a month is plenty for us to live on—although we feel a bit tight every time Kemei's college charges come due," Judy said. "How about you? Any regret about coming to Nanjing?"

"I enjoy teaching, and my work in the lab keeps me busy."

"You and Calvin are the same animal—nothing but work!"

"Calvin's crazier than I am," John said. "I'd never keep a cot in my office for spending the night." He poured tea from a thermos bottle and handed Judy a bowl of sugar. "Working constantly at a breakneck pace is not good for his health."

"I worry about that too," Judy said, pouring sugar grains into her teacup. "Oops! Too much. You really should get yourself some teaspoons, John."

"Sorry."

"Calvin is abusing his body like there is no tomorrow," Judy continued. "I tried to get him to relax, but he says his work can't wait."

"Many Chinese people I know are workaholics," John said. "Your father, for one. He worked from ten in the morning till eleven at night, day in and day out, but hardly spent any money."

"I hope Calvin will not end up like him: dying in a hospital bed before his time," Judy said.

"Your father passed away? When?"

"Several months ago. I got a telegram from my aunt telling me that he had only days to live. I had no idea that I would feel this way, but it was like being hit by a hammer over the head. I broke down and couldn't stop screaming. Calvin got me a ticket for a commercial airplane," Judy said.

"I have never been on one," John said.

"It was my first time too. Do you know, John, that there are only fourteen seats attached to the wall of the airplane cabin, and that one has to use cotton balls to protect one's eardrums? But I had trouble finding a taxi to take me to the airport. Fortunately, the good policeman in our neighborhood gave me a ride on his motorcycle."

"I had wondered why your father returned to China in such a hurry. He probably knew his time was coming."

"Dying at home meant a lot to him," Judy said. "He used to say: 'A leaf must fall on its own root.'"

"He must be happy that you came to see him in the hospital."

"Yes, he said it gave him a chance to apologize to me."

"What? Coming from a man who had never admitted to having hurt you, and thought that every time you two had an argument, it was your fault?"

"Well, he finally admitted that he was wrong to shack up with Sally," Judy said. "He said that a Chinese man in America is allowed neither to marry a white woman nor to bring a woman over from home, and that such a man has no diversion, no woman, no respect. This made me realize why he had dreamt of building a school in China: he wanted the respect he had been denied in America."

"Did you accept his apology?" John asked.

"I finally saw the lonely man he was under that impassive facade. I understand loneliness, John, so yes, I forgave him," Judy said and dabbed a handkerchief around her eyes.

"That's good, a closure of your relationship with your father!" John said.

"Not quite. Next thing I knew, he showed me a stack of papers that looked like sheets of huge stamps. He said they were called *Jiu Guo Gong Zhai.*"

"What do those words mean?"

"Save the Nation Bonds. They were signed by Kong Xiangxi, finance minister of the Nationalist Government."

"Bonds are safe investments," John said.

"Not those bonds, John," Judy said. "They issue no interests. You don't even get your equity back."

"Really?"

"I got angry and shouted at him!"

"Judy, the man was dying!"

"I know, but he sounded like an idiot again and I couldn't control myself," Judy said. "Then he said he could explain."

It was a long explanation. Briefly, he fell sick before he had been able to build a school in his name.

"He made a phone call to a banker friend ," Judy said. "The friend told him that the government needed money to buy machine guns, cannons, tanks, and airplanes from the West, all those weapons China couldn't produce herself. The Chinese soldiers needed these weapons to defend themselves. The friend also said that if Japan had been allowed to conquer China, all of the Chinese people would've have become second class citizens in their own country. They would've been more miserable than the black people in the United States, having to bow to any Japanese soldier they met in the streets—or be ordered to kneel and be slapped in the face."

Judy added that she finally understood her father.

"I had dismissed him as a crude, uneducated, and self-centered man," she said. "I never thought he would be willing to spend all of his precious money on Jiu Guo Gong Zhai. He was really no different from Calvin, a proud man who wants respect for his countrymen."

* * *

A week later, a limousine driven by a uniformed chauffeur took John to the front door of a house on Huangpu Road. One of the many aides on the lawn escorted John inside. A grand piano under a glittering chandelier stood in the large living room. Most guests were Westerners standing in groups, chatting. No one took advantage of the hardwood chairs with silk cushions.

An aide announced John Winthrop; another led him to Madame Chiang.

The First Lady looked resplendent in a dark blue qipao under a black vest, her padded shoulders tapering to a slim waist. The beauty of the qipao's embroidered white flowers was outshone only by her jadeite rings and bracelets. John knew the translucent gems of Imperial green were as valuable as the finest diamonds.

Madame Chiang granted John her hand as he bowed his head. He watched with awe as her delicate fingers disappeared into his pale hand.

"I've heard a lot about you," Madame said in fluent English, formal and with a slight tinge of accent giving away her years of living in Tennessee and Georgia as a child. "Welcome to China!"

Madame looked about his age. But John knew she had studied in Wellesley College years before his time.

The First Lady was familiar with MIT's new campus by the river. She told John she had arrived at Wellesley soon after MIT's move from Boston to Cambridge, and laughingly described how she had gotten lost in a very long hall.

"The infinite corridor that joins all MIT's main buildings!" John exclaimed.

Madame Chiang reminisced about a regatta race on the Charles River called the Head of the Charles. But when John mentioned the MIT football team, she seemed surprised that MIT had one.

She asked him about the changes in the Boston area, particularly her alma mater's new Gothic buildings atop the campus hills. John felt that they talked like old friends. Then she glanced at the long queue of guests waiting behind John and told him that aeronautical technology was much needed in her country. Realizing that he had been dismissed, John bowed to her again as she thanked him for coming to China. Then she turned to people obviously more important than he.

Among the guests drifting over to surround John was a well-dressed gentleman with a strong scent of cologne. Introducing himself as Gregory Evans, the cultural attaché of the American Embassy asked what Madame Chiang had said to him. John told him briefly about their conversation.

"I bet she had many Harvard suitors in her days," a lady in a pink hat whispered after hearing John's brief answer.

Her comment evoked much interest.

"Her elder brother Song zi-wen was studying at Harvard at that time," another lady in a very large hat said. "To go out with her, a young man had to earn his approval."

A middle-aged lady said that she and Madame Chiang had attended college about the same time. Had she chosen to go to Wellesley instead of Smith, they could have met some twenty years earlier.

"And you might have been her best friend by now," said her husband standing next to her. He gave a nervous little laugh.

Evans told John that Madame was the Secretary General of China's Aeronautical Affairs Commission. She had just given a speech on how the invention of airplanes had made communication easier and the globe smaller.

John exchanged addresses with everyone. All promised to look him up. Greg Evans remained by his side when they walked out of the Generalissimo's house. They traded stories about life in Nanjing. Soon they were addressing each other by first names.

John told Greg about his interest in Chinese antiques. Greg warned that most wares on the market were of poor quality—even fakes.

John knew this only too well. Just the day before, he had thought he had found something special in an outdoor antique booth. He told the story to Greg.

* * *

The peddler had shown him a carved Ming ivory figurine and asked for ten yuan. John, having been forewarned of inflated asking prices by Chinese peddlers, countered with four yuan—about a dollar.

The peddler accepted the offer without blinking.

Later, one of John's co-workers, Lin, advised John: "Given what the peddler had asked, you should've offered no more than half a yuan."

"Why didn't you tell me this earlier?" John was miffed.

Still, four yuan was cheap for something three hundred years old.

"I hate to tell you, Professor, but it's not Ming," Lin said after taking a close look at the figurine.

"Which period is it from?" John asked, concerned that he had been duped.

"From yesterday," Lin said. "It looks old because it has been stained." Then a final blow: "And it's made of bone, not ivory."

* * *

John climbed into his limousine. "Well, Greg, I guess I have a lot to learn."

Greg gave a compassionate chuckle and offered to go antique shopping together some day.

October 20, 1936

My dearest Cynthia,

I am happy to report that my students address me as "professor." It feels great not to be a lowly instructor any longer!

But I had misunderstood the meaning of the professorship they conferred on me. The Chinese academia has only two professorial ranks: associate professor and full professor. So an associate professorship in China is not as eminent a position as I thought.

Attendance at my classes has not dwindled much after a month. I lecture mostly in English. My students are getting the MIT treatment: a problem set every week.

The most enthusiastic responses to my teaching come from students in the lab. I have been pleasantly surprised by the quality of the papers they've turned in—despite the rumor that Chinese students are poor in performing experiments.

The social life of an engineering student here reminds me of MIT. All of my students are male. There are few opportunities for them to meet girls. Indeed, I have never seen a young man and a young woman hold hands on campus—although plenty of young women do that with one another. I asked my students about it, and they just laughed at my stupid question. I am glad girl problems are not mine any longer, for I have you, my darling!

The wind tunnel I am building is coming along nicely. It is going to be bigger than the one at MIT. I must ask Calvin why he wants it this way.

Here, with no distractions, I find out what work means to me. I am happy for being useful. On the other hand, I truly miss you, my darling—indeed very, very much.

Love,

John

P.S. I have been searching the antique market but have had no luck so far. The antique stores in Chao-Tian-Gong do carry high quality Ming and Qing porcelains, but their prices are not much better than those in New York and Boston. One dealer treated me as a special customer, taking me upstairs and drawing all the curtains. But four hundred yuan (about one hundred dollars) seems high for the wucai (five colors) Ming vase he offered me—with or without curtains.

* * *

One night John brought a load of notes home. The next morning he forgot them in a drawer. The notes contained nothing but equations. He rushed back at noon but couldn't find them.

Calvin returned from Beijing Saturday afternoon and dropped into John's apartment. Apologizing for not having been able to take John sightseeing, he said, "Let's do it tomorrow."

John thanked him and mentioned the missing notes.

"Heavens!" Calvin seemed alarmed out of all proportion. "Did they contain anything important?"

"The final formula. It took me four months to derive it."

"Where did you keep your notes?" Calvin asked, looking around.

John pointed to the top drawer of his desk.

"Damn! I should have warned you. Never take your notes home! Lock them up in the lab and let our armed guards watch over them."

"Armed guards, Calvin?" John asked.

Calvin did not answer the question. "Do you remember the formula?" he asked.

"I wrote down what I could, but something is wrong with it."

"Show it to me."

John handed a sheet of paper to Calvin, who took a glance and began muttering: "Set x to zero. The right-side vanishes; the left-side is equal to one-third. Hmm. What if we change this to . . . no no no, that won't work . . ." He closed his eyes, opened them again, and pointed at a term on the paper. "There must be a factor of one-fifth missing here. How long will it take you to confirm it?"

"About twenty minutes," John said.

A while later, John raised his head and broke out a big grin. "You are simply amazing, Calvin."

"Let me tell you something, John." Calvin didn't smile back. "Nanjing is a dangerous place. You want to be very careful with everything you do."

"All right, chief!"

"You don't understand, John. As a matter of fact, neither did our former premier Wang Jing-wei—until someone pumped three bullets into his body."

"Is he alive?"

"Only miserably so. One of the bullets is still lodged in his lung. He stepped down from office last December, telling his wife he had no more than ten years to live."

"But, Calvin, you are flattering me. If there is anything good about being an associate professor, it must be that he doesn't have to lose any sleep over an attempt on his life—unless he seduces someone's young daughter."

"This is no joking matter. We need to talk, John."

Upon hurrying out, Calvin said again, "For tomorrow, how about meeting at nine at the bus stop in front of the convenience store?"

"Fine. I've been thinking of delivering a doll to May's little sister," John said. "That will be killing two birds with one stone."

Chapter 11

The Mausoleum Builders

When John and Calvin walked into the convenience store the next morning, they saw the baby girl Wumao sitting on her mother's lap hitting the countertop with a chopstick.

"My husband is not in," the mother said.

"That's all right. We are here to see Wumao today." Calvin beamed at the baby girl. "Isn't that right, little princess? Am I getting a kiss from you today?"

The baby quickly hid her face in her mother's bosom, her hair a whirl of black waves.

"Sorry. She is shy early in the morning waking up," her mother said.

John clapped his hands to get the baby's attention. "Hi, Wumao! See what I've brought you?"

The toddler showed half her little face. When she saw the doll in John's hands, her eyes turned into two smiling half-moons.

"Come and get it," John beckoned.

The mother put her daughter on the floor. The little baby tottered forward jerkily. She was about to stumble when John caught her. The large man and the tiny girl fell into a squealing heap. Everybody laughed when she grabbed the doll from John.

A teenage girl was standing in a corner, wearing a pair of black trousers and a white tunic. Both looked cleanly washed but were one size too large for her.

"Heimao!" Calvin called in Mandarin. "Say, you must have grown another centimeter since I saw you last. I swear you are now taller than Judy."

"You are teasing me again, Professor Ren," the seventeen-year-old girl replied, her voice raindrops on a bamboo roof.

"Not at all. I mean it," Calvin said. "Do you see who is here? I thought you wanted to talk to him."

John handed the baby girl to her mother. "Hi, Chen May! What's on your mind?" he asked in broken Mandarin.

"The teacher in my English class entered me into a city-wide English speaking competition. I'm very nervous." The color on May's cheeks deepened. "Mr. Tang suggested that I practice speaking English with a foreigner."

"You are looking at one, Chen May," John said. "Practice away!"

"I can't impose on you like that, Professor Winthrop." May blushed even more. "It would take up too much of your time."

"I'll enjoy every minute of it. We can start right now." John switched to English. "Let's begin with how to address people. Call me John. Go on."

May tried and stopped.

"What's the matter?"

"I can't say it."

"Why?"

"You have a doctoral degree!"

"So?"

"Even our principal doesn't have one."

"You and I are friends, May. You're my little friend, I'm your big friend," John said. "In my country, friends call one another by their first names."

May looked at John dubiously.

"Let her think about it, John. She is terrified," Calvin said. "She is not used to this."

"All right," John said. "How can we talk, May?"

"I've found a way for us to talk a lot," May said, "and it won't take up any of your time."

"That's interesting," John said.

"I heard you're shopping for antiques in the market," May said. "I can go with you and interpret for you."

"May!" Calvin said. "John needs no interpreter. He has managed quite well on his own."

May's face reddened to her ears. "Of course, Professor Winthrop's Mandarin is very good."

"You both are lying." John laughed. "Too much kindness. I may have picked up some Chinese, but I've absolutely no idea how to bargain with peddlers."

"I can do that for you," May said quickly.

"And I'll speak nothing but English with you," John said. "Shake hands?"

May hesitated.

"I don't think she cares to touch a man's hands," Calvin said.

* * *

At the bus stop, Calvin said that the first thing he wanted to show John was the mightiest river in China.

They took the bus to Lion Hill northwest of the city. Upon arriving, John followed his friend climbing to the top of the little hill, where they could get a good view of the glimmering Yangtze River . The day was breezy, and their clothes flapped in the wind. John thought the view of rolling waves spectacular. The distant city looked quaint and mysterious in the mist.

"Over there is the *Jinghai Temple*, John." Calvin pointed to a group of old buildings with gray tile roofs. "That's where the Chinese and the British signed the Nanjing Treaty."

"Didn't it legalize British opium in China?"

"It did more than that, John. It also forced the Chinese to hand Hong Kong to the British, open five ports for trade, and pay for the opium she had burned. Eventually, it reduced China to a semi-colony."

"Why did China agree to such a brutal treaty?"

"Because China's bows and arrows were no match for British cannons."

"I'm glad we Americans never sold opium to China." John sighed. "Otherwise, you might have hated me too!"

"I'm afraid you've got the facts wrong, John. Four Boston families—Perkins, Forbes, Russell, and Sturgis—controlled the American opium trade."

"Oh, I didn't know that." John said.

"The essence of Americanism is 'all men are created equal,' yet the American government forced unequal treaties on us."

"Calvin, how much money has China paid the US and other powers over the years?"

"The total reparation was about twenty-five times China's national budget."

John did a calculation in his head. "If the US government were to take up a debt twenty-five times the federal budget at the rate of four percent, it would have to double the federal income tax just to pay the interest," he sighed. "The impact would have created an economic storm many times that of the Great Depression!"

"The Western exploitation of China is the reason why *capitalism* is a dirty word in the Chinese dictionary," Calvin said. He took out his wallet, rummaged through it, and showed John a faded photograph. "This is a snapshot I took of my best friends in high school, Liu and Sze. Look here, Liu is the one on the right; Sze is on the left."

John squinted at the bright faces of two young men standing in front of a brick house, thick hair flying in the wind, hands on their hips, thumbs at the back, their arms and elbows forming proud triangles with their bodies. "Sze is a handsome young man," John said.

"He was our class president," Calvin said. "The teacher in charge of our class regarded him the most promising of us."

"Both of them look so confident and full of hope, they might as well be carrying China on their shoulders," John said. "Did they go to college in America?"

"Didn't want to. They hated America," Calvin said. "In fact, the day before I left for the US, the three of us debated till daybreak over who was China's worst enemy, Japan or the United States."

"Did they attend college?"

"Yes—in China. Liu studied electrical engineering, and Sze studied law," Calvin said.

"Why did they think these two disciplines would save their country from the powers?" John asked.

The Chinese intelligentsia, Calvin explained, regarded Western science and Western democracy—nicknamed *Mr. Sai* and *Mr. De*—the answers to China's difficult problems. Students in these fields were in demand. Indeed, Sze and Liu had promising careers upon graduation.

"But several weeks after Japan had seized Manchuria, both of them quit their jobs," Calvin said.

"Why?"

"They blamed Chiang Kai-shek for the loss and went to Jiangxi province to join Mao Ze-dong," Calvin said.

"You mean your best friends in high school were communists?" John was shocked. This was a part of Calvin's past he had never suspected.

"Yes. A couple of years later, both of them were captured in Shanghai by Chiang Kai-shek's security agents. Refusing to sell out their comrades to save their lives, both sang communist international songs and shouted, 'Long Live the Chinese Communist Party' as they faced the firing squad."

"Oh my God!" John exclaimed. "Calvin, are you a communist too? Please tell me the truth!"

Calvin said he was not. He added that while most of the serious students in his class favored communism, he believed the United States was not China's worst enemy.

"Who is?" John asked

"Japan, who took Taiwan from us forty years ago. Manchuria in 1931. Rehe last year—and our Generalissimo didn't put up much of a fight. So Mongolia will be next. Our country will cease to exist if we don't stop her."

John looked at his friend and felt a tinge of envy. He didn't believe that China would cease to exist, but he had been motivated by personal goals such as buying a three-bedroom house.

"China is not a nation of military might," Calvin continued. "If anything, she is a nation of wrath—and that can be more dangerous to the world in the long run."

John asked what he meant.

"You remember what I did the day I heard that the Japanese had invaded Manchuria?" Calvin asked.

"You hit your fists on the wall and broke four of your knuckles." John said. "I thought you were going to hit me!"

"I'm sorry, John, but there are many angry men in China. You don't see them. The wrath is hidden deep. But one day it will come up and explode with the fury of a thousand suns. The world will tremble, John, when the eruption comes."

John was not sure if Calvin was being melodramatic.

* * *

Calvin told John that the next place they should visit was Sun Yat-sen's Mausoleum—a must-see tourist spot.

They hired two rickshaws to take them to the east side of the city. When his rickshaw slowed, John saw a large structure of blue tile and white marble standing high up on a hill.

After getting off the rickshaws at the foot of the hill, they climbed a stair of white-stone steps—almost twenty stories worth of them, each measuring fifty meters wide. John was exhausted when they arrived at the entry of the mausoleum, a tri-arched marble gate headed by four large characters in Dr. Sun's calligraphy: *Tian Xia Wei Gong* (What Is under the Heaven Is for All). At the highest point of the tomb, Calvin stopped in front of a huge marble figure, losing himself in thought for several seconds.

Calvin indicated little interest in the rest of the tomb. He showed John the sarcophagus where Dr. Sun's body lay; then he took John to the surrounding pine trees and sat him down. "I'll take you to another mausoleum—the one built for the First Ming Emperor who drove the Mongolians out of Beijing," Calvin said.

It was past noon. The air had heated up. Calvin led John zigzagging down a slope with no road, seeing no one but squirrels leaping from tree to tree. John was about to ask his friend why they were doing this, but a look at Calvin's taut face shut him up. After a long trek they came to an open field. Calvin took off his glasses, wiped off the perspiration around his eyes, and gestured for John to sit on a bench overlooking a road.

"This is the Ming Tomb's Sacred Way," Calvin said.

"Where is the tomb?" John asked.

"At the end of the road—more than a mile from here," Calvin said.

A couple stood in front of a giant stone elephant about fifty meters away. A man aimed his camera at them. Farther down were more stone animals and stone officials. The statues, all of them larger than life size, dwarfed the handful of leisurely tourists around them.

"They were chiseled from huge boulders some five hundred years ago," Calvin said.

"Magnificent!" John said, putting one aching leg over the other. "These statues tell me how grand your Ming Empire must've been."

"If you get closer to them, John, you will see the large cracks on their bodies, works of art no longer. The Ming Tomb is a huge waste of human labor, if you ask me," Calvin said.

"How many laborers and how long did it take?" John asked.

"A few hundred thousand men toiling for several decades."

"Goodness gracious! I bet you and I could build thousands of airplanes a year with such human resources."

"But we won't have that kind of manpower, John. Our resources will only allow us to build airplanes at the rate of one a year, if that." Calvin frowned. "Moreover, our products would not be very useful unless we can make them world class."

"I think we can do that," John said.

"Come on, John. You and I learned everything from books and academic journals," Calvin said. "How can we compete with the engineers who have honed their technical skills through years of work in Lockheed, Boeing, and Douglas?"

"You may be right, Calvin, but just for the sake of argument, let's review what we've got between the two of us," John said.

He listed three areas of expertise for building airplanes: aerodynamics, structure, and internal combustion. "No human being has been able to command all three areas," he said. "You are a theorist. You can make a good design for the airplane."

"I can try," Calvin granted.

"I'll build the parts and test them in the wind tunnel," John said.

"That takes care of aerodynamics," Calvin conceded.

John said he could assemble the parts into a flying machine, given a number of skilled workers.

"Where do we find them?" Calvin asked.

"The engineers and the students in our lab would make a nice start, but we may need to hire some specialty mechanics from the United States," John said.

"What about the internal combustion engine?" Calvin asked.

John paused. "This is the area where we'll need the most help," he finally said. "I worked under Professor Mark Taylor for a summer, but my experience is very limited. We can start by buying the engines from General Motors and tweak them to fit our needs."

"China has repair and maintenance facilities," Calvin said. "She also has factories that make engine parts."

"Great. Some day we can convert them and build our own engines."

"OK, where do we start?" Calvin asked.

"We start small," John said. "If we work hard, we can probably build a prototype airplane in a year."

"A crude product," Calvin said, "at best."

"True. We will need to fine-tune it before going into production."

"How many airplanes can we produce in a year?"

"I would say ten the first year," John said slowly. "One hundred in two or three years. Four hundred in a couple more years. Then we will be on our way!"

Calvin looked around before slapping his thigh. "You know what, John, I've been thinking along the same lines. As a matter of fact, I submitted a proposal to the university last year. It was very close to what you just said."

John stood up. "You must be joking!"

"Japan acquired their first warplanes in 1910," Calvin said, "but was already building aircraft carriers in the 1920s. I don't see why we can't do just as well."

"What did the university do with your proposal?" John asked.

"President Lu forwarded it to the Aeronautical Affairs Commission."

"Did anything come of it?"

"I got anxious hearing nothing from anyone for months," Calvin said.

"Darn!" John said. "Government agencies don't like to take chances, not with a large project and the principal investigator having no track record."

A grin slowly spread across Calvin's face. "You'd better sit down, John. It turns out Madame Chiang Kai-shek is enthusiastic about the proposal."

"Holy cow!" John cried. "You mean you got the money?"

"We didn't get a million dollars, if that's what you have in mind. But the government has approved the budget. They also approved your appointment."

"Aha!" John shouted. "No wonder Madame knew about me."

"Sit down, sit down, John!" Calvin said. "The grant is for three years. We'd better get some concrete results before the money runs out. It's also important to convince China's academic leaders to support us."

"Is this why you left town in such a hurry last week?" John asked. "You must've done a lot of talking in Beijing!"

Calvin nodded solemnly. He tore off a piece of paper from a small notebook and drew a red airplane with his fountain pen.

"Look, John, this is the single-seater Japan has been producing since last year. Maximum speed, four hundred kilometers an hour; rate of climb, one thousand meters a minute; range, eleven hundred kilometers." He pulled out John's fountain pen from his friend's shirt pocket and drew another figure in black around the red figure. "This is my design. I used a number of new methods such as conformal transformations to help me. See the difference in the wing, the contour of the fuselage, and the control surface? Maximum speed, four hundred and fifty kilometers an hour; rate of climb, twelve hundred meters a minute. Range will also be somewhat better."

"How sure are you about these numbers?" John asked, tracing the shape of the black airplane with his index finger.

"They can be off by as much as ten percent, but no more."

Goose bumps broke out all over John's body. "Calvin! You have been planning this for years, haven't you?"

"Yes."

"This is why you dropped out of theoretical physics and went into aeronautics!"

"Right."

"You wanted to build warplanes—something your country needs desperately."

"You've got it."

"And my coming here has nothing to do with helping to update your department."

Calvin patted John's shoulder. "My apologies, John, but I couldn't have written you about a classified project. Top military secret, as a matter of fact. Even with our best attempt at secrecy, your identity had already been leaked out before you left America."

The edge in Calvin's voice gave John pause. He asked, "Am I in some kind of trouble?"

"Not until you work with us. I'll tell you the truth: I cannot guarantee your personal safety in Nanjing. That's why I must ask you one question before we go forward: Knowing what you do now, are you still willing to join our project?"

"What if I don't?"

"We will pay you five hundred dollars plus traveling expenses to send you home," Calvin said.

"Wait! I'm an American citizen. If the Japanese do anything to me, they will have to answer to my government."

"Such considerations will hardly deter them," Calvin said.

"Why?"

"The stakes are too high."

"Explain!"

"The Japanese air force destroyed our airplanes in Manchuria, reducing the 'young marshal' Zhang Xue-liang's soldiers to cannon fodder," Calvin said. "Once we have warplanes as good as theirs, we'll level the playing field."

"Lord Almighty! You expect the two of us to tip the military balance between China and Japan?"

"Yes sir!"

"This is the craziest idea I've ever heard! Tell me one more thing. Why did you choose me?"

"Because you are exactly the man we need!"

"Explain, please!"

"Our project is starting from zero. It will go through crisis after crisis," Calvin said. "No one will be here to help us, so we must solve them on our own and quickly. If you don't mind my saying so, John, your grades in school were not great, but you have an instinct that cannot be taught. Some people are error prone. They may have as much knowledge as anyone else, but they will mess things up if given a chance. Back at MIT, I noticed how you handled yourself during a crisis in the lab, almost always making the right call. You're like some people who have an internal compass—the kind who can drive in the dark better than others. We want a man like you to lead us!"

"You are the only one who thinks so highly of me!" John said in a hoarse voice. "For that reason alone I'll honor my promise to work with you for one whole year, come what may!"

"One year?" Calvin held up a hand. "No, we need you for longer. At least three years, John!"

John's face fell. "I'm afraid I can't do that," he said. "But you don't have to worry. Once we get the project running, you won't need me. You'll be able to continue on your own."

"I'm only a theoretician. Without you I'm nothing," Calvin said with clenched fists.

"Come on, Calvin. You are smarter than I am."

"We have a huge project and zero experience. With you on board we've got a shot. Without you it will be a total disaster. It's that simple. We *need* you!"

"I'm sorry," John said.

"If not for three years, how about two years, John?" Calvin's voice quivered. "Do you need more money? We'll pay you whatever you want."

"It's not money. Look, Calvin, I'd like to stay, but I can't. I've promised Cynthia that I will go home and marry her next summer," John said.

"Our people will not survive without warplanes, John!"

"I am very sorry," John muttered under his breath.

Calvin abruptly got up from the bench and went down on his knees to his friend.

John was frightened. "Hey! Have you lost your mind? What the hell are you doing?"

"John, I beg you!" Calvin said in a trembling voice.

John jumped up. He remembered what Calvin had said to him on the morning after attending a party held by the Boston Chinese Student Association: "I've never *begged* in my whole life, John, and I am not about to start now."

"Don't do this to me, Calvin. Please get up!" John pleaded.

"I won't until you agree to work with me for one more year!" Calvin said.

John went to Calvin and forcibly lifted his small body off the ground, surprised by how light it had become. The man had worked himself to the bone! John was overwhelmed with sadness when he said, "Listen, Calvin, I swear I'll do my best to help you. Any time a problem with your project comes up, just write me a letter. No, send me a telegram. I'll drop everything else and take care of it."

Calvin pushed him away. "We need you to work with us face-to-face and hand-in-hand. What you can do for us an ocean away will not be worth a shit, and you know it!" Calvin's voice was shaking with anger.

It took a long time for Calvin to recover. He sounded like a man totally defeated when he spoke, "Never mind, John, forget I ever asked."

They continued their trek to the Ming Mausoleum in stony silence.

November 15, 1936

Dear Cynthia,

You have no idea how good it felt to receive your first letter to China. I am glad you like your nursing classes but worry about the perfectionist in you. Please promise me not to go to bed later than midnight!

The weather in Nanjing is getting cold. In an apartment without heat, washing up in the morning can leave your teeth chattering. Taking a bath is worse. It requires the patience of waiting for the water to boil and the resolve to expose your body to the frigid air. My neighbors do not believe that there is such a thing as turning a faucet to make hot water appear.

Today I received my salary for the first month in the form of a stack of bills sealed inside a large cowhide envelope. Since the Chinese government collects no income tax, I am able to put most of it in the bank.

A few days ago, I said 'no' to Calvin's request on extending my stay in Nanjing for one or two more years. I fear the damage to our friendship is irreparable.

Love,

John

Book II

Chapter 12

The Collector

Calvin once said, "A brother is like a limb; a girlfriend is like a dress. You don't break a limb to save a dress." John had done just the opposite.

There was only one thing John could do to make amends to his friend. He began to spend all of his waking hours in the lab working like a madman. When his footsteps echoed in the empty corridor late at night, he saw only dour security guards on their rounds.

One December evening, John went to see Calvin in his office. The slight man was sitting under a bare bulb frowning over a pile of drawings, his thinning hair losing much of its luster.

John thought: *My God, he looks ten years older than me!*

Back at MIT, Calvin had been easily one of the youngest-looking students on campus. John had been sure that Calvin would still look twenty when he reached fifty.

"The wind tunnel is ready!" John announced, too loudly.

Calvin started. "Why, it's you, John," he said, sounding distant. But his face slowly changed and light came to his eyes. "Thank God! Thank God! A load off my mind!" He patted his drawings and got down to business. "Here's my final design. Our airplane!"

"That's great! We're ahead of schedule. I'll start building the parts you want as soon as I catch my breath. But I need some sleep right now."

Calvin got up from his chair. "Snore all you want, big fellow. Tomorrow is Sunday. When you wake up, have the biggest brunch in your life."

"You buying?" John laughed.

"Of course!"

The next morning John and Calvin went to a neighborhood noodle shop. Afterwards, they dropped into the convenience store several blocks away.

May was busy taking care of a customer when they came in. "Good morning, Professor Ren. Hello, Professor Winthrop. I've been wondering what had happened to you."

"Sorry, May, I was just a bit over my head," John said. "Say, how about the deal you and I struck the other day? Would you be able to help me shop for antiques next Sunday?"

The girl's face brightened. "I've a better idea, Professor Winthrop," she said, waving goodbye to her customer. "How would you like to visit a collector instead?"

"Love to!" John said.

"You know one, May?" Calvin seemed surprised. "What's his name?"

May smiled. "Mr. Fan! That's who I know!"

"Are you talking about Mr. Fan Dong-mei by any chance?" Calvin asked.

"Yes!" May said. She turned to John. "Mr. Fan has many Chinese paintings on his walls. Why, some of them are so old they are practically in tatters!"

"May, tattered paintings are not what collectors want." John smiled. "They want fine antiques in good condition."

May blushed.

"People tend to think the older an antique, the better it is," John continued. "Truth is, garbage remains garbage after a thousand years."

"Mr. Fan has many fine antiques in great condition!" May said immediately.

"She is right. Fan Dong-mei is a great collector and a fine artist," Calvin told John. "There is a saying: 'Fan Dong-mei owns enough treasures to match a nation's, but he owns no land big enough to stick a nail into.'"

"Is this a Chinese riddle?" John asked.

"It is a statement of fact," Calvin said. "Although Mr. Fan has the finest antiques, he is also constantly broke. At the end of the year—when all debts must be paid, he would paint many paintings and sell them at fire sale prices in a gallery."

"Does he have a job?" John asked curiously.

"He teaches in an art college, which doesn't pay enough to take care of his huge financial expenses," Calvin said.

"On women?"

"No, on antiques. But you asked an appropriate question. Mr. Fan chases after antiques the way some men chase after women," Calvin said. "Pursuing antiques is his love affair. When he falls in love with an antique, he must have it."

"I once fell in love with a Qianlong vase, but I couldn't afford it." John laughed. "Mr. Fan and I are both teachers. Where does he get the money to buy all the antiques he lusts after?"

"Borrowing at high interest rates, forging a painting and selling it to a rich salt merchant, pawning an antique a friend lends him," Calvin said.

"What does he tell his friend?" John wondered.

"Nothing," Calvin replied. "He simply sends him the bill from the pawn shop, and the friend pays it to get his antique back."

"He mustn't have many friends left!" John exclaimed.

"Quite the contrary," Calvin said. "Mr. Fan has more friends than anyone I know. He is generous with them. When a friend of his gets into trouble, he is known to have sold an antique or two to help him out."

"People just die when they get invited to Mr. Fan's parties," May added. "They are not lavish, but Mr. Fan has a chef who can do French cuisine as well as the finest Yangzhou dishes."

"How does a poor teacher afford a great chef?" John marveled.

"And a chauffeur and a horde of maids," Calvin said.

"He seldom pays them," May said.

"I don't understand. Why don't they leave him?" John asked.

"I wondered about that too," May said, "until one of his maids explained to me that if she had quit, she would have had trouble to collect the months of salary Mr. Fan owed her."

Everybody laughed.

"How do the servants survive without pay?" John asked.

"They get tips from Mr. Fan's guests," May said, "and have lots of fun in the meantime. Why, on the old lady's last birthday, they got to see a Beijing opera performed by many famous opera singers."

"That can't be right, May," Calvin said. "Famous opera singers don't accept private bookings. It takes *face* to get just one of them to perform for you, not to mention many."

"Mr. Fan has a big face, Professor Ren," May said. "The performers sang for free. They took turns doing their best pieces until midnight. The old lady, the servants, and the guests—the mayor among them—were all having a wonderful time."

"May, are you sure Mr. Fan will take the trouble to see me?" John asked.

"I have face too," May said proudly. "I delivered to his house the other day and told him about you. Mr. Fan said I could take you to visit him any time."

John wondered if Mr. Fan's antiques could be compared with the Qianlong vase in Yamanaka's gallery back in Boston.

Chapter 13

The Museum Director

John worked on the airplane wings in the lab throughout the week. He got into a mechanical problem and had to stay late in the lab on Saturday night. His head was still spinning getting up Sunday morning. He had time only for some bread and green tea before hurrying to the convenience store.

Baba was sitting behind the counter, his sons snoring in a corner. May was sweeping the floor, the contours of her hips periodically showing through the back of her pants. John was impressed with the determined manner the young girl was putting into her chore.

"Good morning, Professor Winthrop, please stay away from the dust." May brushed the hair from her eyes. "I must finish cleaning for Baba before I go."

John thought her gesture incredibly feminine for a girl so young. He turned to the store owner. "Where's your lovely baby daughter?"

"My woman is picking wild vegetables outside the city wall. Wumao is riding on her back."

John walked around the store consulting his shopping list. By the time he was ready to pay for his purchases, the store already looked spic and span.

May called out, "I am leaving, Baba."

"Where are your sweaters?" Baba grumbled.

"I'm wearing three of them under my blouse, Baba," May said.

Baba slipped a coin into the girl's palm. "Buy yourself a bowl of hot bean soup from the uncle next door, for heaven's sake!"

The sky was a bright blue. May walked with a bounce in her steps. John matched them and hummed: ". . . that's because . . ." which was the only part of a song he knew. He took her arm. "Mind if I drop off my bag first?"

"Not at all, Professor Winthrop," she said and wriggled herself free.

She stayed outside of his door when John went inside his apartment.

* * *

Mr. Fan's house was surrounded by a brick wall. May grabbed the rusted bronze ring and knocked on the gate with peeling paint. After some waiting, the door creaked open.

"Zheng Ma!" May greeted the middle-aged woman in a black satin tunic and white pants. "Where is your daughter?"

"She is here, in Nanjing!" The woman's face lit up. "Very lucky. Her neighbor brought melons to the city and she got a ride on his buffalo cart."

"Is she really pregnant?"

"Yes! My daughter said I'll be holding a fat baby boy in my arms very soon." Her smile broadened.

"How does she know it's going to be a boy?"

"Because her tummy is pointed, not round."

John and May followed Zheng Ma down a narrow pebble path in the middle of an unkempt garden, arriving at a sprawling stucco house with an upturned roof. They were taken to the living room, where the drawn curtains reduced the daylight to a shadow. Sitting down, John smelled a quaint, soothing scent and wondered what it was. As his eyes slowly adjusted to the dimness of the surroundings, the landscape paintings on the wall brightened into his vision. Brought to a serene world of green woods and waterfalls, he forgot about his headache.

A middle-aged man entered the room with a little cough. His gaunt face suggested an undernourished high school teacher, but the fine silk of his gray vest and blue Chinese robe spoke of a man from a family of wealth and status.

May stood up. "I wish you a peaceful day, Mr. Fan. This is Professor Win, the man I told you about."

John got up and pressed the long, slim fingers graciously extended to him. He was directed to another chair at the front side of a huge desk. May moved to stand behind him. The host took the chair across the desk.

Zheng Ma brought a tray with a pot, a creamer, two sterling silver jugs, and two porcelain cups. Next to them stood a tin receptacle of 555—a brand of British cigarettes.

Mr. Fan held his long right sleeve with his left hand as he poured tea into a cup. He served it to John with two hands, his fingers dancing in the air as he withdrew.

John thanked him in Chinese and took the red and blue Worcester.

"Cigarette?" Mr. Fan offered the tin can sealed by an aluminum foil.

John declined politely, helping himself to sugar and cream.

Mr. Fan poured tea for himself. "Heimao told me you collect Chinese antiques. That's remarkable. May I ask what you prefer?"

"I have . . ." John turned to the girl and switched to English. "How do you say Chinese export porcelain?"

The young girl struggled to translate the unfamiliar words.

"We rarely see any of those." Fan nodded. "Few of us collect them. If you allow me, I can show you something we like better."

"Please do."

"Kindly pardon my impudence. I suggest you collect the *guan yao* of Ming or Qing."

"What's a guan yao?"

"Guan yao means, literally, official kiln. Permit me to oversimplify: they are porcelains made for the emperor and his household."

"Are they finer than export porcelain?"

"They are among the finest porcelain Chinese craftsmen ever produced."

John nodded politely. He had heard that the Morgans and the Rockefellers preferred Chinese domestic arts over Chinese exports, setting the taste for the American wealthy. Upper-class families in Manhattan matched their French furniture with domestic Chinese antique porcelain, but John found out long ago that the imperial peach bloom vases of the Kangxi reign, the blue-and-white porcelain of early Ming, the mysteriously blotched Jun earthenware, and the delicately carved Ding bowls of the Song dynasty were beyond his reach.

"How can one tell a fake?" John expressed his constant worry.

Mr. Fan stroked his chin and produced several delicate coughs. John waited, wondering if he had intruded into a sensitive subject.

"I will tell you a little story." Mr. Fan settled back in his chair and began. "A young man asked an antique scholar in Beijing to accept him as a student. His wish was granted.

"On the first day of class, the eminent teacher gave the student a porcelain vase to hold and left the room. He returned an hour later to take the vase away. Then he sent the young man home.

"The next day the teacher gave the young man a shallow bowl to hold, returning an hour later to end the lesson.

"This wordless play repeated every day for a month, and the student began to feel unhappy. He had paid a hefty tuition and had been taught nothing.

"On the first day of the second month the student was given a charger.

"He roared as soon as he touched it," Mr. Fan said. "Please excuse my language, Mr. Win, but these were his words: 'Why are you giving me a piece of crap this time?' He threw the porcelain on the floor, shattering it into many pieces.

"His teacher smiled and told the student that he had arrived. There was no need for him to come again."

May broke out laughing.

It took a split second longer for John to follow her. "I see, I see. Mr. Fan, thank you very much. But where do I find a guan yao to hold for an hour?"

"Please wait here, Professor Win," Fan said and left the room.

The host returned holding a little blue satin box. He carefully laid it down, bringing John's eyes to the dark, purplish desk.

"Intriguing timber," John commented. "Is it *zitan*?"

"Yes. A zitan timber of this quality could only be imported from India five centuries ago," Fan said.

"That's before Columbus discovered America!" John exclaimed. "I heard it is very heavy."

"Enough to sink in water," Fan said.

"Why is it so?"

"A zitan tree grows slowly, Professor Win, taking about a thousand years for it to develop into furniture timber."

"That's amazing!" May exclaimed. She caressed the surface of the desk and declared, "It feels as smooth as a baby's bottom!"

Fan opened the blue satin box on the desk, revealing a dish about six inches in diameter resting on silk padding. Its outside wall was decorated with white plum blossoms on a yellow ground.

"What a perfect balance of form and color!" John exclaimed.

Mr. Fan picked up the dish and turned it upside down. He read John the four Chinese characters on its bottom.

"A Yongzheng guan yao!" John repeated, awed. Yongzheng Emperor was the father of Qianlong Emperor.

"It's a little more than that, Professor Win. This is a *falangcai*, the most exquisite of Yongzheng wares. Indeed, the artwork on this dish was done in the imperial workshop, under the personal direction of the Emperor."

John asked about the fourteen characters painted in black enamel on the interior rim of the dish.

"It's a poem praising the indomitable spirit of winter plums, which blossom at the harshest time of the year," Fan said. "Professor Win, what would a dish like this cost in the United States?"

"I once saw a vase with a Qianlong mark," John replied. He described it to Fan. "It had the exorbitant price of two thousand dollars. I'm no expert, but I would say your dish is finer and should be worth at least twice as much."

"Two thousand dollars is quite reasonable for the vase you saw in Boston," Fan said. "I suggest you buy it."

"I wish I had that kind of money."

"That's too bad," Fan said. "Chinese porcelains are relatively inexpensive today because our people are living from hand to mouth. Once China gets out of this mess, her antiques should cost more."

A knock came from the front gate outside. Zheng Ma hurried out. Uneven footsteps approached. A middle-aged man limped into the threshold of the living room.

"Director Yao!" Fan stood up and put his left fist into his right paw. "What an honor to have you grace my humble abode!" He introduced his guests to one another.

"My big friend's full name is Dr. John Winthrop," May offered. "He is from MIT University."

John smiled but didn't correct her.

The deputy director of the Shanghai Museum wore a Chinese cotton robe of faded blue. If not for the thick eyeglasses, John would have taken him for a store clerk.

Zheng Ma came in with a red lacquer platter. She poured tea into a tiny cup decorated with roundels of flowers on a bright yellow ground with feathery scrolls.

The director reached for the cup but withdrew his fingers as if they had been burnt. "Is this what I think it is?" he asked, a quizzical expression on his face.

"Indeed, Director Yao," Fan answered. "It's a Qianlong guan yao."

John stared at Mr. Fan in disbelief.

"We have those in our museum," Yao sighed, "but only our specialists are allowed to touch them. This is extravagance unsurpassed!" He picked up the cup gingerly. After a sip, his eyes widened again. "Longjing tea with Hubao spring water! How did you know where I was born?" he exclaimed.

"Just a lucky guess, Director Yao."

"Your hospitality exceeds your reputation! I can't imagine the trouble you must have gone through for me."

"No trouble at all, Director Yao. A friend of mine is a train conductor. He acquired the Longjing tea leaves from a farm in a Hangzhou suburb. At the very top of a mountain, as a matter of fact."

"And the spring water?"

"Hubao Fountain is not far from the Hangzhou train station," Fan said.

"Your generosity knows no bounds, Mr. Fan."

"Would you care to see the *li* now, Director Yao?"

"Nothing would give me more pleasure," Yao answered.

"What is a li?" May whispered to John, who shrugged.

"A rare form of archaic bronze cooking vat, Heimao," Yao said.

"One of those ancient tripods used in rituals?" John asked.

"Yes, this one was made in the tenth century BC," Yao answered.

"Wow! How do you know Mr. Fan's li so well?" May asked.

"By studying photographs of it," Yao said. "In fact, they were in the textbooks I studied as a graduate student. However, no one in my field of study has seen it in real life. The academic world was beginning to wonder if it had been destroyed. I was most happy to learn of its survival. I can't wait to hear how you found it, Mr. Fan."

"I'm afraid there isn't much to tell, Director Yao. I gave a party several months ago, and the media described me undeservedly as a collector. A few days later a man showed up at my door and offered it to me."

"Not a word more, Mr. Fan. You bought it before the man had a chance to finish his sentence. Right?"

"Wish it had been that easy, Director Yao. Problem was, the asking price was beyond my means. I had to haggle with the man back and forth for a month. Finally, he came down to what he called the jump-off-the-skyscraper price."

"What's that, Mr. Fan?" Yao asked.

"The price under which he would rather leap off the tallest building in Shanghai than sell it."

Yao smiled. "I see. So you traded in a house or two to pay for it?"

"Pretty close, Director Yao. I talked my mother into selling her family farmland in Yangzhou."

John was stunned.

"Congratulations, Mr. Fan." Yao nodded. "It will be a privilege to see it!"

Fan stood up and left the room. Soon he staggered back cradling a large bronze object. It had three legs, two upright handles, and a surface covered by archaic patterns. Fan heaved out a long breath as he laid the bronze on the table.

May tugged at John's sleeve. "See the green and red rust on the outside wall? It looks older than the broken wok Nainai threw out the other day!"

"It has . . . an aura that makes one sit up," John said.

"For a moment I had the strangest sensation," May said. "I saw a temple with this tripod lying on its altar. People in long robes walked around it humming a quaint song. And sounds of chimes and bells rang in the background."

Director Yao took out a magnifier and moved it slowly over the bronze's exterior. Then he examined the inside of the bronze with a flashlight. Once in a while he jotted notes in a booklet, seemingly unaware of the people around him.

Mr. Fan ushered John and May to an adjacent room. He showed John a few porcelain vases before hurrying out again. John could hear whispers in the next room.

"You have written me about its dimensions, but I am surprised at how large it is in real life." It was Director Yao's voice. "Look at those powerful legs!"

When Mr. Fan returned, May asked, "Is the li worth more than the falangcai?"

"You cannot compare them that way, Heimao," Mr. Fan said.

"Why?" May asked.

"For one, the li is priceless."

"But the dish has a price?" May asked.

"The falangcai is two hundred years old, the *non plus ultra* of eighteenth-century craft," Fan said. "It can be sold for a huge sum of money. Some people might even kill for it. But the value of this li goes beyond money, or even its three thousand years of age. Most archaic bronzes of comparable vintage have no inscriptions. Some are inscribed with a few. This li has sixty-five archaic pictograms on the inside—more than any other li known to man. Those old scribbles have been obsolete for two thousand years. Only a few people can read them."

"What use do we have with something almost nobody reads?" May asked.

"The pictograms on this li recorded an event that took place nearly three thousand years ago. Those words are cast in bronze and unchangeable, whereas oral information can be distorted down the centuries."

"I see," May said.

"Tell me what you are thinking." Fan smiled at her.

"Last week I asked a girl to tell my best friend to meet me at the school library," May said. "Instead, my best friend waited in front of Baba's store for an hour. The two girls are still mad at each other."

"Exactly," Fan said. "Information can be lost during each step of communication. Therefore, rarely are we absolutely certain about any part of our ancient history. But we can rely on the pictograms to reconstruct the cultures of the earliest Chinese society. They carry a message handed down from our ancestors three thousand years ago. Not many pieces like this li have survived. It's invaluable for this reason alone."

"What message does your li carry?" John asked.

"Director Yao is translating the inscriptions right now. He will let us know," Fan said.

* * *

Yao entered the living room looking tired. He showed Fan his Leica and said, "I hope you don't mind, Mr. Fan, but I have taken photographs of your li. I am excited about the new insights it offers and would like to share them in an academic paper."

"That would be wonderful," Fan said and put his left fist into his right hand again.

The director handed Fan a handwritten note. Fan coughed a couple of times before reading it aloud:

"Duke Mu built his temple
In the sixth month, during the phase of jishengba, on the day of Yimao
The Empress Dowager, not forgetting how Duke Mu had served the late king, came to the temple at Yulin
She praised Duke Mu and bestowed four horses and five pieces of jade on him
Duke Mu bowed his head and pledged to defend her kingdom with his blood:
No land too small to lose; no man too big to fall."

A hush followed.

* * *

Walking home, May couldn't stop talking. "Professor Winthrop, I think this is the most wonderful day of my life. I've learned so much!"

"I'm glad."

"Did you notice, Professor Winthrop? The director called me Heimao. With so much knowledge fighting for attention in his brain, he still remembers my name! Think of that!"

It was past lunch time, and John suggested they should get a bite.

"Please wait here, Professor Winthrop," May said and ran away. She came back holding high a steaming loaf wrapped in dark lotus leaves. "Eat!"

"What is it?" John asked.

"The tastiest rice cake in the world!"

John peeled off layers of lotus leaves and found a rice ball covered with rich patches of red, green, and purple syrup.

"Bite!" the young girl urged.

"What's it called?" John mumbled, chewing the sweet pulp in his mouth.

"Babaofan—sticky rice with eight kinds of sweet delicacies. My favorite dessert, Professor Winthrop."

"I don't believe I ever had anything better."

May brightened. "Professor Winthrop, may I ask you a question?"

"Of course."

"Ever since Professor Ren let me use his books, I've been wondering. You'll laugh at me, but I've been wondering a lot. Professor Ren often helps me. He has been like a father to me. The math problems I have had trouble with are nothing to him. But he always takes me seriously and explains everything patiently to me. He is so smart, but he never looks down on me . . ."

May hesitated, and John gestured for her to continue.

"Professor Ren thinks I have what it takes to go to college. So I was wondering—I just wanted to know: Am I really smart enough to study for a college degree?" May blushed.

"I certainly think so," John replied.

"Even a doctoral degree?" May asked hopefully.

"Why not? You are smarter than I—and I have one."

"That is good. I mean . . . I mean it is good you think I can handle graduate school."

John laughed. Then he turned serious. "But being smart alone is not enough."

"I will work so hard you wouldn't believe," May cried.

Before it occurred to John that he should repay the girl the copper she had spent on him, she was already standing on the tips of her toes and gave him a peck on the cheek. Her wind-swept hair, thick and black, fell all over his face. For a moment his world was a blur.

"Thank you, John!" the girl said happily. "Bye!"

John touched the wet spot on his cheek, the fresh smell of her hair still lingering in his nose. While his sight had been hindered, he could see the shyness on the girl's face as she tiptoed. She had been unwilling to shake hands with him the week before, but now she kissed him so naturally. It surprised him that he had forgotten how warm and moist a young girl's lips could be.

And what had she just called him? John! He walked back to his apartment with a smile on his face.

Chapter 14

The Xian Incident

One cold morning in December, John was in the hangar examining the airplane fuselage he was building. Calvin found him and dropped a bombshell: "The Generalissimo has been arrested!" He added that the coup had been led by a general named Zhang Xue-liang.

"The yellow-bellied 'young marshal' who surrendered Manchuria to the Japanese?"

"The same," Calvin said.

Calvin explained that the Young Marshal had been sent to a northwest city named Xian, joining forces with General Yang Hu-cheng, commander of China's Northwest Army. They carried the order to wipe out the communist soldiers holed up in a rural area one hundred and fifty miles from Xian.

"The generals made only token efforts," Calvin said, "so Chiang Kai-shek went to Xian to push them. The generals rebelled and arrested him."

"Where did the timid man find the courage to go against the Generalissimo?" John asked.

"That surprised me too. Zhang Xue-liang used to worship the Generalissimo. He could have kissed the ground Chiang Kai-shek walked on. No one expected this about-face," Calvin sighed and added, "He and Yang also arrested all the government officials accompanying the Generalissimo. A couple of them have been shot."

The last sentence gave John a jolt. Calvin had warned him about the risk he would be taking if he joined the classified project. Those words finally sank in.

* * *

A few days later, a bulging letter was delivered to John's apartment. He opened it, and a bullet fell out. Inside the envelope was a sheet of crude paper with the boldfaced English words:

AMERICAN CAPITALIST, GO HOME! OR YOU WILL DIE TOMORROW! CPC.

Skeletons and bones were drawn around the border.

"Nanjing is a dangerous place indeed," John told himself.

* * *

In the lab that afternoon, John showed the letter to Calvin. The latter turned pale and cursed: "Damn those Japanese agents!"

"Calvin, CPC stands for Communist Party of China." John tried to calm his friend, although he was shaken himself.

"That's just a smoke screen, John."

"But, Calvin, if the Japanese meant to thwart our project, the first person they would get rid of would be you."

"You are the highest paid."

"How on earth do they know that?" John asked.

"The salaries of our personnel are listed in our budget, which they have a copy of."

"But if they wanted to kill me, they wouldn't have alerted me." John argued.

"They are giving you a warning, John. They will get nasty if you don't listen."

"I've never run away with my tail between my legs," John tried to sound tough, although his heart was beating faster. "If they think they can scare me with a cheap trick, they don't know me."

Violent barking broke the morning quiet. John went to the window and peeked through the thick curtain that had been put up for secrecy.

"Step back, John!" Calvin shrieked. "There may be a sniper waiting for you out there!"

"You are getting paranoid, Calvin," John said, but he quickly moved away from the window.

"Our lab hounds are well-trained. They don't bark without reason," Calvin said.

"John, we will have to give you security protection. In the meantime, please watch out for yourself too. Always plan escape routes before you go out."

"Hey! I am John Winthrop, the man who couldn't find a good job in America, remember? Don't worry about me," John said and changed the subject. "Say, I've been wondering, why did Zhang Xue-liang go against the Generalissimo?"

"They have a conflict of interest," Calvin said. "The general's first priority is to drive the Japanese out of his turf. He prefers not to expend his military resources on the Chinese communists."

"How is the Nanjing government dealing with the situation?"

"The ex-premier Wang Jing-wei argues that the rebel generals have broken the law and must be brought to justice. He is supported by the young military officers. Madame Chiang Kai-shek hopes to negotiate with the generals, but she is not allowed to join the official discussions."

"How can the renegade generals fight against a whole nation?"

"They are appealing to the nation to unite and make fighting the Japanese the first priority."

John thought the Generalissimo's life was in danger.

* * *

May would be delivering the Declaration of Independence in the English-speaking competition. John helped her to rehearse. He didn't let her get away with the slightest mispronunciation. May kept trying.

During a break, May told John what she had heard about the coup. Mao Ze-dong, the communist party chief who was in charge, wanted the Generalissimo executed. He sent Zhou En-lai to Xian to talk to the renegade generals. Separately, Madame Chiang flew to the northwestern city to join her husband in detention.

* * *

The experimental tests on the airplane wings had been completed. The results indicated that Calvin's calculations were correct. Everybody was ecstatic.

Judy held a Christmas Eve party in her apartment for her husband's group. She bought a carp as long as a man's arm. The broiled fish was surrounded by dishes of chicken, shrimp, pork, and beef. Bowls of rice, noodles, vegetables, and fruits vied for space on the dining table.

Calvin couldn't stop blabbering about what a goddamn genius John was. The American pleaded with him not to swear in front of the students.

The radiant hostess was beaming all night. At the height of the celebration, she brought out two bottles of American whiskey—no doubt purchased from a foreign liquor store, probably costing as much as a month of her salary.

The hostess kept filling up John's glass. The American drank an inordinate amount. At one point he climbed up a chair and toasted everybody in the room, singing "Jingle Bells" at the top of his lungs.

Calvin must have gotten drunk too. He kissed Judy right in front of everybody! Only on her cheek, of course. But that was enough to send all the students grinning.

In the midst of the celebration an engineer rushed in waving a newspaper with a large headline: "THE GENERALISSIMO HAS BEEN RELEASED!"

Cheers and shouts drowned out all other noises in the room.

* * *

The newspaper reported that the Generalissimo had accepted the generals' demands, promising to stop fighting the Chinese communists and start resisting the Japanese. He was allowed to go home. All dignitaries of the city went to the small Xian airfield to see the First Couple leave. Just before the airplane took off, the 'young marshal' climbed on board and left with them. His military officers were stunned. Certain that their leader had fallen prey to a communist plot, they drew their pistols at Zhou En-lai and demanded to have their "young marshal" back. It took all of Zhou's diplomatic skills to get out of trouble.

As soon as the plane touched down at the Nanjing airport, the Generalissimo put Zhang Xue-liang under house arrest.

February 12, 1937

My dearest Cynthia,

You may be interested to know that Calvin has become a legendary teacher. Here is how the students describe him in the classroom.

He enters the room empty-handed—no books, no notes. Before you can say "Chiang Kai-shek," elaborate equations have already appeared at the upper-left corner of the blackboard. He almost never erases his equations. If he makes a rare misprint, he looks very irritated with himself. As the lecture progresses, the equations steadily spread to the right side of the blackboard. Students can tell time from where he stands. If he is filling up the space in the board's lower-right corner, then the class must be ending. Sure enough, the school bell rings exactly at the time he finishes. From where he is, it takes him only one step to get to the door, leaving several students chasing after him in his wake.

I have no magic to wield on my students. In fact, I am barely able to handle the elements in the classroom. As I have told you, rooms here are unheated. I wear my overcoat during my lecture. Since I cannot put on my gloves and hold a piece of chalk too, I leave my fingers bare to the weather, rubbing them once in a while to keep them from getting stiff. Fortunately, the radiation from one hundred young bodies slowly warms up the room—if only moderately.

Life in China is different from the one we know in America. It lacks much in material comfort. I've learned that people can manage with less, unaffected by what they are missing.

There was this woman who sold bamboo baskets.

"Four cents for a big one," she told me. Four Chinese cents is about one penny. "Two cents for a small one."

I wanted a big one. So I dug out four coins from my pocket.

Instead of taking them, the woman burst out laughing.

"You are so dumb!" she exclaimed. "Don't you know you are supposed to bargain with me?" Before I had time to retort, she added, "OK, OK, you can have a big one for two cents."

By the way, I did receive a threatening letter, but it was just a prank. Please don't lose any sleep over what Judy wrote. Right now, at the most critical phase of the project, I cannot leave Nanjing.

Love,

John

* * *

President Lu invited John, Calvin, and Professor Zhu to his home. After dinner, the host brought his guests to lounge around the fireplace. In the warmth of the leaping fire, the president toasted everyone on their last progress report. He also informed them that the funding for the internal combustion engine had been approved.

The red sorghum liquor was excellent. The atmosphere became more relaxed as President Lu opened the third bottle.

The conversation drifted to politics. Professor Zhu asked President Lu for any insight on the renegade generals' refrain from shooting the Generalissimo.

"As you know, Professor Zhu, there are many theories about that," President Lu said. "But I think the decision was made in Moscow, thousands of miles away from the China theater. Russia and Japan are rivals in Asia. Joseph Stalin recognizes that Chiang Kai-shek is the only viable man to lead China against Japan. He made the reluctant Chinese communists exert pressure on the generals."

"I still don't understand. Why did Zhang Xue-liang voluntarily fly to Nanjing with Chiang Kai-shek?" John asked.

"Zhang Xue-liang is as compulsive as he is young," President Lu laughed. "I think the young man wanted to repair the damage he had done to the Generalissimo's image of authority."

"What is going to happen to Zhang Xue-liang now?" Calvin asked.

"Nobody knows, but he himself said that he would've shot any subordinate who had plotted against him," President Lu said.

John wondered aloud how this incident would change China.

"The Generalissimo's first priority had been to annihilate the Chinese communists, but Zhang Xue-liang made him alter it," President Lu said. "Now our national leader will not allow the situation in Northern China to deteriorate any further. A war with Japan is going to break out sooner rather than later."

"What a drastic change to China's strategy!" John exclaimed.

"Perhaps even more than you realize, Professor Winthrop," President Lu said. "The Generalissimo has just formed a united front with the Chinese communists, giving them a reprieve. In the long run, this may lead to very serious problems for the Generalissimo."

"Such as?" John asked.

"The Chinese communists were on the brink of insignificance holing up in a rural area. Now they are being handed a golden opportunity to recoup. They may grow into a formidable force."

"Do you think the Generalissimo will keep his promise to them?" John asked.

"Chiang Kai-shek may have many faults, but he understands that a national leader must regard his words as weighty as the Tai Mountain."

In early March, the internal combustion engine from General Motors arrived. When John came to work one morning, he noticed the machine guns that had been added to the security unit patrolling the lab. John tried not to think about them. He had to concentrate on assembling all of the parts of the airplane into a flying machine.

Chapter 15

The Red Face and the Black Face

One Sunday morning, Judy went to the convenience store and saw May counting change for a customer.

"Heimao," Judy said in Mandarin. "I heard the good news. Congratulations!"

"Thanks, Mrs. Ren," May replied in English.

Judy immediately understood that May was trying to practice speaking English with her, so she switched to her mother tongue. "I see why you won the first prize in the English competition, May. No wonder. Your pronunciation is perfect."

"I couldn't have done it without John," May said, her young face shining.

"Really?" Judy said.

"Mrs. Ren, do you have some time?" May whispered. "I would appreciate being able to talk to you in private for a few minutes."

Judy paid for the newspaper she had come to buy for Calvin. Then she took May to a small park several blocks away. On a bench, Judy asked May about the azure flag she had received from the city's Education Bureau.

"The citation says: Excellently Fluent English Speaking," May said.

"Nice!" Judy laughed. "I heard that all the kids are talking about the box of chocolates the city gave you."

"Actually, Miss Vautrin gave me that. She is so kind."

"You've been doing very well with your school work, May. Now this honor from the city. I am proud of you!"

"I have John to thank for that. He taught me so much!" May said.

"He is very nice," Judy agreed.

"Mrs. Ren, I was wondering. I would like to express my gratitude to him in some way. Do you think it would be proper if I gave him the chocolates?"

"What a lovely gesture!" Judy said. "But, have you had chocolates before?"

"No."

"How about sharing your chocolates with him?" Judy asked.

"I cannot thank John enough. I want to give him all the good things I have."

"All right then. Do it! Is that what you wanted to talk to me about?"

"There is more," May said in a small voice. "Mrs. Ren, I'm having butterflies in my stomach. It feels worse than the time when I was made to take a math exam unprepared."

"Do you know why you're having this problem?"

May looked down at her fingers and nodded. She said, "Mrs. Ren, you were raised in America and have seen more of the world than any of us. I hope you can advise me."

"I'll try," Judy said and settled back on the bench.

"I had a dream last night . . ." May said and stopped.

"What was it about?"

May hesitated. "It's embarrassing."

Judy assured her that whatever she said would be kept in strict confidence.

"I had this dream in which someone . . . someone . . ." May blushed.

"Go on," Judy encouraged her with a smile.

". . . kissed me." May barely managed to say the first of these two words.

Judy laughed. She told May not to worry: such a dream was perfectly normal for a teenager. "Did you recognize the person in your dream?"

"That's the most scary part," May said, so weak that her lips barely moved.

"Who was he?"

"It was . . . John."

"What? What did you say?!"

"John—John Winthrop." May repeated.

"No! It can't be!" Judy cried.

"But it is, Mrs. Ren," May said and buried her face in her hands.

"John is *twice* your age!" Judy pleaded.

"I know."

"And he has a fiancée in America. You should never think of him romantically!" Judy angrily hit her hand on the bench with each syllable.

"Please help me, Mrs. Ren. Am I a bad girl?"

"Not if you handle this properly," Judy said sternly.

May asked what she should do.

"The English contest is over. You have no reason to see him any longer. Stop shopping for antiques with him. If he comes to the store, leave!"

"I will do what you say, Mrs. Ren," May said in a small voice. "Please don't tell anyone about this, will you?"

"I won't. Now you go home and share your chocolates with your family. Give the ones with the largest nuts to your Baba!"

* * *

Principal Yang of Zhong-Shan Middle School sat behind a large desk across from Judy. "How long have you been working for us, Ren *lao shi*?" *Lao shi* meant teacher.

"Over two years, Principal Yang," Judy answered, shifting nervously in her chair.

She had never been inside the principal's office alone.

"How do you like your experience so far?" he asked.

"It's wonderful to see the kids learn," Judy answered cautiously. She had had words to say about Mr. Yang's divorce and the following marriage to a young teacher. She wondered if the principal had caught wind of them.

Principal Yang continued to flip through the papers inside a large binder without saying a word, and Judy was getting more frightened by the second.

"We didn't have the budget to hire new teachers two years ago. That's why we haven't been able to pay you a regular salary," Principal Yang finally said. "I'm looking to change that."

"Thank you very much, Principal Yang," Judy said, greatly relieved.

"I have a question, if you don't mind." Principal Yang looked up from the binder. "Did you take a trip to Guangzhou?"

Judy tensed up again. "Yes. My father was dying. The telegram came on a Sunday. Your office was closed. I asked my husband to take over my classes. I hope that was all right." She had never felt so scrutinized before.

"Your father led a difficult life in America, didn't he? No woman, no diversion, no respect."

"That's what he said."

"Ren lao shi, are you aware that the Chinese are the only people in the world who have been categorically denied immigration to the United States?"

"There are Chinese people living in the United States," Judy offered timidly.

"The descendants of coolies who risked their lives dynamiting mountain rocks to build the railroads," the principal sneered. "Even these coolies are not allowed to return to America once they leave to see their families."

"True," Judy said.

"The Westerners are racists," the principal said. "First they sent missionaries. Next they sent trade representatives. Then they sent gunboats. Have you ever watched a Beijing opera? The black face enters the stage when the red face exits it. Good guy, bad guy. Every foreigner shows us a different color and sings us a different song. But all of them are after the same thing: money. Woodrow Wilson's Fourteen Points were supposed to espouse national self-determination, but the Americans joined the powers to hand our Shandong peninsula to the Japanese."

"My husband told me that international justice belongs to those who have the most advanced warplanes," Judy said.

"Your husband is wise. National borders shift with military powers. That's why the world will always have wars. The Americans are doing their part to keep that going. You and I are always the ones being robbed."

"Actually, Mr. Yang, I'm an American myself," Judy said.

"Really?" Yang raised his eyebrows.

"Well, I was born in the United States," Judy said.

"Oh yes, I forgot that. Your husband too?"

"No. He was born here—in Nanjing."

"I understand your husband was the best MIT student ever. Why is he working under an American not half as good as he is?"

"Principal Yang, my husband is working *with* John—not *under* him."

"Then why is this American making ten times your husband's salary?" The principal seethed. "And what has this fellow done for us for that kind of money?"

"I am sorry, Principal Yang. My husband forbids me to talk about the work he is doing with John," Judy said.

"The only people I detest more than the Americans are the Chinese who think they are Americans," Principal Yang said. "We call them *bananas*: yellow outside, white inside!"

"That's not fair, Principal Yang."

The principal stood up, his face bright red. "You left your teaching duties without permission. You are fired!"

* * *

When Calvin came home that evening, Judy was in tears.

Calvin frowned after hearing the story. "No woman, no diversion, no respect—how did he learn about it?"

"I don't know! I only told my best friends in school—and the good policeman who took me to the airport." Judy wiped her eyes. "Calvin, there is something else I must tell you. I think a man is following me."

"What does he look like?"

"He has dirty hair, sort of haggard looking—like a beggar. He scares me."

"Don't worry, Judy. I will take care of him," Calvin said.

"You made me feel better, Calvin," Judy said. "One more thing. That woman in the convenience store is going to ruin John Winthrop!"

"Whom are you talking about?"

"May, May Chen! Who else?"

"What?"

"You should see the way she walked with John, laughing and talking! It was disgusting."

"Judy," Calvin said, "May is helping John to shop for antiques. They've been at it for some time now. Why does it suddenly bother you?"

"She is coming between John and Cynthia—that's what she is doing!"

"Don't be ridiculous," Calvin said.

"Cynthia is your friend too. I'm surprised you don't care," Judy said.

"You worry too much, Judy. John and May are just helping each other."

"You don't understand, Calvin. That woman is scheming after John."

"For what?"

"For John to marry her—and take her to America."

"That's absurd. May's much too young and innocent to have such thoughts," Calvin said.

Judy snorted. "A child from a poor family has no right to be innocent. There's a lot you don't know about women!"

"What are you talking about?"

Judy did not answer.

"Well?" Calvin asked again.

"Like something I have been trying to tell you for years, but couldn't bring myself to," Judy said in a barely audible voice.

"What's that?"

"You remember the Harvard guy I used to go out with?"

"The law school student I stopped you from seeing? What about him?"

"He doesn't exist!"

Calvin almost fell into the chair behind him.

"I shouldn't have done it, Calvin. I'm sorry! But in three years you never did what it took my father one day to do! I thought the only way to draw you out of your shell was to make you jealous. I am very sorry! I've never gone out with anyone but you!"

"That's all right, Judy," Calvin said, reaching for her hands. "Neither have I."

Judy was happy again. "You are so funny, Calvin!" she said, breaking into a smile.

Chapter 16

The Wine Houses on the Qinhuai River

On a cold, rainy April afternoon, John found Calvin in his office and showed him a letter from the University of Michigan.

Calvin took a glance and exclaimed, "Offer of an assistant professorship! John, Michigan is one of the best engineering schools in the United States. Congratulations!"

The school bell rang. In running out, Calvin called over his shoulder that they should meet again and talk more about this offer.

* * *

The rain had stopped, but a chill still hung in the air. In John's favorite restaurant, several blocks from the bank of the Qinhuai River, Calvin ordered a bottle of warmed rice wine. John asked for a whole soy sauce duck. "I've been thinking about it all afternoon," he chuckled.

The wine arrived first.

"A toast to your future, John." Calvin raised his little wine cup. He asked, "What do you think Cynthia will think about it?"

John swallowed his wine. "She will not be thrilled, I'm sure. She prefers not to leave Boston."

"If you don't mind my saying so, I never understood why you let Cynthia walk all over you," Calvin said. "No one turns down a tenure-track offer, John."

"I hope Cynthia sees it that way."

Calvin sighed and changed the subject. "When does school begin in Michigan?"

"Early September."

Calvin made a quick calculation. "Then you'll be leaving us in five months' time."

"A little sooner, I'm afraid," John watched Calvin's face. "Don't forget it takes three weeks just to cross the Pacific."

"When do you have to leave?" Now Calvin looked nervous.

"First of August—at the latest."

A waiter came to lay a dark brown duck on the table. A strong aroma spread in the air as he sliced it with a long knife.

Calvin paid no attention.

"School will be over by that time," John said sheepishly, picking up a piece of dark meat with skin.

"School is nothing! I am worried about our project!" Calvin almost shouted. "We just started to tune the engine. I see no way to get the airplane flying before you leave!" Calvin fell into ominous silence. Suddenly he exploded. "God damn it, John, you are not going to do that to us!"

John was shaken by the violence of his friend's outburst. "Please understand, Calvin! I must show up on time in Michigan to teach my classes," he pleaded.

"We need you here more than Michigan does."

"I know, I know. But I have only one chance to make a good first impression on them."

"We've shelled out a lot of money on you," Calvin's words were as cutting as a knife. "You must finish your job before you can leave."

"Calvin, I only promised to work with you for a year, remember? My obligation to you is just that—no more."

John regretted it as soon as his words left his mouth.

"Alright, let's see where this leaves you," Calvin said savagely. "You arrived on October 11 last year, so you owe us till October 10 this year."

"Calvin, have a heart. I promised Cynthia that I'd be back in a year. She won't be very happy if I don't keep my word. To tell you the truth, I am worried. There is a young doctor Cynthia mentions in her letters. Physicians are good providers. You don't want to ruin my life, do you?"

Calvin shrugged.

"Besides, if I leave here on October 10," John continued, "I can't possibly report to Michigan before mid-November, which will be two months into the fall semester."

"Write your department chair that you'll be late," Calvin said.

"Sure, he will be happy to ask the students to sit around waiting for me." John was upset.

"Tell him to cancel your classes," Calvin said.

"You are impossible, Calvin. I'm a free man. I quit! My letter of resignation will be on your desk first thing tomorrow morning."

"Request for resignation denied! You will honor your obligation like a man." Calvin pointed a finger at John's nose.

A waiter in thin black trousers came to spread several more dishes on their table. John suggested they postpone the discussion.

Calvin fell silent. "Sorry I yelled," he finally said. "Let's eat." He picked up his chopsticks, but held them in the air for a long time. "John, can you see the river from here? How about a stroll after dinner?"

"That would be great! I always wanted to get Cynthia some of those colorful agates sold in the shops down there," John said, relieved that Calvin was making an effort to be civil. "What do you call them again?"

"Rain flower pebbles," Calvin said. "According to a Chinese legend, they are the pieces of a broken rainbow."

* * *

For two millennia, the bank of the Qinhuai River had been a favorite haunt for poets and scholars alike. Literary people, young and old, had come to drink wine, compose poetry, and listen to fair maidens singing the beauty of springtime.

By now the sun had set. Only a strip of the sky above the western hills retained a few bold strokes of amber. The pleasure boats lit their lanterns, sending zigzagging gold ripples on the lazy water. The twinkling windows overlooking the riverbank, Calvin said, belonged to the wine houses that offered entertainments for men.

* * *

Sitting in an ornate bedroom behind one of those windows, Fan Dong-mei tapped a folded ivory fan rhythmically on a redwood table. A woman standing several feet from him was singing "Spring Comes to the Jade Hall." The black color of her long robe was cut in the middle by the dazzling red of her silk belt. Her exaggerated eyebrows rivaled those of fierce warriors in a Beijing opera.

Fan Dong-mei clapped his fan on his left palm. "Excellent, Black Cat! My compliments to Master Tuan," Fan said as she finished.

"Thank you for your generous praise, Mr. Fan." The woman sat down with a pretty smile. "I am sure my teacher will be very pleased to hear that."

Fan pointed his ivory fan at the Go chessboard on a side table. "I'd like to finish the match with you. Please go to tell your mama that there will be no table-hopping for you tonight."

"Master Fan!" The woman stood up, the snapping of her handkerchief wafting a strong dose of perfume. "Who in Nanjing has the imprudence to take me away from you?"

"Flattery, flattery! But I like it," Fan murmured. "Seriously, I am surprised at your attainment in Go! You've given me the tightest encirclement I have seen in weeks!"

"Just a stroke of luck, Master Fan, but I'm not clever enough for you. You must yield me one more stone in the next match."

"You're driving a hard bargain, girl!" Fan reached for her hand. "You may underestimate me, but I am a master at it as well. You will get no concession from me." He was about to caress her round wrist when his eyebrows arched up in surprise. He looked again before releasing her hand and poked his head out of the window. "Mr. Win! Mr. Win!"

The brown-haired man in the street below looked up. "Hello, Mr. Fan!" he exclaimed. "What a pleasure to see you again!"

"The night is too fine not to have a drink in a wine house. Would you join me?"

"I have a friend with me, Mr. Fan. This is Professor Ren Kewen. I'm working with him at the university."

"A great honor to meet you, Professor Ren," Fan said. "Are you by any chance related to Professor Ren Guo-hua, the eminent historian?"

"He is my father," Calvin answered respectfully, lowering both hands to his sides.

"I've heard that the old professor has a brilliant son. You must not deny me the pleasure of getting to know the baby phoenix who has a better chirp than the father bird!"

"Thank you, Mr. Fan. We accept your gracious invitation," John said after exchanging a look with Calvin.

* * *

As the professors were entering the brick house in gaudy red, John was startled to hear muffled shouts behind a closed door.

"They are playing Guess the Fingers," Calvin explained, "a game in which the loser empties a cup of wine."

Two stories of red doors surrounded the spacious receiving hall, those on the second floor connected by a gallery.

"Serve the tea!" sang a husky voice from a male servant in a black brocade tunic standing by the front door.

Two young maids in red silk qipaos appeared, each holding a red lacquered tray.

"If it pleases our honored guests," the servant intoned.

Calvin dug into his pocket and threw a bill on one of the trays, the holder of which curtsied and retreated. While John stood puzzled, Calvin reached into his pocket again and came up with another bill to dismiss the other maid.

"Honored guests are here!" sang the baritone.

Up went all the silk curtains on the red doors. From each of the doors emerged a pretty woman. All of them wore silk shoes and long, flaring pants, their black translucent cotton jackets heightened by shell-shaped collars and their jadeite earrings jingling in competition with their gold-flower bracelets. The women from the ground floor arrived first, forming a moving helix around the visitors, while the women from the second floor continued to come down the staircase. Soon the young women, the silk scarves around their waists whirling up a wind of perfume, took turns urging the professors in a coquettish voice to make their picks. They paid particular attention to John. It was clear that they had never come this close to a Caucasian man before, for all of them were giggling behind their delicate hands.

A man appeared from the gallery upstairs. "These gentlemen are my guests," he called down. "It will be my honor to do the picking for them. Ladies, you can return to your rooms now. And you, young fellow, escort my guests up here."

The servant clapped at the women, who turned around and disappeared into the red doors, still giggling.

It took a while before the hall cleared, when John wiped his forehead mockingly.

Calvin laughed. "John! Have you ever seen so many pretty girls in one place before? Cynthia better not know about this."

John heard none of Calvin's teasing. Climbing the stairs, he was wondering how Mr. Fan dared to visit such a place so openly.

Chapter 17

The Little Maid

Fan Dong-mei was born in 1893 in Beijing, eight hundred miles north of Nanjing. As the saying went: *Dong fu xi gui* (east is wealth, west prominence). Fan's father, a deputy-minister in Beijing's imperial court, lived in a western suburb.

Fan Dong-mei was eighteen when the Qing dynasty was overthrown and China declared a republic. His father, now a commoner, sent him to Beijing's central district to live and study.

As Fan Dong-mei left home, a little maid named Little Green followed him to the front door. She was in tears. Officially, she was an adopted daughter of Fan's father. In reality, she had been bought four years earlier from a poor family. In his spare time, Fan Dong-mei had given the little girl a few reading lessons and occasionally a pear or a dried prune. Sometimes he even teased her. She seemed to be the saddest in the house to see him leave.

* * *

In the private school of thirty under the care of a tutor, Fan Dong-mei developed a voracious appetite for classic poetry—but not the Confucius analects for which he was being sent. He lived in a temple near the glass factories area. The industrial buildings had been dismantled years earlier, and the area had become the city's antique market.

A fine antique was worth many times its weight in gold, but its allure went beyond money. It was art, culture, and history all rolled into one—a symbol of class and good taste.

Fan had a discerning eye honed by living and breathing antiques in a fine home as a child. He could pick out a Ming vase from across the room. He was also able to declare a Kangxi bowl a fake with but a glance. His arrival at the glass factories area was impeccable timing. The imperial collection had suffered great losses. Foreign soldiers had plundered the palace. The imperial family had pawned its valuables. The eunuchs had stolen from their masters. Many palace antiques wound up in the glass factories area.

Without a generous allowance, Fan rarely felt comfortable climbing the green stone stairs of the elite antique stores. Rather, he spent hours upon hours browsing the stands outdoors. Such a limitation hardly curbed his enthusiasm. Picking out an authentic item from a pile of fakes was a challenge. The young scholar was no easy prey for the cunning peddlers.

When one of them invited the young man to rummage through his goods, Fan would quickly spot a very fine item in the pile. Instead of asking for its price, he would cast it aside, declaring it the first one to *eliminate*.

"But this is an excellent piece," the peddler protested, putting it back into the pile.

"It's a fake." Fan said with an air of authority, taking the piece out of the pile again.

"Keep your voice down, sir. What's the matter with you?" the peddler whispered.

After going back and forth a few rounds, the peddler capitulated. "Give me a little face, will you? If you take this piece, I will give you the piece over there, which is my best one."

So Fan got two good pieces for a pittance.

Often enough, Fan would not leave the area before spending the last copper in his pocket. Then he had to prevail on a friend for a bowl of noodles for dinner.

At the end of the year, his tutor wrote a letter to his father praising the son's talents for classic poetry, which, he added caustically, hardly a serious scholar made.

When Fan came home for the New Year holidays, his disappointed father gave him a severe tongue lashing, dampening the festive mood of the household. The only person happy to see him appeared to be the little maid. She followed him around, bringing him tea, dried watermelon seeds, and prune rice cakes. At night she served him a bowl of bird's nest soup, taking as much as an hour to clean out the tiny feathers in the nest.

For a year the father heaped reprimand after reprimand on the son—all to no avail. The former deputy-minister had to face facts. There was no doubt the young man was gifted. His Go game had no match within five miles of his residence. But he excelled only in frivolous matters—not serious scholarship.

* * *

Fan Dong-mei took private lessons on brush-painting. One day Fan's art teacher showed Wu Chang-shuo, the most prominent artist of the Shanghai school, a selection of Fan's work in the classic style. Wu exclaimed that while most landscape painters touched only the skin of the ancient Song art, Fan's work reached the core.

With high praises from an eminent artist , several galleries carried Fan's work. The young man spent all of his new revenues on antiques. To compensate the friend who had bought him noodles, Fan would do a "Song" painting. He drew it on a silk scroll browned over a candle and forged the signature and the seal marks of an artist long deceased. The friend, having been caught in bed with a woman and coerced into signing an IOU to the wronged "husband," would sell it for a hefty sum of money.

One day a matchmaker called on Fan's father. The young lady in the proposal was a daughter of a household more prominent than Fan's. The senior Fan was overjoyed. He had been unable to get his wayward offspring married to an illustrious family.

But by this time, Fan Dong-mei had already heard of Western courtship. He had no inclination of marrying a young woman he had never met. His father pressured him. Fan's resistance melted after learning that the young lady happened to like a poem he had composed and brushed on a painting. Indeed, she was the person who took the bridal proposal to her father. The contract for marriage was struck and gifts for betrothal exchanged.

When Fan went home for the New Year, he found Little Green no longer little. Indeed, she had grown to be as tall as his mother. She had also grown a temper. Everything he asked her to do was done with spite.

At first he ignored it, knowing that teenage years were difficult. Later, when they were alone in his room, he asked her if there was anything wrong. She turned her back on him. When he asked again, she grabbed the blue-and-white palace bowl from his desk. The Ming guan yao with a Chenghua mark was his prized find in the glass factories. He had told her it was worth the price of a Beijing mansion.

She threw it at him!

He tried to catch it, but his hands had been frozen by fear. As the bowl sailed past him, his heart broke with the crashing sounds. He shut his eyes and then opened them again, and saw shards all over the floor.

Trembling in rage, he ordered the little maid to bring him the ruler. In the past, the threat alone would have been enough. The girl would beg for mercy and wail that she was very, very sorry, and that she would never dare to do it again. There had never been any need to use the ruler on her flesh. But things were different this time: she stood and glared at him. In fury, he picked up the ruler from the desk and told her to open her palm. When she didn't, he smacked the ruler on her shoulder. An expression of hurt came to her eyes. He hit her again, and she fended it off. Her unexpected defiance made him angrier. He proceeded to hit her all over her body: arms, chest, head, stomach, and legs—harder and harder.

Then her eyes showed fear. "Stop! I can't take it anymore!" she cried.

Taking a look at the young woman cowering in front of him, he was shocked to see the bruises on her arms and the streaks of blood on her face. Panting heavily, he threw down the ruler and left his room.

After his anger had waned, shame took over. Little Green was not a little girl any more. She was fighting for the respect for the woman she had become. And he had dragged her nose through the mud!

He tried to avoid her for the rest of the day. But when he returned to his room at night, he saw the place had been tidied up. Not even one broken porcelain piece could be found. Then he saw the little maid still in the room cleaning. There was a steaming bowl of bird's nest soup with lotus seeds on his desk and two dishes of dried nuts by its side.

He thought of tiptoeing out of the room, but the little maid had already turned around, her eyes full of tears. "I know you didn't have the heart to hurt me," she said in a trembling voice. "I could feel your ruler coming down lighter and lighter every time."

It made him feel worse. He had harbored nothing but savagery when he hit her. Was she trying to find a reason to forgive him? Or was it a desperate denial of reality?

He escaped to school the next morning.

* * *

A few months later, there came the sad news of the death of his fiancée from consumption. The arranged marriage ended a month before it was supposed to begin.

Fan Dong-mei remembered how he had once playfully sought the advice of a fortune teller, who told him that his zodiac numbers were too intense for any woman to bear. He had dismissed the remark as superstition. But now he wondered if he should have yielded to his father.

* * *

Two years later, his father died. At the age of twenty-four and still floundering, Fan became the improbable head of his family. His mother wanted to move back to the city of her birth. He sold the family house and took her and the little maid to Nanjing.

It was good to start over.

He entered a Go tournament and won it. With great fanfare he was matched with the Go masters in the area and beat all of them as well. Newspapers and magazines ran stories about this meteoric star who had never lost a single game since defeating his father at the age of eight. He made friends, many of whom would come to his house to watch a Go match—and stay for dinner. His reputation as a generous host spread. More people came to his house, ate, and left. Sometimes he did not even know their names.

Then he was seen standing and applauding in the midst of a Beijing opera. The next morning his review of the play appeared in a local newspaper. It showed deep understanding of a performing art that owed its origin to his birth city. The article was well received by the critics. The publisher of the newspaper, a friend of his late father, gave him a column in the supplementary pages. He used it to comment on all matters of culture: opera, arts, antiques, Go, classic Chinese poetry. His knowledge and engaging writing style won him a following. With time, he became an influential arts critic in the city.

He went out to sing Beijing opera with friends every evening till the wee hours of the morning. The little maid always waited up for him. She never went to bed without serving him the bird's nest soup with lotus seeds.

He could now recount to his new friends the loss of his Chenghua palace bowl. "I was willing to break my knees diving for it." He embellished the story, eyes wide with wonderment. "But my fiery maid missed me by two feet!"

His listeners, shocked by the loss of a fortune, did not know if they should laugh.

* * *

One day the little maid came to his study and asked if it had become illegal to buy or sell a girl—now that the republic had replaced the Qing monarchy.

Fan admitted that he had heard a proclamation of that nature, although it had not been strictly enforced. But if freedom was what she wanted, he would grant it.

"Where would I go if my young master frees me?"

"You could go back to your parents!"

"I wouldn't know where to find them."

Fan rummaged through a drawer and took out a piece of paper. "This is the contract your father signed when he sold you to my father. Here is his address. I think I can help you."

"I thank my young master. But that is not what I want. Ever since they sold me, I stopped regarding them as family."

"Then stay with us!"

"If I do, would you grant me a new status?"

"Sure, take this piece of paper. Tear it up. Now I don't own you any longer. You will be paid a monthly wage and will be free to leave here any time you choose."

She said she wanted to think it over.

The next morning she came back and told him she found it difficult to leave.

"Why?"

"Because you are all I have," she answered in a voice that was barely above a whisper.

There was a shade of rouge on her cheeks and a faint smell of cassia flower oil in her hair. At the age of nineteen, she was blossoming into womanhood. Her eyes were as clear and innocent as a child's. Her skin reminded Fan of the finest silk woven in the gentle breeze of the Yangtze Delta. Her hair, now combed into a stylish bun, brought out the beauty he had never suspected.

She told him, however, that she would not stay as a maid—not even with a wage. Instead, she said with downcast eyes that she wanted to be his concubine. She would eat very little and would take no money from him.

Shocked, Fan mumbled that concubines had also been banned by republic laws. Then he stammered and couldn't continue.

A fire built up in her eyes. He looked around to make sure his prized porcelains were beyond her reach.

She bit her lower lip. Fan looked away, fearing to see the blood that would be bursting out like a ripe cherry being pierced by a needle. He heard her venomous voice: "People say you are good at art and poetry. But you don't even know how to tell a woman you want her. Do you have an inch of manhood between your legs?"

Then she turned and ran away, leaving him like a fish on a chopping board with its belly cut open.

It was past midnight when Fan was awakened by a gentle hand. He opened his eyes and saw the crescent moon hanging in his window like a crystal hairpin. The little maid was kneeling by his bedside, her body bathed in a haze of moonbeam. She put a finger on his lips and slipped under his blanket. The breathing in his ears was louder than the roar of the wind over his tile roof. As his hands glided over a body that seemed to have caught fire, she closed her eyes so tightly the skin around them wrinkled. The fire spread to his body. When he entered her she grabbed his hands desperately—as if fearing he would vanish into the silvery air if she ever let go.

* * *

It was his first time making love, and he dozed off in exhaustion. When he woke up, the little maid was sitting up holding the blanket to her chin staring at his face. He urged her to get some sleep. She nodded but did nothing. He sat up with her, and she rested her head on his shoulder, turning her face to kiss his ear time and time again.

"Dong-mei," she whispered his name, then kissed him again. "Dong-mei!"

Suddenly he found himself sobbing uncontrollably, her soft voice melting away the self-doubt accumulated inside him over years of paternal reprimands. This was the first time a woman had ever told him he was worthy of her love. His sobs subsided as she continued to kiss him, pampering him into a contented unconsciousness.

When he woke up in the morning, the little maid was gone.

The only traces she left behind were several small pink stains on his sheet and a slip of paper on his desk. He read her childlike scrawl:

You brought me so much happiness and so much sorrow.

There was neither a salutation nor a signature.

She had given him something a Chinese girl would die to preserve for her wedding night.

In the following days Fan Dong-mei was in bad temper. Nothing seemed right. He yelled at the servant who took too long to answer his nightly knock at the front door. He blew up when he didn't get his bird's nest soup.

With great remorse Fan decided that the fortune teller had been right: he would always ruin the women who loved him. Resisting his mother's nagging to get married, he would see only the women in the wine houses on the bank of the Qinhuai River. Such a house, called a *chang-san*, offered the highest services of pleasure. In days long past, a courtesan entertained by singing songs, drinking wine, playing chess, even composing poetry. They did not have to do anything else unwillingly. Things had changed since. The indulgence of the flesh could now be bought. Nevertheless, it was rare for Fan to do much beyond holding hands with a courtesan.

He became known in the houses of pleasure as having the heart of a monk.

Chapter 18

The Huangpu Military School

As John and Calvin entered the ornate bedroom on the second floor of the wine house, Fan stood up and put his left fist into his right palm.

"Mr. Fan," John began as he settled into a chair by the redwood table, "it's very kind of you to invite us up. But Professor Ren and I are both teaching in a university. We can't be seen in the company of courtesans."

Actually, John had seen his share of professional women. Years ago, they had been standing at street corners in Boston downtown at night. John had stolen glances at them, and his heart had fluttered. But he had never talked to them, not to mention having a dalliance with one of them in a dimly lit hotel room charged by the hour.

"Ah, professor Win, put your mind at ease," Fan said. "Many fine scholars—eminent Confucians among them—have spent their best days in wine houses."

"You are right, of course," Calvin said. "But I agree with Professor Win. Our university is funded by the government. We must set a good example for the students. Drinking wine with courtesans is hardly one of them."

"Many prominent members in the Nationalist Government have frequented the wine houses here, Professor Ren. So have many presently in the communist government at Yan'an, if you must know."

John raised his eyebrows.

"Some of these luminaries met in the wine houses when they were revolutionaries," Fan went on, "using the houses as their covers. The courtesans contributed to the overthrow of the Qing dynasty, don't you agree? This is not to say these dignitaries have not been back since coming to power."

"Interesting," Calvin said. "However, we really don't feel comfortable choosing courtesans. I hope we are not being disrespectful to you, Mr. Fan."

A servant slipped into the room and handed Fan a stack of papers. Fan signed them one by one. He then pointed to the wine ewer and wine cups on the table: "Take these things away and bring us some decent tea instead."

"May I ask what is your pleasure today, Master Fan?"

"The *Biluochun* you served last time is not too bad."

As he turned to leave, the servant bumped into a chessboard and sent the stone playing pieces flying.

"Oops!" Fan cried, trying in vain to grab at the stones darting through the air. Some of them fell to the side table, while others rolled on the floor.

"I-I am very sorry, Master Fan," the servant stammered. "Very, very sorry indeed."

"What a pity!" Fan lamented. "I just thought of a maneuver to turn the game around."

Calvin stood up. "If you will allow me, sir, I'll see what I can do." He started to put the displaced stones one at a time in their former positions.

Fan watched with an amused smile, which slowly disappeared. "Your memory is as magnificent as your reputation, Professor Ren," Fan sighed, when Calvin put the last displaced stones on the board. "You've spared me the agony of a sleepless night!"

The woman in black came back, went to Fan's side and sat down. Fan handed her the signed papers and she wrapped them up in her handkerchief.

"You may go now, Black Cat," Fan said, pressing something into her palm. "I won't be needing you tonight."

"Thank you, Master Fan." The courtesan closed her palm. "But I was looking forward to finishing the game with you," she purred.

"We will do that tomorrow."

"You must give me more opportunity to please you then," the courtesan said. She turned to Calvin and clasped her hands on the right side of her waist lowering herself: "And here is wishing you a peaceful day, Little Master Ren." She then gave John a curtsy as well before taking her strong scent of perfume out of the room.

The servant came in with a tea set, served everyone, and left.

Fan examined his cup and frowned. "This teacup is an affront to good taste. You must allow me to invite you to a tea house next week." He raised his cup.

John and Calvin did the same.

"Thank you, Mr. Fan," John said. "Please pardon my curiosity, but what are the papers you just signed?"

"*Jupiao*, bills for the courtesan's service," Fan said, moving his cup to his nose breathing deeply.

"How much does a jupiao cost, may I ask?" John said.

"Each costs one yuan."

"So Black Cat gets twenty yuan and a good night's rest?" Calvin asked.

"Very good, Professor Ren, but no. All the money goes to the house."

"That's not fair," John protested. "What does the courtesan eat?"

"A courtesan eats and sleeps in the wine house. Her music lessons and dance lessons are also on the house. She gets gifts from the clients too—if she is lucky. This is on top of the two hundred silver dollars paid her family up front."

"I've been wondering," Calvin said. "How did Black Cat know my name?"

"You've met her before, Professor Ren," Fan said. "Didn't you recognize her?"

"No."

John broke out laughing. "Calvin is quite sincere. He would have a long conversation with a person at a party. Then he would come to ask me whom he was talking to."

"Black Cat's given name is Qian Ying," Fan said. "Her mother Qian Ma lives in your neighborhood."

"Oh no!" Calvin exclaimed. "Qian Ying was a little girl. The last time I saw her, she was hanging onto her mother's apron in our kitchen."

"Time flies, Professor Ren. That little girl has grown into a ravishing woman!"

"Mr. Fan, can a courtesan leave the wine house and have a life for herself?" Calvin asked.

"Sure, if someone pays enough money for her," Fan replied.

"How much would that be?" Calvin asked.

"That depends. If a courtesan brings good income to the wine house, the Mama may ask for as much as ten thousand yuan."

John whistled.

"But if the courtesan has little business," Fan went on, "the Mama could take less, like a hundred yuan, just to eliminate a mouth from the dining table."

"Do the incomes of the courtesans differ a great deal?" John asked.

"Did you see the 'water plaque' hanging near the front door?" Fan answered the question with a question.

"Is it the blackboard with many names on it?" Calvin asked.

"Right," Fan said. "The female names are those of the courtesans. The male names under each of them are her clients.'"

Calvin said that one of the courtesans had twenty-one names below hers.

"That's unusual," Fan said. "What's her name, Professor Ren?"

"I only remember numbers and geometric configurations, not names."

"Of course. It's Professor Win's business to keep track of such nonsense for you."

All laughed.

"Does Qian Ying have many clients tonight?" Calvin asked.

Fan said that the jupiao he had signed removed Qian Ying's name from the water plaque.

"How about other nights, Mr. Fan?" Calvin asked.

"Er-er, I think she has been busy the last several months."

"Mr. Fan, are you saying that this had not been the case months ago?" Calvin asked sharply.

"She was once . . . in some trouble with the Mama, yes," Fan admitted.

"What happened?" both guests asked.

"Well, a young military officer named Sun Chi patronized her every night. Then he ran out of money."

"Seems to me the young man should've been the person in trouble, not her," Calvin said.

"True, if she hadn't received the young man on the sly," Fan said.

"Really?" John exclaimed. "A courtesan falling in love!"

"Actually, Black Cat and Sun Chi went back a long way," Fan said. "Their mothers were both widows and often got together. When the little boy Sun Chi was brought to her house, the baby girl would jump up and down, her thin hair bouncing on the top of her head. Old folks still laughed at how a mite of a girl would stomp on a cockroach crawling toward the bigger boy."

Calvin wanted to know why Qian Ma sold her daughter to the wine house.

"Money, or the lack of it, what else?" Fan said. "Qian Ma fell ill, and debts piled up.

"Couldn't Sun Chi have helped her?" John asked.

"Sun Chi was only a teenager then. He asked Qian Ying to run away with him. But Qian Ying was her mother's only asset. The woman would've had to hang herself if the girl had disappeared. So Sun Chi left for Guangzhou alone and wound up as a cadet of the Huangpu Military Academy."

"What's that?" John asked.

"The school founded by Dr. Sun Yat-sen," Fan said. "Chiang Kai-shek is its president."

"The Huangpu graduates have formed the backbone of the Chinese National Revolutionary Army," Calvin added. "They enabled Chiang Kai-shek to reach the pinnacle of power."

"Has Huangpu helped Qian Ying in any way?" Calvin asked.

"Not really. By the time Sun Chi came back to Nanjing years later, he could see Black Cat only as a patron," Fan said. "When he ran out of money, Black Cat sneaked him into her bedroom."

"She's got spunk!" John said with admiration. "You mean they—?"

"I think so," Fan said. "Indeed, it was Black Cat's first time. The groans behind the closed door alerted a male servant, who knocked to ask if everything was all right. Sun Chi jumped up and ran away. He reappeared in the front hall of the wine house the next evening, but the Mama ordered her servants to give him a thrashing. She also locked Black Cat in a room without food for three days."

"That's excessive!" Calvin fumed.

"Well, the Mama was upset. She had been saving Black Cat's *melon breaking* for a generous client," Fan said.

"Poor girl!" John exclaimed.

"A few nights later," Fan said, "Sun Chi came back to the wine house with his buddies. They beat up the servants and smashed all the vases in the foyer. After the soldiers left, the Mama ordered the servants to flog Black Cat twenty times."

"My God!" Calvin exclaimed. "She could die from that!"

"I stopped the nonsense by offering to pay for the damages," Fan said.

"What a good deed, Mr. Fan! No wonder Black Cat is so respectful to you," Calvin sighed in relief. "Did Sun Chi make any effort to rescue Black Cat from the wine house?"

"No. He never showed up at the wine house again."

"Do you know why?" both professors asked.

Fan shrugged. "Who can fathom a man's mind?"

It was drizzling again when John and Calvin biked home.

"Oh, I forgot to tell you," Calvin said. "My father looked into some city files. He found a few things about your grandfather. During the 1892 famine, for instance, your grandfather had served free porridge to the refugees and had saved many lives."

"I'm proud of him," John said hoarsely. "Please thank your father for his trouble."

"Not at all. My father said that he has the highest respect for your grandfather. He will be happy to send you the other information he has gathered."

They pedaled for a few more blocks before Calvin spoke again. "Judy is pregnant."

"Congratulations! You must feel great."

"If only for getting my parents off my back," Calvin laughed.

* * *

Early the next morning in the hangar, John was trying to start the airplane motor when he felt a cold hand on his arm. It was Calvin. The Chinese professor grabbed John's hands, pulled him into the corner office and closed the door. "John, pack up and leave Nanjing. Right now!" he whispered, his face as pale as a ghost.

"What? Why?"

"There is a ten-thousand-dollar reward on your head!"

"You must be kidding!"

Calvin fished out a ticket from his pocket. "This is for the ocean liner leaving Shanghai tonight. A car will pick you up in an hour at your apartment." He pushed John toward the door. "Go home and pack only what you need. I'll send the rest of your luggage to Michigan."

"Wait a minute!" John wrestled. "Was it the Japanese again?"

"Who else? You'd better run! Our intelligence has found out that one of their agents is planning to kill you."

"Who is he?"

"Probably Lin Hong-feng," Calvin said.

"Little Lin? It can't be! What's the proof?"

"He just moved to the apartment next to you and has taken up an unusual amount of your time."

"Talking about vases," John sneered.

"His father has many Japanese visitors. Our security people are checking them out right now," Calvin said.

"You will find that all of them are in the antique business."

"You may not have noticed it, but we have an armed detail following you everywhere."

"Ha! That motorcycle."

Calvin jumped. "We have three men in the detail, but none of them rides a motorcycle. Describe the cyclist to me."

"I never saw his face, those huge goggles! He motored away as soon as I turned to take a look at him."

"Go home and pack, John, for heaven's sake! Don't forget your passport." Calvin started pushing John again.

John resisted. "Listen, Calvin," he finally said. "I've been thinking things over for several days. I asked myself what Grandfather would've done if he had been in my shoes. I found the answer just now: he would have stayed to work on this important project. To hell with you, Calvin, I will be here for another semester!"

* * *

In the afternoon, John saw on a newsstand a picture of himself standing outside of a wine house. He brought a copy of the newspaper to the lab and asked a coworker to translate for him.

Headlined "An American Professor Visits a Whore House," the article reported that John had had a party in a wine house before he took a courtesan to the Jinling Hotel. Such a deed, the article went on to say, was the moral equivalent of raping a Chinese woman empowered by the money the Nationalist Government had paid him.

The next day, a student demonstration rocked the campus. Professor Mo, an eminent writer, took a number of students to call on Principal Lu and demand the dismissal of one American John Winthrop.

* * *

April 3, 1937

My dearest Cynthia,

Please don't be upset, my love, but I have decided to stay in Nanjing for another semester.

I have not forgotten my promise to you, Cynthia. But I also promised Calvin to spend a full year on his project. As I just realized, it is impossible to honor both promises. I must choose between them.

This morning Calvin helped me to do that. Informed that Japanese agents are trying to harm me, he urged me to leave Nanjing immediately.

He is putting my life over his project, which is his life. I cannot leave a friend and run away because things have gotten difficult.

Don't worry about me, my love. I am very well protected by armed guards. Nothing will happen to me. I am perfectly safe in Nanjing.

I pray you will find forgiveness for me in your heart.

Love,

John

He also sent a letter to Michigan, asking his appointment be postponed for a semester.

* * *

The last breath of the bleak winter was a dash of cold rain. John shivered in bed all night. In the apartment's staircase the next morning, John bumped into the limping custodian, who reminded him that today was the day people celebrated the *Qingming Festival*, when the sky was supposed to turn *qing-qing ming-ming* (clear and bright). "Open the windows and let the warm air come in!" he said.

"What warm air?" John wondered.

As soon as he stepped out of the building, he was greeted by a gentle breeze. Walking in the balmy atmosphere was like taking a comfortable bath. He took off his jacket after half a block.

It was a delight to see the streets filled with young girls dressed in myriads of colors. His spirit soared watching the kites of all shapes and sizes flying over the river bank. The ground seemed to have turned green overnight. The lunar calendar was amazing! The Chinese were a farming people. They must know exactly when to sow and when to harvest—or starve. Being able to predict the weather was a matter of life and death.

Having a tighter schedule than ever before, John had skipped antique hunting for weeks. He missed May and Wumao, the baby girl who had been reluctant to call him "*Shu Shu*" (Uncle). When her mother had urged her, she had hidden her face behind the woman's neck. Then May's family took him to a temple gathering. Wumao was in her mother's arms looking at him with a thumb in her mouth. Suddenly he was being swallowed up by a large crowd. He heard a little voice calling, "Shu Shu! Shu Shu!" Seconds later, the call turned into a scream. He pushed his way through the crowd and ran to her, and the baby girl wrapped her thin arms tightly around his neck.

* * *

In the convenience store, May came up to him with a face as bright as the sunshine outside. She had changed into a spring dress, and John was astonished to see her breasts pushing her thin blouse into a delicious contour.

The last time he saw her, she had been flat-chested under a heavy cotton jacket!

May fired rapid questions at him asking how he had been. John put on a straight face and answered in monosyllables. It was silly to act as if he had something to hide. He had done nothing wrong. But the girl had grown up. He didn't want Baba to have any suspicion about his intentions.

May apologized that she could not go antique hunting with him that day, the Qingming Festival being the time to go to the mountains and sweep the ancestors' graves.

Walking home alone, he continued to visualize her well-shaped breasts. They reminded him of his first night in Nanjing, when the steaming buns in a downtown restaurant had captured his attention.

Is that what they look like under that blouse?

"Stop it, John. She is one month shy of eighteen!" he chided himself.

That night in bed, little devils tempted him with naughty thoughts. He tried to drive them away: "Do the right thing, John!"

But the devils kept coming back.

He was no longer sure if his staying in Nanjing had nothing to do with May.

Chapter 19

Meeting the Generalissimo

On the seventh day of July 1937, the Sino-Japanese War finally broke out.

A minor incident sparked the conflagration.

A Japanese garrison stationed near Beijing had launched a military exercise at the historic Marco Polo Bridge. A local Chinese squadron, enraged by the effrontery, staged their own exercise at the same time. Several shots were heard in the dark, and a Japanese soldier went missing.

The Japanese demanded entry to a nearby city named Wanping to search for their comrade.

Ji Xin-wen, the commander of a Chinese regiment in Wanping, flatly denied the request. He declared that the Marco Polo Bridge would make a sacred burial ground for him and his soldiers, if necessary.

The missing Japanese soldier returned after peeing, but his temporary absence started a violent chain reaction that couldn't be stopped.

Japanese artilleries and airplanes blitzed the Chinese installations. Chinese soldiers returned fire. Their shots, heard all around China, gave the Japanese the excuse to invade Beijing as well as Tianjin, a major city seventy miles southeast of Beijing.

Chiang Kai-shek announced his support of the Chinese soldiers in Northern China, sending them six divisions of reinforcements.

Still, Beijing and Tianjin fell. A month later, China and Japan came to blows in Shanghai. The combatants between the two nations totaled more than one million—the most ever.

* * *

August light was barely breaking in the east when John left his apartment building. Not a soul was in sight. Several sandbags had been left helter-skelter on the ground. John didn't pay much attention. He was a little tense over the upcoming meeting with the Generalissimo.

A black Cadillac limousine glided to a noiseless stop at the curb.

"Good morning, Professor Winthrop," an elderly man in a Stetson hat greeted John from the backseat.

"Good morning, President Lu," John said as he climbed aboard, surprised how well the Western hat went with the traditional Chinese robe.

The limousine driver was in military uniform. Lu's own chauffeur and aide sat on the passenger seat in front.

"Thank you for joining me so early," President Lu said.

The car began to move.

"Not at all. I'm glad that this gives me the opportunity to thank you in person for supporting me when the students attacked my character," John said.

"My friend Professor Mo—or should I say my former friend?—still doesn't speak to me. But I'm well aware of your moral fiber. Please don't be offended by the storm in a teacup. It was all politics."

When John had been scandalized a few months earlier, President Lu had stood by him. Calvin corroborated that the two of them had left the wine house and gone home together.

"I apologize for this insane hour, but the Generalissimo has a lot on his plate."

John nodded.

President Lu pulled down the partition separating the rear seats of the limousine from the front seats. "Not many people are aware that it was our Generalissimo—not the Japanese, who started the Shanghai warfare," he whispered.

John was astonished. He had assumed the Japanese had struck the first blow, as they always had.

Seeing the expression on John's face, the man with silvery eyebrows explained. "The clashes in Shanghai between the two nations had been skirmishes, until our Generalissimo sent his airplanes to bomb the Japanese flag ship Izumo in the Yangtze River."

John was stunned.

"This is part of his grand strategy," President Lu continued, his eyes suddenly flashing. "He wanted to lure three hundred thousand Japanese soldiers to Eastern China."

"My God! Why did he do that?"

"The axiom for conquering China is to start the military action in the north and push it to the south, proven centuries ago by the Mongolians and the Manchus, both horsemen coming from the northern steppes," President Lu said. "Had the Japanese marched south from Beijing along the Beijing-Hankou Railway, they would have cut China into two halves, driving China's best troops to the Pacific Ocean, where Japanese warships are waiting."

"The war would've been over in months!" John almost lost his voice.

"Heaven bless China!" President Lu said. "The Japanese disagreed among themselves if and when to start a whole-scale war with China—many of them preferring to devour us bit by bit. Now that the fighting has begun from the east coast, they will find it hard to push their way westward, over mountainous terrains with mostly country roads."

The limousine passed Xinjekow, Nanjing downtown, where a mock bomb stood in the middle of a plaza. It was supposed to warn people of the real ones dropped from the sky. The admonition was no longer needed—not with the Nanjing populace reeling under repeated aerial bombardments. John had taken a hike on the Bell Mountain the week before, and he had seen most of the buildings in the city camouflaged by painting their roofs black.

"At this moment, the Generalissimo must have his hands full," John said. "How did he find time to see you and me?"

"Actually, he has no time for me." President Lu smiled. "But he wants to see you. No need to feel flattered, Professor Winthrop, you are building airplanes for him."

"But meeting so early in the morning?"

"The Generalissimo always gets up before dawn," President Lu said. "That's the time for him to groom his horse—a routine of his since his days as an artillery cadet in Japan."

John couldn't conceal his surprise. "Really!"

"The Generalissimo has his flaws," President Lu nodded. "But he also has a number of strengths."

"Could you tell me some of the former?"

"One of them is his distrust of people. He doesn't delegate enough and works himself to exhaustion. He'd be better off turning a blind eye to blemishes."

"What are his strengths?"

"A clear vision and a steely resolve to pursue it," President Lu said. "But not the least is his willingness to spend money."

"Did he come from a wealthy family?"

"His father was only a middling merchant," President Lu said. "But the Generalissimo understands the power of money and never hesitates to employ its force in full."

"Could you give me an example?" John asked.

"Only a few months ago, the Guangdong governor was about to declare his independence from the central government," President Lu said. "On the eve of the announcement, he found his airplanes had suddenly been moved to Nanjing. The governor renounced his plan. The million pieces of silver dollars paid to his chief of air force were obviously worth it."

"Last I heard, bribing was immoral, not to mention illegal," John said.

"You will never make a wily politician, Professor Winthrop," President Lu laughed. "Have you ever been told the noble end justifies the ignoble means?"

"But bribing by a head of state?"

"A person capable of the highest form of treachery is not necessarily one without a code of honor."

"Would you care to elaborate?"

"When the Generalissimo makes a promise, whether to an ally or a foe, he keeps it," President Lu said.

"I'd expect the same from our FDR."

"I'm not sure your FDR can keep some of the promises Chiang Kai-shek has made."

"Name one," John shot back.

"The Generalissimo had sowed his share of wild oats as a young man, but he has been a faithful husband since he married Madame."

"You consider that exceptional?"

President Lu laughed again. "Mencius—considered by many as the greatest Confucian who'd ever lived—admitted that no human is a saint. Who knows what one would do wearing the Generalissimo's powerful pants?"

John couldn't argue with that.

President Lu changed the subject. "Professor Winthrop, how is your project with Professor Ren coming along?"

"At first it went beautifully. Calvin's design is splendid. Our lab tests have verified all of his numbers down to the last decimal point. I don't believe I'm saying this, but Caltech's Von Karman couldn't have done better."

"But I heard the professor is distraught."

"Well, the war has disrupted our aluminum supply, and Calvin hasn't gotten much sleep since."

"Poor fellow."

"I told him the problem is mine. But he simply won't let go."

"I know you can fix anything with your wonderful hands, but how do you make a mountain of aluminum appear?"

"Do without it."

"Pardon?"

"Replace it with bamboo, of which China has an abundant supply."

"Great idea!" President Lu exclaimed.

"But our bamboo plane has inferior speed and poor maneuverability."

"Oh no!"

"We need a bigger engine. But bigger means heavier, which slows down the plane—a vicious cycle."

The limousine stopped in front of a large house at Huangpu Road. An aide in a dark Zhongshan uniform opened the rear door. "Welcome, President Lu. Please come this way, Professor Win."

The visitors were led to the large lawn behind the house.

A mustached man with a shaved head was caressing the back of a horse. From a distance, the trim figure standing very straight in military fatigues bespoke of a person in his twenties. But up close, John could tell from the lines on the face that the man couldn't be much younger than fifty. John was electrified by the intense pupils under the thick, sword-like eyebrows.

The Generalissimo said a few greeting words to President Lu before turning to John. "Thank you for coming to China, Professor Winthrop. I hope your living quarters have been comfortable." The Generalissimo extended his hand. When John was slow to react, the Generalissimo added: "Please pardon my appearance."

John was glad to have been given an excuse for his manner. "I see you are washing your horse, Generalissimo." He hastily grabbed the Chinese strongman's hand, and was surprised by how soft and warm it was.

"I was forging a bond with him," the Generalissimo said. "While I'm doing it, I must pay attention to details."

John understood, details being important to an engineer.

"The water you use, for instance," the Generalissimo continued. "On a hot day like this, it has to come straight from a well. Splash him with the crystal clear fluid, and he will raise his neck and neigh. You must scrape the water off him quickly, or he will stamp his hooves on the ground. You caress his body and brush him from head to tail until his coat shines in full splendor. Talk to him at the same time. Show him you care about him, and he will prance every time you come near him."

The Generalissimo's Mandarin was laced with a Southern accent, which John had to labor to understand. An American politician with a similar deficiency would find it difficult to win an election.

"That's a great deal of attention you pay to a horse," John said, slowly regaining his bearing.

"But care alone is not enough, Professor Winthrop. While you want the horse to love you, he must also fear you. Spoiling the horse is no way to train him. If he gets too comfortable, he will be no good to you. Set up rules for him to keep. If he violates any of them, whip him without mercy. Do it right, and the horse will leap over a river to carry you to safety."

"Well said," applauded President Lu, lifting his gray Stetson hat in salute.

"Thank you, President Lu. But you didn't come here to hear me talk about horses. Neither do I have time today to hear your lecture on the thoughts of Zeng Guo-fan." The Generalissimo turned to Winthrop. "Professor Winthrop, thank you for the progress report you submitted. I am happy to know that your warplanes will stand up to Japanese fighters. We'll do everything possible to get the aluminum you requested." He took John's hand with both of his and continued: "You are a true friend of the Chinese people. We'll never forget how you left your country and came here to help us. Please think of my house as your home in China. Our door is open to you at all times." A pause. "Now if you will excuse me, I must change for breakfast."

"Wow!" John uttered a little exclamation as soon as the Generalissimo's back disappeared from sight.

An aide escorted the guests to the living room. A maid served tea.

"President Lu, I was wondering," John whispered. "Who is Zeng Guo-fan?"

"The scholar general who, some eighty years ago, quelled the Taiping uprising led by a self-proclaimed brother of Jesus Christ."

"What blasphemy! But, President Lu, in China's long history, there must have been military feats greater than the suppression of an uprising. Why did the Generalissimo single out Zeng Guo-fan?"

"Good question," President Lu said and took a sip of his tea. "I have a humble theory for that. In China's past, a powerful general was a threat to the throne and a subject of the emperor's suspicion. Zeng Guo-fan was one such man. He avoided the guillotine by holding fast to his personal motto: seek *imperfection*. The moon, when full, starts to decline; a high position is fraught with perils. Zeng saved his own life by disbanding his army as soon as the Taiping rebellion had been crushed. I imagine the Generalissimo respects Zeng Guo-fan for his ability to handle attacks from two directions: front and back."

"Is the Generalissimo handling attacks from two directions?" John asked.

"Three, actually." President Lu made a sign with the last three fingers on his right hand. "Opinions on the Generalissimo vary: hero or villain? But it's not difficult to understand him. Keep in mind just one thing: he is, first and foremost, a nationalist."

"One who dreams of a strong and independent China?"

"Exactly," President Lu said. "Japan is destroying his dream and is his number one enemy. But going to war with Japan meant certain defeat. Therefore, when the Japanese invaded Manchuria, he swallowed his pride and ordered Zhang Xueliang to emphatically avoid conflict. You probably know that."

"No!" John exclaimed. "I thought the young marshal was afraid to fight."

"He hated the Japanese with a passion; they murdered his father and took away his turf," President Lu said. "He would've thrown every one of his soldiers against them had the Generalissimo backed him up."

"Now you make me curious," John said. "Who is the Generalissimo's enemy number two?"

"His own countrymen."

"I don't understand!"

"His people blamed him for handing Manchuria to Japan. Students demonstrated against him. Politicians demanded his resignation." President Lu lowered his voice to a whisper. "The media spread ugly rumors about his personal life."

John's face changed.

"I know, I know." President Lu patted John's hand. "It's frustrating when someone does that to you, and you get more muck on your face trying to clean it."

"People told me the Generalissimo is corrupt, and that he leads a decadent life," John said.

"Give me a sample of what you heard."

"Well, in his days as a cadet in Japan," John said, "the Generalissimo is supposed to have shared a whore's bed with his best friend. The woman got pregnant but couldn't determine the father of her baby. Chiang Kai-shek took the responsibility and the boy became his second son Chiang Wei-guo."

"You may say half of this rumor is true."

"What is the whole truth?"

"A good friend of the Generalissimo had an affair with a Japanese woman and couldn't tell his wife. Chiang Kai-shek raised the illegitimate child as his own."

"How did the Generalissimo defend himself against the defamation?"

"He uttered not a word."

"That's incredible!" John shook his head. "Did you say the Generalissimo has more enemies?"

"That would be the Chinese communists, his most deadly enemy," President Lu said. "I'll quote him verbatim: 'The Japanese are an affliction of the skin, while the communists are a disease of the heart.' He waged five expunging campaigns to push the Chinese communists to an area near Xian, where his Northeast army and his Northwest army were supposed to join forces to wipe them out. You know the rest."

"The Xian Incident changed the Generalissimo's plan!" John exclaimed.

An aide came to apologize for the delay: the Generalissimo was taking an urgent long distance call from Shanghai.

They were led to the breakfast room. Madame Chiang Kai-shek, looking elegant in a casual black qipao, asked John warmly how he had been doing in Nanjing.

A few minutes later, the Generalissimo arrived in full uniform. All of them sat down and lowered their heads in a prayer led by Madame Chiang.

"This is my translation of Ambassador Wang Zheng-ting's telegram this morning," Madame Chiang said, handing her husband a sheet of paper. "Washington is concerned about China's abilities to hold off the Japanese in Shanghai."

The Generalissimo read the translated script, the furrows on his forehead deepening.

Breakfast was served: porridge with peanuts, pickles, and salted duck eggs for the Generalissimo and President Lu, ham and eggs for Madame and John.

No one began.

After waiting quietly for the Generalissimo to finish reading, Madame Chiang broke the silence. "Well, what do you think?"

"We will not pull out of Shanghai!" the Generalissimo said flatly.

"Even if we lose all of our troops?" President Lu asked.

"We have no other choice, President Lu!" The Generalissimo replied.

"How about asking the West to intervene," Madame Chiang suggested.

"We did that when the Japanese invaded Manchuria," the Generalissimo said. "The League of Nations gave Japan a reprimand—words, words, words! No one was willing to use economic sanctions, not to mention military means, to make the aggressors leave our country."

"Russia gives us military aid," President Lu said.

"Sure, to shield their Siberia for them," Chiang Kai-shek said gloomily.

"Germany sends us weapons," Madame offered.

"In exchange for tungsten, or Germany goes dark."

"When I was a student in the United States, I was impressed with the American sense of justice," Madame Chiang said. "This is only a thought, but perhaps you could send me to America to talk to President Roosevelt."

"And beg that grandson of an opium dealer for a handout?" Chiang Kai-shek shouted. "May-ling, Roosevelt has his own political agenda. A bullet costs five cents. Each nickel in the industrialist's pocket jingles when he sells ammunition to the Japanese. We can't afford Western bullets, so we order our soldiers to hold their fire until they can hear the encroaching footsteps."

"I thought thwarting the Japanese advance in China was consistent with American interests," John said.

"Thank you very much for sharing your insight, Professor Winthrop. But your government wants to see returns on their investments. It doesn't send military aid to a nation that loses every battle."

"How can we fight without tanks and warplanes?" Madame Chiang widened her eyes.

"Look, China is a weak nation," Chiang Kai-shek said. "The last thing we want is a war with Japan. That's why we cooperate with them in every way possible. But there is a line in the sand: Our national sovereignty must be respected, and our national territory must be intact. Manchuria is part of China. If we accept Japan's occupation of our provinces, we will have no face and no eyes to meet our ancestors in the netherworld. No matter if you live in the East, the West, the South, or the North. It makes no difference if you are male, female, old, or young. Now that the line in the sand has been crossed, all of us must be prepared to sacrifice our lives. We have no option other than to choose a city, send our best troops, and show the world what we can do without their help!"

"Why Shanghai?" John asked.

"It has the largest foreign population, hence it is the best choice," Chiang Kai-shek said, his voice cold and angry. "We will lose. Perhaps few of our soldiers in Shanghai will come out alive. But only by doing so can we convince the world that we will stand up for our rights and are not afraid to die."

Madame Chiang stared at her husband, and her eyes began to well up.

"Maybe I can pull out some of our troops," Chiang Kai-shek said in a softer voice. "We will need them to defend Nanjing."

Nobody spoke.

China's strongman took a sip of his tea and stood up. His guests did likewise. The Generalissimo gestured for them to sit and keep Madame company. He followed a guard who walked backward to the door holding a pistol in each hand, eyes darting left and right. Other armed guards covered the Generalissimo's back.

Through the window of the breakfast room Madame Chiang quietly watched her husband disappear. Then she asked her guests to have their breakfast. But they only chose a few morsels to pick at before taking their leave.

Madame Chiang went to her piano in the living room and quietly played a hymn.

* * *

It was still early in the morning. Few people were out on the streets. Inside the black limousine, President Lu's chauffeur whispered to his master some gossip he had heard from the Generalissimo's aides: "He is screaming in his sleep again!"

"Can they tell what he was saying?" President Lu asked.

"Only something about sending his young sons and young brothers to their early graves."

"He must have scared them out of their wits!" John exclaimed.

"They've heard it before. Only the screams are getting shriller these days," the aide said.

President Lu shook his head whispering to John, "The Generalissimo's carrying a heavy cross. The casualties keep piling up. The pressure keeps rising. I hope he doesn't lose his resolve, for thousands of lives are hanging in the balance."

The limousine wheeled into the spacious Zhongshan Road. President Lu changed the subject to a lighter topic. "How is your antique collecting coming along, Professor Winthrop?"

"Frustrating."

"How so?" President Lu asked.

"I don't think I will ever learn to tell a fake from an original."

"What happened?"

"Last week a dealer sold me a blue-and-white vase with a Xuande mark," John said.

"Ah! An early Ming guan yao. Very lovely!"

"The dealer said it had stood in Prince Gong's chamber thirty years ago."

"How much did you pay for it, may I ask?"

"Two thousand yuan."

President Lu nodded. "Quite reasonable—provided it's genuine."

John sighed. "I showed it to a friend's father, who told me it's a modern imitation."

"Goodness! What are you going to do?"

Before John answered, a truck burst out of a side street, sealing off the intersection. As tires screeched, the limousine came to a halt, abruptly throwing John forward against the partition. He froze when a pistol appeared outside the window pointing at his head. A ragged young Chinese man held it, his vaguely familiar face cold and steely. As John searched his memory bank, his eyes were blinded by fiery explosions.

In one quick motion the big Cadillac shot backward. It made a U-turn over the sidewalk, knocked over several rickshaws, and sped away from more popping sounds.

"Good move!" President Lu's aide exclaimed in a trembling voice. He looked at the cracked window at John's elbow and said: "Thank heaven for the bullet-proof glass! It would have shattered had we allowed this rascal to pour one more round of bullets into it."

As the sound of sirens filled his ears, John touched his head carefully and was relieved to find it whole.

* * *

Late that evening, Calvin braced the rain on his way to John's apartment to tell John that the failed assassin had been captured. John could not conceal his surprise that the hired man was Police Officer Wang, the patrolman of their neighborhood.

"Sorry that we messed up!" Calvin apologized. "Our men were guarding your apartment last night. But when you left home this morning, the Generalissimo's secret service stopped them from following you."

According to Calvin, Wang had been hired by a Japanese spy who was holding Wang's little son hostage. The Japanese threatened to slit the child's throat if Wang betrayed him. The policeman didn't—even with a pistol cocked to his temple.

After Calvin left, John sank into the sofa. He had been lucky this time. But there would be a next time—and a next time and a next time. He couldn't be lucky always.

What he couldn't accept was not so much death itself. Rather, it was death *before* ever having slept with a woman.

At MIT, John had led a Spartan life. His days of heavy academic pressure coincided with those of strong sexual needs. Cynthia never allowed him to go very far with her. He was sustained only by the hope of a good future. That future had arrived: a tenure-track job awaiting him in Michigan, and a bank account that made him smile every time he looked. But now he might not live long enough to get married.

* * *

At noon the next Sunday, John and May were strolling in his neighborhood when a sudden storm caught them. Lightning cracked the sky like a long whip. A splashing rain followed. May took John's arm and ran for his building. This was her first implicit declaration of how she had come to regard him. John's heart beat wildly.

Thunder exploded overhead when they reached his apartment door. She withdrew her hand, but the warmth of her fingers on his arm remained.

John unlocked the door. "Don't worry, May. There is a lightning rod on the top of this building. We're safe here."

May entered the apartment. "My, so many rooms!" she looked around and exclaimed. "A bedroom, a kitchen, a bathroom, and a foyer—I just learned that word." She beamed. "Your house is so clean, John!"

"This is not a *house*, May, just an apartment."

As John steered May to his bedroom, she continued to stare at her surroundings, seemingly struck by the bright-red bedspread on his narrow bed.

"It's a present from Judy. She did the embroidery herself," John explained, handing her a towel. "You may want to dry yourself. You are dripping wet."

When John returned from the kitchen with two cups of tea, May was drying her hair with his towel. She wore no bra—probably had never seen one. Her breasts pressed on the wet spots of her blouse, the healthy brown skin showing through the semi-transparency.

John swallowed hard and put down the tea cups. He walked up, put his arms around her from behind, and bent down to snuggle his face against her ear.

She squirmed. "I think you should've bought the red lacquer box." She talked quickly. "The dealer wanted two yuan. That's outrageous, but you liked it so much," she said even faster. "Did you notice his crooked nose? It looked so funny. He reminded me of my history teacher. All of my friends thought he was good looking, though. Imagine that!"

"Who is good looking—your history teacher or the dealer in the antique store?" John's voice trembled a little.

"My history teacher. He smokes nonstop, you know. You should see the yellow stains on his teeth! And that gold crown! My classmates are so foolish . . ."

"Why're you talking like that, May?"

"What?"

"You sound like a chatterbox."

"I do that when I am scared," she said, her face flaming.

Encouraged, John took a deep breath and pushed her down on his shiny bedspread. She didn't fight him, only kept turning her face to avoid his lips. But she kissed back when he finally succeeded in covering her mouth with his. Emboldened, John forcibly undid a couple of her buttons, but he met firm resistance trying to do more. Reaching inside her blouse, he filled his palm with her warm fullness. Her teeth chattered. His hands must've been chilled by raindrops! Her skin was so delicate that his hand glided to her armpit. He was surprised to find her hairless there too.

But she recoiled when his finger moved down to her belly. "No!" she cried—her voice more grown-up than he remembered. She pushed his hand away and jumped off his bed.

Thunder exploded outside the window. Lightning blinded his eyes with repeated flashes of fury. When the blasts ended, he sat up sweating. What would she be thinking of him now?

"Where-where are you going?" he stuttered.

May buttoned up her blouse.

"I'll get you an umbrella," he said.

But she had already stormed out of the door.

* * *

John didn't go antique hunting the following Sunday. It took some time before he could brace himself to walk into May's store. She acted as if they had made an agreement to forget that stormy afternoon. Polite and distant, she seldom talked to him. John was relieved that the store owner was as respectful to him as always.

John carefully avoided bumping into May's shoulders. Baba might kill him if he found out what he had done to his daughter.

Book III

Chapter 20

The Great Enigma

November 11, 1937.

At the foot of a forested hill, inside an ordinary building unusual only for its camouflage, a mustached man in military uniform was entering an ordinary room. The clock had just finished chiming seven times. An aide announced the arrival of the leader of China. Everyone in the conference room—a graying Caucasian among them—stood up.

Chiang Kai-shek nodded at the men stiffly standing around the conference table. He gave his words of approval "Hao! Hao!" (Good! Good!). "Please sit down, everyone. Thank you for coming."

He went to the head of the table and began. "Generals! Our soldiers have fought a valiant battle in Shanghai. The Japanese boasted that they would conquer China in three months. It took them almost that long just to take one harbor city. The Western Powers, seeing what we are capable of, will come to our aid."

Everybody applauded.

"Now that Shanghai has fallen," the Generalissimo continued, "Japan's next target will be Nanjing. Generals, I seek your esteemed opinions on how to defend our capital!"

His eyes fell on General Li Zhong-ren, a dark man whose rustic look and small frame gave away his Southern rural origin.

Only in his forties, Li was already a seasoned military man. Ten years earlier, he had led the Seventh Army to join Chiang's Northern Expedition, the success of which united the nation.

But back in August, Li's had been one of the loudest voices objecting to pitting eight hundred thousand Chinese troops against three hundred thousand Japanese soldiers in Shanghai.

"The city has no fortresses," Li had argued. "Our soldiers will be pounded by Japan's firepower from the air, sea, land—and melt like a bar of iron in a furnace. It's not the best place for us to expend our military resources."

"Which place is, pray tell?" the Generalissimo countered.

"None," General Li had answered. "We should engage the Japanese in a long war over China's vast territory. Trade space for time!"

But the Supreme Chinese Commander had rejected General Li's advice and had given him no explanation.

After enduring almost three months of brutal attack, the Chinese army in Shanghai began to show signs of weakening. But the Generalissimo, informed of the Nine-Power Treaty Conference being held in Brussels, ordered his generals to fight on for ten more days, hoping for a sanction against Japan to come out of the conference.

None did.

When a reinforcement of sixty thousand Japanese soldiers landed on the north shore of the Hangzhou Bay, the Chinese troops completely collapsed. By the time Chiang Kaishek consented to the retreat, more than half of his soldiers already lay dead on the battleground.

The Chinese army tried to make another stand inside the fortresses on the Defense Lines named Wu-fu and Xi-cheng—the Chinese counterparts of the Hindenburg Lines. But the local authorities had fled, taking the keys to the fortresses with them. Chinese soldiers retreated farther inland.

* * *

"Elder brother De-lin," the Generalissimo addressed General Li by his style name—a first name chosen by a person for himself—"Your opinion on how to defend Nanjing?"

"There is no way to defend it," General Li replied.

"What do you propose?"

"Evacuate before the Japanese arrive!"

Without any expression, the Generalissimo turned to the next person at the table. "Elder brother Jian-sheng, what do you think?"

Jian-sheng was the style name of General Bai Chong-xi, one of the shrewdest military minds in the nation. During the Northern Expedition, Chiang Kai-shek had asked General Bai to serve as his de facto Joint Chief of Staff. At that time, this handsome man had been only thirty-three years old.

The Generalissimo's question to the General was followed by several seconds of silence.

"Nanjing is a city easy to attack and difficult to defend," General Bai said. "Our capital is surrounded by flat lands on three fronts: east, west, and south. If the Japanese launch a three-pronged drive against us, our lack of geographical protection will be exposed. We lost Shanghai only days ago. Our soldiers are not ready to fight another battle against great odds."

"How long do you think we could hold them off—if we tried?" the Generalissimo asked.

"Three or four days—at most."

"And after that?"

"Calamity!"

The Generalissimo's voice turned just a tad sharper: "How so?"

"At our back is the Yangtze River. We don't have enough ships to carry our troops across. It will be impossible to execute a timely evacuation."

"What should we do then?" The Generalissimo sounded impatient.

"Abandon the city before the enemies arrive. I beg for your wise judgment, Generalissimo, to choose our battle at the best time, the best place, with the best harmony of human resources."

The Generalissimo turned to Alexander von Falkenhausen, the military adviser Hitler had sent to Nanjing. The Chinese generals referred to him as the German, his name being too long for them to remember. The handsome blond man, in spotless army uniform decorated with shiny hardware, nodded gravely.

The Generalissimo's eyes moved down to his other Chinese generals, and saw all of them nodding.

The face of the Generalissimo darkened, and the atmosphere in the room suddenly turned frigid.

"Generals! We are soldiers of Revolution," Chiang Kai-shek roared. "We pledged our lives to defend our nation and our party. Nanjing is our national capital. The Bell Mountain is the final resting place of our party's founder. Are we going to invite the Japanese to enter our capital? Are we going to let them plunder the tomb of our National Father?"

Every man in the room shrank deeper into his seat.

"General He, what is your opinion?" The Generalissimo no longer bothered with courtesy, his patience apparently wearing thin.

During the Xian Incident, General He Ying-qin had advocated using military measures against the rebels. Since then he had been plagued by the criticism of having little regard for the Generalissimo's personal safety. Then, the man second only to Chiang Kai-shek in the Huangpu military hierarchy said: "As a soldier of revolution, I follow all of the Generalissimo's orders."

"And you, General Xu?" The Generalissimo turned to his Defense Minister sitting at the end of the conference table.

"I obey every order from our supreme leader," echoed Minister Xu Yong-chang.

The last officer at the table to be consulted was General Tang Sheng-zhi, a tall man with a mustache. To the surprise of everyone in the conference room, the former warlord jumped up. "I completely agree with the Generalissimo. All of us must be prepared to die defending our capital, and our soldiers must fight to the last man."

As Tang sat down, a shadow of a smile showed on Chiang Kai-shek's lips. The thunderstorm had blown over, and the Generalissimo reverted back to the benign and magnanimous leader he had been. He summarized: "Our opinions are unanimous. We will defend Nanjing! There is only one question remaining: Which one of you will volunteer to be the commander of the defending army?"

As his generals cast glances at one another, the Generalissimo locked eyes with General Tang. "If nobody does, I will stay in Nanjing to direct the defense myself."

Tang jumped up from his chair again. "Generalissimo, I will be honored to lead our Nanjing army! I, and every man under my command, will live or die with the city!"

The Generalissimo snapped to attention clicking his heels. He raised his right hand over his eyebrow in a solemn salute, the ultimate tribute from China's supreme commander to his sacrificing general. Instantly, everyone else in the room stood up and did the same.

"General Tang, we express to you the utmost gratitude of our nation," Chiang Kai-shek said in a strong voice. "Your name will be recorded in history. I hereby appoint you the Commander in Chief of our Nanjing army. You will be responsible for the security of our national capital, with all power to prevail over any and all issues in this matter." The Generalissimo thanked his generals for their dedication and marched out of the conference room.

Li whispered to his good friend General Bai as they followed the Generalissimo out, "Why does he insist on fighting an impossible battle *again*?"

"A riddle worth one hundred thousand lives," General Bai replied.

* * *

People fled the city in droves; trucks and buses jammed the streets.

Ten thousand crates of ancient art from the Palace Museum, accumulated by Chinese emperors over one millennium, went to the harbor. They included the Song paintings brushed five hundred years before the Renaissance, the archaic bronze vessels cast a thousand years before Christ, and the Ru ceramics fired in the twelfth century—the quality of which remained unsurpassed. Another seven thousand crates of treasures had already been loaded on trains bound for Baoji in Western China. The cultural as well as market value of these antiquities was beyond estimation.

The once boisterous city had turned into a ghost town.

Chapter 21

Welcome, the Great Japanese Imperial Army!

December 4, 1937.

Midnight darkness engulfed all but one of the buildings on the campus.

Calvin looked up from a desk at the far end of the lab. "It will work, John!" he cried. "It will certainly work!"

"Take it easy, Calvin," John said. "No need to wake up the entire Nanjing City!"

As if on cue, a siren blared. The frightening pitch rose to an ear-splitting crescendo, faded, and repeated itself:

WOOwoo—WOOwoo—WOOwoo—!

Calvin answered with a fit of violent coughs.

"To the air-raid shelter." Old Tang, the foreman, jumped up. "Run!" he yelled.

"And feed the mosquitoes again?" Lin murmured, extinguishing his cigarette as he stood up.

"Please! I'm too tired even to crawl," complained Zhao, a student who had taken a couple of courses from John.

But Calvin paid no attention to the threatening visitors in the sky. "Start building the engine, John. Right now!" he said between bouts of coughing.

"And throw out the GM engine we paid good money for?" Lin piped in. "You must be joking!"

"That engine doesn't have the five hundred horsepower we need for a bamboo airplane!" Calvin answered.

"Any such engine will be too heavy," Lin shook his head. "We've gone over that."

"I've done the numbers." Calvin grinned through another coughing fit. "John's engine will weigh no more than GM's. Five hundred and fifty horsepower! We'll blow those Japanese bastards out of the sky."

"Really?" everyone in the room cried in chorus. "What's the idea?"

"Add a supercharger to compress the air," Calvin said.

The room fell silent.

Tang finally nodded. "Very tricky. But if anyone can pull it off, Professor Win can."

"I've heard many good ideas in this room before. This tops them all," Zhao sang.

"Goddamn genius!" Calvin said, shaking his head while blowing his nose loudly with a handkerchief.

The siren pierced the air again, one long and three short blasts:

WOOO—WO WO WO! WOOO—WO WO WO—!

It was the signal that the Japanese planes had invaded the Nanjing sky!

"Too late to run! Turn off the lights!" John yelled. "Find a table to hide under."

Quickly, darkness fell on the large room. All noise in the lab stopped.

Distant explosions caused John to hide deeper under his creaky desk.

Outside the window, a flare shot through the sky.

The explosions came nearer. Another flare. Whistles of dive bombers. A series of explosions. The ground shook.

"Jesus!" John swore.

The roar swooped over their heads. Explosions danced past them. Silence again.

One of the workers broke the stillness: "Whew! That was close. It felt like they had something against us personally."

"I wouldn't be surprised if that's exactly what it is," Tang said ominously.

Calvin muttered under his breath: "God damn it!! When are we fighting back?"

"When we have a couple hundred warplanes in our hangar, Professor Ren," Lin said softly.

The buzz of the planes returned.

"Hey!" said a voice. "That's not fair!"

Flashes illuminated the sky. A series of explosions shook the room. A corner of the roof collapsed. Debris rained down. Everybody hid his head under his hands.

Another bomb landed at a faraway corner of the building. Crumpling sounds.

John said a silent prayer.

Then they heard a long startling hiss followed by an overwhelming explosion in the air.

"Hey, we got them!" shouted a joyous voice. "Our anti-aircraft artillery!"

Gradually the noises in the sky sounded more distant. Finally, Calvin's periodic coughing was all that remained.

An even-toned horn signaled the end of the air raid. People exhaled and slowly crawled out from their hiding places.

John's hands were shaking when he reached to switch on the light. Thank goodness the bombing had not put out their power. Then he heard Calvin murmur, "There is one more problem to solve: the vibration of the fuselage."

Hysterical laughter broke out across the room, diffusing the tension in the air.

"Forget the darned fuselage, Calvin! Our problem is to get the *bird* out of Nanjing," John said.

Calvin coughed again, his ashen face looking like those wounded soldiers carried into the city by continuous streams of trucks.

"Are you all right, pal?" John asked.

"No problem," Calvin answered.

"If you don't mind me saying so, my friend, you've got to take care of yourself," John said. "We need you around."

"Sure, sure."

Tang came back after a quick inspection of the building. "Hit by three bombs," he said. "Lucky, nobody hurt. How you doing, Professor Ren?"

"Fine," Calvin said. "Look, John, I need two days to get the fuselage fixed."

"No, Calvin, you are taking too long! Now we don't even have two lousy hours to spare!" John said.

Calvin slumped into his chair.

John reacted. "Sorry, pal. You need to go home and sleep like the rest of us," John said as his eyes swept over the workers in the large room. "The guys need their rest too."

"Just give me a few more minutes," Calvin said.

"Come on, Calvin, these people have worked awfully hard." John lowered his voice. "One of them told me they've been on half salary the last three months. Yet everybody keeps coming back. In case you didn't know, Calvin."

"I do. It's my job to stuff their cowhide envelopes with cash every month."

"Calvin! Have you been on half salary too?"

"I've not been paid all semester."

"What?" John raised his voice.

"I'm an employee of the university. No classes, no salary."

"The technicians and the engineers, who pays them?"

"The Aeronautical Affairs Commission."

"How come I got full pay?" John asked.

"You're the foreign consultant."

"What do you eat without money? How do you pay your rent?" John was livid now.

Calvin looked at his hands.

Barking came from outside, then shouts. Several workers ran out. Tang came back and said: "Professor Ren, the police have caught the *turtle egg* who sent up the flares. They arrested him, a Chinaman!"

John hit the desk with his fists. "Let's pack up, Calvin. We've got to move the airplane!"

"OK, John."

"Have we gotten the steamship yet?" John asked.

"Madame Chiang Kai-shek stepped in and secured one for us—with the Generalissimo's direct order. It'll be in the harbor tomorrow."

"How do we move the airplane from the basement to the waterfront?"

"We've got two army trucks for that. We can drive them out through the underground tunnel."

"What tunnel?"

Calvin handed over a large bronze key. "You will see it after you open the steel door in the basement."

"The door with the big, rusty chain!" John exclaimed. "Where does it lead to?"

"An alley three blocks away."

"Son of a gun!" John said.

Calvin stood up and clapped. "Go home, everyone. Get some sleep. Be back at seven o'clock tomorrow morning—sharp!"

People slowly filed out of the lab.

Calvin sat down, his face looking pale.

"Let's go, Calvin. It's already midnight."

"Just a minute! I have an idea I must write down before I lose it."

"You must go home like the rest of us," John said, taking the pencil from Calvin's grasp.

Calvin cursed.

"If I were you, Calvin, I wouldn't keep my pregnant wife waiting up all night."

Calvin, looking defeated, rose, and dragged his feet to the front door.

* * *

John and Calvin cycled side by side as they left the campus.

"Doesn't this street give you the creeps?" John asked. "It feels like a graveyard. See that building over there? Riddled with bullet holes and barely standing."

They biked for another block before John said: "I went to the bank today and took out all of my money. They told me banks are closing."

Calvin said, "So are the post offices."

"Is that right?" John said. "I'd better mail out my letter to Professor Dickinson tomorrow."

Gradually, Calvin fell behind. John slowed down for him.

A little girl sat in front of a burning stucco house crying. John looked at her and then back to Calvin, shaking his head.

"It's not safe for Judy to stay in the city," John said. "You should take her to the USS *Panay* tomorrow."

"And leave you with the dirty business?" Calvin said, breathing hard. "I can't."

They came to Drum Tower Square, where all windows and doors were boarded up. The chilly December wind mercilessly tossed wastepaper and empty bottles around. The area, lit at this hour weeks ago, had been largely deserted since the decision to defend the city had been announced.

Turning a corner, they happened onto a large square. A sea of soldiers lay side by side on the ground covering themselves with burlap bags shivering. A few people in white robes walked between the tightly packed rows.

"Miss Vautrin!" John called in surprise, and braked his bike to an abrupt stop.

The woman turned. She moved toward John like a large white crane in her stiff garment. The two young professors got off their bikes.

"Is it you, Professor Winthrop?" the principal of May's school asked. "And is this Professor Ren?"

"Yes, it's us, Miss Vautrin," John said.

"Professor Winthrop!" Minnie narrowed her eyes. "I haven't seen you in our church for weeks. We miss your little donations."

"I'm very sorry, Miss Vautrin," John said. "The war . . . I've been over my head."

"Well, I understand." The woman laughed shortly. "Everyone is trying to get out of Nanjing. When are you leaving, John?"

"As soon as possible."

"The sooner the better. You might not find transportation if you wait any longer."

"The USS *Panay* is patrolling the Yangtze River. I can always embark at the harbor," John said.

"What if the city gate is closed?"

"I'm carrying a rope to help me go down the city wall."

The American missionary nodded and turned to Calvin. "How about you, Professor Ren?"

"I'll go with my wife to the *Panay*," Calvin said in a low voice, moving his eyes away from the one-armed man on the ground immobile except for occasional twitching.

"Will they accept you?"

"I hope so. My wife is an American citizen."

"Oh, I forgot about that. That's good. It's almost impossible to get a train ticket right now."

Calvin had another coughing fit.

John took over the conversation. "The other day Calvin took me to the train station to see his family off. Someone offered Mr. Ren twenty times the price of his ticket. He turned it down."

"Very wise. Where was your family going, Professor Ren?"

"Changsha, where they will hopefully hitch a ride to Chongqing," Calvin said.

"How did your parents feel about your staying behind?"

"Mother was upset," the Chinese professor answered.

"Calvin kowtowed to his parents in the train station," John added, "apologizing for putting his duty to his country ahead of his filial duty."

"Miss Vautrin, help! This man is vomiting blood," rang a voice at a distance.

"I must go," Minnie said and hurried away.

Calvin took the opportunity to cough to his heart's content. John watched with a frown.

When the woman missionary came back, she made a cross across her chest. "Another soul gone home."

They shared a moment of silence.

"Miss Vautrin, I would like to ask you the same question you asked me," John said. "You must be aware that the

American Embassy has ordered all of us to leave the city. Why are you still here?"

"I've schools to look after. I explained at length to Ambassador Johnson about that, until his Excellency yawned and nodded off."

"If that's what you're doing, why are you miles away from your schools?" John asked.

"Because the American Red Cross needs help. There aren't enough hands to help these wounded soldiers to take care of their nature's calls. So they are lying in their own waste. That soldier you saw over there, Professor Ren, lost an arm to a grenade. You wouldn't believe this, but we don't have any painkiller to give him. Not even medical ointment for his wounds, for heaven's sake! So he will die soon. Can you smell the stench from here? His flesh is rotting.No, no, don't go any closer. You will throw up."

"I can't stand seeing human beings . . . so tortured," Calvin said.

"I know," Miss Vautrin said. "There is a smell of death hanging over here. Even after I go home, it stays in my nose. I rub my hands over and over again. My skin gets raw, but the smell still clings."

"It's late, Miss Vautrin," John said. "Why don't you get some rest?"

"I feel better when I am with these men, although there is not a whole lot I can do for them."

"There are so many . . ." Calvin's words were interrupted by another coughing attack.

"Some of them are barely fifteen," Minnie said. "Only the good Lord knows if they can survive without their mothers, let alone going to a war. It makes me wonder how such an unprepared army can fight the Japanese."

"They can't. That is why you see so many of them lying here," Calvin said.

"Their wails make my skin crawl," John said.

"One must learn to live with human crying, professors, or he goes raving mad."

John changed the subject. "Is your school closed?"

"What school? All my students have stopped coming. How about yours?"

"Most of my students—if not all—have left the city," John said.

"I'm worried about the people without the means to leave. We hope the Japanese Army will respect the sanctity of the Nanjing International Safety Zone," she said.

"Sorry, Miss Vautrin, I wouldn't count on that," Calvin said. "The Japanese soldiers are killing and raping their way into town."

"Please don't scare the good woman, Calvin," John said. "Much as I dislike Japanese soldiers, they are human beings too—just like you and me. They're not fiends or demons."

"Hallelujah!" Minnie said.

"On my way to China, I stopped over at Tokyo," John added. "I found the Japanese people extremely polite and civilized."

"My experience exactly," Minnie said.

"There's always a small number of bad apples." John continued, "but I expect the soldiers of a fine people to have some discipline."

"John, aren't you ignoring the gory stories pouring in every day?" Calvin said, his face growing red. "Why do you do that?"

"You just said it: stories."

"Didn't you see the photograph on the front page of the *Nanjing Sun* today? A Japanese soldier held the decapitated head of a Chinese man in one hand and a long katana in the other. From the smirk on his face, he might have been coming back from a fishing trip."

"It's just one photograph." John spread his hands and looked to Minnie for support.

"I'm afraid you don't see the facts even when they are staring you in the face," Calvin said, his voice shaking with anger.

"Gentlemen, gentlemen!" Minnie pleaded. "These are inhumane times. We are doing all we can to help the refugees."

"You people are incredible," Calvin said. "You are like John's grandfather, who did similar things during a famine."

"I'm proud of him," John said, "so proud!"

"I know that funny look in your eyes, John. Don't you dare!" Calvin said. "No need to be a hero. The Japanese will not treat you kindly if they get ahold of you."

"I hear you, Calvin."

"Oh, I almost forgot, John," Calvin said. "Mr. Fan came to the university today looking for you. He asked you to please go to his house tonight."

"Now? After midnight?"

"He said no matter how late," Calvin said, his breathing more labored.

"Hey! You look like you're about to collapse, Calvin," John said.

Minnie came over to feel Calvin's forehead. "You have a fever, young man." Calvin slipped down like a puppet with its support pulled away. Minnie tried all she could to hold him up. John came to take over.

The missionary woman gave John some pills. "This may help Professor Ren."

Calvin grunted his thanks.

"He can't bike," John observed. "Rickshaw!" he shouted so loud that Minnie jumped.

* * *

Judy was reading under a dim light when John helped Calvin through the door of the small apartment. Her book fell to her lap.

"Don't worry, Judy. Calvin just has a cold," John said as he half carried Calvin to his bed.

"That's right, Judy," Calvin said, slurring.

Judy took off Calvin's shoes and busily pulled blankets over him.

"Go to sleep, Calvin," John said. "I don't want to see your face in the lab tomorrow, right? Don't worry about a thing."

Calvin propped himself up halfway but fell back onto his pillow.

John handed Judy some pills. "Make sure he drinks plenty of water. Take him to the gunboat first thing in the morning. The ship's doctor will take care of him."

"Judy," Calvin called feebly, "where-where's the money I asked you to keep?"

Judy dragged out a trunk from under the bed, unlocked it, and pulled out from its lining a large envelope with a red numeral on the cover. A camphor odor spread in the room.

"What's this for?" John asked.

"The evacuation of our team," Calvin grunted. "Three thousand yuan. Tell our workers to have their families ready to board the steamship the morning after tomorrow."

"Alright. Judy, you need me around?"

"No. Go home and sleep."

"Can't do that yet. I've got to make another house call."

* * *

Mr. Fan's house was dark. John grabbed the bronze ring and knocked at the gate. The dull echo reverberated in the cold night air. Silence. John knocked again, harder. He heard some faint voices rising in the house. One of the windows lighted up. After a long wait, he heard light footsteps. The door in front of him creaked open.

A young girl held up an oil lamp. Mr. Fan was in his pajamas behind her.

"Please come in, Mr. Win," Fan said gravely. "I've been waiting for you until minutes ago. Sorry I gave up and went to bed. Please forgive my appearance."

"Where is Zheng Ma?" John inquired about the middle-aged servant who had opened the gate for him every time he came to visit.

"In the hospital. She had a heart attack the other day."

"I'm very sorry to hear that. Please give her my best wishes for her recovery."

John followed Fan to the house, the girl lifting up the oil lamp for them to see their way.

In the living room, John was given a chair. The girl fussed with the candle on a side table and left.

"Mr. Win, please excuse the lighting in the house." Fan sighed and lowered himself to a chair across the table from John. "The electricity in this part of town has been out all day. I'm afraid the power plant by the river has been unable to recover from the pounding the Japanese bombers dealt it this morning."

"I know. Many areas in Nanjing are dark right now."

"The Japanese have sacked Suzhou, Mr. Win, halfway to Nanjing from Shanghai. They're marching toward us as we speak. I am surprised you're still in the city."

"I'll leave as soon as I get a few things done."

"Let me tell you something, Mr. Win. Zheng Ma's family lived in a village fifty miles away. A few days ago the Japanese soldiers passed through. Words fail me to describe what happened there." Mr. Fan paused, his eyes dark.

"Try anyway, Mr. Fan."

"Someone told the villagers that they had nothing to fear, that when the Japanese soldiers arrived, they should all come out of their houses to greet them, and that the Japanese would treat them well. So the villagers made little white flags with large characters: WE WELCOME THE GREAT JAPANESE IMPERIAL ARMY!"

"That sounds too weak to me," John said.

"Hard to blame them. Who doesn't want to live?"

"You are right. Please go on."

"A villager sighted a platoon of Japanese soldiers approaching and shouted for everybody to come out. They stood at the sides of the village's thoroughfare holding the flags with their heads bowed. The soldiers passed through the village peacefully."

"Really?"

"Soon another platoon arrived," Fan said. "The villagers came out again with their welcome flags. A bearded Japanese officer riding on a horse ordered them to line up in the open field where the peasants thrashed their rice stalks during harvest. The soldiers picked out from the crowd all the young men, tied them together with ropes, and led them away like pulling a long string of beads."

"Did the Japanese conscript them as coolies?"

"That was what the villagers thought. A fellow, daring devil that he was, followed the soldiers at a distance.The Japanese stopped at a forest, disconnected four prisoners from the ropes, and tied them to several trees. With bloodcurdling screams the Japanese rushed the prisoners with their bayonets. It turns my stomach to tell you, but the hapless men twisted on the tree trunks groaning : "Ma ya! Ma ya ! Tong si wo le!" (Mamma mia! Mamma mia! This pain is killing me!)

"No!" John stood up from his chair.

"The soldiers took their time putting the young villagers to death, and the groans faded into whimpers. When the bodies finally slumped, the soldiers dragged them away and did the same to four others."

"Impossible!" John shouted angrily. "This makes no sense! What purpose did it serve?"

"One theory is that the Japanese were eliminating future soldiers. But I think the true reason is more basic than that. The Japanese regard their race as superior to the Chinese. They think they can do whatever they please with people as cheap as vermin."

"Please forgive my asking, Mr. Fan, but how do you know those terrible things really happened?"

"One of Zheng Ma's cousins escaped to Nanjing a few days ago. I heard it from him."

John fell back on his chair.

"But there's more," Mr. Fan continued. "Another platoon of Japanese soldiers went to the village looking for *hua-gu-niang*, the derogatory words for the females toward whom they have less than honorable intentions. Each of the 'flower young girls' was stripped bare and tied face up on a *tia-odeng*—a narrow bench—with her legs spread apart. Then ten or more soldiers took their turns on her."

"Mr. Fan!!! Please pardon me, but I must ask again. Is this story from a reliable source?"

"It's from a woman whose daughter was raped."

"Perhaps atrocities in wartime can take place in a village where nobody looks," John murmured to himself, little beads of sweat gathering on his eyebrows. "But they are unlikely to happen in Nanjing."

"Why not?" Fan asked.

"Haven't you heard?" John said. "General Matsui, Commander in Chief of the Japanese army in Central China, has issued a military decree, ordering his troops to exercise the strictest discipline and control their excitement over the capture of the Chinese capital. Anyone who disgraces the Japanese Emperor by looting or setting fires, even inadvertently, will be severely punished."

"Do you believe such an order will be obeyed?"

"The last thing the Japanese government wants is for the international community to witness atrocities committed by their soldiers. There may be a few rogue recruits, but an entire army can't go against General Matsui."

"I fear you will be disappointed," Fan said.

The young girl reappeared with a tray. John took the teacup brought to him. He immediately laid it down on the side table, his shaking fingers unable to hold it steady.

Fan continued: "Unfortunate as the situation is, Mr. Win, I thank you for coming. This could be incredible luck for me."

"When are you leaving, Mr. Fan?"

"As soon as I can," Fan said. "But I owe people money. I can't leave without settling my debts."

John began to see where the conversation was going. He didn't like it.

"Few have money to lend. Everybody needs cash," Fan mumbled before coming straight to the point. "I believe you can help me, Mr. Win, if you'll be so kind."

John could sense his host's anxiety under a layer of measured composure.

"What can I do for you, Mr. Fan?"

"I've a proposal I hope you will kindly consider," Fan said.

"Yes?"

"Do you remember the falangcai I once showed you?"

"How can I forget? It's the most beautiful object I've ever held in my hands."

"I hope you will consider acquiring it."

"Me? Are you serious?" John was stunned.

"Yes, Professor Win. You are the only person I know who can."

"Why . . . I never thought you would ever consider parting with a treasure like that."

"People will suffer—even die—if I don't. The choice is obvious, don't you agree?"

John paused for a long time. "Mr. Fan," he said. "People probably think all Americans are rich. But your falangcai is beyond a teacher's means."

Mr. Fan frowned.

"I have some savings," John continued. "But the money does not compare with the value of your dish."

"Which is?"

"Four thousand dollars."

"Professor Win, I am offering my dish to you for four thousand yuan."

"*Yuan*, Mr. Fan?" John sat up.

"Yes, Professor Win."

"Why, that's less than one thousand dollars at today's exchange rate!" John exclaimed.

"Right."

"That's much too low!" John shook his head. "I'm afraid I can't accept it."

"Why?"

"I would be taking advantage of you."

"Quite the contrary, Mr. Win. My mother is anxious to leave the city. You would be helping me."

"The price is outrageous—for lack of a better word!"

"Mr. Win, we have a saying: 'Acquire antiques in peacetime; acquire gold in wartime.' Antiques are worthless when you are running for your life."

John thought. "All right, here is my counteroffer: eight thousand yuan."

"Refuse!"

"Please let me finish, Mr. Fan," Winthrop said, holding up his right hand. "I wish I could offer you more money. But this is all I can spare."

"I see you've learned to drive a hard bargain," Mr. Fan smiled. "But I don't *sell* an antique to a friend. I let him *acquire* it. It is an exchange—not a sale. The money I'm asking is not the price in the commercial market. I need four thousand yuan. I will take no less—and no more."

Fan brought out the antique blue satin box from one of his drawers and opened it. The enamel on the dish glittered in the dim candlelight.

"Pay me any time, Mr. Win, but the sooner the better. My creditors are anxious. Indeed, I think all of them are listening to this conversation behind that door right now."

"I can pay you this very minute, Mr. Fan. By a fortuitous circumstance, I'm carrying all of my money with me."

"That would be wonderful!"

John took out a thick roll of bills from the inner pocket of his jacket and peeled away about half of it. "You are helping me in another way, Mr. Fan." He handed the money over with a smile. "Now I'm less worried about being robbed."

"Congratulations, Mr. Win! Please take very good care of the dish."

"Thank you very much, Mr. Fan," John said, taking over the blue satin box. He closed it and put it into his backpack. "I must say what's happened seems unreal. It will take me some time for it to sink in!"

"I'm happy that the dish finds an appreciative owner," Mr. Fan said. "One more thing, Mr. Win, could you kindly tell me what you are going to do with it?"

"First, I'll find a safe place for it." John laughed. "Then I'll go to see it every morning and smile at it. I'll probably keep doing that for about a month."

"Please excuse me again, Mr. Win, but would you ever consider selling it?"

"I'll tell you the truth. I'd like to buy a house for myself and hopefully another one for my mother. Selling this dish is the only means I have to realize it."

Fan was silent for a long time. "Mr. Win, one day China will be prosperous again," he finally said. "When it happens, this dish will get you ten times—even one hundred times your investment. I suggest you hold on to it for as long as you can!"

John was surprised at Mr. Fan's optimistic prognosis of his country. "I will," he said and put on his backpack. "Goodbye, Mr. Fan, it has been a great pleasure."

"Wait, Mr. Win. When you want to sell the dish, would you kindly let me know?"

"Of course. But where can I find you?"

Fan scribbled something on a slip of paper.

"Is this the address of your farmhouse?" John took a look at the slip handed him before heading for the door.

"No. I just received a letter from a friend with whom I had lost contact for years." Fan walked his visitor to the front gate. "She suggested that I join her several hundred miles out west."

John stopped at the gate. "Mr. Fan, if I may ask, what happened to those women who had been raped?"

"None of them could walk afterward," Fan sighed. "Some died. Others killed themselves in shame—or anger—or both."

John felt as if he had been punched in the gut. The little noise he made sounded like air leaking out of a tire.

"Soldiers are killed in a war and we have a tough time dealing with it," Fan said. "Women and children die too, and it is even more difficult to accept. But what puts bitter hatred in our hearts is the humiliation the Japanese put us through, leaving us with not a shred of dignity. That's what we'll never forget. We'll keep fighting as long as there are three houses left standing in China."

"I see," John said. "Last question, Mr. Fan, may I ask what has remained of Zheng Ma's village?"

"It's completely empty now. Everybody ran to the mountains."

"Zheng Ma's daughter must have given birth to a baby just before then. Did she run too?" John asked.

A look of pain crossed Fan's face.

"I'm sorry," John said. "Did I say something wrong?"

"Well . . . the villagers didn't want her to run with them."

"Why is that?"

"They feared the baby's crying would give away their hiding places."

"So the young woman had to run away alone?"

Mr. Fan did not answer for a long, long time. His voice cracked when he finally spoke. "No. Her companions helped her strangle the baby girl to death."

John began shaking.

"I know," Mr. Fan said. "It is the most goddamn, bloody, soul-ripping story I've ever heard, if you'll pardon the language."

When John found his tongue again, he could only murmur, "No wonder Zheng Ma collapsed. It must've happened when she heard the bad news."

Fan didn't answer.

"Goodbye, Mr. Fan. I wish you a safe journey," John said in a coarse voice.

"Thank you very much, Mr. Win. You take care of yourself too!" Mr. Fan said. "I can't emphasize enough how you must leave the city as soon as you possibly can."

"I'm afraid I'll not be leaving the city at all."

"How's that?"

"I just made up my mind to stay and help out with the Nanjing Safety Zone Committee," John said. "I cannot abandon the people whose leader has treated me so royally."

Chapter 22

The Panay Incident

On the morning of December 6, 1937, the Generalissimo and his wife paid a visit to the Sun Yat-sen Mausoleum on Bell Mountain. After climbing the numerous wide stone stairs without handrails, the First Couple and their entourage reached the main hall of the mausoleum. Military cap in hand, snow blowing in his face, the Generalissimo bowed three times to the huge stone statue of his mentor. Then the leader of China stood pensive for several minutes, his back erect and his eyes misty. When it was time to go, the Generalissimo walked away slowly, turning around several times.

"Premier Sun, Reverend Teacher, I'll be back!"

That evening, the Generalissimo, in his splendid green-yellow cape, gave his final instructions to General Tang and other defending generals. All were heartened to see the supreme commander in the city when Japanese cannons were heard in General Tang's living room.

The next morning, the First Couple left for Hankou.

Two days later, on December 9, the Japanese army arrived at the foot of Nanjing's city wall. Their artilleries shelled the city heavily, and their airplanes blanketed it with flyers demanding surrender no later than noon the next day.

"*Muddled eggs!*" General Tang swore. He ordered all ships be moved from the harbor, making it difficult for any of his soldiers to flee.

* * *

That evening, John Rabe, German businessman and chairman of the Nanjing International Security Zone, proposed a ceasefire to preserve the historic city: the Chinese soldiers would evacuate Nanjing within three days, during which time the Japanese soldiers would stop shooting.

Two committee members, Dr. Bates and Reverend Mills, carried the proposal to the Japanese military. Rabe, John, and others sought an audience with General Tang.

The general told his visitors that a ceasefire was a decision for the Generalissimo to make. Subsequently, Rabe wired the American Embassy at Hankou for them to deliver his proposal to Chiang Kai-shek.

The Supreme Chinese Commander rejected it.

On December 10, Japanese soldiers resumed their attack, penetrating Zhonghuamen, a southern city gate. The Chinese soldiers counterattacked, storming the gate with grenades and bayonets. They recaptured and re-lost this key entry several times. Hundreds of Chinese bodies were left on the ground during each retreat.

Every hour General Tang sent the Generalissimo up-to-date bulletins on the grave military situations: All front lines were under heavy pressure. The defenders fought stubbornly, but they were devastated by the superior Japanese air forces.

On the following day, December 11, a long-distance phone call to General Tang exploded like a bombshell. "This is the Generalissimo's order," General Gu in Hankou declared. "You must execute an immediate evacuation from Nanjing."

"What? After all we have been through?" General Tang cried. "Didn't he say fight to the last man?

"Get all of your soldiers out of Nanjing right now!"

"But most of our communication lines have been disrupted. An immediate retreat will spell disaster for every one of my soldiers," General Tang said.

"The Generalissimo's order is for your troops to cross the river tonight," General Gu repeated.

"Tell the Generalissimo that's impossible!" General Tang shouted and slammed down the phone.

Minutes later, General Tang received two telegrams from Chiang Kai-shek ordering him to withdraw from Nanjing immediately: "You must preserve your forces for a future counterattack. You will be court-martialed if you disobey my order."

At three o'clock the next morning, General Tang, angry and dispirited, met with his staff officers to prepare for the evacuation.

At one o'clock that afternoon, the generals of the defending army received their marching orders.

* * *

In the meantime, twenty-eight miles upstream of Nanjing, the USS *Panay* was bobbing peacefully in the yellow waves of the Yangtze River.

If not for the two cannons and the eight 50-caliber Lewis machine guns pointing outward from its sides, the gunboat was a dead ringer for a Mississippi riverboat. Two huge American flags were glued to the roof. On the deck, a six-by-eleven foot American flag flapped mightily in the wind. Anchored across the river were three Standard Oil tankers with strange Chinese names—Mei Ping, Mei An, and Mei Hsia—which the gunboat had the duty to protect.

Holding her bulging belly, Judy Ren stepped out of a lower cabin of the *Panay* and climbed awkwardly to the upper deck.

A handsome young sailor stood by the railing near the bow shielding his eyes from the bright sunlight.

"Good afternoon, Mrs. Ren," Fon Houseman said. "How's the professor doing?"

"He finally dozed off, Fon. Thank God! It gives me the chance to come out and ask the cook if he could make some porridge for my husband tonight."

"Ask him! Yuan is wonderful," the sailor said. "You can order anything from ham and eggs to Shanghai noodles, and he'll make it for you."

"Good to know."

"You look a bit worn out, Mrs. Ren. You'd better order a good meal for yourself too."

"Thanks, Fon, I appreciate that. But I don't have much of an appetite."

"Same here. Didn't sleep well last night. Never thought the Japanese would unload their whole artillery on us."

"Artillery is not the only problem, Fon. Machine-gun bullets were hitting the hull right outside my cabin!"

"It was scary," Fon admitted. "I think Captain Hughes made the right move. No need to get into a shooting war with those lunatics."

"You don't get out of trouble by running away from it, Fon," Judy said. "Where is the self-respect of the US Navy?"

"That's true, Mrs. Ren. Indeed, we almost got into a fight this morning with another bunch of Japanese soldiers. What gall to shout for us to stop and let them board the boat!" The sailor shook his head.

"I was shocked that we let them do it," Judy said.

Gregory Evans, the cultural attaché of the American Embassy, walked over with his scent of cologne, his slightly graying hair going well with his blue jacket and snow-white pants.

Judy said, "Good afternoon, Mr. Evans. Fon and I have been talking. Yesterday the Japanese shelled us. We have the holes in the hull to prove it. Will our government ask the Japanese for compensation?"

"I doubt it, Judy," Greg replied. "We are trying very hard to look the other way. No one wants to confront the bull in the china shop."

"I wonder if someone should," Fon said. "Did you see how their aircraft sprayed machine gun bullets over the fleeing refugees? I couldn't believe my eyes!"

"I know, I know." Greg sighed. "They treat the Chinese worse than they do cattle!"

"Greg, you said no Japanese soldiers would board the gunboat," Judy said.

"Sorry, Judy. It's a good thing that the captain rejected their demand to search the boat."

"I don't mind to tell you: I was shaking in my shoes when they argued and screamed," Judy said. "The Japanese would have taken Calvin away if they'd found him."

"They have no right to do that," Greg said.

"Neither did they have the right to demand information on Chinese military installations." Judy raised her voice: "But they did!"

"Captain Hughes made it clear to them that the United States is friendly to Japan and China alike," Greg said. "We provide military information to neither side."

Fon stretched his limbs and yawned. "See you later, Mr. Evans and Mrs. Ren. I must get some shut-eye before my shift." He disappeared to the lower deck.

"Have you had lunch, Greg?" Judy asked.

"Yes. The chicken was excellent. Those cameramen from Universal Newsreel are napping happily in their lounge chairs right now." Greg chortled. "Where have you been all morning, Judy?"

"I was with Calvin."

"How's he doing?"

"His breathing is labored. Dr. Grazier said we must check him into a hospital, preferably one in Shanghai." Dr. Grazier was the ship's doctor.

"We can arrange that. There is a British vessel going to Shanghai today. We can radio her for help."

"Thanks. But Calvin doesn't want to go to any place occupied by the Japanese."

"The French Concession in Shanghai isn't."

"Dr. Grazier said that too. But Calvin still refused," Judy said, fighting tears.

A trim officer wearing a military cap with a crisp fold walked over.

"Good afternoon," Judy and Evans hailed simultaneously.

Judy asked, "Tex, the Japanese attacked us yesterday. Why didn't we fire back?"

"Washington instructed us not to overreact, Mrs. Ren," Arthur Anderson, the *Panay*'s executive officer from Texas, replied. He removed his military cap, revealing his hair combed flat and parted in the middle. "Hate to tell you, but our machine guns are from the Great War. I'm not sure they could've stood up to the Japanese artillery if things got nasty."

A drone was heard from what seemed like a great distance in the eastern sky. It sounded like the buzz of giant mosquitoes.

Greg looked up. "What's that?"

Judy put a palm over her eyes searching for the source of the annoying hum. "An airplane. No—three! Where're they going?"

Arthur squinted. "They are Japanese heavy bombers all right, probably on their way to attack the Chinese installations. Excuse me, Madam." He put on his cap and shouted: "Man the guns! Man the guns!"

Sailors poured onto the deck, one man without his pants.

"Nothing to worry about," Greg told Judy. "Whenever there are warplanes in the vicinity, we must make sure that our guns are ready."

The droning grew louder.

"Hey!" Judy cried. "They are coming straight at us!"

The sound of the bombers overhead became deafening.

A bomb broke free from a plane and missed the ship by only a few feet. The explosion in the water rocked the boat, throwing Judy and Greg to the deck.

Glass shattered. Arthur staggered and fell.

"What the devil!" Greg exclaimed, his once carefully coiffed hair now a mess.

"They are bombing us! Why are the Japanese doing this?" Judy sobbed, her nose bleeding.

Greg dragged Judy by her arm and ran toward the anteroom.

Another boom!

"Lie down! Lie down! Flat on the deck," Greg yelled.

Both were hanging onto the railing as the second bomb struck. A huge column of water shot up close to the bow. The *Panay*'s nose rose out of the river. Water gushed down on them.

"Shit," Greg said.

A sailor holding on to a door latch said: "Hundred pounders, two of them. Dropped by a Yokosuka. Damn!"

Da Da Da—Da Da Da Da Da Da.

"Oh my Lord! I'm hit!" a voice wailed.

"Gary, help that man," came another voice.

"Yes, sir."

"Get into the anteroom, all of you!" another voice shouted.

Running feet.

Da Da—Da Da Da Da Da Da . . . Sa Sa Sa Sa.

Shrapnel hit the decks and the walls. The sky seemed to be hurling storms of fire.

"My leg! My leg!" another voice moaned.

"Judy, where do you think you're going?" Greg cried and grabbed the hand of the little woman. "You stay right here!"

"Let go of my hand! LET ME GO!" Judy shrieked.

"Ouch!" Greg yelled as Judy bit his fingers.

Judy ran down the left side of the deck. Splintering sounds followed her trail. Small holes opened up around her feet. Wood fragments zoomed around her ankles. She dashed down the staircase to the lower deck. As if by a miracle she outraced the bullets.

Calvin opened his eyes as Judy burst into the cabin. "What's going on?"

"Japanese bombers," Judy said, breathless, cradling her abdomen with both hands.

"Impossible," Calvin coughed. "This is a US ship."

They heard another thunderous explosion. The walls shook violently. Judy threw herself over her husband.

"No, Judy!" Calvin struggled. "For heaven's sake, let me cover you!"

"No!"

"I've got to protect our child!" Calvin started to cough again.

"No!"

"She is the daughter we always wanted!" Calvin said.

"No!"

"She will be as pretty as you are!"

Judy stopped wrestling. "What was that, Calvin? You never told me I was pretty."

"But I always think you are."

Tears welling in her eyes, Judy bent down murmuring, "Now he tells me."

"Stop this nonsense and do as I say," Calvin said.

"No!" Judy wrapped her arms around Calvin's head again. "You are more important than we two girls put together."

Bullets rained on the outside wall. Another explosion shook the keel from bow to stern. The boat tilted slowly to one side, then righted itself to the other. Judy and Calvin rolled and fell off the bed.

Chapter 23

The Refugees

At this time, inside the city, May Chen and her family were walking toward Jinling Women's College.

It had been relatively warm earlier in the afternoon, but snowflakes began to fall when May followed Baba into Neiqiao. She had a cloth sack tied to her shoulders and a handful of silver coins inside her waist pocket. Her four younger brothers, loaded with clothes and groceries, puffed behind her. Ma shuffled along, Wumao riding on her back.

The baby girl was clutching the cotton doll John Winthrop had given her. "We go live in another place," Wumao told the doll. "Don't worry. We go home soon!"

Panicked refugees, coats covered with snow powder, joined and trudged with May and her family.

The sky was a gloomy gray when a squadron of Chinese soldiers stopped them at a downtown intersection. A heated exchange broke out.

Ma tried to lower Wumao from her shoulder. But the baby girl clung to Ma's neck complaining that her doll was cold. Ma fastened a coat around Wumao's shoulders.

Baba went to the front and joined the argument. "Would you kindly let me and my six children pass, boss?" he begged the commander. "We are on our way to the International

Safety Zone, not to bother anybody. If we get through this alive, we'll burn incense to the gods and wish you the life of a hundred years."

"You've your problem, and I've mine," the captain said, pointing to a poster on the wall. "See? Nobody goes through this checkpoint after four. It's a military order!"

Wumao started to cry, saying her doll was hungry. Ma unbuttoned her jacket and stuffed a nipple into Wumao's mouth.

The refugees behind Baba began clamoring. The captain drew his pistol. The noises grew even louder. The captain fired a shot into the air. The crowd shrieked and retreated to an alley.

A middle-aged man came out of a door. He calmed everyone down by saying that the captain had been telling the truth: "Not even a dog can get through the Winter Plum Alley checkpoint at this hour. The curfew will be lifted at sunrise. Why don't you people find a place on the street to rest for the night?"

Some of the refugees began to clean out the snow over the tree roots. Others just dropped on the ground, exhausted.

* * *

Inside the *Panay* on the Yangtze River, Judy lay on the floor massaging her belly. "Calvin, I'm scared. Let's go join the people in the anteroom."

"I—I can't move." Her husband opened his eyes.

"Let me help you."

She got off the floor and tried to lift her husband up from the ground. After a few tries, hot fluid rushed up her throat and she vomited into a corner.

"Judy!"

"Don't worry, Calvin. It's just my morning sickness," she lied.

"You've got to get out of here, Judy," Calvin said.

"I'm not leaving without you!"

"Don't worry about me. Find some place safe for you and the baby. She is due soon."

"No!"

"There's still time," Calvin said, his eyes suddenly shining like torches. "Once you get on the shore, you can do a few things for me."

Alarmed by the urgent tone in Calvin's voice, Judy straightened up. "What do you want me to do, Calvin?"

"Listen . . ." Calvin said, before being caught by another coughing spell. "Listen, I regard John as my best friend, but I've never told him that—we fought a lot. Go find John and tell him how sorry I am to have made him stay in Nanjing."

"Don't talk like that, Calvin!" Judy sobbed.

"Then find my team and apologize to them for the flaws in my design."

"You have done all you could, Calvin."

"Let them know that John will leave us soon, and that they mustn't be upset with him. My fault. We should've built the airplane on our own, not depending on others to do the job for us. My team must finish the project without John—or me!" Calvin closed his eyes as he finished, his face the color of death.

"Stop talking like that! You'll be all right, darling." Judy wept.

"There is one more thing." Calvin opened his eyes again. "It's very, very important, so don't interrupt me. Promise?"

Judy nodded.

"Judy, I've always thought you were the best wife in the world—please don't cry. I wanted to ask you. I thought of asking you many times, but never found the right moment. So I am asking you now."

"I'm listening."

"Judy, will you marry me in your *next* life?"

Judy started to laugh and cry at the same time, sobbing "yes, yes, yes," and "no, no, no." Finally, she wiped her face with her hand. "Now you listen to me, Calvin," she said. "I cannot leave you, period! No *if*, no *but*, no *unless*, no *until*. This is it. QED. So you just have to get out with me—because I'm not leaving you behind."

Another explosion swayed the boat. A loud, long grating sound came from the keel.

"Mercy, Mother of God!" Judy wailed.

An ear-splitting horn overpowered all the other noises.

"What . . . what's that?" Judy asked. Hearing no sound from Calvin, she answered the question herself. "They're abandoning ship, Calvin. We've got to get out of this cabin!"

Her husband opened his eyes and moved his lips many times. Only one word came out: "Go!"

Judy took a deep breath and tried to pull her husband up one more time. She succeeded in getting him on his feet. They staggered a few steps. Then she stumbled and both of them fell to the floor, Judy on her belly.

* * *

Over in the Chinese military headquarters in downtown Nanjing, General Tang was holding the final briefing for his generals. The air in the room seemed to freeze when he announced that the evacuation would start at six o'clock in the evening—an hour from then. The 36th division and the military police would evacuate via the Xiaguan harbor.

"The rest of you must break *outward* from your present positions," General Tang said gravely. "You will penetrate through the Japanese encirclement and regroup in southern Anhui. Good luck to all of you!"

Stone silence.

A white-haired general finally protested: "You are ordering us to walk through a tunnel of deadly fire!"

A burly general shouted: "I request that you assign four more divisions to the pier!"

General Tang tried to control the uproar, but he couldn't. Chaos erupted as the generals in the room started to argue with one another.

"Give us your orders, General Tang," a voice boomed above the din.

"All right!" Genera Tang capitulated. "The 74th corps, the 87th division, the 88th division, and the military training corps will also go to the harbor!"

This was more than doubling the number of soldiers assigned to the waterway.

The generals filed out of the conference room silently.

* * *

Judy was struggling on the floor when footsteps approached. Judy lifted her face and looked up. She saw the silhouette of a sailor in the door of her cabin, blood staining his right shoulder.

"Fon! What's happened to you?" Judy cried.

"Just some damned shrapnel," Fon Houseman said. "I'm OK. You need help?"

"Yes! Please carry Calvin out of here."

The young sailor came over to help Judy get up before putting Calvin on his back. "Can you walk, Mrs. Ren?"

"Yes. Just take care of Calvin."

Water rushed into the cabin.

"Is the boat sinking?" Judy stopped at the foot of the staircase, alarmed.

"I'm afraid so."

"What are we going to do?"

"Officer Anderson has given the order to abandon ship."

"Isn't he hurt?"

"Yes. He was hit in the throat with shrapnel. He can't talk, and had to write his orders dipping his fingers in his blood."

Judy followed Fon to the upper deck, water lapping around her ankles.

"The pumps are losing the battle with the leaks," Houseman said, putting Calvin down on a wooden crate.

Judy stooped to feel Calvin's forehead. It was burning. When she asked him how he was feeling, he answered with coughs. She looked around anxiously for Dr. Grazier.

On deck, some sailors threw wooden gratings overboard. Others lowered the twin-motor sampans to the water. Two sailors kicked gas cans out of their way carrying Captain Hughes's limp body to one of the sampans.

"What happened to the captain?" Judy whispered, seeing the captain's face covered with soot.

"Also hit by shrapnel," Fon said.

"Who is in command?"

"Officer Anders, but he is not in much better condition."

A loud voice from the main deck: "Listen, crew! Order from Officer Anderson: All wounded on the sampans, right now! Dick and Jim, you take the wheels! Get as close to the shore as possible! Everybody ashore. Then come back for the rest of us."

"Yes, sir!"

"There's a pregnant woman here," someone yelled. "Get her to a sampan."

Judy turned gratefully and saw Greg Evans a few steps away pointing a finger at her.

"Give my place to Calvin," Judy screamed. "He is very sick! I can swim! I can swim!"

"In your condition?" Greg scoffed. Then he yelled to the sailors below, "Take this man down too."

Two sailors carried Calvin to the bobbing boat. Another sailor helped Judy down the ladder.

Fon disappeared below deck.

The voice on the deck again: "Life jackets on! Now!"

One of the newsreel cameramen on the deck looked around frantically. When Fon reappeared on the deck, he took off his life jacket and gave it to the startled cameraman. The sailor leaped to a wooden grating on the water and paddled his way toward the shore. Judy screamed when he was swallowed up by swirling waves. Dick, the pilot of her sampan, gunned the boat and caught up with him. Several hands pulled the drenched sailor up and slapped him on the back until water gushed out of his mouth.

Nine airplanes with sun logos circled overhead dropping bombs on the Standard Oil tankers. Two of them burst into flames, a funnel of black smoke rising from each.

"They'd better douse the fire," an older sailor said. "Those tankers are filled to the brim with oil!"

Judy had other worries. As if to answer her worst fear, two airplanes turned around and went at her sampan. A bomb dropped to loud screams. To Judy's relief, the planes flew away after spraying a few more rounds of bullets at them.

"I could see the faces of the pilots in those airplanes," one of the sailors said, his voice shaking. "They should see we are not Chinese. They better not come back!"

"Don't fool yourself, mate," Fon said, wringing water out of his clothes. "They've known who we are all along. Couldn't have missed the Stars and Stripes."

"No way the Japanese are feeling friendly," an older sailor said. "They left because their ammunition ran out. They'll come back after loading up."

"Let's get the hell out of here, Dick!" another voice urged.

Having gunned the boat to maximum speed, Dick needed no reminder. "Why did you run back into your cabin like fire was burning your ass?" he asked Fon Houseman.

"I went to lock up my cabinet," Fon replied.

Dick laughed so hard he nearly lost control of the wheel. "Jerk! No one but a deep-water diver will be able to steal your dirty toothbrush."

Fon hit his forehead and joined the laughter.

When the sampan approached the river bank, the passengers got into the water and sloshed their way to shore. Two sailors carried Calvin between them. A third held Judy's arm. Once on land, everyone went to hide under the tall weeds in the marsh.

Judy saw the *Panay* sinking slowly. Two of the oil ships were burning. The Chinese crew on them leaped into the water and disappeared in the eddying currents. The third oil ship drifted with the flow, finally beaching at the riverbank five hundred yards downstream.

Judy gasped when a Japanese powerboat burst into the scene and strafed the *Panay* with machine gun fire. Japanese soldiers jumped into the gunboat and ran to the radio room. They ran back empty-handed. Moments later, the *Panay* capsized and completely submerged.

The Japanese powerboat turned around and headed straight toward the marsh. Judy's heart jumped to her throat when they sprayed the marsh with machine guns. She ducked lower into the weeds, and the bullets whipped over her head.

The airplanes came back several times circling over the bamboo grove. The survivors kept very still. The planes finally left.

* * *

The snow had thinned around downtown Nanjing. But as the night wore on, the air was growing colder. In the Winter Plum Alley, May sat with Ma and Wumao. The baby girl nagged Ma to go home. Soothed by the woman's gentle hands, she sang a lullaby to her doll in a tiny voice.

A round woman stepped out of a small house and distributed bowls and chopsticks to the refugees. Several young girls carried wooden buckets of porridge. After having some hot food, May felt better and dozed off.

* * *

Dr. Grazier, the *Panay*'s doctor, made his rounds in the bamboo grove. He recorded the casualties: forty-eight wounded, fourteen seriously. None dead so far.

Greg Evans, the cultural attaché, his white pants soiled and his hair awry, found Judy kneeling in the mud, both hands on her belly.

"What's wrong, Judy?"

"Calvin threw up. His breathing is getting heavier," Judy said.

"Did something happen?"

"One of the sailors carrying him slipped, taking him into the water. I tried to dry him as much as I could, but he has not stopped trembling."

"His temperature?"

"Dr. Grazier just took it: one hundred and three."

"You don't look too good yourself, Judy. You're shivering. What happened to your overcoat?"

"I'm covering Calvin with it. The blanket they gave him isn't enough."

"Take mine, Judy."

"I don't know if I should. You need it too," Judy said as she wrapped the coat around her. "You are a prince, Greg!"

Dr. Grazier arrived at the scene. "Professor Ren needs a hospital."

"Captain Hughes has awakened and has already ordered the formation of a search party," Greg said. "I hope they find one."

"A local hospital will be helpful to most of the wounded men. But it won't do Professor Ren much good."

"Why?" Greg asked.

"Professor Ren needs a real hospital in Shanghai—not merely one for wound care."

"Calvin can't go to Shanghai." Judy's voice interrupted the exchange between the two men.

Startled by the finality in her tone, the men turned to look at the woman with pale lips and strands of hair on her face.

"Judy, let me explain," the white-haired doctor said in a fatherly voice. "I know Professor Ren doesn't want to go to any place occupied by the Japanese. I understand his reason perfectly. But this is no time to stand on principles. Your primary concern should be saving Professor Ren's life."

"It is. That's why the answer is *no*. Only this morning . . . didn't you say something about sending Calvin to a local hospital?"

"Your husband's condition has taken a turn for the worse. We need to send him to the best hospital in China—which is in Shanghai's French Concession."

"No! End of discussion."

"Judy, I can't emphasize enough how a local hospital is unlikely to have the specialists and the facilities Professor Ren's state of health requires," Dr. Grazier said.

"You don't understand." Judy's tears began to flow.

Spreading his hands in exasperation, Greg asked: "Enlighten us, Judy!"

"If Calvin goes to the French Concession, the Japanese will come and take him away. The French can't do anything about it. The Japanese have the guns."

"Why would they go to such lengths to arrest Professor Ren?" Grazier asked.

"They want his classified research." Judy shuddered. "Once they get him, they will force him to talk."

Greg and Dr. Grazier looked at each other.

"Calvin will not tell them anything." Judy raised her head proudly. "But that won't stop them. They may cure him, but they will turn around and torture him. He will die in their hands."

The Americans fell silent.

Greg made a motion with his chin, and Dr. Grazier followed him to another bamboo tree.

"Is Professor Ren's condition serious?" Greg asked.

"Yes!"

"What's his problem?"

"I looked at his spit. 'He's bleeding from the lungs. He needs a blood transfusion—should have had one hours ago. Then he'll need surgery. This is not something I can do."

"We may have to shoot him," Greg said. "We can't leave him to the Japanese."

"Don't tell me about your sordid business," Dr. Grazier said. "Mine is to save lives."

"All right!"

"If we can't send Professor Ren to Shanghai, his best chances are with a hospital in Hankou," Dr. Grazier said.

"Our radios went down with the *Panay*. We have no means to arrange transportation," Greg said. "I hope something will turn up soon."

"Speaking of the radio," Dr. Grazier said, "it looks to me that the United States has gone to war with Japan. But why didn't our Shanghai navy headquarters radio us?"

"My thoughts exactly!" Greg sighed.

"Japanese soldiers could be in the area, looking for Professor Ren as we speak," Dr. Grazier looked grim.

"If they find us with him, they may shoot us too."

They fell into another silence.

* * *

On a city road to the Nanjing harbor, Sun Chi—the officer who had grown up with Black Cat—was running. His soldiers followed him fully armed. They must reach the harbor before the Japanese caught up with them—or die. The sweaty men shoved and knocked over one another. Some tripped. Their trampled bodies produced logjams, making it more difficult to get through the city gate. Some soldiers went to the top of the wall and climbed down on the outside. They slipped and yelled all the way to their deaths.

Those who got through the gate couldn't find the boats to carry them across the river. Panicked, they took off their uniforms, threw away their guns, and ran back to the city.

Sun Chi tried to stop them—then ran himself. He was lucky. Unlike so many others, he had a home in Nanjing.

* * *

General Tang boarded a steamboat at the Navy harbor. It had been procured by a staff member violating his direct orders. General Tang withheld departure for an hour, waiting for two staff members who never showed up.

As his steamboat slowly pulled away from the shore, Tang watched fires rising to the sky from all quarters of his city.

"Generalissimo!" he murmured. "Why did you change your mind?"

Chapter 24

The Japanese Enter the City

Early the next morning, May felt a chill infiltrating her thin covers. Drawing her cotton jacket around her, she slowly realized that she was sleeping in open air. Ma was snoring on the snowy ground under a tree, Wumao on her ample bosom. Baba and the boys stretched out under another tree. Lying farther down the pavement was a sea of bodies in dark, puffy coats.

May yawned, aching from the little pebbles under her.

The quietness of the morning was suddenly broken by the high-pitched hissing of a cannonball. It landed behind a wall, and a fierce explosion shook the earth. People on the ground leaped up and screamed. Ma put Wumao on her back. May dragged Ma and ran for the bomb shelter near the end of the alley.

As soon as May entered the pitch-dark cave, she smelled a revolting stench. "Cow dung!" she thought in disgust and held her breath. She probed deeper into the cave one step at a time, and was relieved to find no sinking pulp under her feet. The smell must've come from a mixture of wet soil and rotten grass, not cow dung.

As soon as she could establish a foothold, May looked for Baba. She found him standing in the brightness of the cave entry. "Get in, Baba!" she yelled angrily. Baba waved without turning his head, busy helping his other children to get inside.

Cannonballs continued to rain. The shelter shook with every explosion. A voice said: "The cave was constructed with wood and soil. It will collapse if it is directly hit by a bomb."

May was terrified at the thought of being buried alive.

"The sounds come from the south," Baba said. The voice was close-by, but she couldn't see where Baba was in the darkness of the cave. "They must be attacking Zhonghuamen!"

Which was close to Baba's convenience store!

When the thunder eventually stopped, May thought the silence seemed like the lull before a storm. But after a long wait during which nothing happened, people grew impatient and slowly filed out of the shelter

"*A-mi-tuo-fo*," someone murmured the Buddha's name. "We are still alive!"

Having adjusted to the blackness of the cave, May could see that Baba was following the crowd. She did the same.

"The attack is over," Baba said. "Things are looking up. Let's get on our way to the Safety Zone."

May had been worrying about the sack she had left behind. As she started to run for it, frightened shrieks came to her. The earth vibrated with trampling feet.

Another shriek—much closer: "The Japanese are coming!!"

Dark brown faces poured in from the street corner. In shabby dun uniforms and flapping hats, rifles at eye level and daggers dangling, the Japanese soldiers looked like savages from the jungles.

May's teeth clattered. She was in a dead-end alley!

* * *

She looked around for Baba and found him behind her grabbing Damao with one hand. She reached for his other hand, feeling much better when his gold ring rubbed her palm.

The Japanese opened fire: *Bon! Bon! Bon!* White smoke rose. Bodies fell. The soldiers marched forward and stabbed people left and right. The refugees ran away. In their panic, some of them collided with the nearby walls. They looked like flies hitting a frosted window on a cold evening.

With a human wave sweeping over their family, May's hold on Baba's hand was broken.

"Baba!!!" she cried.

Some of the refugees fought the soldiers with their bare hands—Baba among them. May cheered when Baba's fists landed on a soldier's head. Then a clutch of soldiers swarmed over Baba. One drew a pistol and pointed it at his forehead. May covered her eyes and screamed. An explosion pierced her eardrums. It was like the firecrackers on New Year's Day—only louder. When she peeked tremblingly through her fingers, Baba's knees were buckling, his body slowly sinking to the ground.

"Baba!!!" May cried in despair.

Now she knew she had no one to protect her. Yet she couldn't stop thinking how much pain Baba must have suffered from the bullet.

A gang of soldiers holding bayonets marched toward her. People in front of her fled like water in a river breaking away from a boulder. She was standing alone, looking at soldiers uglier than the demons roaring out of the wall paintings in a Buddhist temple.

A hand went around her shoulders. She jumped, then realized it was only Ma with a baby girl lying on her back! She heaved out a breath of air from her lungs.

May's sense of relief didn't last, for she soon found that Ma was shaking worse than she.

A Japanese soldier wearing eyeglasses raised his rifle to stab May. Ma stepped out and grabbed the bayonet with one hand. She grimaced as blood dripped from her palm.

"Ma!" May cried.

The soldier twisted his bayonet and pulled back, taking Ma stumblingly toward him. Wrestling the bayonet away from Ma's grasp, the soldier thrust it into her abdomen. Ma made a dull groan and dropped to the ground. Wumao fell from Ma's back.

The soldier turned to the little girl who was kneeling in the slush hugging her cotton doll saying "*bu yao pa, bu yao pa*" (no fear, no fear), her soft hair flying in the wind. The eyes, one thousand questions in them, kept shifting between her mother on the ground and the grotesque man towering over her.

The flashing blade penetrated the little chest.

"Ma!" the baby girl wailed.

A kick sent her body flying. The doll fell to the ground. The baby girl's skull cracked on the cobblestones. "You bastard!" May screamed.

The soldier turned to stab May. She ducked. The bayonet went through the left sleeve of her cotton jacket. She fell. The Japanese soldier stabbed her stomach. The blade stuck. He pulled it out, went back to Ma, and stabbed the writhing body again and again.

Things happened even faster with May on the ground. Simao—Ma's ten-year-old son from her former husband—had never shown much emotion. With a deranged look he now grabbed the soldier's pants from behind and bit his leg. The soldier let out a howl. Ermao and Sanmao, May's two other younger brothers, hit the ground and bit the soldier's other leg. The Japanese hopped and yelled. But before May could rejoice, the soldier kicked all three boys to the dust. Then he put his bayonet through their hearts.

A human wave raged over, trampling May under their feet. Her view became dark, and it was hard to breath. She saw too late a boot coming at her head. Her mind went completely blank.

* * *

Yuan, the Chinese cook on the *Panay* who knew the local dialect, was able to find a hospital in a small town called Hexian a few miles from where the gunboat had been sunk. It was held by the Chinese army. The unheated building had stone walls and a dirt floor.

Two of the wounded had died. Judy had collapsed. The sailors made litters to carry her and her husband to the hospital. Dr. Grazier wasn't sure if he could save her baby.

Lying in a hospital bed being tended to by nurses, Captain James Hughes called the American embassy at Hankou.

"We are lucky! War has been averted!" The ambassador's delight burst through the phone.

"How?" Captain Hughes asked.

"The attack on the *Panay* was unintentional. Their pilots couldn't see the American flags in the fog."

Captain Hughes blew up: "*What* fog?"

"We've received many telegrams from Japanese civilians apologizing for the American deaths. What wonderful people!" the ambassador said.

The captain hung up.

Greg Evans arranged a British ship to carry the survivors to Shanghai. He also found a ship to take Calvin and Judy to Hankou.

* * *

May felt a hand rock her shoulder. A voice called: "*Jiejie, Jiejie*." The blackness in her head slowly receded.

Who would call her *elder sister*? She opened her eyes and saw fifteen-year-old Damao kneeling by her side. The pain in her left arm returned.

"Are you all right, Jiejie?"

May climbed to her feet, feeling woozy. "Go find Baba, quick!!!"

"I did."

"How is he?"

"Dead!" Damao said and trembled. "Those God-damned Japs killed him."

It couldn't be true! Baba couldn't have died. Not the Baba who had carried her on his shoulders to see the lantern festival. Not the Baba who had wept over giving her away. Not the Baba who had worried about boys touching her. No, Baba must be alive!

She felt empty, a dam in her chest blocking all of her emotions.

"That's all right, Damao. Don't cry!" she said.

"I'm not, Jiejie. *You* are crying!"

That was when May realized her tears had flooded her cheeks. The dam suddenly broke, and waves of emotions washed over her. A rage made her want to raise her head and howl at the top of her voice. Then she remembered what Baba had once told her: "Heimao, Baba cannot bear to see you cry." She must get ahold of herself.

"I won't cry, Baba," she said to him with all the love in her heart.

She felt Damao shaking her shoulder. "Don't faint on me, Jiejie! I am so scared. What are we going to do?"

May shook her brother's shoulders. "Damao, don't you give me that *dog shit* again!" she shouted. "We are *not* scared. An eye for an eye; a tooth for a tooth—that's what it will be! One day we will find those assholes and make them pay—ten times—for everything they did to us today. Don't you ever forget that!" Then her voice grew gentle. "How's Ma?"

"She gave me this and spat blood." Damao showed her a red satin purse with dark, wet spots.

"This must be the blood from Ma's hands. She grabbed a bayonet for me today," May murmured. She felt dizzy again and had trouble putting the purse into her waist pocket.

"How did you escape?" May asked.

"They shot the man in front of me. I played dead lying under him."

Damao took her to Baba. Something stuck to her shoes. It was the blood congealed on the pavement. She took care to step away from the sticky dark spots on her path.

Baba was lying on his back. The morning sun cast a gold film on his face, masking the red smudge on his forehead. May knelt to touch his hand. It was still warm. She lifted it and put it on her cheek. It felt so soft.

"You are only sleeping, Baba, looking so beautiful," she whispered. "I will sing a song for you."

She sang the lullaby Wumao had sung to her doll:

"Row, row, row to the bridge,
Row to the house where Nainai lives.
Nainai calls me a good little baby,
A box of fruit, a box of candy,
A box to go . . . to eat slowly . . ."

She couldn't continue.

"Baba, I swear to you . . . If it takes me to the end of the earth or the edge of the ocean, I'll avenge your death!"

She got up with Damao's help and went down on her knees again, touching her head on the ground to Baba three times. She got up and did it twice more, completing the most respectful rite of *three kneels and nine kowtows*.

She heard random footsteps from the boulevard outside the alley. Damao ran to the street corner and ran back. "We need to hide, Jiejie," he said breathlessly.

"Why?"

"People are running. They say Japanese soldiers are behind them. We've got to run too!"

"I want to say goodbye to Ma."

"There is no time!"

Damao dragged May to the back of the closest house. He broke a window pane, climbed inside, and opened the back door to let May in. Both went to hide under a bed covered by a large mosquito net.

Soon they heard heavy boots pounding the pavement.

The noises outside subsided. Damao wrestled away from his sister's hand and crawled out. He advanced on all fours to a window and rose above the windowsill. He quickly ducked down and crawled back to his sister.

"There is a Japanese soldier holding a flag with a scary red sun," he whispered.

"Where?" May whispered back.

"Right next to the window."

"What are the soldiers doing?"

"Stripping bodies. They are taking away necklaces, rings, and hair pins. Some are loading the dead bodies into a big truck."

"Did somebody see you?"

"A-a little soldier might have . . ." Damao stuttered.

"Why do you say that?"

"He turned and looked in my direction."

They heard noises from the front door. A splintering sound! Footsteps entered the front room and fanned out in different directions. The floor in their room creaked. Husky voices snarled. Drawers were opened and banged shut. Under the bed, May held Damao's trembling hand.

* * *

Pon! Pon! Pon! Half a city away, some Japanese soldiers were banging at the front door of a house, shaking the living room.

Sun Chi went to open his curtain a crack. Sun Chi's wife and children ran to hide under a table.

Sun Chi thought of getting his firearms: the grenades and the semi-automatic pistol buried in the backyard.

He didn't mind going down fighting—and taking a few of them with him. How many? One would make it even; two would give him a profit!

But the Japanese would shoot all of his family.

He threw a long cloth over the table concealing his wife and children, and opened the door with an ingratiating smile, hoping the soldiers would find nothing and leave.

The Japanese shoved him aside and poured in. Then they tied him up, brought him to an empty lot, and threw him in with many others.

Now it was too late to rebel. Even if he could break the ropes on his arms—an unlikely scenario—machine guns were pointing at him from all sides.

From where he stood, he could see the small mud house in which he had grown up.

* * *

He was eighteen when Qian Ying, the girl he had vowed to marry, was sold to a wine house. The young man took a train to Guangzhou, putting all his rage into passing the entrance exam for Huangpu Military Academy.

On that spring morning, the sky had been as blue as the water in Xuan-Wu Lake. His mother, her brown face expressionless, had prepared a sumptuous breakfast for him.

As he slurped down the noodles topped by two half-eggs dyed in red, she handed him a small red pouch.

"What's in it, Ma?" he asked, hoping it was money or jewelry.

"A little chunk of earth from under the stove," his mother said in a hoarse voice. "I dug it up last night."

"What did you do that for?" He was irritated. "No wonder you complained about your fingers."

"They'll be fine."

He loosened the strings and peered at the clump of soil that had been blackened by years of cooking.

"Make sure you don't lose it, hear? This is a piece of our land. It will bless you . . . keep you safe," his mother said. "I won't stop you. A man must leave his home one day. Just keep the pouch with you. Your father didn't. So a bullet found him."

She seemed to want to talk more, but the train waited for no one.

"I'll send the fare back, Ma." He went to pick up his sack.

His mother turned to wash a turnip in the water basin.

"As soon as I get my first living subsidy."

"What if you don't pass the entrance exam?" she asked with her back to him.

"That won't happen!"

His mother put the vegetable into a pot.

"Goodbye, Ma."

No answer.

She never hears me, he thought, irritated again. "Goodbye, Ma!" he shouted.

"All right, all right! Just go!" Her voice cracked.

He heard a stifled cry as he walked out, but the pain over losing Qian Ying to the wine house was louder than his mother's sorrow.

* * *

Ten years had elapsed. The sky today was as blue as it had been. But this was December—not April. The willows no longer bent at their waists, swaying with the gentle breeze. They were hanging their heads, surrendering to the harsh icy wind. Frozen snow crushed the wilted grass, and wild dogs sniffed the garbage on the ground. One bared its teeth at him.

Sun Chi spat, knowing these beasts were waiting to fill their empty stomachs with his meat.

Two sitting Japanese officers were talking beside a leaping fire. Their voices were out of Sun Chi's earshot. He only saw them slap hands, their faces glowing in the glare of the fire.

The officers beckoned the Chinese interpreter standing deferentially behind them. The little man listened with frequent nods before hurrying away.

Soon afterwards, five Chinese prisoners were brought to a pit at the far side of a grove. Since the leaves had mostly fallen, Sun Chi could see through the black branches capped by white snow. The prisoners were given spades and made to climb down the pit. Soil flew up and fell on the ground. A prisoner stopped to wipe his forehead, and a soldier hit him with a rifle butt. The prisoner resumed digging. When shoulders were sinking below the surface of the ground, the soldiers barked for the prisoners to hand the spades back.

Another Japanese soldier wheeled a machine gun over and started to adjust its muzzle. The prisoners saw the gun and struggled to climb out of the pit. They were beaten back by rifle butts. Then the barrel of the machine gun shook, raining bullets. Arms and legs flapped inside the pit. Soil particles shot up like a fountain mist and settled on the ground. Silence.

Another group of five prisoners was taken to the pit and made to kneel on its edge. An officer at the fire leisurely sauntered over with a long katana in his hand. He stopped behind the first prisoner and lightly touched the man's neck with the saber. The officer then nodded to the Chinese translator, who nodded back and glanced at his watch. The officer raised his katana and swung. The prisoner's head flew. A jet of blood squirted out from where there had been a face. A headless body fell into the pit.

The officer then executed the rest of the prisoners in the same ghastly manner. It was over in a few minutes. The little Chinese man looked at his watch and scribbled on his pad.

A third group of five. Another Japanese officer. Similar efficiency. The little Chinese man looked at his watch and scribbled on his pad again.

Sun Chi knew that if he didn't do something, one of those sabers would be severing his own neck.

His family was standing behind a pile of rubble. The children hung on their mother's arms, their eyes windows of anger and fear.

His wife had been a peasant girl before her father had accepted his marriage presents: a silver ingot and ten boxes of wedding cake. People envied the young woman, a beggar in the city being better off than the richest of the villagers. She was marrying someone who probably had a trunk of gold bricks under his bed.

Sun Chi's daughter was now four, and his son two. A few weeks earlier, Sun Chi's unit had been deployed to Nanjing, and he got to see his son for the first time. The little boy wrapped his thin arms around his father's neck and called him Baba in the cutest voice.

Sun Chi had taken his children for a stroll in the streets. In his military uniform, the emblem of a white sun on his cap, he looked large and dignified. Several Chinese soldiers snapped to attention and saluted. Awestruck, the son asked the daughter whether Baba's position was higher than that of the Generalissimo.

But now he would be executed by the Japanese, suffering the worst humiliation imaginable for a Chinese man. People would talk about his decapitation by the *turnip heads* years after his death.

Burning with anxiety, Sun Chi struggled with the rope on his wrists—to no avail.

* * *

Over in Plum Blossom Alley, hiding under a bed, May and Damao were startled by the loud knocks on the window above them. A voice inside their room shouted in response. Chaotic footsteps went to the front door. A motor roared after an agonizingly long wait. Then all noise moved away.

May crawled out from under the bed with her brother. They tiptoed to the window and found the alley empty. Both exhaled.

"I guess that little soldier didn't see you after all!" May said.

"How could he? I ducked so fast!" Damao boasted.

Walking back from the window, May tripped over a pile of clothing. She stooped to choose several items from the floor.

"Go to face the wall," May told her brother. "Don't turn around until I say so!"

May hid behind the mosquito net to change. She took off her jacket and blouse, grimacing as she peeled the blood-stained sleeve from her skin. Then she bound up her mangled arm with a handkerchief. Fortunately, the wounds on her stomach were not very deep, the silver coins in her waist pocket having deflected the Japanese bayonet. She came out from the mosquito net wearing a large pink blouse over three sweaters.

Pointing at his sister and laughing, Damao nagged her to go out and look for food. While considering this idea, May heard rustling noises coming from the other side of the wall. She and her brother slid under the bed again like scared little rats. Footsteps came to their room and a pair of shoes stopped close to May's nose. With her heart in her throat, May took a look and let out a breath of relief. The shoes were *embroidered* and made of *cotton*. She stuck her head out and met the round face of a woman bending down to check under the bed.

The woman backed away, the flesh on her rotund body shaking.

"I know you," May said. "You are the nice lady who gave us porridge last night!"

The woman stared at May. "Why are you wearing my blouse?" she demanded.

"I'm sorry. A soldier stabbed me, tearing my . . ." May said and started to unbutton.

"Hold it. What happened?"

May told her about the massacre that had taken place out in the alley. All color fled the woman's face. "Oh my goodness, oh my goodness!" she kept saying with a hand on her heart.

"Where were you when the Japanese searched this house a moment ago?" May asked.

"Hiding in my cellar."

"Are your daughters still there?"

"No, they fled to the International Safety Zone at daybreak."

"Why didn't you go with them?"

"Someone had to watch over the furniture," the woman said.

Damao interrupted the chatter. "Hey, lady, stop jabbering away. I'm hungry. Got something to eat?"

The woman took a look at Damao's face. "You poor child!" she exclaimed. "Come! I'll fix something nice for you."

But she stopped at the kitchen door and uttered a cry of dismay. May peeked inside the kitchen and saw bowls, dishes, and woks lying on the floor. Even the table was overturned. It was as if the room had been hit by a tornado.

"Where did my groceries go?" the woman asked herself.

Damao's face grew red, and May quickly squeezed his hand. She thanked the woman for her kindness and promised to return the clothes as soon as she could.

But the woman didn't seem to hear anything May was saying. Patting her forehead, she reached under the counter and a bowl of noodles in brown soup emerged with her hand!

"I hid my breakfast when I heard gunshots," she beamed. "Ain't I smart, or what?" She got busy lighting the kindling in the stove.

May told Damao to help her right the table. They pushed it against the wall and cleaned up the floor. Damao resisted his sister's plea to go out and pee. Instead, he pulled up a chair and sat down at the table, watching the woman cook.

When the water steamed, the woman put the noodles into three small bowls and passed chopsticks to everyone. Damao grabbed one of the bowls. After shoveling everything down his throat with a few plows of his chopsticks, he dipped his chopsticks into May's bowl. May slapped his wrist and made him withdraw quickly.

An icy gust swept into the room. May shuddered involuntarily, and the fine hair on the back of her neck stood up. In the ghost stories she had heard as a child, such a bone-chilling wind was the prelude to a ghost descending to prey on a household. She looked to the door, and saw two Japanese soldiers walking into the kitchen!

The soldiers nodded at each other, ugly grins spreading across their faces. A stench floated to May's nose. It was worse than Damao's when he had refused to take baths for weeks. Those soldiers mustn't have washed for a long time.

Everybody sitting around the table put down the chopsticks. They stood up and backpedaled till their backs were stopped by the kitchen wall.

The taller soldier nudged his companion and whispered: "*Bi, kan kan.*"

The last two words sounded like *lookie lookie*. But *what* did the soldiers want to see?

The smaller soldier seemed nervous. He shoved his companion away. The taller soldier laughed. He strode to the woman and grabbed her pants with his brown hands. The woman shrieked and stomped her feet. A whack on the mouth stuffed the sounds back into her throat. Blood oozed out of her nose.

"*Bi, kan-kan*," the soldier said harshly, trying to pull the woman's pants down.

May turned to Damao in horror.

The woman pushed the soldier's hand away. She got another smack. Blood streaks stained her cheeks and tears rolled out of her eyes. The soldier put an elbow to her neck nailing her to the wall, using his other hand to jerk her pants down. The woman was wearing no underpants, and her black triangle was being exposed. She screamed and moved to cover herself, her face turning beet red. The soldier drew his dagger and set it at her throat.

Although she was trembling at the other side of the table, May could not help but yell: "Hey, wait a minute!"

The soldier paid her no heed. He pressed the dagger down, and a thin streak of blood dripped down the woman's throat. The woman screamed again and dropped her hands.

The soldier laughed. He returned the dagger to its sheath, lifted the woman up, and dumped her on the top of the kitchen table. One of the noodle bowls toppled over and soup flowed out dripping to the floor. The woman wriggled as the soldier opened her legs into a wide angle. Two more slaps made her sit still. The soldier swaggered back to join his comrade. They stood side by side to gawk at the woman, pointing at her, and then broke into loud laughter.

The woman quickly closed her legs, and the taller soldier stopped laughing immediately. He ran back to her, his footsteps shaking the floor. The woman hastened to open up again. But the soldier grabbed her hair with one hand, pulled her off the table, and dragged her out of the room.

Shrieks sounding like the howling of a pig kept coming from that room. Then May and Damao heard a long, piercing scream!

The echo still rang in May's ears when the smaller soldier sidled up to her and said sheepishly, "*Bi, kan kan!*"

"Damao, help!!!" May cried.

Damao didn't move.

May spat, and the soldier stepped back to wipe off the saliva on his chin, his face darkening. May lifted her only good arm to defend herself. But when his thunderous punch arrived, it blew past her hand and landed squarely on her nose, sending her head bouncing several times against the wall.

In a daze, May only had enough sense to hold onto her pant strings. "Damao!" she cried again.

Urine ran down Damao's legs.

The soldier stepped forward to ply May's fingers away from her pants, scratching bloody streaks on the backs of her hands. May fought back by bumping his crotch with her knees, making him bend down and yell.

The soldier took half a step back to get away from her attack. Then he slapped her left and right with an open hand. May gritted her teeth and didn't yield an inch. Thwarted, the soldier balled his fists and hit May's head again and again. May kicked him with her long legs, reaching him not once, but several times. The soldier shouted in frustration.

But the heavy poundings on her head, each landed with the man's grunt, made her brains shake inside her skull. Then a punch in her eye sprayed bright stars across her field of vision. Feeling dizzy, she rubbed her eyelids to clear it, and found the soldier she was seeing split into two identical images. It looked like a two-headed monster was battering her with four arms.

Rapidly losing consciousness, May held up her pants with the desperation of a drowning woman hanging onto a straw. She might get herself killed, but no ugly Japanese would be seeing her down there and laughing!

One of his punches landed on her bayoneted wound. The sharp pain sent her gasping for air. He hit her again in the same spot, and the stars in her eyes broke into a sheet of gold dust. No longer able to determine where her enemy was, she could only tell that her hands were being grabbed and wrung. An acute pain followed the cracking sounds of her finger bones, and a kick sent her crumpling to the ground. She fainted.

Awakened by a cold draft on her legs, May opened her eyes and was scared out of her wits. She was completely naked below the waist!

Pee and shit burst out of her damaged body. She wanted to cry, "You filthy man! I'll castrate you and grind your penis into the ground!" But her arms felt as heavy as the stone grinder in Baba's backyard, and she was so tired she couldn't move even her little fingers. There was nothing she could summon up to ward off the ultimate humiliation.

The soldier climbed on top of her. He put his mouth over hers, scraping her delicate skin with the prickly stubble on his oily chin. He thrust his tongue inside her mouth, smothering her breath with the smell of dead fish. Then he hunched up his behind and unbuckled his belt.

She heard a tinkling sound. A wide-band gold ring fell out of the soldier's hip pocket and rolled smoothly on the ground.

The tiny noise might have been thunder to her ears. As if a bolt of lightning had struck, she found her limbs moving again.

She tried to shout: "Asshole! That is Baba's ring!" But the soldier's tongue in her mouth prevented her from making any sound. So she bore her teeth down with all of her might. The soldier shrieked, and a trickle of warm fluid flowed down her throat.

He pounded her head madly with both of his fists. Yet she would not let go. She was beyond pain. "I'm going to take it with me, you asshole!" she swore, continued to bite down, and felt a piece of the tongue in her mouth come loose. "There! This is for Baba!"

The soldier shrieked again, rolled off her, and hopped around. May scrambled up and seized the dagger tied to his trousers belt on the ground. Drawing it speedily, she stabbed him in the belly. The soldier howled and jumped on her, all red eyes and bloody mouth. He punched her arm, and the dagger dropped to the floor. Then he flung her to the ground, kicked her legs, and stomped on her face.

As May curled up to absorb the punishment, Damao ran over from a corner. The husky boy picked up the dagger from the floor and buried it into the soldier's back. The soldier howled again and fell. May spat out the piece of bloody tongue in her mouth and got up. She snatched the dagger from her brother and stabbed the soldier with both hands again and again until his body stopped twitching.

When her brother helped her to get out of the house, she saw the woman's body in the living room, her mouth open and her eyes glazed—with a bottle stuck up her vagina.

Chapter 25

To Hell's Gate and Back

In an open lot two miles from Plum Blossom Alley, Sun Chi stood with scores of other prisoners, his body frozen by the thought of his imminent decapitation.

Four Japanese soldiers were carrying a large desk out of a stucco house down the street. This house belonged to a Mr. Fan, and this very desk belonged in its living room. As a child, Sun Chi had been intrigued by the patina of its dark, purplish surface. Once he had tried to touch it with his fingertips. His mother had pulled his hands back. "This is a zitan table," she said. "If you break one of its legs, you will have to sell me to pay for it."

Moving in quick little steps, the Japanese soldiers arrived at the fire by which two Japanese officers sat warming their hands. With a thud the soldiers lay the desk down. Then they took a deep breath, raised it a few inches off the ground, and shoved it into the burning logs. The flame darkened for a long time before a fiery tongue licked up and devoured it.

The leaping fire momentarily took Sun Chi's mind away from his predicament. He saw the face of a little girl in the fire. She was Qian Ying, his playmate when both were children. Growing up, she became his girlfriend. When she refused to run away with him, he took a train to Guangzhou in fury.

The train derailed at Hengyang, and he spent the night sleeping on a bench worrying about missing the entrance exam. When the train resumed, he annoyed the conductor by constantly asking for the time of arrival.

Two weeks later, he went to the front gate of the Huangpu Academy with a sense of misgiving. To his surprise, he found his name on a large poster glued to a wall. He had been accepted!

On the first day of school Sun Chi lined up in the courtyard to have his head shaved. A cadet standing next to him offered him a cigarette.

"Oh . . . I don't know how," Sun Chi stammered.

Everybody around him laughed. They patted his back telling him he was a good boy. Sun Chi was happy. This was a place he belonged.

The cadets came from all provinces in China. Those who spoke Mandarin with a twisted tongue came from northern provinces. Those who spoke sing-song Mandarin came from southern provinces. Those who hardly spoke any Mandarin at all were locals raised in Guangdong province.

Most of the cadets were older than he. A few even had the rank of officer. Endorsed by senior party members, these young officers had been accepted without examination.

Sun Chi was given a razor to shave off the long, sparse hairs sprouting above his upper lip. But the next morning he failed face inspection. It took some time to find out the reason: he had used the razor to sharpen his pencil.

Life was full and disciplined. He shared a bedroom with twenty-nine other cadets in a two-story stucco building with dark brown banisters. The horn blew them out of sleep at five o'clock in the morning. He folded and smoothed his blanket into a mound which must have the sharp edges of a rectangular tofu. He then carried his copper basin to the courtyard to wash up. Ten minutes later in the dining hall, in military uniform complete with leg bands, he sat waiting for the presiding officer to give the signal to start breakfast. Talking was prohibited while they ate, and the only sounds in the hall were made by chopsticks knocking the porridge bowls. He put down his chopsticks as soon as the presiding officer did his.

At six o'clock, he stood with other cadets on the drilling field doing the ten-minute calisthenics led by Chiang Kai-shek.

Sun Chi was given two military uniforms, two sets of underwear, two pairs of socks, and three pairs of straw shoes. He learned how to use weapons of all kinds: rifles, semi-automatics, pistols, grenades, machine guns, bayonets, swords, fists, teeth, and feet. He also learned how to read maps, how to build city walls, how to gather intelligence, and how to survive in the wilderness. Some of the best lessons were given by the Russian advisers who had real war experience. They also brought gifts with them: the weapons the cadets would need in future battles.

Sun Chi did not like the political courses in the school's curriculum. The academy was serious about instilling in the cadets the *Three People's Principles*—the thoughts of Dr. Sun Yat-sen. Sun Chi couldn't keep the three different principles straight in his mind.

Chiang Kai-shek's Monday speech was Sun Chi's weekly highlight. The president of the academy stood on the podium, two crossed party flags behind him, and the plaque of the school motto, "Fraternity, Dexterity, and Sincerity," on a side wall. He put his left hand on his hip and used his right hand to drive home every point. Mesmerized by the gestures, Sun Chi noticed neither Chiang Kai-shek's boring tone nor his heavy Ningbo accent.

President Chiang Kai-shek inspired enthusiasm. Everybody worked to keep the school clean and orderly. Posters on every wall exhorted the cadets to make sacrifices for the revolution: Go elsewhere if you want money and power. Don't come here if you are afraid to die.

Sun Chi was summoned to meet Chiang Kai-shek in person. He arrived at the small office twenty minutes early, his chin cleanly shaven, his uniform ironed, and his Russian shoes, Russian belt, and Russian whip shining. To his surprise, seven other cadets were already there waiting to be called.

When his turn came, Sun Chi entered the office and sat facing the great man across the desk. Handsome and dignified in his tight military uniform, Chiang Kai-shek gave Sun Chi a fatherly smile. He asked the new cadet for his parents' name. Had his father served in the army? Excellent! How many siblings did he have? Ah-ha! Did he like the academy? *Hao, hao* (good, good). Throughout, Sun Chi's mouth felt stiff and the sound of his laugh hollow.

"Your uniform is a little short. I'll get you a new one," Chiang Kai-shek said. "Listen, this is important: A young man must take good care of his health. Make sure you don't catch cold. Do you have enough spending money?"

The president of the academy then turned stern and lectured Sun Chi on disciplining his mind and body to prepare for the great role he would be filling for his country.

Chiang Kai-shek's eyes shone with wisdom. At that moment, Sun Chi would have jumped off a cliff had his principal so commanded him.

Later, Sun Chi felt a letdown learning that Chiang Kai-shek had talked to every cadet in a similar way at least once. To a cadet from Zhejiang province, Chiang Kai-shek would say: "Your hometown is less than thirty miles from mine. My son

Jing-guo, now attending Sun Yat-sen University in Moscow, is four years your junior. Think of him as your younger brother. When he returns to China, you two really should meet."

Sun Chi excelled in hand combat, winning the nickname *Sun the Fierce Kid*. The only criticism of his techniques was on his defense—he had little. He was elected by his peers to lead them during field maneuvers.

He graduated after six months and was dispatched to join the Northern Expedition. In the famed Dragon Lagoon Battle, he led dozens of his men to attack Green Dragon Hill, burying the defenders in a hail of grenades. After they won the battle, the commanding general gave Sun Chi his personal pistol, an American-made M191.

A telegram arrived in the glow of his success informing him of the death of his mother. He looked for the red pouch she had given him but couldn't find it.

For the funeral, Sun Chi returned home to Nanjing. The neighbors marveled at his steely grip and the hand that seemed to have been made of sandpaper, but they said nothing of the dangling pistol on his bullet belt. They helped him to prepare a chicken and a bottle of rice wine to pour on the ground of his mother's grave.

After the funeral, his neighbors pointed him to the wine house where Qian Ying had been sold.

Sun Chi went to ask for Black Cat. Not knowing that he should tip the tea maid, he waited a long time before Qian Ying came out.

Black Cat looked like she was going to faint seeing him in the foyer. Then she covered her face and wept. He tried to hold her hand. She pushed him away.

"You leave now! I can't see you here," she said.

Sun Chi was stunned.

The next day he went to the wine house again. The servant was brusque with him. "Miss is not here," he hissed. "You get the hell out!"

A friend figured out what she was telling him, so Sun Chi booked a private room in a restaurant and sent ten jupiao to the wine house. An hour later, a rickshaw carried Black Cat to him.

Sitting stiffly in her chair across the table from him, Black Cat said little and looked away, even after he had promised to take her out of the wine house as soon as he had the money.

Every day afterwards Sun Chi sent ten jupiao for her service. But Black Cat remained cold—until one day she got angry.

She called him a dumb donkey. As if a floodgate had suddenly been flung open, a torrent of words tumbled out of her mouth: "Do you know a man is always in love with the last woman he has slept with, but a girl the first man she fell for? Do you have any idea how many clients a girl can take before she stops caring? Can you imagine how long the days are when a woman waits for letters that never come? Do you know your mother cried for almost a month after you had left? Did it ever occur to you that she went to the barracks and asked everyone if they had seen you? For the sake of the woman who died calling your name, would you please bother me no more!"

The following day Sun Chi bought ten jupiao as usual, but for a change he just sipped his rice wine and did not try to engage her in conversation. When Black Cat's rickshaw came to take her to another client, Sun Chi stood up and told her this was their last meeting. His money was running out, and he was leaving for another city in days.

Black Cat stopped in her tracks, and when she spoke her eyes had a fierceness that frightened him. "Wait for the moon to rise to the tip of the willow tree tomorrow night. Knock three times at the little red door at the back of the wine house. Someone will let you in."

He followed her instructions. A maid opened the door and led him to a room where Black Cat was pacing. With a sweaty hand she pulled him to a large bed under a red canopy and peeled off all her clothes. She lay down with her eyes closed, her lips open, and her arms forming a lazy triangle over her head. The blatant offer of her white body reminded Sun Chi of his first prostitute, to whom a fellow officer had taken him for his initiation. The prostitute had droopy breasts and was missing a front tooth, but her nipples had the surprising pink of a girl of sixteen, into whose skimpy blouse he had once peeped. She pushed his head to them, and he was able to finish what he had paid her to do.

But this encounter with Qian Yong was entirely different. When he entered her, she suddenly came alive, groaning and digging her nails into his back. He was determined to tame the woman who had put him down, and the battle between the sexes quickly became a mismatch. Only half of his weight, she asked for mercy, her hair soaked with perspiration.

"Please stop!" she pleaded, panting. "You are driving me to death!"

But when he slowed down she cried "no, no, no, no, no" and clung onto his neck begging him to go on. Her loud groans of pain and ecstasy were not the artificial grunts made by his whore, and her brazen display of sexual zeal left him dumbfounded. She had seemed as pure as a lotus in the pond—a delicate flower to appreciate at a distance. Now this!

Years ago, when they walked together in the woods, she once stooped to pick up a pretty pebble. The front of her blouse fell open. She quickly pushed her blouse closed—but not before he had gotten a glimpse of her upper bosom. At that time, it was no more than the suggestion of a gentle slope.

Today, her breasts were still small, but her writhing was natural and instinctive. Did she learn it from her other lovers? Or was it a birth gift that sprouted out as she grew into a woman?

What intimidated him most was how much she enjoyed their intimate act—more than he did. She kept holding him tight to her bosom, suffocating him with her burning skin. By the time the roosters crowed at the eastern sky, Sun Chi was spent. As he rolled off her, he could no longer suppress his jealousy.

"How many men have you had?" he asked, out of breath.

Fire turned into ice. "Get out of here, you no-good, farting, stinking *turtle egg*!"

Her shrieks went on and on, waking up the whole household. Someone knocked at her door. Sun Chi had to wrestle a large servant to get out.

A year later, he married a country girl through a matchmaker. She was clumsy on the wedding night, and he was delighted. Once on furlough in Nanjing, he saw Black Cat in a rickshaw, her red, thick lips shining. She turned her face away.

Times were not good for sorting out personal troubles. As the Japanese marched toward China's capital, Sun Chi's unit was dispatched to hold the enemy troops off at the Guanghuamen city gate. When the order for evacuation came, Sun Chi's soldiers were among those selected to leave the city by the harbor. Unfortunately, they found no boats to carry them across the river. In panic, they ran back to the city looking for places to hide. Sun Chi was luckier. He had a home in Nanjing.

His wife was overjoyed to find that the man pounding her door was her husband. She helped him bury his uniform and his weapons in the backyard. But the Japanese soldiers came to their neighborhood rounding up every man who had a shaved head or calluses on his hands, declaring that such a man was a soldier. Sun Chi was angered by the rudeness doled out to him. Never could he have anticipated what horrors awaited.

* * *

A sharp blade at his back brought Sun Chi out of his reveries. A shove on the shoulders sent him stumbling. Sun Chi was forced to walk to the pit filled with headless bodies and kneel. When a Japanese officer sauntered over with a long, glimmering katana, Sun Chi knew his head would soon be flying. His heart almost jumped out of his mouth.

The Japanese had decided to make examples of those despicable Chinese soldiers. They drove all the Chinese spectators over to witness the decapitations. Sun Chi saw his son in the crowd. The little guy looked furious. He must be angry at the Japanese for not saluting his father. Sun Chi's vision blurred. He turned his head away. A soldier could shed blood but never tears—especially not in front of his little son.

A face flashed in his mind. It was his mother's. She had hidden it from him at his departure from home. Now he understood why.

He heard some strange noises made by the prisoner standing next to him. They disrupted his train of thought, and Sun Chi was annoyed. Then he realized that the man was actually humming a tune. Sun Chi knew only a few songs, but "The March of the Brave Guerrilla Soldiers" was one of them. Without realizing it, Sun Chi hummed along with his neighbor. Their combined voice was small at first, but it grew stronger and stronger, as one by one the other prisoners joined them:

"Rise, all ye who refuse to be slaves.
With our blood and flesh,
Build us a new Great Wall.
The Chinese people have arrived at the moment of truth,
The whole nation must burst out our final roar:
Rise! Rise! Rise!"

"Stop!" shouted the Japanese officer coming over.

No one did.

Enraged, the officer ran to the first prisoner and hurriedly swung his katana down. The saber landed obliquely on the prisoner's neck but failed to sever the head from the body. In frustration, the officer gave the body a vicious kick. It fell into the pit with a flapping head.

The prisoners hushed. Singing halted.

The officer went to the prisoner standing next to Sun Chi and carefully checked the placement of his feet.

A distant voice came to the pit: "Wait a minute! Wait just a minute!"

A middle-aged man in a Western suit sprinted toward the scene. The officer lowered his katana as the man arrived gasping for air.

"Who the devil are you?" the Japanese officer asked.

"I am Tanaka Ichiro, a reporter from Tokyo's *Asahi Shimbun*." Still panting, the man handed a card to the officer.

"What do you want?"

"Some of these men are not soldiers. You cannot kill them," Tanaka said.

"Show me one."

Tanaka pointed to the last prisoner in the line.

"How the hell do you know?" the officer asked.

"He was my servant until this morning—when your soldiers took him away from my house."

"All right," the officer roared. "Untie him!"

Two Japanese soldiers came forward and took the ropes off the prisoner, who ran and stumbled his way to the street corner.

"There may be others civilians here," Tanaka said.

"Boy, what a pest you are! How many servants do you have?"

"See the woman under that tree?" Tanaka asked. "She said your men took her husband."

"Bring her over here!" the Japanese officer bellowed.

The trembling woman was made to stand in front of the officer.

"Which one is your husband?" the reporter asked.

The woman pointed at the man who had started the singing.

"Is he a soldier?" the Japanese officer asked.

"No! He has been a barber all his life."

"Release him!" the officer yelled.

The barber was let go.

"Are you satisfied now?" the officer shouted.

"I apologize for the inconvenience, sir, but could you possibly ask those women if any of the prisoners are their husbands?"

The officer beckoned the Chinese translator, and the little man hurried over to listen to instructions. He went to the Chinese spectators and announced: "The Great Japanese Imperial Army is kind to the Chinese people. If your husband is being arrested here, speak up. He will be freed! Now bow to the Big Man for his generosity!"

Heads went up and down randomly.

The Japanese officer beckoned, and the little man ran back to listen to more instructions. He went back to the front of the crowd and began to shout. "I hope you fools have learned your lesson: All those idiots who dare oppose the Great Japanese Imperial Army will be beheaded. If you try to cover up for any of them, the Big Man will chop off your head too!"

The crowd quieted down.

"Let us begin with this fellow." The little man pointed to Sun Chi. "Is he your husband?"

Sun Chi looked for his wife, but the woman avoided his eyes. *Damn it, woman, say it! What are you waiting for?*

Then a thought dawned on him: "Shit! The bitch is not going to risk her neck for mine!"

A voice in his head said: "Look, she is doing the right thing! Who will take care of the kids if she lies for you and the Japanese find out?"

Another voice sneered: "Listen, she don't want you around no more. You don't stay home enough, and the bitch gets itchy. You could tell something was stinking when she bared her breasts in front of a neighbor."

The Japanese officer set his feet behind Sun Chi.

"No woman claims this one." The officer raised his saber. "If you will excuse me, Mr. Tanaka, I must finish the competition with my colleague."

A scream!

"What now?" The officer stopped his saber in midair, annoyed.

"Someone fainted," the translator said, pointing at the woman who was being pulled up some distance away.

"Don't kill him, please!" the woman shrieked as soon as she was able to stand on her own. "He is my husband!"

All spectators turned their heads. Even though the woman was wearing a gray dress and not her signature long black robe, some of them recognized her as Black Cat, the courtesan who had grown up with them.

She was brought to the Japanese officer, who lowered his katana. "Your husband, huh? Prove it."

"Tell the officer something only a wife would know," the journalist said.

"He has a scar on his right thigh."

With a violent jerk the officer ripped off the tattered front of Sun Chi's pants. "Ha, a bayonet wound!" he roared. "He must be a soldier!"

"It is an old scar from a pocket knife," Black Cat said, entirely calm now. "A man did that to him when he was sixteen. They were fighting over me."

"Liar! I am going to chop off your head!" The officer raised his saber.

"I've known him since he was five, and that's the truth," Black Cat said without flinching. "He used to beat up every boy who tried to talk to me."

The officer laughed uproariously. "What took you so long to come forward, woman?"

"He doesn't want me anymore!" The woman broke down and wept. "He thinks I'm not good enough for him, having slept with other men before him."

"Slut!" The officer made a sweeping gesture with his right hand. "I'm sick of women of your kind. Get the hell out of here before I vomit on you. And take this rat with you!"

A soldier untied Sun Chi.

Walking away, Sun Chi tried to think of something to say to the woman holding him to keep him steady. But no words were adequate for thanking a woman who had saved your life—particularly if you had broken the promise to rescue her from the wine house.

The Japanese officer turned to Tanaka. "Get the hell out of my sight, little man. I'm not going to say it again!"

Many women begged Tanaka to stay and save their husbands. In order to leave, the Japanese newsman had to tear away many hands grasping at his sleeve.

The Japanese officer decapitated the lone prisoner left by the pit.

Chapter 26

The Nanjing Safety Zone

Early the next morning, hundreds of Chinese women, children in tow, gathered outside the front gate of Jinling Women's College. Some of them had smeared their faces with soot. Others had put on male clothing. All had cut their hair jagged and short—like men's.

The gate slowly opened, and a group of men and women walked out. In front was Minnie Vautrin, the American woman who had become a legend. The Goddess of Nanjing was not afraid to confront Japanese soldiers. Even after being slapped by one of them, she made them move their machine guns away from her front gate.

Behind Minnie walked a slim Chinese woman who spoke to the brown haired man pulling a bike with him: "John, Mr. Rabe left this in Minnie's office last night. Could you drop it off at his house on your way to the hospital?" She handed him Rabe's brown jacket, which had a swastika emblem on its sleeve.

"Sure," John Winthrop said and stuffed it into the knapsack on his back.

"How's May doing, John?" Minnie turned her head and asked.

"She is not healed yet. But the hospital needs her bed for a critically wounded patient. I'm going to the hospital and check her out."

The refugees outside the campus fell on their knees and kowtowed on the ground.

The Chinese woman frowned. "Shall we let them in, Minnie?"

"Yes," Miss Vautrin said, "but tell the children that no one is allowed to enter this campus wearing a Japanese badge. They will defeat the Japanese one day—provided that they don't forget who they are!"

John Winthrop ran a few steps, hopped onto his bicycle seat, and off he went.

Rabe's house was only a few blocks away, but John forgot to stop and drop off the jacket. His mind was dwelling on what the chairman of the Nanjing Safety Zone had told him the day before.

"The other night I caught a Japanese soldier raping a woman refugee under my staircase," Rabe had said, lighting a cigar taken out of a silver case. "I put my sleeve in front of his eyes and ordered him to get the hell out of my house—in the same way he had gotten in. The rascal scaled the wall without his pants."

"I understand. Your front door is for gentlemen only."

The German businessman did not answer, puffing on his Havana cigar, frowning.

* * *

Several days ago, John had taken May to the Drum Tower Hospital in Rabe's car with German national flags on its windshield. No Japanese soldiers bothered them. May worried about her brother Damao, who had been turned away at the gate of Jinling Women's College. John promised to find him. Relieved, May put her battered head on his shoulder. But she suddenly jumped up.

"Baba's ghost is following me!" she yelled.

"There is no such thing as a ghost, May," John said, stroking her soft black hair.

"But, John! Baba died an unjust death. His ghost will not rest until I avenge him!"

The hospital was in chaos when they arrived. Three Japanese soldiers had sneaked into the building through the back door, and two of them went to the nurses' dormitory. Slinging their pistols loosely, they lined up the six nurses inside the dormitory and proceeded to rape them one by one. An American doctor discovered them. Furious, he told the soldiers to get the hell out. The Japanese claimed visiting rights and refused to leave. So the doctor ordered all non-patients to vacate the hospital immediately. Before May had a chance to see a doctor, John was being shoved out. When the door slammed in his face, May pushed her way to the front and pressed her palms on the glass partition. John covered them from outside, and a chill went from his hands to his heart. May frantically moved her hands around the window pane, her mouth moving.

"What?" John yelled, his hands following hers. "Louder!"

She mouthed her words to him one by one, fogging up the pane around her lips. But John could only read the angst in her eyes.

* * *

John was not watching the road when a bike overtook him. The rider, a dark man with dirty hair, turned his head and gave him a sneer.

Anyone looking like a coolie shouldn't have a new bike, and if he had one, he wouldn't dare ride it openly—or a Japanese soldier would beat him up and take the bike away.

Was he even a Chinese, or a Japanese?

Calvin Ren's voice rang in his head: "John, don't you ever give any bloody Japanese soldier a chance to see your big pale face!"

The warning had been delivered just before Calvin boarded the *Panay*.

"I'm not afraid of Japanese soldiers," John had answered. "I happen to know my rights."

But now cold sweat soaked the shirt on his back. He made a swift left turn into a side street and then a sharp right, pedaling as fast as he could. Houses blurred by him. Icy wind whipped over his ears. He was breathless when Drum Tower Hospital came into his view.

Perhaps he really had nothing to worry about. Why should he be wary of someone who looked like a beggar?

Then he heard loud whistles coming from several blocks away. A squadron of soldiers in yellow uniforms jogged through a street intersection in chaotic steps, lithe, panting hounds running with them. The coolie on the bike must have reported him!

The sounds of whistles soon spread to the street blocks all around. He was trapped! There was no time to waste. He must decide what to do immediately.

There were two options: escape into a small alley and speed his way out, or hide in one of those dusty, low-lying houses of the industrial neighborhood.

But it was impossible to slip away without being seen. Once you've been seen, you'd better stop. Japanese soldiers shot at anything moving.

That left him only with the second choice: hide. But he could hear the sounds of crashing doors all around him. The soldiers must be breaking them down searching for him.

Suddenly, an idea came to him. Quickly braking, he got off the bike and pushed it into a bush. Then he took off his black overcoat and tossed it away as well. Finally, he pulled out Rabe's brown jacket from his knapsack. He was putting it on when another squadron of Japanese soldiers emerged from the street corner.

A Chinese peasant in a black pajama turned and dashed madly toward a house. The soldiers raised their rifles. Several explosions—a muffled cry. The man fell to the ground, convulsed, and lay motionless.

John continued to walk.

One of the rifles turned, then a forest of muzzles followed.

John raised both hands and yelled, "*Deutschland! Doitsu! Deguo!*"

Some of the soldiers lowered their guns.

John walked up to the military man with red straps on his shoulders. "Heil Hitler!" he said, raising his right hand and clicking his heels.

The officer, eyes narrowing, examined the swastika emblem on John's arm. He touched his cap and mumbled a few words.

"Nein, nein. Sprechen sie Deutsch?" John said.

The Japanese officer did not answer.

"English?" John ventured.

The Japanese tilted his head.

"Chinese, yes?" John asked in the third language.

"Yes," the officer responded in Chinese with an odd accent.

"What's going on, officer?" John asked airily.

"We are here to catch a *spoiled egg*."

"What did he do?"

"I ask question. Did you see a big American riding a bike around here?"

"I saw no one like that," John said. "But if he is around here, you must have him cornered. Carry on, officer!"

A hand on his shoulder stopped John from walking away. "Your name, sir?"

John stared at the officer for several seconds before he said, "Hans Jauch." He took out his US passport, turned it to the first page, and put it under the officer's nose.

It worked! The Japanese officer made no attempt to read the English words on the passport. He only looked at the photograph and compared it with the face in front of him.

"All right. What's inside that thing on your back?"

"Some personal letters and a porcelain dish."

"I look."

John took out a stack of letters and a blue satin box from his knapsack.

"What's this thing?" The officer's eyes immediately fell on the antique box.

John opened the box. The falangcai shone like a large jewel in the bright sunlight.

All soldiers stepped up to take a look at the glittering object.

"Shitty gift shop merchandise." The officer snickered. "You didn't pay much for it, yes?"

"I acquired it for less than it's worth."

"You did good," the officer said, sounding almost like a friend now. Suddenly his face changed. "What are you hiding in that big pocket?" he demanded.

Surprised, John felt himself all over before pulling out a shiny silver case from somewhere. "Have a cigar, officer," he said.

"German cigar?"

"Cuban."

"Ahhhh! Cuban cigar. Very good. Very, very good!" The officer was smiling.

The soldiers stepped even closer. John passed the cigars to everyone until they ran out. A soldier struck a match.

"Cuban cigar!" the soldiers told one another.

"To be perfectly precise, they are called Havana cigars," John said.

"Havana cigars!" the officer repeated.

"Havana cigars!" the soldiers shouted.

"Shut up, all of you. Where you going, sir?"

"The Drum Tower Hospital."

"Good day, sir!" the Japanese officer touched his cap.

John put everything back into his knapsack and started to walk. The hospital was only two blocks away.

He heard stomping footsteps coming from afar: a light one alternating with a heavy one. John continued walking, three hundred feet to safety.

Someone behind called out in a high pitch: "Professor Win!" The voice was familiar, with a heavy accent just like the Japanese officer's.

John stopped and turned. A short, stocky Japanese officer was standing in front of the smoking soldiers, his body slightly tilted to one side. John recognized the face, but for a moment he had trouble connecting it with the man's mustard-colored military uniform with red straps on the shoulders.

"Old Yen!" John finally blurted out. It dawned on him that the accent of the custodian in his apartment building was Japanese—not Nanjing.

The limping man barked an order in Japanese, and John was surrounded by men with Havana cigars in their mouths.

"I am a citizen of the United States of America," John protested. "You can't arrest me. I demand to see your superior officer."

A dark Chinaman pushed himself out of the crowd laughing. "Sure, we will introduce you to General Matsui." He jabbed two fingers at Winthrop's chest. "Mr. Win, too bad you chose to be an engineer. You would've made an incredible professional biker."

John flicked the fingers away.

"But you can't escape the Japanese secret service," the Chinaman said and pointed to John's former custodian. "Haven't you heard of Captain Suzuki, division three, the Intelligence Bureau of the Japanese Imperial Army? Now let me see you outrun his bullets."

The speech was interrupted by a slap on the Chinaman's face. "Dog! You are being impolite to a distinguished foreign guest," the former custodian shouted at the Chinese man, who staggered back and whimpered.

John Winthrop knew he was in real trouble.

Chapter 27

The First Blossom

Calvin Ren died in a Hankou hospital. The only family member accompanying him for burial was his wife Judy.

The coffin, carried on a pole by two quick-step coolies, had been nailed together from four pieces of thin boards. Judy, with her bulging tummy, struggled to follow, wearing a burlap sack over a shapeless long gown. Her head bent, she held a small bouquet of white flowers in her hands. Two nurses hovered behind to help just in case.

They were on a hilly road. Not a soul was in sight. Slush covered the ground. Socks were soaked by the melting ice on the long flattened grass.

"This must be it," one of the nurses said in a barely audible voice, craning her neck to look at a roped-off hole in the ground off the mountain path.

The coolies laid down the coffin in front of the hole and stretched their limbs.

"It should be a little bigger at the corner," one of the coolies observed.

He went over and tore away the ropes. Both coolies climbed down the hole. They removed small spades from their belts and started digging. The hole grew as the hands moved rhythmically.

"Would you like to sit down, Mrs. Ren?" one of the nurses asked, wiping off the dirt on an exposed root and spreading a handkerchief on it. "You should take care of yourself in your condition."

Judy shook her head, her face pale and expressionless.

"We are done!" one of the coolies shouted from the hole.

Both coolies climbed out. They grabbed the ropes on the wooden box, lifted it to the cavity, and lowered it slowly.

"Careful," one of the nurses said.

The ropes broke, and the coffin landed on the ground with a thud. Everybody was startled, but the wooden box looked intact. The coolies rolled up the ropes, picked up their spades, and started to fill the hole with soil.

"No!!!" Judy howled, covering her face with her hands.

The coolies stopped, stunned.

The nurses came over and patted Judy's back. One of them said: "It's all right, Mrs. Ren. Please let your husband rest now." She used a handkerchief to dab off the tears on Judy's face.

"I want to see him one more time," Judy wailed.

Everybody looked at one other. Finally the second nurse said: "Mrs. Ren. We can't do that. We've been told to keep the coffin closed."

Judy howled again.

"People are coming," the first nurse whispered, peering in the direction of the bottom of the hill.

The second nurse turned and looked. "I don't think they are from the hospital. Do you know them, Mrs. Ren? Over there. No. There. See?"

"I don't see very well," Judy said, wiping away her tears.

"There are twenty or thirty of them. All men," the first nurse said.

"Mrs. Ren! Mrs. Ren!" someone at the front of the crowd called to her.

Now Judy could make out that person, a husky man. "Why, he looks like Tang," she said, then called, "Is it you, Big Tang?"

"Yes, Mrs. Ren, it is me—and all of us," called the foreman who had worked for Calvin.

Soon all of them arrived and surrounded Judy. Tang's hot breath was on her ear, his big hand around her shoulders.

"I can't see, I can't see," she murmured as her tears flowed again.

A hand held hers. "I am Pan."

"I am Little Lin." Another hand touched her shoulder.

A third held her other hand. "I am Zhou."

"All of us are here," another voice said.

Her vision slowly clearing, she could see them now. Everybody was dressed in white. All of them held flowers in their hands. Some also carried candles and incense sticks. Lin grasped a paper airplane. Others brought paper horses, paper carriages, stacks of mock paper money, and two paper servants—one male and one female. All of the paper was metallic and in bright colors.

"Thank heavens that all of you are safe. Oh, I am so happy to see all of you!" Her tears flowed harder. "How have you been?"

"Fine, Mrs. Ren."

"And your families?"

"They are safe, thanks to the steamboat Professor Ren provided for us."

"Calvin would have been so happy to hear that!" Judy said. "How did you find me?"

"We asked everywhere in Hankou about you and Professor Ren," Lin said. "But even the Aeronautical Affairs Commission didn't know."

"In fact, they asked us about Professor Win," Tang added.

"Why?" Judy asked.

"They have a Cai-yu medal to give him, the highest honor China bestows on a foreigner—from the Generalissimo," Tang said.

"We went to the American Embassy," Pan said, "and they told us about Professor Ren. We are so sorry."

Tang made a signal, and everyone lined up in front of Judy and bowed deeply to her. Judy returned the bow, her vision blurring again. Tears darkened her burlap sack.

There was a long silence. "I inquired about John at the American Embassy," Judy finally said. "Greg Evans, the cultural attaché, told me that John went out one morning several days ago and never returned. Miss Vautrin suspected foul play. She urged Greg to do everything possible to find him."

"When did you last talk to Mr. Evans?" Lin asked.

"Two days ago," Judy said and tried to lean back on a tree. "Have you found out anything since then?"

"To make a long story short, Mr. Evans found Professor Win."

"Alive?"

"Yes!" everybody shouted and grinned.

"Thank the Lord! Thank the good Lord! What happened to him?" Judy asked, teetering. Tang held her arm.

"Well, I will let you hear it directly from Mr. Evans. He should be here any minute. Even better, hear it from Professor Win himself. He is coming too," Tang said.

"I think they are here already!" Lin pointed at the bottom of the hill. Everybody turned to look.

"There is John!" Judy exclaimed. "Greg is right behind him. But who are the other two?"

No one answered.

"Judy!" The brown haired man arrived and gathered the small woman into his arms.

Judy kissed and hugged him. "John!"

"You'd better take it easy, Judy," said the man arriving next.

"Greg!" Judy cried.

"Would you let go of the poor fellow, Judy?" Greg said. "Look at the grimace on his face. You're going to break every bone in his body the Japanese didn't."

Judy immediately released John. "Are you all right, John?"

"I'm fine. You can thank Greg for that."

"Greg, thank you! Thank you! Thank you! How did you find him? How did you get him out?"

"It's a long story. Let's talk about that later. Do you see whom else we've brought?"

Judy turned and saw May and Damao—both in burlap sacks. "It is a long way for you to come," she said. "Why are you dressed like this?"

"May told me that Calvin was like a father to her, although he was not that much older," John explained. "She wants to fill the role of his daughter at the funeral."

"Very thoughtful, May! How did you get here?"

"In Mr. Evans's embassy car," May said. "He let us come along."

"Wonderful!" Judy said.

The two nurses approached. "Shall we start?"

Everyone gathered around the grave. By now, the sun was at its height, but not warming.

John took out a small box from his pocket and opened it, his eyes misty. "Calvin, you never received much recognition. But no one gave more than you did, for you gave your all. You are the person who deserves the Cai-yu medal, not me." He threw a shiny blue-and-white metal on the top of the coffin.

It was time to seal the grave. Someone gave Judy a handful of soil, but she pushed it away and cried. A nurse took the soil and threw it to the coffin for her.

One by one people took their turns dedicating a handful of soil to Professor Ren. After a moment of silence, the coolies filled up the cavity, built a small knoll, and marked the grave with a wooden stake.

Judy lit an incense stick and set it in front of the grave. She knelt down, kowtowed three times, got up, and repeated this ritual two more times. She then went to kneel on the right side of the grave. May and Damao did the same and went to kneel behind Judy.

Each of the guests set down his incense stick and made his bows. Judy and her borrowed children, as Calvin's closest family, kowtowed in return. Calvin's former colleagues built a fire near the knoll with the colorful papers. Lin threw the paper airplane into the fire. When it was consumed by the flame, all gasped.

Judy added a stack of mock money and prayed: "Calvin, you never had much money when you were alive. I am sending you this so that you will have plenty to spend in the netherworld."

The fire rose. The stack slowly turned into smoke and ashes.

* * *

Walking down the hill after the funeral, John told Judy what had happened to him after he had been kidnapped.

Suzuki, the custodian-spy formerly known as Old Yen, had taken John to an office in a drab building. With a clink he had put two glasses on the table.

"I know you like whiskey," Suzuki said, taking a bottle out of a drawer. "You got drunk on it last Christmas. I helped you up the stairs, remember?"

John looked down at his shackled hands and feet and told Suzuki he drank only to celebrate.

"Mr. Win, I want you to know we've been trying to save your life," Suzuki said.

"By offering a reward on my head?"

"We warned you, Mr. Win, but you wouldn't leave Nanjing."

"I will—the day the massacre stops."

Suzuki came straight to the point. "We have no quarrel with you, Mr. Win. We just want to know where the airplane is. Give us this information, and we will let you go."

"Why didn't you say so? I can give you the information right now. The airplane is in Hankou."

"Impossible! We had our men watching your hangar."

"You should have paid someone smarter."

With the conversation at an impasse, the limping officer hung John with a rope from a rafter and beat him with a stick. John told himself not to give his torturer satisfaction, but Suzuki knew his vulnerability: the shoulder separation from a football game. He directed his hits only to his right shoulder. The pain was excruciating. John let out a long scream and fainted.

He woke up in a cold dungeon, still bound.

The next day he had a new interrogator who offered him a friendly smile. "Suzuki could have killed you. I convinced him to enlist your help instead."

"I have some difficulty in helping people who torture me."

"So sorry, Mr. Win, so sorry. We didn't mean to hurt you, but Suzuki must find this airplane. He already shamed his family by letting it slip through his watch. If he doesn't recover it, he will have to commit harakiri—opening up his belly with a dagger and disemboweling himself like this." The Japanese made a twisting motion with his hand.

"I am not going to stand in his way."

"The man is crazy, you know. He enjoys chopping off men's male organs," his interrogator said. "But don't worry, Mr. Win, I am here to help you. Where are you hiding your airplane? We will take you home in a limousine as soon as you give us this little information."

John repeated the answer he had given Suzuki.

"Then give us the numbers of your design. Otherwise Suzuki will have to take over the conversation again."

"He can do whatever he wants with me and my work is still classified."

With a smile his interrogator tied John to a board and covered his nose and mouth with a towel. John tried to keep calm, but he couldn't when the Japanese poured water on the cloth.

Ever since one summer afternoon many years ago, John had been terrified of drowning. All of six years old then, John Winthrop was sitting with his father in the back of their fishing boat watching the green waves spreading over the Nantucket Sound, fishing pole in hand. The sea wind blowing his hair onto his face and soothing him into sleepiness, he was unprepared for the sudden jerk of his fishing pole. Before he realized what was going on, he was already gurgling in the chilly ocean sinking into a bottomless void, utterly confused how a comfortable environment could so abruptly change into this hostile darkness. Panicking, he prayed to the Lord and promised to be a good boy. A hand grabbed his shoulder and pulled him into the boat, coughing and vomiting.

Now, some twenty-one years later, he once again experienced the frightening feeling of cold water going down his throat.

It became hard to breathe.

Well, it really isn't too bad, he encouraged himself, drops of perspiration popping out on his forehead. *I can handle it.*

But things got worse—much worse. His windpipe felt as if it were tearing as water flowed into his lungs with a burning sensation. He opened his mouth gasping for air. More water came in. Struggling wildly, hands and feet against the ropes, he tried to yell, "Stop, you bastard!" But only muffled sounds came out.

His interrogator patted his shoulder.

John blacked out.

A bucket of cold water hit his belly. The interrogation continued.

Breathless and indignant, he declared that they had violated the Geneva Protocol. His interrogator put more water into his lungs.

John kept on passing out and waking up by cold water thrown on his abdomen. The suffocation after suffocation was harder to endure than he could have imagined.

When the Japanese torturer woke him with cold water for the eighth time, John's will weakened. He prayed to God. No help came this time. Disappointed, he cursed God.

Years ago, when John had had a tooth drilled, the pain had penetrated into his skull. He tried to get away from the dental tool, but a firm hand held him. Although the drilling lasted only a few seconds, his shirt was soaked with perspiration when the ordeal was over.

The water torture was worse—and endless. Buckets of sweat poured out of his body. The degree of suffering kept rising even after it exceeded his level of endurance.

John lost touch with his body.

His vision fading, he gave up the hope to live. He had heard that the last scene a man would see was a parade of the women he had slept with. It would unfold like a slide show. He still had not had sex, but death was preferable to this never ceasing torment. Cynthia walked past him, glum and wordless. May flew by, a floating angel. The last time he saw her, she was mouthing words to him behind a glass window. He had been trying to figure out what she was saying, but he would die without knowing the answer.

John apologized to God. His prayers were wild and wordless.

The pain went up another notch.

A miracle happened. He was flying out of his body in a column of warm light. There was no pain whatsoever. As he floated through the window, he could see his contorted face on the torture board below him.

Deliverance, he exulted, *into the infinity of space*!

Rise, rise, and rise! Bright and comfortable. Light and free. Not a worry in the world. Drifting into a sweet drowsiness. Happy! Happy! Happy!

Then things went wrong, terribly wrong. A pair of hands came out of the cloud and pulled him down, down, down.

They slapped his face. A voice called his name. He opened his eyes—and pain attacked every inch of his body again.

"What the hell are you doing?" he shouted at the man cuffing him. "Let me die!"

He felt another smack on his face. He closed his eyes, too weak to resist. The slapping stopped. Someone untied and toweled him off. It probably took only a few minutes, but it seemed an eternity. Awareness slowly returned. The pain receded.

After a long time, he heard footsteps approaching. There came a familiar smell of cologne. He opened his eyes and saw directly above him a shining face and impeccably groomed pomaded hair.

"How are you doing, old man?" asked a friendly voice.

It was Greg Evans!

"Never felt better," he said.

Greg helped him get up from the board. John tried to look normal but could not. He had no way to control his coughs.

Suzuki, the custodian-spy, was standing near a window. At his side was a Japanese officer with white strands in his sideburns. Greg introduced him as General Watanabe Hisahi. John ignored the extended hand. He wanted to punch Suzuki in the nose, but he knew the swing would have toppled him backward. He looked around for a chair to sit down.

"I had a chat with Mr. Winthrop," Suzuki told Greg. "It seemed his old shoulder injury bothered him."

"It looks to me he has recovered very nicely. Can he leave now?" Greg asked, in an obviously forced pleasant tone.

"Of course," Watanabe said.

John dropped on a metal chair and asked for his personal belongings. He was surprised to see his falangcai being used as the container for his passport and personal letters.

"Where is the blue satin box for it?" John asked.

"So sorry. I forgot," Suzuki said, his face reddened.

Suzuki unlocked a drawer and brought out the antique blue satin box. Wrapped in an exquisite silk handkerchief, it looked like a million dollars.

John was about to put the dish into the box when Watanabe asked: "Excuse me, sir. Is this a falangcai?"

John did not answer.

"The finest porcelain dish I've ever seen." Watanabe murmured. "You must have gotten very lucky, sir."

"It takes a little intelligence to tell the real from the fake," John said. "Brute force only gets you so far."

"I apologize for the inconvenience my ignorant officer might have caused you," Watanabe said. "He told me you two had a good conversation."

"The pleasure was all mine, thank you very much," John said. "I just hope to reciprocate the favor to your officer one day."

"Can we offer you a car?" Suzuki asked quickly.

"Thank you, Officer Suzuki, but no. Our embassy car is waiting outside," Greg said. He shook hands with the Japanese officers.

John pointedly ignored everyone as he got up and limped out.

* * *

Greg told John what had happened to Calvin. John broke down and cried. After he gained control of himself, Greg changed the topic. "The Japanese made sure to eliminate all possible witnesses in the streets when they kidnapped you," he said. "But everyone standing inside Drum Tower Hospital could see through the windows what was happening. A

French employee followed the Japanese to a house in downtown and informed the American Embassy in Hankou.

"Remember the letter you sent your MIT mentor three weeks ago? Although the words were cryptic, Professor Dickinson could tell that you and Calvin had made some kind of a breakthrough. An adviser to the War Department, he suggested to his division chief that you be invited to D.C. and give a full report on your work. The War Department sent a letter to the State Department, and it became my job to find you.

"The information provided by the hospital employee couldn't have come at a better time. The Japanese government, embarrassed by the *Panay* incident, was not ready to provoke another international furor. We pulled some strings and the Japanese agreed to release you if we kept everything quiet.

"A military plane is waiting for you in Manila. Would you accept our government's invitation to go to Washington?"

"Yes sir! I want to help our country shoot down as many Japanese planes as possible when we go to war with them," John said.

"Great!" Greg said. "But again, how are you feeling, old man?"

"I'll live," John said. "Greg, do you remember a Chinese girl named May Chen? You know where she is?"

"Minnie told me that May is now living in Jinling Women's College," Greg said.

"I would like to see her," John said.

"Sure. We can make a stop at the college before we go to Hankou."

* * *

After Calvin was buried, everybody went down the mountain. At the bottom of the hill, the workers took the bus to a vacant building where they were allowed to stay. Judy joined John, Greg, May, and Damao to go to the embassy. On the way, Judy expressed to John the wish to go back to America. There was space on the military plane in Manila, and Greg suggested that Judy take a train with John to Hong Kong, where they could catch a commercial flight to the Philippines.

All went to the train station the next evening. John asked the workers to take care of May and Damao as a personal favor to him. Everybody shook hands. Judy and John waved to their friends before entering the hall where they would wait for their train.

They had a problem with their sleeping car arrangements, and John went to the ticket counter to resolve it. Judy wandered in the large hall, her belly feeling heavy. Looking for a place to sit, she saw someone walking toward her and immediately knew who he was.

"Calvin!" she cried in delight, going up to him.

But the man just walked on without acknowledging her.

She was left standing, staring at the man's receding back, confused. Then she saw Calvin walking toward her from another direction. "Calvin!" she cried again, louder this time. But the man walked past her without turning his head. She watched the man disappear into the crowd, her heart pounding. Then she saw Calvin again. This time there were many of them. All were walking toward her—all from different directions.

"Calvin! Calvin! Calvin!" she cried to each and every one of them.

None of them turned their heads. All continued to walk, passing her and receding from her sight.

"Calvin! Why are you abandoning me?" she cried in despair.

When John returned, a crowd was surrounding a woman who had collapsed in the middle of the train station.

* * *

Before dawn the next morning, John was sleeping soundly in his bunk bed inside the train to Hong Kong. Judy was wide awake. Outside, the snowy ground reflected the moonbeams, which filled the air with silvery dust. The northern sky was an eerie, unexplainable crimson.

Through the window, Judy saw ice trees moving past the train one after the other—like a row of crystal chandeliers.

The train made a loud, long whistle. Judy watched the sky break. She saw a bush of winter plums blosssoming on a frozen cliff. The frail flowers, blown by the wind, bounced back proudly.

The baby inside her stirred. She was kicking again.

"Oh no, I've been getting it wrong all along!" Judy sat up. "My baby has got to be a *boy*. Calvin, you are going to have a son! I will work hard to provide him a good education. Don't worry about a thing, Calvin—he will grow up just fine. He will be just like you!"

She heard Calvin's feeble voice: "Judy, will you marry me in our next life?"

A flash of lightning broke through the darkness in her brain. She saw her parents meeting for the first time in their previous life, her mother giving her father a shy, almost invisible smile. She also saw her own future with perfect clarity.

"Calvin, we will meet again—in our next life," she said. "When it blossoms—the first branch of winter plums—one spring morning, I will be there, standing by a country well, in a small village, waiting for you."

Chapter 28

Victory!

Years later, Chen May still thought of Professor Ren. He had been the person who had put into her head the idea of attending college. He was the one who had influenced her the most. She would be grateful to him always. She would miss him forever.

A little man, very intense, always nervous—even crazy perhaps. Imagine, one man trying to tip the military balance between China and Japan! She admired that.

"It is a law of physics, May," Professor Ren had once told her. "Given the force field, given the initial position and the initial velocity, you can predict the position and the velocity of a particle at all subsequent times."

She had been fascinated. The statement was so precise, so beautiful, and yet so powerfully frightening! It was like peeking at a page of *Divine Design* in the handwriting of the Almighty.

"Is it true, Professor Ren? What makes it so? Can you say the same about human behavior too?"

"You know, May, I am not sure if Sir Isaac Newton ever gave us enough clues for that." Professor Ren sighed. "Chinese philosophers have debated for over two millennia whether human nature is good or evil, and they have never managed to settle even that simple question."

"What do you think, Professor Ren?" May asked reverently.

Professor Ren paused. "A human being is an amphibian between good and evil," he finally said. "All of us, you and I no exceptions, have the seed of a demon and that of a saint inside us. We can grow into either one."

"No!" May cried.

"So perhaps you are right. Given a number of initial conditions, the group behavior of humans is as predictable as that of particles."

"What are these conditions, Professor Ren?"

"I don't know." Professor Ren sighed again, a faraway look in his eyes. "You are a smart girl, May. One day you may figure it out. When you do, will you tell me?"

She promised, although not entirely sure if she understood everything he had said.

* * *

After Professor Ren's funeral was over, everyone straggled down the hill where a wooden stake bearing his name had been planted. May prayed silently: "Goodbye, Professor Ren! Thank you, Professor Ren! I love you, Professor Ren!" over and over in her heart.

Strangely, his ending had marked a new beginning for her life.

She wanted no part of the Nanjing occupied by the Japanese, but where could she go? Who would help her? Baba was dead. So was Ma, and so was Professor Ren. Nainai, with two bad legs, couldn't make it to the Nanjing Safety Zone. "Not even a wild wolf would kill an old woman who doesn't walk," she told others.

She was wrong. A Japanese soldier knifed her dead when she wouldn't let go of her duck.

And John? The day before, after picking her up from Jinling Women's College, he told her that he would be returning to America the day after next.

May was dumbfounded.

She had feared that the two of them had different destinies. They would forever part ways the day he left. And he had made the decision to leave China without talking to her first.

She felt a chill. She had imagined it would be impossibly difficult to say goodbye to her young American hero. But now it didn't matter.

She heard him saying, "Are you all right, May?"

"Yes. Just a grain of sand in my eye."

Nanjing doesn't cry! Nanjing doesn't cry! But a fog covered the narrow road the car was taking. Rain was dribbling against the windshield. How she hated this rain! Wait, what was wrong with her? She used to love the silky spring drizzle falling every early April, deepening the lush green color on the ground. Once she pointed out to John the different hues in various parts of the park, laughing heartily as the engineer, failing to see the distinctions, stood in puzzlement. On a rainy morning before school, she would run out into the street alone without an umbrella, letting her hair get wet by the gentle drops, spreading her arms dancing and singing—in a joyful world of glorious apricot blossoms.

But those drops had been spring rains. Now it was December.

It had been so much fun going antique hunting with John, seeing him wrinkle his nose weighing and tossing a small sculptured stone in his hand—with the concentration he must have called upon to solve his engineering problems. Told that the asking price was one yuan, he turned to her happily. "Gee, that's cheap!"

"Don't be a fool, John! It is just a pebble—not jade."

He uttered a cry and made a face at her, one eyebrow up and the other down. The two of them would laugh together, as if they had heard the funniest joke in the world.

Looking at the man sitting next to her in the car, she said to no one in particular: "What are you going to do, May? There is no going back any more!"

* * *

When the crowd at the funeral walked down the mountain, Lin, one of Baba's regular customers, helped May down the slope. In front of her, John was holding Mrs. Ren's arm.

A stranger in Hankou, May was facing the harsh realities of wartime on her own. The only person who mattered to her now was Damao. She would do everything to ensure that he lived. He was Baba's eldest—and the only surviving—son!

Biting her lips, she asked Lin if he and his group would take her and Damao along—to wherever the airplane would be shipped. She begged him to convince his colleagues, assuring him that they would be no burden.

"We have plenty of money. We will be able to pay our own way," she pleaded. "Please help me!"

She spent the night in the embassy, where John gave her the addresses of his parents and his university. He would try to find a high school for her, perhaps a college later. He asked her to be patient. It would be no easy task. The Chinese Exclusion Act had made it difficult for a Chinese female to immigrate to the US.

She felt insulted.

He asked what she had been mouthing to him when they were separated by the glass partition in Drum Tower Hospital.

She didn't tell him. He wanted to give her some money. She refused and looked away.

The next day she and Damao went to the train station to see John and Judy off. Both hugged her. At departure he said to her again: "Drop me a line on your way whenever you can. Write me after Chongqing. Don't forget, May!"

She said nothing.

Judy cried as she entered the waiting hall in the train station, but May had no tears to shed. She lovingly touched the red silk purse in her pocket. Baba's silver coins had disappeared after she had been stripped by a Japanese soldier. The money inside Ma's purse was all she had left. Ma had been saving it for her son's education. Her son was dead, but her money would keep Damao alive. Even in death, Ma came through for her children. May tore up the addresses John had given her. The wind blew the tiny pieces out of her hands.

* * *

May and Damao went to the government building to spend the night. The workers held a group meeting. None of them knew Chen May well, but Lin reminded everyone that May and her brother had stood in as Professor Ren's children during the funeral. Shortly after, May was told to get ready: they would be leaving for a faraway western city called Chongqing.

Except for a few engineers and mechanics chosen to escort the airplane on the steamship, the rest of the crew and their families set out on foot for China's wartime capital.

They walked from dawn to dusk for months, covering more than one thousand miles of mountainous terrain—a vast wilderness dotted by small villages in China's heartland. This was difficult enough to do for an able-bodied person. It was harder for May. The wounds on her head, her legs, and her arm had not healed.

The travelers ate frugally on their way and slept in temples, school classrooms, or whatever public places they could find. May handled her money with an iron fist, buying food for one person and splitting it with Damao. She picked up every grain that fell to the ground, blew on it, and swallowed. She licked her fingers clean after finishing the food in her hands.

It hurt her to see Damao accept the food and make no attempt to rob her of her share. The wife of an engineer, seeing how little Chen May allowed her brother, offered him some noodles. Chen May refused for him, insisting that her brother had enough. From then on she gave half of her share to Damao.

A constant pain gnawed at her stomach, making it difficult for her to walk. Then the hunger sensation dulled but she felt faint. Much of the time it was like floating in a fog as she staggered along. The weather was cold, and the frozen roads slippery. She stumbled and bruised her knees. Blisters formed and broke on her soles. Blood stained her rubber shoes. The pain all over her body constantly told her to give up. She kept looking at the sun, hoping for the group to stop and rest. But when it thankfully did, she never got to stay for very long, and the food she allotted herself was just enough to make her want more. It was strange that her face, instead of thinning, became grotesquely bloated. Her skin, once moist and shiny, was peeling. When she pressed the flesh on her arm, it stayed sunken. Some mornings she cleaned out handfuls of hair from her wooden comb.

She dreamed of the freshly cooked rice at home, all of the grains shining as bright as pearls, piling high in her bowl like a snowy mountain. Sometimes she had even eaten a second bowl! She licked her lips thinking about the steaming vegetables, eggs, and meat on Baba's dining table.

May was thankful when the group hired a boat to take them across a river. The boatman dug a long bamboo pole into the muddy water and pushed against the riverbed. May rested her aching feet watching the monotonous motion, and her mood of despair deepened. For months now, she had coaxed her hungry body every morning to carry on for just one more day, telling herself that plenty of food would appear the next. She and Damao would be hungry no longer. Now she could no longer believe her own words. Both of them were doomed! She should pass the red silk purse to her brother and slip quietly into the muddy water. Damao, getting her share of food, would survive.

Lin came over and sat with her, pressing something into her hand. It was a whole loaf of steamed bun! Before she could refuse, he shook his head at her and shuffled away. Her eyes welled up with tears. She fought them down. Nodding at Lin's back, she shared the loaf with her brother. Feeling some strength returning, she vowed silently that if she managed to pull through this nightmare, she would return the same kindness to a hungry man one day.

As the snow first softened and then melted into little rivulets under her feet, the group arrived in Chongqing, a foggy city in Sichuan province.

As early as 1935, two years before the Marco Polo Bridge incident, Chiang Kai-shek had designated Sichuan as the base province to lead China in the impending war against Japan. He picked Chongqing for his wartime capital, its fog and surrounding mountains offering some protection from Japanese bombers.

By the time of arrival, May's red purse was nearly empty. Foreman Tang heard that the government had built many schools for exiled students. May found two—one for herself and the other for her brother. Both were in Chongqing's outskirts. Tuition, room, and board would be free.

After registering, May sought out the dining hall. A woman working in the kitchen took a look at her face and warned her not to eat too much or too fast. "Break up your meal into several small ones," she said, "or you will have a terrible stomach ache and may even die."

Inhaling the hot steam rising from buckets of cooked rice, May couldn't control herself. She fought tooth and nail with the woman and gobbled down thirteen bowls of rice! She had thought eating a full meal again would be like living in heaven, but tears kept rolling into her bowl. She was haunted by the hardship of the long journey to Chongqing.

That night, an acute pain attacked her stomach, causing her to curl up like a cooked shrimp. Lest the good woman in the kitchen would know, May stuffed a handkerchief in her mouth to prevent herself from crying out. Wave after wave of pain surged for hours. It hurt so much she wished she would just die and be done with it. She drifted off to sleep only when the early morning light broke through the window pane. Hours later, she was awakened by something burning her face. It was the sun. Most of the pain was gone.

* * *

For two years, May attended classes in a room with a leaking roof. She slept on a straw mat separated from a pigsty by a water trough. Large rats ran around her all night. She brushed her teeth with salt. Her meals consisted of rice mixed with chaff and sand of various sizes, nicknamed babaofan because of its numerous foreign ingredients. She had night blindness. People in the school clinic told her it was malnutrition.

Although life was hard, it was harder for Damao. Mr. Tao, the teacher in charge of Damao's class, told May that her brother daydreamed much of the time and failed all his tests. May saw the change. He was no longer the rambunctious child she had known.

May decided to treat Damao to a good meal. One weekend she took out one of the remaining crumpled bills in her red silk purse, bought a fish from the market, and begged a cook to let her use the school kitchen. When she turned her back to tend to the rice, a crow swooped through the window and snatched the fish away from her bamboo basket. While the fish was not very big, the loss was devastating. She couldn't afford another fish.

Beyond the physical hardships was loneliness, the memories of her family's demise haunting her. She contracted malaria from the mosquitoes swarming around the pigsty. Burning with fever, she hallucinated that Baba got up at night to feel her forehead and tuck in her blanket. She woke up with the pillow thoroughly soaked.

While the Japanese foot soldiers could not reach Chongqing, Japanese bombers filled May with terror. Ever since the beginning of the Sino-Japanese War, Japanese planes had been dropping incendiaries almost exclusively on China's civilian areas. Even with the protection of its fog and mountains, Chongqing was the world's most bombarded city during World War II. Each aerial attack blanketed city block after city block with white smoke. The bombers came not only in the daytime but also during moonlit nights. May rarely had a restful sleep. She went to bed with her clothes under her pillow. As soon as the horns blared, she threw her dress on and ran to the bomb shelter, a tunnel dug into mountain rocks.

One Saturday morning Chen May had unexpected visitors: her former neighbors Sun Ma, Sun Chi, and their two children. After hopping, screaming, and laughing, Sun Ma told Chen May that she and her children had escaped from Nanjing with the help of several strangers—all of them communist guerrilla who controlled much of the area outside the city.

Sun Ma took a long look at May's face and exclaimed: "What's the matter with you, Heimao? Where is the hair that used to look like the finest black satin in Nanjing? And your eyes are so sad. In the old days, you were madly in love with everything around you. That's gone. Who *are* you?"

Sun Ma's little daughter reminded May of her brother Sanmao. Years ago, the two babies had suckled Sun Ma's breasts together. Life was cruel. Why wasn't Sanmao with her any longer? She had to excuse herself.

When she came back, she noticed the long scar on Sun Chi's right cheek.

"Just a saber wound," Sun Ma explained. "He got it in the battle of Taierzhung—a small city forty-two miles northeast of Xuzhou."

Xuzhou was the main target of the Japanese military after Nanjing.

"I reported to our headquarters in that city," Sun Chi said, "and they sent me to Taierzhung."

"And you came out of that battle alive?!" May exclaimed.

According to Sun Chi, the Japanese sent two of their best divisions to capture the city. They fired six or seven thousand rounds of artillery a day at the Chinese military installation, obliterating most of it. Then the Japanese tanks came and wiped out the rest.

Behind the tanks marched Japanese soldiers.

The Chinese army, commanded by General Sun Lianzhong—no relation—fought the Japanese outside the city wall for three days, losing over half of its men. The surviving soldiers went inside the wall and fought street by street and house by house. Devastated by Japanese airplanes, they were driven to the edge of the city six days later.

A general named Chi asked General Sun for permission to pull the troops out of the city and take up a position south of the Grand Canal.

General Sun called headquarters in Xuzhou to inform them that his army was facing total annihilation. He begged General Li Zhong-ren, his superior, to let him save some of his men. "It will be your highness's kindness and compassion to leave me some seeds so that I can grow my army back."

General Li replied. "I'm giving you two orders: number one, hold on at all costs till noon tomorrow; number two, you will launch a counterattack tonight!"

To make sure that he had heard them right, General Sun asked his superior to repeat the orders.

When General Chi called again to inquire about the evacuation, General Sun said: "The moment your last soldier falls, you will step in to fill his position. The moment you fall, I will step in to fill your position."

General Chi dynamited the bridge on the Grand Canal, doing away with the only escape route from the garrison.

"Your generals were crazy!" May cried.

"We organized a dare-to-die column of five hundred," Sun Chi said. "Many of the recruits were cooks or medics. Each was armed with two grenades and a large sword. No guns. We attacked under the cover of night, catching the Japanese by surprise. By daybreak we recovered most of the garrison."

"Well done!" May jumped up.

"The next morning we heard cannons booming from the northern hills," Sun said, "signaling the arrival of our reinforcements. General Li Zhong-ren and General Bai Chong-xi came from Xuzhou to direct the military action. We unleashed an all-out attack. The Japanese fled after a day of fighting, leaving behind tanks, cannons, machine guns, and bodies. We had broken the myth of the invincibility of the Japanese Imperial Army."

"Bravo!" May clapped.

"We lost Shanghai," Sun Chi continued, "but bought time to move our vital industries and key personnel into the interior. Then we turned around at Taierzhuang and gave them the shock of their lives. After the victory, we pulled our troops out of Xuzhou."

"Why?" May asked.

"To preserve our strength," Sun Chi answered. "We pulled out of Hankou for the same reason."

"Pull out, pull out, pull out! Are we ever going to stand up and fight again?" May cried.

" Our General Xue Yue has already done that—at Changsha. Our soldiers fought them at the front; other troops came down from the mountains and cut off their supply line in the rear. We beat the shit out of them—the first time we have been able to do that in a major regular battle."

"How are we doing overall?"

"We are at a stalemate. Whatever we lack in modern armament we make up for with determination. Japan and China are like two heavyweight boxers facing off in the twelfth round: neither can land a punch to knock the other off his feet. It has become a grueling fight for both sides."

* * *

One day Japanese airplanes darkened the sky to bombard May's school. After it was over, May came out of her bomb shelter and waved off the smoke stinging her eyes. Her pigsty mud house had disappeared. A direct hit had wiped out one of the air raid shelters. Twenty youngsters were buried in the avalanche. Three of them were May's classmates.

People dug out the blackened bodies and took them to the hills. May was the only one watching with dry eyes.

The school's choral society gave a memorial performance at the snow-covered soccer field. That wintry night, some people walked ten miles from Chongqing to attend the concert.

On the stage, May stood with tens of other chorus members singing the songs that had become popular throughout the country. The first one was "China Is Not Going to Perish":

"China is not going to perish,
China is not going to perish!
At Si-Hang warehouse our eight hundred strong,
Held up a whole Japanese army for long . . ."

A hum went up from the audience. The deep voices merged with the young voices on the stage. By the time they got to "The Great Yellow River Chorus," most of the audience had already stood up clapping, their singing rising to the sky:

"The wind is bawling,
The horses are neighing,
Roars the Yellow River,
Roars the Yellow River . . ."

Then they sang the nostalgic "On the Bank of the Pine Blossom River":

"My home is on the bank of Northeast's Pine Blossom River,
Where forests, coals, sorghum, and soy beans abound . . ."

At that point, onstage, all of the exiled students from Manchuria broke down. Feet stomping, they sang the "March of the Brave Guerrilla Soldiers":

"Rise! Rise! Rise!
Ten thousand in one mind,
Break through the enemy fire,
Advance!

Break through the enemy fire,
Advance! Advance! Advance and advance!"

They repeated these songs until their voices grew into a roar to heaven, rising above the whistling of the wind over the treetops. The moon grew pale, yet the soccer field became brighter. May looked down from the stage and saw thousands of faces lit up by the torches in their hands, mouths opened wide, tears flowing down, the rubble of burned buildings behind them bearing solemn witness to their pledge for their country.

* * *

Passing an entrance examination, May entered Chongqing Normal College as a freshman of foreign languages. Her dormitory room, shared with seven other girls, had no smell of pig excrement.

But food remained scarce. The only dishes served at meals were stale vegetables, overcooked and oversalted. No meat. No fish. No fruit. Her stomach rumbled as she sat in the classroom listening to lectures.

One of the rare pleasures at a wartime campus was meeting fellow students of the opposite gender. May showed little interest in young men. When one of them tried to strike up a conversation with her, she answered in monosyllables and walked away as quickly as possible.

The only male she saw regularly was her brother Damao, who continued to do poorly in school. More than once he had to repeat a year of study.

"A traumatic experience destroys a child's mental health," said Mr. Tao, Damao's teacher. "There is little I can do for your brother. He is too far gone."

* * *

On December 7, 1941, Japan attacked Pearl Harbor. The United States declared war on the Asian aggressor. President

Roosevelt asked the Chinese government to assist the British military efforts in Burma.

Chiang Kai-shek rallied his countrymen: "Spill an inch of blood for each inch of our mountains and rivers; build an army of one hundred thousand with one hundred thousand of our youths." Students all over China volunteered for the Chinese Expedition Army to Burma. Sun Ma told May that her husband Sun Chi was with the American-equipped 38th division. In April 1942, Sun Chi's regiment of eight hundred defeated seven thousand Japanese soldiers in Yenangyaung, rescuing American missionaries, women and children, and the seven thousand British soldiers who had been sieged.

* * *

When May graduated from the normal college two years later, the US Flying Tigers had shot down twenty-five thousand Japanese warplanes from China's skies. May was hired as an interpreter for the American airmen she adored. Her salary was higher than that of a schoolteacher's—the position she had been trained for. She rented a small room in a mud-and-bamboo house and cooked for Damao, whose body gradually grew thick again.

* * *

It happened one afternoon in February 1945. Shouts of "Extra! Extra!" disrupted Chen May's attention from the telegram she was translating. She went out and bought a copy of the newspaper. Two hundred US bombers, the low-flying B-29s, had taken off from the Pacific islands to attack Tokyo. Two weeks later, almost three hundred B-29s dropped two thousand tons of explosives on the Japanese capital. Over one hundred thousand Japanese civilians died in a fire raging through the narrow lanes hugged by small wooden houses.

May found little pity in her heart. "Serves them right! Now they get a taste of what they were doing to us for the last eight years."

That evening, in a restaurant with friends, May ordered her favorite dish of shrimp over burnt rice. As the waiter poured the sweet-and-sour sauce on the rice, white smoke rose from the steel plate with a sizzling sound: "zzzzzzz." The little man in a black tunic announced that the restaurant had renamed the dish "Bombarding Tokyo." Everybody at the table clapped.

In two more months the war in Europe was over. Hitler killed himself. Germany surrendered.

Then came the day when everyone talked excitedly about *the bomb*. A middle-aged fellow interpreter, saliva flying out of his mouth, told May that the atomic bomb was as small as a grapefruit. Another interpreter disagreed, insisting that it was a little bigger than a basketball.

No matter its size, people spoke in awe of how one such bomb had leveled the entire city of Hiroshima.

Three days later, another atomic bomb wiped out Nagasaki. More than two hundred thousand Japanese civilians died in the two cities.

"Don't forget! More people were killed in Nanjing," one man shouted in the crowd.

"Judgment Day! The bombs are thunder from heaven!" shouted another.

Everyone praised America and American culture: her science, her technology, her democratic form of government, her willingness to stand up to the bullies. Good, good, good, good.

A colleague asked May: "Did you watch that American documentary film on construction machines? An airfield appears in a wilderness just like this!" He snapped his fingers. "So does a whole highway."

"And what equipment do *we* use? Spades, hammers, and stone rollers! *Dog shit!*" Another colleague shook his head.

May had seen a photograph of a giant stone roller hauled by hundreds of coolies. At first glance, she had taken it to be a praying mantis carried away by a swarm of ants.

"The Americans eat canned beef and chocolate, and even their *drinking water* is delivered by *airplane*," another colleague marveled.

"And we? *Buffalo carts* for our *rice*." the first colleague sneered.

"They own all kinds of weapons we can't even name," a third interpreter said. "Why, those people are so advanced, yet they are so easygoing and never put on airs. Have a Camel, they say, offering a cigarette. Always giving chocolates to the kids. They helped us beat the hell out of the Japanese." The man showed his crooked teeth with a big smile.

May agreed wholeheartedly.

Still, China and Japan had been going at each other for fourteen years! When was the war going to end?

* * *

It came as a total surprise. On August 15, 1945, dusk was settling on Chongqing Normal College. People sat and chatted around their dining tables after having their meager meals. Suddenly, they were shocked by insistent gongs. May stepped out of her house to investigate. She saw men and women running down the hill carrying torches. Others banged gongs with big padded mallets.

"*Bong! Bong! Bong!* Extra! Extra! Extra! *Japan has surrendered unconditionally!*"

"Listen up! Listen up! The war is over! All hail! *Victory to China!*"

Students came running out of the dormitories, took a look, and ran back to tell others. In no time young men and young women poured out of the dorms screaming hysterically. They danced. They sang songs. They hopped up and down shaking hands with one another. As the sounds of celebratory firecrackers flooded the campus, students filled the soccer field, jumping and hollering. A few of them shimmied up the goal posts hooting and waving towels. One slipped and fell on his back, pounding the grass and kicking his legs in the air laughing.

May joined the crowd, tears streaming down her face. She hugged everyone—even men. *We won! We won! Now we can go home.*

We are going home!

Chapter 29

The Locket

March 1946, seven months after the end of the bloodiest war in human history.

Dawn was slowly breaking over Nanjing. In the Chinese capital, China's national flags flew everywhere.

In an alley off an avenue, peddlers were setting up carts of dumplings, steaming soy milk, fried pancakes, fried crullers, and sticky-rice balls. Customers lined up. The weather being a little nippy, they rubbed their hands waiting impatiently.

Ten Japanese prisoners of war in yellow wool overcoats and yellow uniforms were cleaning the streets. They swept the soil to the unpaved edges of the road, scooping the waste into a dirty metal barrel.

A young Chinese soldier in olive green fatigues stood at the curb, his cap cockily aslant. With a pistol dangling on his belt and a cigarette hanging from his mouth, he pointed his finger at the ground once in a while. A Japanese prisoner would scurry over with his broom and clean the spot again.

Most of Nanjing was still asleep. At the corner of the alley, a large wall poster fluttered in the wind. The yellow stains on its flayed edges indicated that it had been exposed to the weather for a long time. Nobody bothered to read its large characters anymore.

A shrill cry broke the stillness of the early morning: "Murderer!" It was a female voice. "Police, police! Arrest this man!"

Everybody around the breakfast carts turned. They saw a young, pretty woman in a blue qipao beating up a mustached Japanese prisoner. The rugged man hid his head behind his hands, but the woman scratched his face. Bloody streaks appeared on the prisoner's cheeks, his short legs buckling and his cap sliding to one side. Yet he made no attempt to strike back. Neither did the other Japanese prisoners help him. They just stopped working and watched in silence.

The cigarette dropped from the Chinese soldier's mouth. "Stop!" he shouted. "Stop it!"

The Chinese woman redoubled her efforts. No longer able to reach the prisoner's face, she kicked his shins and genitals. The Japanese prisoner doubled over.

The Chinese soldier ran to the woman and grabbed her from behind.

The woman spat at the prisoner's face. "Japanese asshole! This is for Baba!"

She spat again. "This is for Ma!"

Then she spat again, again, and again. "For Ermao and Sanmao! For Simao and Wumao! This is for Baba—again!"

The customers around the breakfast carts drifted over to surround the commotion. Passersby added to the circle.

A portly, elderly policeman in uniform pushed his way through the crowd, as did an officer with the insignia of winter plum blossoms on his shoulders.

"What's going on?" the officer snarled.

The Chinese soldier saluted. The policeman looked at the officer's shoulders and said: "We are investigating, Colonel!"

"This animal killed my Baba!" The woman lunged for the officer's pistol in the holster. As the officer stepped back, she pointed a trembling finger at the prisoner and screamed at the officer: "What's wrong with you? Shoot him!"

The crowd roared its approval.

"Baba! I have finally found the beast who shot you," the woman howled. "They will execute him. Baba, your ghost can rest now."

"Take it easy," the young colonel said.

The policeman took out a notebook. "When did he commit the crime against your father?"

"December 13, 1937," the woman said.

"A long time ago," the policeman murmured. "The place of the crime?"

"Winter Plum Alley, seven blocks from here."

The policeman jotted down the information.

"Didn't you say he killed your mother too?" the Chinese soldier chimed in. He was still restraining the woman, though loosely now.

"Another Japanese animal did that."

"Whom else did they kill?"

"My baby sister and three of my brothers . . ." the woman said.

The crowd roared.

"Anyone else?"

"About one hundred other defenseless civilians."

The spectators edged closer. Some of them shook their fists at the Japanese prisoner.

"You must be talking about one of those mass slayings during the Nanjing Massacre," the policeman said. He turned to the officer and offered his notebook. "I think this matter belongs to the military tribunal court. You'd better take over, sir."

The officer took out a Parker fountain pen from his breast pocket and importantly twisted off its cap. "Were you present at the time and place of the crime?"

"I was!"

"What was the mode of killing?"

"He pointed his pistol at Baba's forehead and pulled the trigger. Oh Baba!"

The officer winced. "Your name and address?"

"Chen May, 125 Qinghua Road."

"Profession?"

"Assistant editor of the *Nanjing Daily News*."

"Other witnesses?"

"My younger brother."

"Name and address?"

"Chen Li. We call him Damao. He is living with me."

"What does he do?"

"He's a longshoreman at Xiaguang."

"Other survivors in your family?"

"No! All my other family members—six of them—were killed by this animal and other animal soldiers."

The crowd moaned.

"I'm really sorry to hear that, Miss Chen," the officer grimaced. "But how can you be certain that this man is the soldier who committed the crime?"

"There is no question about it."

"But that incident happened more than eight years ago."

"I refresh my memory of his face every night before I go to sleep."

"Every night for the last eight years?"

"Yes, sir. Didn't miss a single day. I etched every detail of his face in my brain. I could identify him if you showed me just one of his eyes."

The crowd gasped.

"How did you run into him?"

"I began searching for him after returning to Nanjing about half a year ago. One day I noticed some Japanese soldiers disappearing into a horse stall. People told me they are cleaning our streets every morning. I bought a city map and drew ten vertical lines and ten horizontal lines, separating the city into one hundred squares. I've been inspecting one of these squares every morning, crossing out the ones I have covered. This is the forty-ninth day, and, God willing, I found him."

"Wow! You certainly have a head on your shoulders!" the officer said. "What did you want to do to him?"

"I heard of a man tearing out the heart of a wolf that had gnawed his son to death. I wanted to do the same with this beast. But an explosion went off in my head. Boom bang! My mind went blank until I felt this soldier's hands on me."

The officer put the Parker pen back into his pocket and took out a card. "We'll take him in. Here is my name and telephone number. Contact me any time you want me for any reason."

May didn't move.

"I've got your address. You can go now," the officer said.

The young woman stared.

The officer looked away to avoid her intense gaze. His eyes landed on a banner five-stories high hung at a building a block from them showing a smiling Chiang Kai-shek.

"You must have heard our Generalissimo's speech: 'Dwell not on past wrongs; do good to others,'" the officer said. "With thirty-five million of our people killed and twenty-five-billion

US dollars of property destroyed, he has not asked them for any war reparation—not a single copper!"

The woman glared.

"We should never forget what had happened, but the war is over," the officer repeated.

The woman looked over the officer's head, and people followed her eyes to the wall poster on the street corner, whose large characters now shouted out to everyone:

CITIZENS, STEP FORWARD AND IDENTIFY THE WAR CRIMINALS WHO RAVAGED OUR NANJING!

"The war will never be over for me," the woman said in a low voice. "Yes, the Japanese lost and surrendered to us. But how can I forgive the animal who killed my Baba?"

* * *

The trial against Private Sakai began in the summer of 1946. May was one of the witnesses. Several Nanjing residents, on seeing Sakai's face in the newspapers, came forward to give their testimonies. The courtroom was packed.

May, cool and composed on the stand, gave precise details about a mass murder committed nearly nine years earlier.

After returning to her seat, May had trouble breathing. She got more agitated listening to the continuing interrogation and almost blacked out.

The court adjourned. Sakai was being led away. May stepped out into the aisle firmly blocking his path. She looked at the Japanese straight in the eyes and said: "Private Sakai, you killed my Baba. Would you please tell me why?"

She asked the question first in Japanese, which she had learned in college. Then she repeated those same words to him in Chinese. Finally, she said them in English. She wanted to make sure that Sakai understood every word she was saying.

But the Japanese prisoner just stood there, his waxy face impassive. Not a muscle moved. May detected no trace of remorse, or guilt, or emotion of any kind on his face. He seemed affected neither by what she had said nor by the trial he had just gone through.

She was disgusted. "You killed Baba and don't have the decency to answer me?" She spat on his face.

A court officer pulled her away.

* * *

The next day was a Sunday, but the questions that had been haunting May for nearly nine years remained unanswered: *Why did you open fire on us? Didn't you see we were civilians? Do you have a daughter? Do you know how a daughter feels when her father is being killed? Do you care about the pain you inflict on other people? Are Japanese human beings? Do you have any feelings? How can human beings do the kind of things you Japanese did to us?*

She wanted to know the answers. She had to understand!

She was restless all Sunday morning and couldn't eat. In the afternoon she went to the prison with an empty stomach and told the guard she had come to see Sakai. Expecting to be refused, she was surprised that her wish was actually granted.

The dirty corridor was lit but dimly. The wet concrete floor smelled of urine. It reminded her of the pigsty in Chongqing where she had lived for two years.

Sakai was sitting quietly on the concrete floor of his prison cell leaning on a wood grating. He had his back to her. The Japanese must have heard her footsteps, for he quickly put away something shiny in his palm. He didn't move when she stopped behind him, nor did he answer her questions given in three languages. Seeing May's face reddening, the prison guard put his hand on her shoulders. She spat at the prisoner through the bars and left.

May attended every session of the trial but learned nothing. Every day she went to the prison to visit Sakai. But not even once did Sakai acknowledge her presence.

She talked to the prison guard.

"He doesn't have many visitors," the guard said, "only you and the peddlers who sold him cigarettes."

"I never saw them," she said.

"They stopped coming after his money ran out."

"Is he that poor?"

"Well, he traded a watch, a ring, and his winter coat too. He is going to shiver when winter comes."

"I once saw something shiny in his hand."

"A silver chain with a little locket? He wouldn't trade that."

"Why not?"

"There is a photo of a woman and a child inside."

"That animal has a family?"

"I guess so."

* * *

It took May weeks of daily visits to get some kind of reaction from Sakai. Not that he did anything very different, but several times he looked at her hand. Then she realized that he was eyeing the loaf of babaofan she happened to be carrying with her.

A hungry face appeared in her mind. It was Damao's on his way to Chongqing. She saw the steamed bun Lin had given her and remembered how it had pulled her back from the brim of suicide. The vow she had made to herself resounded in her head: *One day I will return this kindness to a hungry man.* Reluctantly, she handed the loaf over to Sakai, who tore off the lotus leaves and wolfed down the rice cake.

On her next visit, May went to a roadside stand before entering the jailhouse. She bought a loaf of babaofan and gave it to Sakai after spitting on him.

One day coming out of the courthouse, she was surprised to see a man in a military uniform waiting for her. He had a long scar on his cheek.

"I don't read newspapers and didn't know about the Sakai trial until yesterday," her former neighbor Sun Chi apologized. "I thought I might find you here."

Sun Chi was no longer the fierce young man he had been. Now he looked almost like a middle-aged country gentleman.

He suggested they have a cup of tea. May followed him to a tea house and sat down. He asked her how the trial was going.

She told him it was about to end. All witnesses had been called.

"He pleaded not guilty," she said. "Can you imagine that?"

"What did he say for his defense?"

"He said: 'As a soldier, I had to follow orders.'"

"What did the prosecuting attorney say to that?"

"He raised his voice: 'Were you following orders to kill war prisoners?'"

"Useless question. What else did the attorney ask?"

"'How about killing civilians? How about raping women? Were those your orders too?'"

"What did Sakai say?"

"At first nothing. Then he said everybody was doing it." Chen May's face was suddenly aflame. "I know a criminal rapes and kills, being an aberration of humanity. But I don't understand how a whole race of human beings can murder and rape the way the Japanese did to us. How could these people, supposedly decent human beings at home, turn into animals after landing in China?"

The waiter came over and poured tea for them.

Sun Chi said the Japanese had done that to everyone, not just to the Chinese. He gave the example of an American soldier who had been taken prisoner in the Philippines.

"The American was straggling his way to the prison camps during the Bataan Death March," Sun Chi said. "A Japanese officer whipped his horse and overtook him. For no apparent reason, the Japanese slashed the Caucasian's back with a saber. Later, the cut from neck to waist became infected, and the man grew feverish. He said years later that the Japanese would have shot him and thrown his body into a ditch had two fellow prisoners not put his arms across their shoulders and dragged him along with them."

"A Chinese would have met a worse fate under the same circumstances," Chen May said. "I don't think the Western world is aware of the degree of inhumanity the Japanese put us through."

"I met a Canadian after the war," Sun Chi said. "An emotional wreck, he wouldn't tell anyone what the Japanese had done to him in the prison camp."

May looked out the window. The bustling street was filled with men and women in white tunics and black pants. There were more of them in other cities of the province and still more in the provinces beyond. Baba had said, "When we get together, we can drown those midgets with our spit alone."

She asked: "Do the Japanese enjoy hurting people?"

"I can't speak for them, but the war taught me something about myself," Sun Chi said.

"Like what?"

"A few years ago, I fought in Bhamo, a city in Burma, and I felt a thrill seeing a Japanese soldier drop to the ground after I pulled the trigger. I kept shooting even after they had stopped shooting back. I must have gone mad. My men said the whites of my eyes had turned blood red."

"That's different," May protested. "You were shooting at enemy soldiers. Baba was a civilian. My brothers and my sister were children. You'll never meet a woman nicer than Ma. The Japanese slaughtered them all."

The waiter brought over two dishes of dried nuts.

"All right. Let me tell you what happened after we captured Bhamo," Sun Chi said.

"Please do!" May said, settling back in her chair.

Sun Chi scooped up a handful of nuts from one of the dishes. "We wiped out most of the Japanese soldiers in that city," he said, popping a few nuts into his mouth, "and took about one hundred of them prisoners. General Sun Li-ren gave us the instruction on how to interrogate them: '*Ask them if they have been to China. Shoot them if they say yes.*'"

"Bravo!" May clapped.

"Summer in Burma was even hotter than Nanjing," Sun Chi said. "With giant trees blocking out the blazing sun, the lighting at noon inside the jungle was as dim as in late afternoons elsewhere. We took the prisoners out of their bamboo cages to execute them. One of them was a little man. He walked slowly, his feet shackled. One of our soldiers gave his shoulder a shove. It reminded me of myself shuffling my way to the death pit in Nanjing. I ordered to have him spared.

"Later that afternoon, I sat outside his cage and struck up a conversation with him. His name was Igi. He told me about himself in broken Chinese.

"As a child, Igi learned that the American 'black ships' barged into Tokyo Bay and forced Japan into opening two of her ports for trade. For decades after that, Japan had been getting nothing but insults and exploitation from the West. At the beginning of the twentieth century, Japan defeated Russia in Manchuria. During World War I, Japan joined the side of the eventual victors. Even so, at the end of the war, the West rejected a Japanese request to include a sentence for racial equality in the League of Nations Covenant.

"Igi was determined to help Japan free Asia from Western dominance.

"When he was seventeen, Igi joined the army. He had a difficult time dealing with military training. Sometimes his sergeant slammed his face against the wall. Other times he hit him with a baseball bat until he fainted. At the end of training camp, Igi got used to physical punishment. In fact, he doled it out to recruits junior to him.

"Igi was angry at Chiang Kai-shek for rejecting a ceasefire proposal over the Marco Polo Bridge Incident. When Chiang Kai-shek sent the Chinese air force to attack the Japanese armada in Shanghai, Igi couldn't wait to teach the Chinese strongman a lesson.

"He got his wish: the army sent him to Shanghai.

"Upon his departure, his grandma cried and held him to her bosom, while his mother gave him a pistol. 'Your grandfather took this gun to Korea,' she said. 'Although he lost his life, he brought honor to our family. Keep this gun with you at all times. Don't let yourself be taken prisoner. Use this gun on yourself if needed! We will be proud of you dying for our emperor. Don't worry about me. I have three other sons. They will take care of my livelihood.'

"The people in his village went to the train station singing to send him off.

"He expected the war with China would be short. Chinese soldiers were supposed to flee when they were being fired upon. Arriving in Shanghai, he was shocked to see many Japanese corpses piled up on the beaches.

"Igi was given the duty to watch over military equipment. He argued hotly with his superior and won the right to go to the front, where he witnessed his comrades being blown to pieces by cannonballs. He vowed revenge.

"After a hard-won battle in Shanghai, Igi and his regiment chased the Chinese troops to Changzhou, a city farther inland. The journey was not the romantic march he had imagined. There were no pretty girls waving handkerchiefs at him. Most of the people he saw were half-naked children with bulging tummies staring at the roadside. Covered with dust and sweat all day, he tired easily and missed the baths he had taken daily in the wooden barrel at home.

"But the worst part of the march was hunger. The army's food supplies were scarce. They were not allowed to take a grain from the Chinese people. The Great Japanese Imperial Army had strict orders."

"Liar!" May pounded the table and shouted. "Those Japanese bandits took whatever they pleased from us!"

The nuts in Sun Chi's hand fell to the floor. "I am sorry, Miss Chen," he murmured. "But that's what Igi told me. You want me to go on?"

"Sorry, Mr. Sun. I'm not upset with you. Please do ."

"All right," Sun Chi said. "One day Igi and his regiment came to a deserted village and saw food in a kitchen. The soldiers told one another, 'We can't fight on empty stomachs, and the food will rot. Why don't we eat it and leave money on the table?'

"That was what they did with unattended food for a few days. One morning one of the soldiers forgot to leave money on the table. Soon afterwards, everybody did the same.

"Then they demanded food from the Chinese peasants they ran into, beating up those unwilling.

"First they asked for chickens. Then they asked for pigs. Finally they asked for buffalo."

"Uh-oh," May said. "Buffalo are family to the peasants. They till the land for them."

"Exactly. The farmers hid their buffalo, and the soldiers shot them."

"Why doesn't it surprise me?" May said.

"One day the Japanese took over a village," Sun Chi said. "One of the soldiers came out of a white brick house grinning from ear to ear, clutching a fistful of money. Igi felt contempt for this fellow. How could a soldier of the Great Japanese Imperial Army steal from people? Igi entered that house and found antiques neatly arranged in a glass case. He 'confiscated' several items. From then on he looked for antiques everywhere he went."

"Oh no! This is worse than stealing money from us," May said. "Antiques are our cultural heritage."

"I don't like that either, but this is not as bad as other things they did to us," Sun Chi said.

"What are you talking about?" May asked.

"Well, the Japanese soldiers were young men and had . . . ah . . . urges," he looked away from May, "but they were not allowed to touch any Chinese women."

"Lie!" May shouted. "A god-damned lie!"

"Miss Chen, I must apologize to you a thousand times. I have never learned how to talk to a refined lady. Perhaps I should stop now."

"No, no, no, Mr. Sun! It's not your fault. I want to hear the rest of your story. I really do. Please go on, Mr. Sun. I beg you!"

"You will not be angry with me if I say something wrong?"

"You haven't. I swear!"

"All right then, but please let me know if I do," he said. "OK, the Japanese took over another village. Early one evening, Igi walked by a house and heard lewd laughter. He took a peek and saw several shivering Chinese women sitting on a bed burying their heads in their hands. They were surrounded by Japanese soldiers . . . the women without their clothes. Hey, are you all right?"

"Go on. Please go on. I want to hear all of it."

"Igi went inside and asked what the heck they were doing," Sun Chi said. "The soldiers grinned. 'Nothing. We didn't touch any of them—we only *lookie lookie*.'

"Igi walked away.

"But the next morning, Igi heard that the soldiers had done something later that night. Things worse than *touching*, as a matter of fact." Sun Chi stopped and took a glance at Chen May, who was hugging herself with her hands around her knees. "It was bound to happen when you think about it, hot-blooded, gun-toting young men in a room with helpless naked women."

"What *happened* in that room after Igi left?" May demanded in a trembling voice.

"The Japanese killed all of them," Sun Chi avoided the question, "leaving no one to report on them."

May covered her face.

"I am very, very sorry," Sun Chi said. "I must stop now. This is no story to tell a lady."

"Mr. Sun! Some nights I tossed and turned in my bed wondering why my family had to be killed. Believe me, I'll not be able to sleep a wink tonight if you don't finish the story for me. Mr. Sun, please don't make me kowtow to you!"

"All right, then." Sun Chi sighed. "But I would rather leave this incident behind if you don't mind."

"Go on! Just go on!"

"Halfway to Changzhou, Igi's unit received the intelligence that guerrillas were hiding in a village. After a search, they caught an old peasant woman who banged her white hair on the dirt pleading for her life.

"Igi's officer told Igi to kill her.

"'But she looks more like my grandma than a guerrilla,' Igi said. 'Couldn't we spare her?'

"His officer shouted: 'Idiot! She may be unable to hand-combat, but she can gather intelligence. Shoot her!'

"When Igi still balked, his officer pulled out a pistol and shot her in the temple.

"Igi was severely reprimanded for disobeying his superior. From then on, Igi followed every command he was given, including killing the seven Chinese coolies who had dug a trench for him. To save bullets, he ordered them to kneel before bayoneting them one after the other. He had gotten used to killing Chinese—easier than killing chickens, as a matter of fact."

Sun Chi stole a glance at Chen May, who had suddenly turned very quiet, her eyes wide open and shining.

* * *

The Military Tribunal Court in Nanjing announced the verdict on Sakai: "Guilty."

Thunderous applause arose from the audience.

Then the sentence: "Death by hanging."

Pandemonium!

Walking back to his cell, Sakai passed where Chen May was sitting. He stopped, although she was making no attempt to block his way.

For a long while Sakai stared at the Chinese young woman, who stood up from her seat staring back fiercely.

"I am sorry!" Sakai finally said in a subdued voice.

May was stunned.

Sakai closed his eyes and opened them again. He snapped to attention and bowed deeply. "Please forgive me for what I did," he said. "I was wrong!"

Looking straight into May's eyes, Sakai slowly raised his handcuffs and opened one of his palms, showing a shining silver chain.

"A little present," he said hoarsely.

May continued to stare. She didn't want that thing!

"I want to let you know," Sakai said again, "I have a daughter. Her name is Michiko. There is a baby photo of her inside the locket. I hope one day you two will get to meet."

May thought of the question she had once asked Professor Ren. She never completely understood his answer, which now rang in her ears: *A human being is an amphibian between good and evil. All of us, you and I no exceptions, have the seed of a demon and that of a saint inside us. We can grow into either one.*

The words came to her one by one, like thunder from the sky.

"Yes, Professor Ren, now I understand what you are saying." She lowered her head in a prayer.

A song grew into a roar in her head. It wasn't "China Is Not Going to Perish." It wasn't "On the Bank of the Pine Blossom River." It wasn't "The March of the Brave Guerilla Soldiers" or "The Great Yellow River Chorus." It was none of the numerous songs her people had sung with tears and hope during a war that had lasted fourteen long years. Yet it was all of them—and more. It belonged to her, a woman who knew nothing about music composition. It was her song, coming from the depths of her soul. It was everybody's song. It was *The Song of Nanjing*!

Raising her head proudly, she walked toward Sakai, took his trinket and clutched it to her heart.

Epilogue

On a spring day in 2016, when the world was recovering from the worst economic storm in eighty years, a news wire shocked the antique world.

Headlined "A Stunning Sale," it read:

A Chinese porcelain dish, barely six inches in diameter, was sold yesterday at an auction held in Essex, a sleepy little town in Eastern Massachusetts. The dish, made for the enjoyment of the Yongzheng Emperor in the eighteenth century, is decorated in falangcai. An American professor had acquired it in Nanjing four years before Pearl Harbor.

The auctioneer had posted a photo of this dish on the Internet. The low/high estimates were five thousand dollars/seven thousand dollars. His office was quickly inundated with emails, faxes, and phone calls. Many attending the exhibition took photographs of this item.

A local collector was ready to bid as much as twenty thousand dollars for the dish. He didn't even have a chance to raise his paddle.

The bidding started at one thousand dollars. With paddles rising one after the other in the auction room, the price quickly went to fifty thousand. Then someone in the front row made a jump to one hundred thousand. A long silence followed. The auctioneer was ready to slam down his gavel when a deep voice from the back offered two hundred thousand.

The action then turned fast and furious. New bidders, most of them over the phone, joined the bidding. A phone bid of one million dollars silenced everybody in the auction room. Eight bidders remained active on the phone at five million, three at fifteen million. The auctioneer finally hammered it down at twenty-two million dollars—to resounding applause in the auction room. With commission included, the auction result for this dish was almost twenty-four million dollars!

The auction house revealed that the successful bid came from China. For decades, the consigner of the dish had kept it in a glass case in her basement. She put it up for auction before her move to a nursing home.

The old lady was shocked by the auction result. Following the instruction of her late father, a professor emeritus at MIT, she would use the proceeds of the sale to establish the John Winthrop Foundation to help young girls in China go to college.

Memorial Day, 2016